Mirror

Mirror
The Fiction and Essays
of Kōda Aya

University of Hawai'i Press
Honolulu

Kakera, Kunshō, Hina, Mono iwanu isshō no tomo by Kōda Aya
Copyright © 1947, 1949, 1955, 1966 by Tama Aoki
Originally published in Japan

Publication of this book has been assisted by a grant from
the Kajiyama Publications Fund for Japanese History, Culture,
and Literature at the University of Hawai'i at Mānoa.

© 1999 University of Hawai'i Press

Printed in the United States of America

04 03 02 01 00 99   5 4 3 2 1

Library of Congress Cataloging-in-Publication Data
Sherif, Ann.
Mirror : the fiction and essays of Kōda Aya / Ann Sherif.
p.   cm.
Includes bibliographical references and index.
ISBN 0–8248–1899–7 (cloth : alk. paper) —
ISBN 0–8248–2181–5 (pbk. : alk. paper)
1. Kōda, Aya, 1904—Criticism and interpretation.
I. Kōda, Aya, 1904–   Selections. English. 1999.   II. Title.
PL832.O33Z84   1999
895.6'45—dc21   99–10672
CIP

University of Hawai'i Press books are printed on
acid-free paper and meet the guidelines for permanence
and durability of the Council on Library Resources.

Designed by Janette Thompson (Jansom)

Printed by Maple-Vail Book Manufacturing Group

I am silver and exact, I have no preconceptions.
. . . .
Now I am a lake. A woman bends over me,
Searching my reaches for what she really is.

. . . .
I see her back, and reflect it faithfully.
She rewards me with tears and an agitation of hands.
I am important to her. She comes and goes.
Each morning it is her face that replaces the darkness.

Sylvia Plath, "Mirror"

Contents

Acknowledgments   ix

A Note on Names   xi

Part One: Life and Writings

1   A Literary Life   3

2   The Father: Kōda's Autobiographical Texts   29

3   *Flowing* and the Literature of the Demimonde   73

4   Narrative Authority and the Postwar Realm:
Two Exemplary Short Stories   105

5   Torn Sleeves and the Anti-Oedipal Family   131

6   Epilogue   156

Part Two: Translations

Fragments   163

The Medal   166

Dolls for a Special Day   177

A Friend for Life   188

Chronology   201

Bibliography   205

Index   219

Acknowledgments

This book is based on parts of my dissertation at the University of Michigan. A Fulbright-Hays Fellowship made it possible for me to pursue research in Tokyo and to interview Kōda Aya. While in Japan, I benefited immeasurably from the resources of the Nihon Kindai Bungakkan and the National Diet Library. The support of Oberlin College and Case Western Reserve University assisted me at later stages of research and revision. A grant from the Kajiyama Publication Fund provided a subvention toward the publication of this book. Kōdansha granted permission to publish the photograph of Kōda Aya. Sharon Yamamoto and Masako Ikeda at the University of Hawai'i Press were fantastic to work with, and I am extremely grateful to have had Don Yoder copyedit this book. I would also like to thank my colleagues in East Asian Studies at Oberlin College for their camaraderie and encouragement.

Finally, I owe special thanks to several other people. Hiroshi Miyaji first introduced me to Kōda Aya's writings, and the late Robert Danly showed great and unlimited enthusiasm for my choice of topics. I am particularly grateful to Aoki Tama for her kindness and support. I would like to thank especially Ken Ito, Marvin Marcus, Noborio Yutaka, Oketani Hideaki, Katie Sparling, Esperanza Ramirez-Christensen, Sue Sherif, and Alan Tansman, who read earlier drafts. I deeply appreciate the encouragement, criticism, companionship, and good humor of many colleagues, friends, and family, especially Maggie Childs, Janet Ikeda, Kurita Akiko, Momokawa Takahito, Ginny Morrison, Sharalyn Orbaugh, Jim Reichert, Joan Sherif, the Uzawas, and the Wilsons. Thanks to Carolyn and Muzafer for giving me two books that they didn't write—the *Webster's Dictionary* and *The Joy of Cooking*. It is with great pleasure and joy that I dedicate this book to Len Smith and Ian Wilson.

A Note on Names

In this book, Japanese names appear with the family name first in accord with the Japanese practice. I refer to some writers by their pen names (Rohan for Kōda Rohan). Kōda Aya is usually referred to by critics and biographers in Japan by her family name. I follow this practice as well.

Part One:
Life and Writings

1

A Literary Life

Kōda Aya (1904–1990) never wanted to be like her father, the dedicated and prolific writer Kōda Rohan (1867–1947). Most of her life, Kōda had stayed at home raising a daughter and caring for her father in his old age.[1] Far from her father's world of art and literature, she devoted herself to work in the kitchen. After Rohan's death in 1947, Kōda took up writing herself, primarily as a means of supplementing her income. In her own words:

> My motivation for writing was purely commercial. Because my father was a writer, I knew what writers were like and I found it most disagreeable. When I was a child, Father always sat at his desk writing, and all we ever saw of him was his back. I thought that writing was a dull, dreadful occupation. After my father died, all I had was myself and my memories. I was asked to write them down, and I did, that's all. No learning, no art, just a way to make it through the world. Japan had, after all, lost the war.[2]

Despite Kōda's practical intentions, her short stories, novels, and essays won high praise from readers and critics. With penetrating insight her works addressed subjects close at hand: the lives of women, the family, traditional culture in a rapidly changing world. Her style proved subtle, elegant, and accomplished.

The reading public took pleasure in the fact that some of Rohan's brilliance and artistry had rubbed off on his child. At the same time, critics found it difficult to compare the works and attitudes of the father with those of the daughter. Rohan was not simply a writer, he was a Renaissance man, the last of the *bunjin,* or literati.[3] Literary historians count Rohan as one of the major figures of modern Japanese letters, and most critics revere Rohan's erudition and his unshakable respect for the Asian literary and philosophical heritage. In his youth, he made his mark as a novelist—above all for *The Five-Story Pagoda* (Gojū no tō; 1891). Later Rohan turned to historical works and also produced books and articles on the classical literature of China and Japan. He wrote authoritatively on a wide range of subjects: urban planning, Edo-period culture and literature, Asian thought and religion, history, the Bible, fishing, and foreign films. Rohan's style varied, but it tended to challenge the reader with difficult vocabulary and allusions to the Chinese classics. Over the course of his long career, Rohan won numerous honors and awards. Kyoto Imperial University (present-day Kyoto University) conferred on him the honorary degree of Doctor of Literature.

While Rohan reveled in portraying historical figures and events on a grand scale and pondering metaphysical and religious matters, most of Kōda's stories, novels, and essays concentrate on the domestic scene. In her eyes, the home is the setting for some of life's most significant dramas: the battles of adolescence, the trauma and disillusionment of adulthood, the acceptance of old age and death.[4] Kōda has created many fascinating portraits of women who are strong-willed, hardworking, and independent: an idealistic teenager who struggles with her troubled, nonconformist family; a woman whose avocation is attending funerals; a middle-age widow who works as a maid in a geisha house. The unity of Kōda's thematically and generically diverse body of writings lies in a positive, mature worldview that is attentive to the forces of time and decay and insists on the importance of past lives. In the ensuing chapters we will look at the forces that shaped Kōda's literary career and her works and examine the place of Kōda's writings in modern Japanese letters.

In a number of ways, Kōda's career as a writer is anomalous. She did not belong to the literary establishment and had no literary ambitions or artistic pretensions. She made her debut during the turbulent early postwar era, when the wartime experience and the nation's defeat figured prominently in the writings of young and old alike. Kōda neither joined the people of her own age in reexamining the writer's place in the military effort and wartime guilt, nor did she share the younger generation's aspirations for a new life and a new beginning for Japanese literature. She entered the debate from an entirely different angle by presenting the positive aspects of tradition and a firm sense of values. Kōda's writings do not represent a nostalgic view of the past; nor do they pander to a desire to return to the good old days. Readers accepted—and continue to accept—her works with enthusiasm because they represent a maturity and certainty missing from much of modern Japanese letters.

The maturity and wisdom evident in Kōda's prose have much to do, no doubt, with the advanced age at which she began her career. Although she had regular contact with writers and publishers from her youth, Kōda exhibited no interest in writing until she produced her first essay at age forty-three. As a youth, she read a wide variety of books—from Thomas Hardy to Edo-period fiction and classical verse at her father's bidding—but was not particularly enthusiastic about any of them. Kōda resented her father's writing and her stepmother's devotion to poetry and the Bible because it took their time and energy away from the family. Because Kōda regarded writing as a solitary, self-absorbed activity, it is not coincidental that she started to write only after her own child had become an adult and her father was dead.

Kōda's Life and Career

Kōda Aya was born on 1 September 1904 in Mukōjima, Tokyo, near the banks of the Sumida River. Her parents came from radically different backgrounds. Rohan's father Kōda Shigenobu (1839–1914) worked as an adviser to the Tokugawa shogunate on matters of protocol and bore the title of *chabōzu* (tea monk), a post that demanded a high level of literacy, and his mother Yū ran a strict household. Like many families formerly associated with the Edo government, the Kōdas' fortunes waned upon the abolishment of the shogunate in the Meiji Restoration. Even though the Kōda family lacked financial resources, Rohan's parents taught all the children attitudes toward study and discipline that contributed to their extraordinarily successful careers later in life. Kōda's mother Kimiko (1873–1910), by contrast, grew up in a merchant family that did not emphasize learning. The Meiji government's reforms had banished the class distinctions that had been central tenets of Edo society, and therefore no one looked askance at Rohan for marrying the daughter of a merchant. Kimiko did, however, encounter resistance to her engagement with Rohan because of his profession as a writer. Writing had not been regarded as a worthy occupation during the Edo period, and this scorn for the creators of fictitious narratives continued into the Meiji period. Despite parental opposition, the couple proved compatible and Kimiko's skills at homemaking and stretching a writer's modest earnings allowed Rohan to write happily and without interruption.

Kōda had an older sister, Utako (1901–1912), and a younger brother, Shigetoyo (known as Ichirō; 1907–1926). Kōda Aya remembers her sister Utako as a bright, well-behaved girl.[5] Rohan doted on Utako and, pleased by her curiosity about the world around her, had their small garden landscaped with fruit trees and plants, so that Utako could study them close at hand. If Utako distinguished herself by merit of her intelligence and enthusiasm, then Ichirō received favor because he was a boy. To the adult Kōda, the writer of memoirs, Rohan did not differ from other fathers in Japan in his desire for a male heir. Indeed, she portrays Ichirō's birth as a moment of ecstasy:

> I can well imagine how my father felt upon the arrival of his long-awaited son. Early spring; sunlight shining softly through the white papered screens; plum blossoms aglow with their sweet scent. In the distance, the drum signaling the

noon hour echoed, low and muted. Father made a toast and sat savoring his wine. In the other room Mother, feeling both satisfied and exhausted, dozed peacefully. When I think of this moment now, I sense a certain poignance in its very auspiciousness. Doubtless that was the happiest time in my father's home life.[6]

During this rosy period when the children were little, the Kōdas moved into a new home in Mukōjima. Rohan, who had designed the house himself, called it Kagyūan, the Snail's Hut.[7] The Kōdas' lot bordered on the vast garden of a fancy, exclusive club *(ryōtei)* called Unsui. Replete with persimmon trees, laurel, arborvitae, tall bamboo, a pond, and even an artificial mountain, the landscape on the other side of the fence could be appropriated to make the Kōdas' modest garden seem lush and even spacious.[8] Rohan forbade Kōda and her siblings from venturing outside their own gates, but the three, weary of the family garden, would on occasion steal into the huge expanse of land next door where they could play and explore.[9]

The Terajima area of Tokyo's Mukōjima, where the Kōdas lived, was located directly across the Sumida River from bustling Asakusa. In those days, the hundreds of cherry trees lining the river at Mukōjima attracted crowds from near and far in the springtime. Strictly speaking, Mukōjima was part of Tokyo's *shitamachi* ("Low City")—areas of the city populated by working people.[10] Merchants, artisans, and others who had served the daimyo and samurai during the Edo period made up the greater part of the *shitamachi* population.[11]

The area around Kōda's childhood home in Mukōjima was partly rural. Rice paddies, vegetable patches, and an abundance of flowering cherry and plum trees flourished in profusion only a short distance from the Kōdas' home.[12] Once Kōda started school and was able to wander beyond the confines of her cultured household, she enjoyed this natural aspect of her neighborhood. At the same time, Rohan would berate Kōda if he spotted even a hint of the countryside in her behavior or speech and would call her "Ayako, the night soil bucket hauler."[13] Although Rohan was among the most loyal of the literary types who had chosen Mukōjima for its natural beauty and relative seclusion, ultimately he retained a deep-seated attachment to his urban origins.

Mukōjima had won fame as one of the most scenic spots in the city. The daimyo, during the Edo period, and the rich and powerful, in the Meiji period, claimed as prime sites for their villas the area's pleasant water frontage, distant as it was from the High City.[14] Mukōjima appears in such Edo-period narratives as Tamenaga Shunsui's (1790–1843) *Shunshoku umegoyomi* (Colors of Spring: Plum Blossom Calendar; 1832–1833). Edo authors chose the area as a perfect setting for "fashionable promenades."[15] Even during the Meiji period, people crowded the Sumida River pleasure boats that floated past Mukōjima's famous cherry trees. Old temples, shrines, and historical sites abounded in Mukōjima. A spacious grove of plum trees, once used by cultured Edo towns-people as a kind of salon for poetry composition, still attracted visitors during the Meiji period. The popularity of Mukōjima as a scenic spot also resulted in the appearance of other types of entertainment for visitors. Customers at Unsui, for example, could enjoy the company of geisha.[16] Before the end of the Meiji period, however, the area began showing signs of decline. The Sumida River had an ugly tendency to overflow its banks, and in the summer flood of 1910 it dramatically displayed its powers by submerging vast areas of *shitamachi*. Mukōjima's residents, dwelling as they did on the banks of the river, suffered great loss. Rohan sent the children to their Aunt Nobuko's in hilly Kōjimachi and then set about the arduous task of drying hundreds of books that had been drenched by the rising waters. After the flood, many of the wealthier people who lived in the area decided to move away. The Kōdas chose to stay put.

When the children were still quite young, Kimiko died, leaving the busy, successful Rohan to raise them by himself. Although Rohan did his writing at home, he was so involved in his work that he found it difficult to devote time to the children's care and maintain the household. Various relatives helped the Kōdas during this trying time. Sorrow visited the family again in May 1912 when Kōda's elder sister Utako came down with scarlet fever and died. In the autumn of that year, Rohan agreed to an arranged marriage with Kodama Yayoko (d. 1945). Since Rohan's life with Kimiko had been happy, the family greeted Yayoko with high expectations. Rohan's first marriage had been one of choice, and his partner was a woman whose self-effacing personality and dili-gence in family affairs complemented Rohan's self-absorption and devotion to his career. His second marriage was prompted less by emotional attachment than by pressure from his family and friends and a personal desire to bring symmetry to his family. The couple did not get along well, however. Yayoko, in her forties when she entered the Kōda household, led an active, independent life as a poet and a devout Christian. She quickly realized that the new roles of housewife and mother did not suit her. Yayoko suffered from various debili-tating ailments, as well, and Kōda therefore shouldered much of the work required to maintain a household, even as a young student. In her early essays from the 1940s and 1950s, Kōda drew a portrait of Yayoko—describing her as inattentive and lacking in motherly attributes—that was far from complimentary. One of Rohan's biographers reinforced this negative view by portraying Yayoko as "cold hearted" despite her avowal of Christian notions of love.[17] In her later works, however, Kōda presented a different picture of her stepmother, one that acknowledged the clash between Yayoko's progressive attitudes and prewar Japan's rigid definitions of female roles in society.

Before her marriage to Rohan, Yayoko had taught in a missionary school and wrote poetry.[18] She devoted much of her time to Bible study, prayer, and church activities. One of the greatest influences in her life was the Reverend Uemura Masahisa (1857–1925), a well-known, charismatic leader of one of the largest Protestant churches in prewar Japan.[19] Uemura denounced the sexism of Japanese society and advocated improving the status of women. He fought for the ordination of women as elders in the Japanese church, and he condemned sexist language such as "*gusai*" (literally "foolish wife" but used to mean "my wife").[20] Although Yayoko adhered to Uemura's philosophy and had remained single for years, life was not easy, either financially or socially, for unmarried women in prewar Japan.

Yayoko did not marry an ordinary man—Rohan stood out even among writers and intellectuals of his generation as an extraordinary and, in many ways, enlightened person—but she did join a household that expected her to play the traditional nurturing roles of wife and mother. Rohan recognized that Yayoko, like himself, would need a place where she could study and write, and he even had a room built for her exclusive use.[21] Both he and the children, however, grew impatient when Yayoko spent too much time away from the rest of the family. When Yayoko would not come home from church or a literary event in time to take care of the evening meal, Rohan complained. Kōda later recalled her fascination with the Bible stories that her stepmother told her. But she feared for her father, who was fond of drinking, when she heard Yayoko talk about sin.

From Yayoko's point of view, the arrangement proved equally unsatisfactory. Not only did she resent the pressure to occupy herself with the care of the children, but she refused to sit and listen passively to Rohan's diatribes on nothingness and other philosophical issues. Disturbed also by Rohan's lack of Christian faith, she would preach about hell and damnation to him and the children. Born to a prosperous provincial family, Yayoko was well educated and sophisticated. She felt out of place in the midst of what she regarded as a bunch of entertainers.[22] Although Rohan devoted much of his time to scholarship, he had started his career as a writer of fiction, even then a despised occupation.

Kōda entered Terajima Elementary School at age six. Because Rohan had not allowed her to play with other children in the neighborhood, this was her first real exposure to the outside world.[23] Although the Kōdas were by no means rich, Kōda was startled by the stark contrast between her own home life and that of the children of the many poor rural and working-class families in the neighborhood. The differences lay not only in financial resources but in education as well. In the memoir *Good for Nothing* (Misokkasu; 1949), Kōda describes her surprise one day at school when she realized that not all of the other children's fathers were as knowledgeable and interested in their children's learning as her father.[24] It was also at this time that Kōda became aware of her father's fame and the extraordinary talents of her extended family.

From 1917 to 1922, Kōda attended a missionary school called Joshi Gakuin (Girls' Academy), located in Kōjimachi Ward in the heart of Tokyo, a considerable distance from her home in Mukōjima.[25] As she had done poorly on the entrance examination for the more prestigious Ochanomizu Middle School for girls, she instead enrolled in Joshi Gakuin, a Christian school. Despite Rohan's Confucian and Taoist leanings, such an education won the approval of the whole family: not only had Yayoko taught at a mission school before her marriage, but Rohan's parents and siblings had converted to Christianity as well. Although Rohan himself was not a believer, he recognized the importance of learning about Western systems of belief and the English language. Each day after classes ended at Joshi Gakuin, Kōda made the long journey through the city and across the Sumida River to Mukōjima. Once home, she began another set of lessons. Rohan taught Kōda about housework, took her to see Western and Japanese films, gave her Edo-period stories and translated English novels to read, and instructed her in the Confucian classics and the composition of traditional Japanese verse. Her mother carefully monitored her studies and classes at school and helped her with English, Japanese, and Bible lessons.[26]

Rohan possessed a definite philosophy of education that was based on his adherence to the principle of *kakubutsu chichi*. This phrase, found in the Confucian classic *Great Learning* (Chinese *Daxue;* Japanese *Daigaku*), means "investigation of all things" with the goal of spiritual cultivation. This principle was elaborated upon and advocated in China by Zhu Xi (1130–1200) and later in Japan by Edo-period Neo-Confucian thinkers. Rohan studied Chinese thought from his youth and passed on aspects of his own Confucian-inspired philosophy to Kōda. Even when teaching his daughter about practical household matters, Rohan told Kōda that one must know things of this world and investigate them thoroughly as a means of self-cultivation. The water in a bucket is not just a tool for cleaning; it is a substance to be scrutinized and contemplated:

> I had lessons in handling water. Father started them with the fearful message that "Water is a frightening thing, and an undisciplined person cannot use it well." I grew up in an area that flooded often, and I feared water in those amounts. But water in a bucket? How could it be frightening?[27]

The years after Kōda's graduation from Joshi Gakuin were difficult. In 1923, the Great Kantō Earthquake and the ensuing fires ravaged much of Tokyo. Because of flooding and an increasing number of factories in the area, most of the other Mukōjima writers had moved away years before, and Rohan had become known as the last of the Mukōjima *bunjin* (literati).[28] The destruction brought on by the 1923 catastrophe, however, made the neighborhood's future uncertain. Although the Kōdas' home still stood after the quake, they decided to leave. The family found a new house in Koishikawa in Tokyo, the neighborhood where Kōda lived until her death.[29]

The Kōda household in Koishikawa had little resemblance to the harmonious young family that had started out in Mukōjima. Both strongly opinionated, self-absorbed people, Rohan and Yayoko either fought or ignored each other most of the time. Adolescence proved to be a difficult time for Ichirō, Kōda's younger brother. He felt alienated from the foreign priests and religion at the missionary school he attended and had trouble adjusting. After being expelled from school, Ichirō fell in with a group of rough boys. Kōda became his most trusted ally and stood up for him even during hard times. In 1926, at the age of nineteen, Ichirō contracted tuberculosis and died. His troubled life later inspired Kōda to write one of her most popular works, the novel *Little Brother* (Otōto; 1956).

Kōda left her father's home in 1928 to marry Mitsuhashi Ikunosuke, the third son of a Tokyo merchant family. In the following year, she bore their only child, Tama. The Mitsuhashi family ran a wholesale liquor business, and they gave Ikunosuke the opportunity to participate in the family business. He did not inherit his parents' business acumen, however, nor the stamina to withstand the rigors of commerce. Despite her lack of experience, Kōda threw herself into running their small retail sake shop. Kōda came from a cultured, learned family, but she did her best to fit into the merchant culture of her husband's family. The marriage, however, proved far from an ideal match. Not only did the couple barely scrape by financially but, to make matters worse, Kōda and Ikunosuke's relationship lacked mutual respect and affection.

Although Kōda refrained from recording her married life in much detail, her essays suggest the unhappiness of this period. In 1938, Kōda divorced her husband and went to live with her father once again.[30]

The reconstituted household now consisted of Kōda, Tama, and Rohan because, several years before Kōda's divorce, Yayoko had left Rohan to live near her family's home in Nagano prefecture.[31] Kōda spent her days in Koishikawa as a homemaker raising her daughter and caring for her aging father. Despite his advanced age, Rohan continued his literary activities. Kōda played hostess to a stream of writers, publishers, editors, and admirers who came to the house to speak with Rohan or assist him with his writing. As Rohan's health declined rapidly in the autumn of 1944, Kōda and several of his loyal colleagues spent countless hours taking dictation of his commentaries on Bashō's poetry, his final works. Rohan's deathbed vigor fit nicely into literary history, as it paralleled the final years of the renowned and well-loved poet Masaoka Shiki (1867–1902)—a fellow devotee of Bashō and reformer of poetry who, although bedridden, spent the last six years of his life working "with almost unbelievable energy . . . writing, dictating, editing, publishing" in the company of his "haiku disciples."[32]

The family was so absorbed in Rohan's care that the raging Pacific War seemed remote. In the spring of 1945, however, the Kōdas, along with hundreds of thousands of other Tokyoites, were forced by news of the U.S. military's massive bombing raids of Japanese cities to consider the personal consequences of Japan's involvement in the world war. Rohan resisted evacuation, but at last the sound of bombs nearby made him acquiesce to Kōda's plan to leave the city. When they finally left Tokyo in March, with books and a few precious belongings, Rohan had to be carried out on a stretcher. The Kōdas evacuated to Nagano prefecture, where they stayed in the house where Yayoko had lived until her death earlier that year. The Kōdas' Koishikawa house was destroyed in May, during the Allied incendiary bombing attacks, and so after the war ended the family moved to Sugano in Ichikawa city, Chiba prefecture, rather than returning to Tokyo. Rohan, who suffered from diabetes, died in July 1947 before a new home in Koishikawa could be completed.

It was during the year of her father's death that Kōda started writing. As Rohan's constant companion, Kōda seemed the logical source for intimate details and a precise account of the frail but venerable writer's domestic life. Noda Utarō (1906–1985), the editor of a literary journal called *Geirin kanpo* (A Stroll Through the Arts), asked Kōda to write about Rohan early in 1947, before Rohan's death, but this first effort appeared in print only after Rohan's death.[33] Even though it was the first thing she had written since her school days, the forty-three-year-old homemaker succeeded in producing a very fine short sketch. In "Random Notes" (Zakki; 1947), "His Last Hours" (Shūen; 1947), "A Record of the Funeral" (Sōsō no ki; 1947), and "Notes from Sugano" (Sugano no ki; 1949), Kōda focused on the subject suggested by Noda and other editors: Rohan and his family life.[34] From the beginning, the inexperienced writer held her audience's interest with her rhythmic colloquial style, sense of humor, and careful attention to detail.

These early works describe Kōda's relationship with her father and her emotional reactions to his illness and death. Her analysis of her own psychological state is nuanced. Kōda could never simply write "I felt horrified when I realized that my father was dying." Instead she evokes death metaphorically, as a visitor, and carefully analyzes its manner of imposing itself on the body. Kōda does not offer rosy sketches of this period when her father died or misty accounts of their relationship. Rather, she presents her father's deteriorating condition in astonishing and vivid detail, from the pallor of his skin to his appearance as death overtook his body. She describes her desperation as she wonders to whom she can turn for help. Far from romanticizing the ailing Rohan, Kōda shows his stubbornness and brutal frankness. Though not consciously the artist, Kōda transforms the events surrounding her father's illness into a literary text through a variety of tropes and a vivid and concise use of language. Aside from these well-received essays about Rohan, Kōda wrote, in the late 1940s and early 1950s, a number of longer works about her own childhood and life with her father in his younger days.[35] These fragments of autobiography exhibit the fledgling writer's surprisingly mature and elegant style as well as her talent for transforming ordinary childhood incidents into appealing stories.

With her father's death, Kōda became not only a writer but a textual persona. The conventions of modern Japanese literature value the evocation of a literary persona that does not differ a great deal from the historical author, as the poetics of the *watakushi shōsetsu* (personal fiction, I-novel) show.[36] Shiga Naoya, Uno Chiyo, Dazai Osamu, and many other writers all presented a literary alter ego in their works—a voice that readers understand as the authentic voice of the "author," performing a discursive version of lived experience, a sincere discourse portraying interiority. For reasons of readerly expectation and authorial self-presentation, Kōda's autobiographically inspired narratives do not fit neatly into the generic category of *watakushi shōsetsu*. As Tomi Suzuki, Dennis Washburn, and others have reminded us, the parameters of the *watakushi shōsetsu* genre have evolved less from formal, rhetorical, or structural features of texts and more from conventions of reading, print culture, and social and critical practices instrumental in the formation of the canon. That is, the reader who seeks a consistent set of common formal features in the corpus of texts conventionally classified as *watakushi shōsetsu* will simply not find them. Rather, as the hallmark of this genre, both the author and reader agree to understand the text as closely related to the life of the historical individual who produced the text and as a work of art/literature. The quality of sincerity *(makoto)* is also demanded of the creative act of writing and being read as *watakushi shōsetsu*. Suzuki further notes that the "I-novel," as she calls it, is a "historically constructed dominant reading and interpretive paradigm—which soon became a generative cultural discourse."[37]

Critics and scholars have amply illustrated the mediating nature of texts and discursive practices—even those aimed at relating actual events and facts or the course of a person's life. Given the evocative, highly idiosyncratic, and refined nature of Kōda's writing style, Japanese readers and critics do not regard Kōda's works that focus on her childhood and Rohan as a devalued form of nonfiction writing. At the start, Kōda concentrated on the past and succeeded through her writing in making herself into something she had never been before in the public's eye: the great Rohan's child, a role she could play only by resurrecting, or creating, her life with him in textual form. Thus Rohan is not the central figure in her narratives. In fact, Rohan rarely appears as a fully developed individual. The father, when he does appear, tends to be faintly sketched and speaks in a stilted, archaic manner. Even the very first essays— ostensibly about life with father—focus more on the daughter and her perceptions than on the famous Rohan. She acknowledges her original audience, made up of Rohan's followers, in various ways. She writes of her own discomfort at having to use her father's famous name in order to get help during his illness, for example, and she describes the involvement of his literary colleagues, such as publishers, editors, and his biographer Shiotani San, in their life.[38]

The voice that narrates all the tales of childhood and the enigmatic father is above all distinctive. It was not until several decades later, however, that Kōda began to write essays that give the reader a sense of the face behind the voice, of a contemporary reality, and this was when she was in her sixties. Even in her fictional works (autobiographically inspired or not), the present is veiled in a cloak of remembrance—not the bittersweet longing of nostalgia but a frank exploration of memories. This quality reflects Rohan's emphasis on the importance of investigating in detail the qualities of the world around us and, in this case, the contents of Kōda's recollections.

During the first several decades of her career, the past offered certainty for

Kōda in the face of an unstable personal life and the uncertain world around her. The bomb and the defeat delivered a devastating blow to national identity. Kōda's reliance on memory and the authority of her father's intellect contrasted starkly with the *sengoha* (postwar school) writers, who sought a new beginning for Japan's literature, and the younger *daisan no shinjin* writers ("third generation of new writers"), who plunged into examinations of the trials and battles of postwar life.[39] For this predominantly male group of writers, the end of the war spelled the "erosion of the deified self" and the collapse of the patriarchal family system that had figured as central tenets of prewar fiction, especially the *watakushi shōsetsu* tradition.[40] Kōda's writings also defy identification with several significant trends in fiction by other female writers of the early postwar era. Even as she was criticized for wartime collaboration, for example, Hayashi Fumiko (1903–1951) produced illuminating portraits of women who were buffeted by the social upheaval and deprivation of the early postwar days. Consistently throughout her career, Ariyoshi Sawako (1931–1984) confronted pressing current social and political issues such as pollution and an aging population in her realist fiction. Kōda's contemporary Enchi Fumiko (1905–1986) boldly explored in her novels the mythical, spiritual, and erotic potential of women, with frequent reference to premodern Japanese literature.

Perhaps the most notable current in postwar literature, for both women's and men's writing, was the growing fascination with stories that celebrated in explicit detail sex and eroticism—those based outside the "real world, in a complete, fully articulated world of fantasy," a fictional realm where "it is possible to explore freely the implications of overturning the dominant hierarchies."[41] While a writer such as Uno Chiyo (1897–1996) had even in the prewar period focused on obsessive love, sex, blood, and death in her fiction, the postwar literary scene is marked by a predominance of fiction concerning what Sharalyn Orbaugh has called "disturbing themes" and images, such as "incest, explicit sado-masochism, amnesia, infanticide, cannibalism, murder, dismemberment, disfiguration, and so on." The writers do not employ such themes merely for shock value or simply to titillate readers. Rather, Kōno Taeko (b. 1926), Takahashi Takako (b. 1932), and others view such "shocking appropriations of violent elements of the discourse of the body" as a means of political expression.[42] Kōda, however, had lived apart from elaborate notions of a deified self and patriarchy and fantasy and the discourses of the body and sexuality. Her starting point, even after she became involved in writing, was that of a homemaker. For Kōda, modesty was a virtue and art was something that belonged to others, such as her father and her aunts, who were accomplished musicians.

When Kōda mentions her writing activities, it is ostensibly to denigrate her efforts. In April 1950, for example, nestled in among peculiar tales of robbery and the latest in Paris fashions, an article by the fledgling author appeared in the *Mainichi Shinbun:*

> Certainly I have worked hard on my writing, but the effort involved is nothing compared with Father. In fact, it hardly qualifies as real writing at all, when you consider that I have never done it with a sense of dedication. . . .
>
> When first asked for an essay, I was so overjoyed that I almost forgot my own family. For forty years, I had always been the good-for-nothing. I had never won recognition for anything. At Father's side, I became timorous, and was constantly being scolded, and never praised. Even when Father was pleased with a meal I had prepared, he would inevitably attribute its success to his own good advice. This, then, was my first experience with love. . . .
>
> To the extent that I do not devote myself to my writing, I have been insincere to those who take the trouble to read my essays. Morally this is inexcusable. . . . I have thus made the decision to quit writing, although someday I may have the urge to take it up again. If that day comes, I must abandon these remembrances of my father and write about other things.[43]

Although Kōda writes extensively about her own life, her works are not classified by critics as *watakushi shōsetsu*. If anything her resistance to the concept of transcendent art and sincerity is a defining characteristic of her texts and career. She lacked "dedication" and devotion and saw herself as working outside the orthodox realm of modern Japanese letters and the hallowed notion of artistic sincerity. This also speaks to the distance between Kōda and the "modern Japanese concern for, and preoccupation with, Western notions of love, sexuality, nature, and 'truth,' which . . . constituted a major axis of I-novel discourse and radiated from the privileged signifier of modernity, the 'self.'"[44]

Titled "Kōda Aya Abandons Her Writing Brush," the newspaper article just cited has been interpreted by some readers as marking Kōda's break with her past.[45] The conceit of humility appears in other essays, as well, but the notion that writing also meant for her recognition and love—her first experience with love—is communicated with even greater force than the recurring humility theme.[46] The praise for her writing from readers and critics and the repeated requests from publishers astonished and pleased her. Kōda had lived most of her life, unknown to the public, in the shadow of a famous, egotistical man.

Kōda's essays suggest that Rohan constantly corrected and criticized her and that she felt unworthy and unloved.[47] She also measured herself against other family members who had earned public recognition and fame, such as her aunts Kōda Nobuko and Andō Kōko, who were renowned musicians and tutors to Japan's imperial family. Her stepmother Yayoko, moreover, possessed an intellect and interests far beyond those expected of a Japanese woman of her day.

If the act of writing and having a reading audience signified love and acceptance for Kōda, then the textual arena itself was a place where she could illustrate the deep bond between herself and the renowned Rohan. Even as she claims that she was an "unlovable child" and last in her father's affections, she asserts the affinities between her father and herself. In "Notes from Sugano," Kōda ostensibly sets out to restate her lack of favor in the family but ends up demonstrating the shared experience that leads to an identification between herself and her father. In one passage, Kōda has prepared a birthday dinner for her bedridden father. Despite the near impossibility of procuring proper ingredients in the lean years immediately after the war, she manages to scrape a respectable meal together. When Rohan sees the tray laden with the dishes she has cooked—sea bream *(tai)* and *sekihan,* a rice dish prepared for special occasions—he smiles broadly. He is so ill that he cannot take a bite of the meal, but even so he does not let Kōda remove the tray. Rohan goes into a daze, and Kōda conjectures that he is recalling a meal that his mother prepared for him as a child. At length, he urges Kōda to eat his birthday meal.

As in many of her memoirs, the reader understands that such subtle depiction of Rohan's pleasure at her efforts represents a recognition of his affection for her. His association of the meal she prepared with one from his past signifies to her the special bond between them:

> Father used to say that his mother did not love him. Despite this, Father surprised me and my brother by collapsing in tears when he heard that our grandmother had passed away. I also thought that Father did not love me. My Aunt Nobuko told me, "Your father said that he didn't really like you, you know. All the kids he loved died and you're the only one left. But you're still taking care of him, even though he's hard on you and makes you cry. I think you're wonderful." Her words of support soothed me in rough times and helped me to survive. Unlike my cousins who had artistic talent and had done well in school, I was qualified only as a homemaker, though an unwilling one.
>
> Mr. Kuramoto, one of Father's students, once told me, "Your father loved Utako and Ichirō so much." I interpreted that to mean that Father didn't love me. I heard that Mr. Urushiyama told Mr. Kobayashi, "Ayako, unfortunately,

was just never easy to like, even as a child." . . . It made me sad that I was always the outsider, and, in time, my sadness grew into resentment. As time passed, I became stubborn. I really wanted to be loved by Father.[48]

Critics and readers tend to define Kōda primarily in terms of her relationship with her father, ignoring others who had a significant influence on her life. Kōda's own writings, however, reveal the importance of women in her life and the wide variety of role models she had, even in a day and age when women's spheres of activity in Japan were severely circumscribed. Kōda indeed struggled with her relationship with Rohan—more because he tended to dominate and demand a great deal of attention than because she wanted to be like him or take his place. She focused on Rohan in her writings in response to the public and the publishing world's interests. In the textual realm that Kōda created, he was a justification for her writing and a reason for the persona to exist. Although she continued to employ this literary creation called Rohan throughout her career, his presence faded in time and portraits of other people, especially other women, came to occupy center stage.

Rohan may not have commended Kōda for her efforts in their home, but neither did he ignore her. Like many fathers in prewar Japan, he reserved his highest hopes for his firstborn son. At the same time, because of the good examples of his sisters and his second wife, he had every reason to believe that women could succeed in public careers and engage in intellectual and artistic pursuits. Rohan regarded his role as parent and teacher to his daughter Aya quite seriously. He taught Kōda about literature, finances, philosophy, housekeeping, and social matters. Kōda took pride in creating a literary persona and a narrative realm in which she stands steadfastly as a survivor and an example of an upright individual steeped in Rohan's intellectual, moral, and literary teachings. She also brings to life the personalities and wisdom of figures such as her stepmother, who, although not nearly so prominent as Rohan in the public's eye, influenced her life profoundly.

Kōda did not spend all of her time writing after her father's death. In the winter of 1951–1952, Kōda worked as a maid for four months in a geisha house *(okiya)* in the Yanagibashi district of Tokyo. Disillusioned with her efforts at writing, despite her success, she decided to make an honest living at a job that did not provoke in her anxiety about dedication to art, sincerity, and her illustrious family's shadow. Her tenure as a maid did not last long, however, because the financially strapped *okiya* demanded that Kōda survive solely on rice and salty pickles.[49] Physically weakened, Kōda returned to her writing desk in Koishikawa.

Kōda was intrigued by the women who worked at the *okiya,* and she observed them closely during her brief stay. She remembered passing by geisha houses as a child in Mukōjima, and her fascination with these seemingly free and vibrant beings had not waned. Several years after her experience at the geisha house, Kōda wrote what was to become one of her most famous works: *Flowing* (Nagareru; 1955). *Flowing* concerns a financially troubled geisha house in early postwar Tokyo and the women there. The central figure is Rika, a widow who has come to work as a maid at the house. Although autobiographically inspired, *Flowing* is regarded by most readers and critics as a novel marking a new phase in Kōda's literary career. It is her first sustained, full-length narrative that focuses on a topic other than Rohan and her childhood.

In the context of Japanese narrative, the alternative of writing "imaginative" fiction about other worlds, times, and characters did not immediately present itself to Kōda. In twentieth-century Japanese literature, the predominance of personal fiction—the vaguely defined genre of the *watakushi shōsetsu*—encouraged Kōda to choose the more familiar route: fashioning personal experience into fictional discourse by blending autobiographical and fictional fact. Kōda's works also reflect the extreme subjectivity and celebration of the artist's consciousness said to be inherent in this tradition. Thus the quality of the narrative voice and the use of imagery tend to be more pronounced than matters of plot or characterization.

During the second decade of her career, Kōda turned increasingly to short fiction and novels. She won literary prizes for *The Black Kimono* (Kuroi suso; 1955), a collection of short stories, and for her novel *Flowing.* Film versions of *Flowing* and *Little Brother* received awards as well. The first multivolume collection *(zenshū)* of Kōda's works appeared in 1958–1959, a decade after she started writing. She also edited volumes of her father's correspondence, essays, and collected works. Subsequently Kōda tried her hand at different types of writing, especially full-length novels. In these novels she employs a third-person narrator and concentrates on the mechanics of the plot. Like many of her works, the novels appeared first in serialized form in journals. *The Sadness of the North* (Hokushū; 1959) revolves around a young woman named Asogi, her failing marriage, and her friendship with her cousin Junji.

The Struggle (Tō; 1965) represents a further departure from Kōda's accustomed realm. It involves the patients and staff at a tuberculosis sanatorium. Kōda drew inspiration from her son-in-law, a physician, and from the loss of her own brother to the disease. In *The Struggle,* Kōda employs an omniscient narrator and tries her hand at fully wrought male characters. *The Struggle* is not so much an effort to emulate Thomas Mann's *The Magic Mountain* as an earnest attempt to portray daily life at a TB hospital in an era before effective treatments for the disease had been discovered. Because of its subject, *The Struggle* appealed to a broad audience and received popular acclaim. In 1973, Kōda was awarded the Joryū Bungaku Shō literary prize for women writers for *The Struggle*.

Kōda as Mature Narrator

During the 1960s and 1970s—an era of high economic growth—Kōda enjoyed the fruits of Tokyo's material prosperity and domestic stability. Her reputation as an author well established and the ghosts of Rohan and her childhood largely quelled, Kōda boldly expanded her sphere of activity and the focus of her writing. Despite her apparent lack of feminist sentiments, Kōda celebrated, in her work from this period, the merits of living independently as an older woman. From the 1960s, Kōda composed numerous essays about growing old: "A Friend for Life" (Mono iwanu isshō no tomo; 1966), "Living Alone" (Hitorigurashi; 1962), "Just My Age" (Onai doshi; 1963), "A Good Day" (Tama no ii hi; 1965), and "Whistle of Grass" (Kusabue; 1977) exhibit Kōda's characteristic style, powers of observation, and interest in the past.[50] In 1966, Kōda published a remarkable coming-of-age novel, titled *Kimono,* in which she frankly and skillfully explores the contradictions of heterosexual marriage and celebrates the sensuality and self-awareness of female adolescence. Because *Kimono* was serialized in a journal and did not appear in single-volume form until after Kōda's death, the novel did not at the time receive the critical and readerly consideration that it deserved.

Consistent in her lack of commentary on pressing political issues, Kōda never became engaged in the U.S.-Japan Security Treaty (ANPO) controversy, or in citizens' movements protesting unchecked economic and industrial growth, or in the debate about war guilt. Even when asked to contribute an essay to a special journal issue on the topic of 15 August 1956, the eleventh anniversary of the emperor's radio broadcast announcing Japan's surrender in World War II, Kōda's response is characteristically oblique:

> The night before, my photography friends had reminded me that they would be coming to take a picture for a book, so that morning I woke up thinking of their visit. I did look at the garden carefully, because I wanted to remember what it looked like that day. I counted seven bright red hollyhock stalks in bloom.

In the morning, I had a bit of writing to get done. Again and again, I would write three or four lines on a piece of paper, only to set it aside and start over with a clean sheet. When at last I finished the essay, I set about erasing all the writing from the wasted pieces of paper and making it into new paper. This was the same way I always treated paper, because I found that it calmed me down after writing.

At 1:30, I did a recording for a radio program. Rather than reading from a written script, I would usually try to speak only from an outline, but that day I realized that I needed two more minutes of material. I added what I thought would take about that much time, but then I ended up going over by a full minute. I became so flustered that I could feel my temperature rise. That, combined with the blast of the air conditioner on my skin, made me shudder.

Though August the fifteenth of this year scarcely differed from any other day for me, I must admit that ever since that day in 1945 I have been able to pray, with my eyes open, even in the midst of a meal. Today I sat, with my cat in my lap, looked out at the green persimmons hanging from the branches, and prayed about the horrors of war. Several friends came to visit.[51]

As Kōda matured, she produced fewer fictional works set in the social realm. Instead she became interested in writing about places in Japan she had visited, especially the sites of huge and catastrophic landslides, tall stands of virgin forest, the high seas—all places far from her home, her childhood, her Tokyo. Kōda's interest in the natural world, apparent in many essays written during the last three decades of her life, makes sense in biographical, narrative, and social contexts. These extended essays about her journeys to places where terrible landslides had occurred include "Ore" (Jigane; 1968), *Landslides* (Kuzure; 1976), and *Trees* (Ki; 1971). Her motives for this unexpected change in focus vary: Kōda reported that she traveled to see old trees and landslides and the like because she found beauty in the process of the earth changing or trees growing.[52] These journeys also provided her with an opportunity to ponder her own life and the process of growing old. In the face of vast and ever changing nature, Kōda expresses amazement at how she survived so long in what she terms her safe and narrow world.[53]

In her own way, in these later works Kōda was also addressing issues articulated widely from the 1960s about Japan's natural environment and the threats posed by rapid and initially unquestioned economic and industrial growth. Kōda's essays remind the reader that Japan is more than just a collection of massive, sprawling urban areas and painstakingly tended and subsidized rice paddies and fields of tea. She examines precisely the barren and eroding mountainsides and steep valleys, the vast and constantly changing oceans, the untouched forests protected from logging companies. Kōda reminds us of the enormous potential for change and destruction—as well as renewal—often forgotten in the seeming certainty and solidity of urban structures, economic affluence, even the earth beneath our feet. Indeed, she comments that most people forget all about natural disasters such as landslides until one happens.[54] In *Landslides*, Kōda recalls her initial efforts to become a student of geology:

> In order to understand landslides, one must start by learning about what is happening deep within the earth, and then about the constitution of the continents and the oceans; how mountains are formed; the properties of boulders, rocks, earth, and sand; the earth's time line; climate change, the four seasons, and botany; the properties of water; the disposition of rivers; and on and on. Only then can one truly understand landslides, I learned to my amazement. It was beyond me. In the first place, I personally did not have that many years left in me, and even as a child I had not had much affinity for studying. . . . So I decided to call it quits as a scholar of landslides. . . . But I did have the capacity to venture out and see landslides with my own two eyes, and to grasp the feeling *(kandō)* of landslides. I would be satisfied if I could create in words that emotion and convey it to my readers.[55]

Her works from this period abound in detailed and precise description: from place-names to dates to detailed descriptions of the sights and sounds of the avalanches of earth and rock and the other natural phenomena she observed. Her method clearly reflects the training she received from Rohan— based on his belief in the investigation of things, careful observation, and narrative expression—and her subsequent refinement of this intellectual, aesthetic, and moral attitude and practice. She expresses only temporary disappointment in her lack of aptitude for the discipline of geology presented in books.

She also takes advantage of the knowledge of her many guides in the mountains, constantly asking questions about the sites they visit. Despite her advanced age and physical limitations, Kōda remains determined to climb Mount Fuji to a famous landslide area:

> Every time [my guide] explained something to me, he would talk about things with which I was not familiar, and I would have even more questions. "Why is that?" I would ask. "Could you explain the reason for that?" And so his explanations became increasingly detailed and complex, and I would try all the

more feverishly to set my poor memory into motion and remember what he was saying. . . . Then I asked, "Basically, what is a landslide? Why does the earth crumble like that?"

"Well," he said. After pausing for a moment, he replied: "It happens at a weak spot in the earth, a structural weakness." A weak spot. Weak. This one word had the effect of calming me, instantly, like a tranquilizer. I felt so surprised at his explanation, because up until that moment I had always considered landslides to be something that one could see happening on the surface—as destruction, as the earth's ruin, as erosion, as an absence. But a structural weakness is not something visible on the surface of the soil. Rather, it suggests the depth of the earth's outer crust, and gestures toward the causes of that weakness.[56]

In her essays about trees and landslides, Kōda rarely mentions Rohan directly or her connection to him. In fact, a pivotal moment appears early in *Landslides* when she visits a bookstore that specializes in geology and science in order to find out more about the natural phenomenon she plans to observe in the mountains. Flustered at the bookstore manager's request for her name card, she simply introduces herself as "an old woman who lives in Koishikawa and writes random essays."[57]

Kōda did not turn away from human affairs entirely, however. She became actively involved in the reconstruction of a pagoda at Hōrinji Temple in Nara and subsequently published a series of essays about the structure. For someone whose life had revolved around the home, such public activity appears unusual. In the context of Kōda's writings, however, her attention to the pagoda seems consistent because it is commemorative in nature.[58] Her father Rohan's most famous piece of fiction, *The Five-Story Pagoda,* concerned an idealistic carpenter named Jūbei who, against all odds, successfully builds a pagoda (an act of great religious merit) and proudly watches it survive a fierce storm.[59] In this way Kōda Aya's writing came full circle: from the depiction of memories of her father to the commemoration of his literary works and ideals in her own narratives.

Since her death from heart failure in 1990, Kōda's fiction and essays have enjoyed new popularity, even with younger readers. This posthumous revival has brought to light her novel *Kimono* (1965–1966), as well as the reissue of *Trees* and *Landslides,* and occasioned a reconsideration of the texts she wrote and indeed her literary career. While some critics laud her works primarily for the excellent style and her beautiful Japanese, others have sought to reevaluate Kōda's writings in the context of feminist and reader response criticism. In the following chapters I discuss the work and life of Kōda Aya in light of changes in critical horizons, readership, and especially constructions of gender and the family in the latter half of the twentieth century. For although Kōda's ideas about herself as a writer and the purposes of narrative seem simple and straight-forward, many widespread attitudes toward the value of prose narrative and the ambiguous zone that circumscribes habits of reading and writing a wide variety of genres—novels *(shōsetsu)*, essays, memoirs, biography, and poetry—are sug-gested in the shifting reception of her works and the course of her professional life as a writer. Moreover, I wish to examine the means by which Kōda estab-lishes her mature professional and artistic reputation by claiming the impor-tance of affect or heightened emotion *(kandō)* in ways that appeal directly to constructions and conceptions of affect in premodern and modern Japanese lit-erature and culture. At the same time, however, I suggest an idiosyncratic spin, or inversion, on the relationship between affect and narrative, text and reader.

Because Kōda Aya was a prolific writer, I have chosen in this study to focus on her most accomplished and provocative works and their reception rather than surveying her entire oeuvre. To broaden her English-speaking audience, moreover, I include a number of my own translations of her essays and short stories.

Notes

1. I refer to this author as Kōda, rather than Aya, because Japanese critics and schol-ars usually refer to authors by their family name rather than their personal name (Enchi, for example, or Tanizaki)—unless they use a pen name (such as Rohan and Ichiyō).

2. Kōda Aya, interview with the author, Tokyo, 17 May 1985.

3. For accounts of Kōda Rohan's life and career see Yanagida Izumi, *Kōda Rohan* (Chūō Kōronsha, 1942); Shiotani San, *Kōda Rohan,* 3 vols. (Chūō Kōronsha, 1965–1968); and Chieko Mulhern, *Kōda Rohan* (Boston: G. K. Hall, 1977).

4. Van Gessel claims that for male authors of the *katei shōsetsu* (domestic novel) genre, the home was "the ultimate human battlefield, the ground on which the most pain-ful conflicts are waged, and where human relations are subjected to their most poignant tests." It is significant that Gessel elects to use metaphors of war (a male arena) for the home. This metaphor assumes that male experience must be used to dignify and justify the works of male authors who write about a traditionally female, and thus marginal, realm. Kōda's works are not usually classified as *katei shōsetsu.* See Van Gessel, *The Sting of Life: Four Contemporary Japanese Novelists* (New York: Columbia University Press, 1989), p. 31.

5. *Kōda Aya zenshū* (hereafter *KAZS*), 7 vols. (Iwanami Shoten, 1994–1996), 2:56–59; and Shiotani, *Kōda Rohan,* 2:172.

6. *Misokkasu, KAZS* 2:6.

7. The family moved into Kagyūan in Mukōjima in February 1908. In premodern Japan, it was traditional for writers to name their residences. See Shiotani, *Kōda Rohan,* 2:36.

8. Ibid., p. 38.

9. Ibid., p. 120.

10. Edward Seidensticker identifies the residents of *shitamachi* as primarily "plebeian" in *Low City, High City: Tokyo from Edo to the Earthquake* (Rutland, Vt.: Tuttle, 1984), pp. 8 and 249.

11. From these parts of the city arose a vital culture—as opposed to the staid milieu of *yamanote,* the "High City," where daimyo and aristocrats had once resided. The Low City bustled with urbanites who valued flexibility and outspokenness. The Low City dweller spoke a direct, crisply rhythmed dialect that differed sharply from the nuanced, refined speech of *yamanote.*

12. Kōda Aya recalls the rural atmosphere of Mukōjima and the many harvest festivals in "Fundo no kaki," *KAZS* 2:237, and in *Konna Koto, KAZS* 1:168.

13. *Misokkasu, KAZS* 2:55.

14. Seidensticker, *Low City, High City,* p. 249.

15. Alan S. Woodhull, "Romantic Edo Fiction: A Study of the Ninjōbon and Complete Translation of *Shunshoku Umegoyomi*" (Ph.D. diss., Stanford University, 1978), p. 361, n. 84.

16. Later, in the 1930s, author Nagai Kafū would write about his visits to the Tamanoi, a less exclusive pleasure district adjacent to Mukōjima. Seidensticker surmises that Tamanoi appeared after the 1923 Great Kantō Earthquake, when geisha and prostitute houses moved there from Asakusa. See Edward Seidensticker, *Kafū the Scribbler: The Life and Writings of Nagai Kafū* (Stanford: Stanford University Press, 1965), p. 144.

17. Shiotani, *Kōda Rohan,* 2:192.

18. Yayoko's poetry appeared in an anthology called the *Shin-Manyoshū* under her pen name, Kodama Teruko.

19. Uemura performed Rohan and Yayoko's wedding ceremony. He also had earlier contacts with Rohan's family because he baptized Rohan's parents and siblings. (Rohan was working in Hokkaido at the time.) Poet Masamune Hakuchō (1879–1962) and novelist Kunikida Doppo (1871–1908) were among Uemura's followers.

20. Richard H. Drummond, *A History of Christianity in Japan* (Grand Rapids: Eerdsman, 1971), p. 219.

21. Poet and sculptor Takamura Kōtarō and aspiring painter Chieko are another example of a married couple who, despite declarations of equal opportunities for both male and female in their artistic pursuits, ended up in a quite traditional division of labor. In Chieko's case, especially, this early attempt at a new type of marriage proved disastrous.

22. Rohan's two sisters, Andō Kōko and Kōda Nobuko, were well-respected Western classical musicians.

23. *Misokkasu, KAZS* 2:91.

24. Ibid., pp. 92–94.

25. Kōjimachi ward bordered on the imperial palace. Joshi Gakuin was founded in the early Meiji period (1870s). A. K. Reischauer was the principal from 1920 to 1927. See Tamura Mitsuru, ed., *Joshigaku hachijūnen shi* (Joshigakuin, 1951), p. 343.

26. *Konna koto, KAZS* 1:164–166. Kōda states that the only time she felt close to her stepmother was during this period when Yayoko showed interest in her studies.

27. The long series of essays titled "Atomiyosowaka" (Incantations; 1948) concerns the way Rohan taught Kōda; *Konna koto, KAZS* 1:121–122.

28. As a result of the prosperity brought to Japan by World War I, a growing number of factories had appeared on the easily accessible east bank of the river.

29. Rohan's sister Nobuko had lived in Koishikawa, but by this time she had moved to Kōjimachi. The sister of writer Higuchi Ichiyō (1872–1896) helped the Kōdas find their first Koishikawa house.

30. Shiotani discusses the divorce in *Kōda Rohan,* 3:264. Okuno suggests that Kōda's divorce was not the act of an enlightened modern woman seeking liberation but an act of desperation on the part of a person caught in an impossible situation. See Okuno Takeo, *Joryū sakkaron* (Daisanmonmeisha, 1974), p. 98.

31. Although Rohan and Yayoko were not compatible, they did not divorce. Divorce was rather uncommon in prewar Japan and would have made life very difficult for both of them. See Shiotani, *Kōda Rohan,* 2:195 and 3:209–210.

32. Brower further comments about Shiki that it "is not difficult to understand why his premature death at the age of thirty-five should have been so deeply felt, or why his memory became a cult with his most loyal followers." See Robert Brower, "Masaoka Shiki and Tanka Reform," in *Tradition and Modernization in Japanese Culture,* ed. Donald H. Shively (Princeton: Princeton University Press, 1971), pp. 386–387.

33. Noda Utarō was active in reviving *Geirin kanpo* soon after the end of the war. He was known as a poet and author of numerous books about literature, including the well-known *bungaku sanpo* (literary stroll) series.

34. All are included in *KAZS* 1.

35. Notable autobiographical pieces include *Misokkasu* (Good for Nothing; 1949) and *Kusa no hana* (Flowers in the Grass; 1951).

36. Edward Fowler points out that when one is reading the *watakushi shōsetsu*, a text's authenticity comes from the author's perceived presence. He also argues that authorial presence is itself a convention and that the illusion of presence comes about through certain modes of presentation. See Edward Fowler, *The Rhetoric of Confession: Shishōsetsu in Early Twentieth-Century Japanese Fiction* (Berkeley: University of California Press, 1988), pp. xxi–7. Scholars of Western autobiography have pointed out the impossibility of demarcating fiction and nonfiction. Eakin notes that autobiography "in our time is increasingly understood as both an art of memory and an art of the imagination." See Paul John Eakin, *Fictions in Autobiography: Studies in the Art of Self-Invention* (Princeton: Princeton University Press, 1985), pp. 5–6. Spengemann, in his historical study of autobiography, observes that while in earlier centuries Western autobiography involved the measure of a man against the ideal image of his creator, modern autobiography "becomes synonymous with symbolic action in any form" because "whatever one writes about will be about the self it constructs. . . . To call any modernist work 'autobiographical' is merely to utter a tautology." See William C. Spengemann, *The Forms of Autobiography: Episodes in the History of a Literary Genre* (New Haven: Yale University Press, 1980), p. 168. This personal bent, furthermore, characterizes much of modern Japanese prose.

    The use of factual materials is not always the sole criterion for distinguishing fiction and nonfiction. Barbara Herrnstein Smith has discussed the importance of the author's and readers' assumptions in defining categories of fiction and nonfiction. See Smith, *On the Margins of Discourse: The Relation of Literature to Language* (Chicago: University of Chicago Press, 1978), pp. 47 and 141–144. Also relevant to this question of literature and reality is Todorov's assertion that while literary works do "evoke life . . . the absence of a rigorous relation of truth must at the same time make us extremely cautious: the text can 'reflect' social life but can just as well incarnate its exact opposite. Such a perspective [of viewing literary works as a means of understanding culture and societies at certain points in history] is quite legitimate, but leads us beyond poetics: by putting literature on the same level as any other document, we are obviously no longer concerned with its specific literary qualities." See Tsvetan Todorov, *Introduction to Poetics* (Minneapolis: University of Minnesota Press, 1981), p. 18.

37. Tomi Suzuki, *Narrating the Self: Fictions of Japanese Modernity* (Stanford: Stanford University Press, 1996), p. 10. Another highly insightful discussion of the genre can be found in Dennis C. Washburn, *The Dilemma of the Modern in Japanese Fic-*

tion (New Haven: Yale University Press, 1995), pp. 139–163. See also Irmela Hijiya-Kirschnereit, *Rituals of Self-Revelation: Shishōsetsu as Literary Genre and Socio-Cultural Phenomenon* (Cambridge, Mass.: Harvard University Press, 1996).

38. "Sugano no ki," *KAZS* 1:13ff; 47ff.

39. See Gessel, *Sting of Life,* and Honda Shūgo, *Monogatari sengo bungakushi* (Shin-chōsha, 1965).

40. Gessel, *Sting of Life,* p. 68.

41. Sharalyn Orbaugh, "The Body in Contemporary Japanese Women's Fiction," in *The Woman's Hand: Gender and Theory in Japanese Women's Writing,* ed. Paul Gordon Schalow and Janet A. Walker (Stanford: Stanford University Press, 1996), p. 124.

42. Ibid., pp. 127–128.

43. *Yūkan Mainichi Shinbun,* 7 April 1950, p. 5.

44. Suzuki, *Narrating the Self,* p. 10. At the same time, Karatani Kōjin reminds readers that "as long as a work is seen as the 'expression' of the 'self' of an 'author,' that work is already located within the apparatus of modern literature, no matter how antimodern and anti-Western it may be." See Karatani Kōjin, "Afterword to the English Edition," in *Origins of Modern Japanese Literature,* trans. Brett DeBary (Durham: Duke University Press, 1993), p. 192.

45. Itagaki Naoko, *Meiji Taishō Shōwa no joryū bungaku* (Ōfūsha, 1967), p. 288. See also Iwaya Daishi, *Monogatari joryū bundanshi,* 2 vols. (Chūō Kōronsha, 1977), 2:117; *KAZS* 4:69.

46. Humility is a common aspect of discourse in Japanese, even in narrative. It is a culturally acceptable form of self-presentation, whether it originates in sincere self-deprecation or as a socially sanctioned rhetorical style.

47. Because Rohan and his biographers did not write much about the dynamics of their life together, there is little corroborating evidence for Kōda's view of her relationship with her father. If anything, the account by Aoki Tama, Kōda's daughter, portrays her mother as a strong and sometimes difficult individual who could hold her own in confrontations with Rohan. See Aoki Tama, *Koishikawa no uchi* (Kōdansha, 1994). See also a public lecture by Kōda on her personal and professional development and her family relations, "Kōen: 'Deai to kandō' Iwanami no bunka kōenkai nite," in *KAZS* 22 (cassette tape).

48. "Sugano no ki," *KAZS* 1:68–69.

49. Interview with the author, 21 May 1986.

50. Many of these essays appear in the volume *Daidokoro no Oto* (Kōdansha, 1992).

51. *KAZS* 7:272–273.

52. Interview with the author, 21 May 1986.

53. Collections of these essays were published posthumously in the volumes *Kuzure* (Landslides; Kōdansha, 1991) and *Ki* (Trees; Shinchōsha, 1992) and also in *KAZS* 19 and 21.

54. *KAZS* 21:26.

55. Ibid., pp. 24–25.

56. Ibid., pp. 28–30.

57. Ibid., p. 20.

58. Vance defines commemoration as "any gesture, ritualized or not, whose end is to recover, in the name of collectivity, some being or event either anterior in time or outside of time in order to . . . animate, or make meaningful a moment in the present." See Eugene Vance, "Roland and the Poetics of Memory," in *Textual Strategies: Perspectives in Post-Structuralist Criticism,* ed. Josué V. Harari (Ithaca: Cornell University Press, 1979), p. 374.

59. See the translation in Chieko Irie Mulhern, trans., *Pagoda, Skull, and Samurai: Three Stories by Rohan Kōda* (Rutland, Vt.: Tuttle, 1985), pp. 21–109.

2

The Father: Kōda's Autobiographical Texts

At the start of her career, Kōda Aya had the advantages of a famous name and a tolerant age. The postwar era encouraged an outpouring of literary creativity and fostered a diversity of voices and interests. In this exhilarating atmosphere, Kōda grappled with the assignment of presenting her father's home life to an admiring readership. But now that she no longer had the responsibility of caring for her father, she also faced the tasks of supporting herself and finding a place in the world. During the 1940s and 1950s, Kōda's numerous autobiographical essays drew the attention of many Japanese readers because they succeeded brilliantly in providing an intimate view of the personal life of the idiosyncratic Rohan who, though a celebrated writer, did not run with members of the literary establishment *(bundan)* and whose revered works held an ambiguous position in the modern canon and the debate on tradition and modernity. Kōda herself acknowledged her father's ambivalent status as cultural figure and family man:

> Some people praise my father as a formidable scholar; others call him an eccentric *(fūgawari na henjin),* but Father had a different interpretation: "It's not that I'm a great scholar; anyone who thinks so must be greatly ignorant," he'd say, or "People who think I'm strange just don't realize how many people don't fit into the same mold as they do." At times I agreed with him. In any case, I did not learn about housekeeping from my father because he was a scholar who felt compelled to teach me. Nor were my lessons the warped inheritance of an eccentric. Rather, it just happened that way naturally; my father acceded to act both as father and mother to me because the circumstances at home demanded it. After my mother died when I was eight, I had to depend on the kindness of my stepmother, a woman who was superior to my first mother, I understand, in matters of learning, but who fell short when it came to managing a home.[1]

In the political atmosphere of the early postwar years, no censor complained that her frank depictions of her father's drinking and irrationality signified a lack of filial piety. Kōda did not have to fear criticism of her divorce or her explorations of women's struggle to find identity outside of marriage and passion. Her willingness to remember the good and the bad, to portray her distinguished father as an ordinary flawed human being, and to write at all is as much a reaction to the repressiveness of those dark years as a celebration of the freedom afforded Japan's citizenry by the nation's defeat. Kōda's many essays about life with Rohan include the early pieces she wrote around the time of his death—"Random Notes" (Zakki; 1947) and "Death of My Father" (Chichi: sono shi; 1947)—and numerous later individual works and collections of essays such as *This Sort of Thing* (Konna koto; 1956), *Good for Nothing* (Misokkasu; 1951), and *Scattered Clouds* (Chigiregumo; 1956).

Finding Her Own Voice

Critics often cite the publication of Kōda's first full-length work of prose fiction, *Nagareru* (Flowing; 1956), as marking the true beginning of Kōda's career because it marked her accession to the position of novelist. The reader can detect a significant shift in her writings much earlier, however, one that determined the form and substance of her essays and established her as an important narrative presence. In her first essays, Kōda obediently responds to the assigned task of writing about Rohan, and her inclusion of minute physical detail, nuances of emotion, and compelling style makes these initial works extremely evocative. In the space of a few short years, however, Kōda developed an approach to narrative form, perspective, and subjectivity that would become her hallmark. This is evident from the essay "Sugano" (1948), which, like the first writings, describes her daily life with Rohan during his later years. Instead of using the chronology of her father's illness as the primary structuring device, however, she organizes the later essays around different tropes, such as wandering *(sasurai),* war, evanescence *(karisome),* confusion *(mayoi),* sudden awareness of absence *(totsuzen no natsukashisa),* potential for failure *(masaka),* waiting, and especially heightened emotion *(kandō).*[2]

Her new method has the effect of altering the nature of the voice, because this formal shift indicates not only a difference in structure—that is, devotion to a thematic conception of narrative that highlights subjectivity rather than a linear temporal strategy—but also a seizing of narrative authority. Long before Kōda joined the ranks of novelists, she asserted in writing that the voice, the subject position, of her creation bore narrative authority—the power to command an audience—that derived not simply from her father's name. This shift has not been obvious to readers and critics, however, because of the expectation that any writer of merit will prove her skill and earn the title of artist through the creation of works of prose fiction, not by dashing off essays. Of equal significance, Kōda's constant pose of humility and insistence on fore-grounding her links with her father have distracted readers from her narrative accomplishment: an opportunity to encounter, through narrative, a symbolic realm of stability, unity, and moral certitude rare in postwar Japanese literature.

Although she denies involvement in the learning and artistic aspirations of her illustrious forebears, Kōda presents a vision of personhood grounded in close observation and sensual and emotional response to the phenomenal world, belief in personal maturity and the possibility of recovery from trauma, and the rejection of loss as a central trope signifying the reality of Japan's post-war culture. The moral certainty and the belief in continuity expressed in her narratives stem from a dedication to the notion of the family, in whatever form, as the primary social unit. Kōda's figuring of gender may initially seem regressive and rooted in conservative constructs of men's and women's social roles because of her biographical adherence to the role of homemaker for much of her life and the reverence accorded to the father. Moreover, Kōda's narra-tives do not share much with texts ordinarily categorized as early feminist fiction, described succinctly by Maryellen Toman Mori as stories that "usually revolve around alienated female protagonists who oppose patriarchal society's values and its prescriptions for women's lives. These protagonists resent or reject marriage, reproduction, and child rearing, because they entail women's subordination to men and their confinement within the domestic sphere." Although writing in the same decades as novelists such as Takahashi Takako and Kōno Taeko, Kōda evinces an indifference to the "search for sexual trans-port and spiritual rejuvenation" and "women's quest for *jouissance*" evident in Takahashi and Kōno's fiction.[3]

Kōda's repeated mention of Rohan in many of the essays that she wrote over four decades would seem to refute the claim of a newfound confidence in her relationship both with her own creative abilities and with her audience, as would her constant unfavorable comparisons of her own abilities with her father's. As Alan Tansman notes, however, this "rhetoric of inadequacy" became a means of fashioning a narrative presence in the world.[4] But on closer examination, this narrative presence bears an authoritative vision of the mean-ing of maturity, of aesthetics and morality, and challenges the reader to recon-sider the notion of a break *(danzetsu)* between tradition and modernity—between prewar and postwar.

Although much of her work is autobiographically inspired, Kōda's signif-icance as a writer does not rest solely on providing autobiographical detail of her father's life and her own personal and creative struggles in reaction to that father. Kōda wanted to portray more than her own historically verifiable life story or that of her father. Furthermore, she affirmed that her imagination, vision, and skill with words would allow her to speak more broadly of human experience and convey certain transcendent meanings as art and literature are meant to do.[5]

The habit of self-denigration goes hand in hand with the powerful emotions with which Kōda regarded her father, whom she portrays in her writing as, in several senses, her partner for life. Rohan, in Kōda's work, becomes variously her teacher, her home, her authority figure, her charge, her muse, her tormentor, her means of support, her companion, and the primary object of her affection. The parent/child relationship evoked in the narrative is, however, conspicuously devoid of sexual overtones. Eroticized parent/child bonds have been given bold treatment most notably by Okamoto Kanoko (1889–1939) in "A Mother's Love" (Boshi jojō; 1937) and by Tanizaki Jun'ichirō in "The Bridge of Dreams" (Yume no ukihashi; 1959) and other works. Only once does the daughter in Kōda's essays, however, wonder about the nature of her feelings for her father. The context for this reflection is the days of the incendiary bombing of Tokyo by the Allied Forces in spring 1945, a time defined by trauma and extreme emotion. Worried to distraction over the safety of her bedridden father, Kōda devises a makeshift bomb shelter for him in a closet filled with bedding. Although she realizes the futility of her attempt, she feels compelled to go any length to avoid losing him. In a sober moment she wonders, "Could my feelings for him be likened to those of a mistress (*mekake*)?"[6] But Kōda purposely phrases this extremely rare flirtation with taboo in the abstract terms of social relations (married man and mistress)—terms lacking the evocative and frankly erotic force of, for example, Okamoto Kanoko's mother character, who regards her son as a "man," or the heady indulgence of Tanizaki's male protagonists who long for the milky scent of mother.[7] A writer such as Kanai Mieko, working in the early 1970s, utilized explicit imagery of the body, addressed eroticized parent/child relations, and was conscious of Freudian and Lacanian "models of oedipal relations" in stories such as "Boshizō" (Portrait of Mother and Child; 1972) and "Usagi" (Rabbits; 1972).[8] But Kōda's education and reading did not include Lacan and Barthes, as Kanai's had, and she constantly looked to Confucian-inspired notions of familial relations based on moral and ethical concepts of propriety and self-cultivation and prohibiting eroticized relations within the family.

Even so, the roles played by Rohan and Kōda Aya remain to a large extent defined by gender. And as we shall see, his identity as the Father has profound implications both for Kōda herself and for her readership. During the postwar decades, Kōda's figuring of the Father was highly anomalous and attractive to readers of a defeated nation who literally had to cross out the lessons of the past, as presented in school textbooks, with opaque black ink. Kōda's essays about Rohan will always be a moving account of one woman's love for her parent and the process of mourning and learning to live on her own. Consciously or not, however, Kōda also invests great symbolic weight in the Father by constant reexamination of the Father as a positive figure whose stability is associated with his grounding in the past and whose teachings and moral outlook, while challenging, were to be embraced rather than categorically rejected. Even if the parent/child bond and the family have primacy, as in Confucian terms, Kōda puts her own postwar interpretation on the relationship. In essays and speeches, she reiterates the dynamics of her relationship with Rohan. At first glance she seems to be placed in a subordinate, disadvantaged position; but the subtext suggests her pride as a survivor and her enjoyment of drawing on the rich material that was her father's life, personality, and narrative, her family, and her own success. In 1977, for example, Kōda delivered a lecture titled "Convergences and Emotion" at the prestigious Iwanami Hall. She spoke about her life and career and, of course, her illustrious family:

> I don't think that he loved me much. . . . I was a middle child, and Father constantly found fault with me. He called me worthless. I suppose that [compared to my siblings], I had the least to offer. . . . But then my father was the fourth child of a large family, and he too was constantly ignored, so perhaps I inherited it from him. . . . My father said to me, "You are rather slow, aren't you?" Not "stupid," mind you, but "slow." [Audience laughter.] In any case, I hated being compared with my older sister.[9]

This "slow" daughter then proceeds to deliver a brilliant oral performance before a large audience assembled for the sole purpose of hearing her speak about herself and her thought. In her clear, melodious voice, Kōda narrates her transcendence of the pulverizing effects of being the middle daughter to her demanding father and speaks of the sources of her strength *(chikara)*, such as her uncle's love, and her ability to respond with deep emotion *(kandō)* to the people and events she has encountered (and, although she does not mention it explicitly, her talent at narrating those encounters).

But this Father also has a negative aspect: he drinks; he scolds; he is unreasonably demanding. He expects others to attend to his needs. But the rewards of association with this Father, it would seem, more than compensate for the drawbacks. Moreover, the historical Rohan has died, and, through narrative, Kōda can rehearse the death of the father again and again—either in great detail, as in her first works, or merely by referring to him as "my late father" (*bōfu*), rather than "my father" (*chichi*), as she does in the later essays. The measure of control afforded by the act of writing—and not only once—ultimately has various benefits: it quells the father's anger, abates the child's fear, and puts an end to his drinking. It also allows the persona to conclude that she has, after all, "pleased him" and earned his love. While the essays display a mixture of both fear and adoration of Rohan, the negative emotion is transitory because the father's anger passes quickly but the sense of debt, love, and longing for their life together remains constant. This expression of affection in the earlier works sometimes is cloaked in the language of extreme emotion, as in the short piece "Fragments" (Kakera; 1948) describing Kōda's visit to the bombed-out ruins of the Koishikawa family home:

> The burnt ruins are a treasure chest, and the earth yields so much. Buried in it are things that, above the ground, had purpose but now, broken, are useless, like fragments of china and dishes, and warped pans and spoons. While the soil seems willing to settle back into its old routine, now dancing up in the wind, now sinking down under the falling rain, the things in the earth are content only if they can push their way up out of the soil so as to see the sun once again. Every object that appears has some memory attached to it, especially the things directly linked to Father. When I come across one of those, I feel like raising my face to the sky in celebration of the opportunity to remember, and at the same time like lying down on the earth to cry over my loneliness.
>
> Just this morning, I could scarcely believe my eyes when I saw a glint of dark blue in the ice that covered the ground. It was a fragment of a tray Father had adored—a nice Kyoto piece of Shōnzui ware with a low rim. . . . I imagine that [my first] Mother used it to carry a bottle of sake, a cup, and some tasty morsel out to Father each evening.[10]

Good for Nothing, which contains a meditation on Rohan's drinking habits, follows a very different course, and the affective declaration takes the form of an apostrophe. In any case, the subjective sense presents itself with immediacy but calm. The memoir traces the discord in his relationship with his second wife that came about because of Rohan's heavy drinking and Yayoko's Christian condemnation of the practice as sinful:

> It requires a large measure of control (*gaman*) to sit here in such memories. I fling away my pencil and stand up to leave my desk, and it takes great effort to calm myself down, to catch my breath [and come back to it]. The range of situations and emotions that well up within me oppress me unbearably. Indeed, the passage of thirty or even forty years between then and now has not

made me an adult. My indescribable anguish as a child presents itself in unaltered form, making me screw closed my eyes and mouth in pain. I am irritated, driven to distraction, and in the end unable even to write. Not that I do not wish to write, or that I have lost the ability to do so—I am, put simply, without words. Please be patient with me. Oh, the image of my father, so beyond my control, that of my mother, and my own heart![11]

Over the course of Kōda's career, the mention of Rohan and her own inadequacy continues, but it becomes markedly more formulaic and occupies less space in her narrative.

Although Rohan had a reputation as a difficult man, lived apart from his wife in his later years, and did not attract scores of followers, Kōda Aya was not his sole companion. Indeed, several of Rohan's faithful admirers and visitors sought to portray Rohan the man. Kobayashi Isamu (an editor at Iwanami Shoten) produced a detailed account of his relationship with Rohan from 1936 to 1947 (Records of My Visits to Kagyūan; *Kagyūan hōmonki;* 1956), and Shiotani San wrote a three-volume literary biography (*Kōda Rohan;* 1965–1968).[12] Among these accounts it was Kōda Aya, inexperienced a writer though she was, who best captured Rohan's many faces, his voice, and moods —in short, she rendered a vivid and extremely moving portrait of Rohan as well as producing something of lasting literary value. As Rohan's daughter, Kōda had different concerns from men such as Shiotani and Kobayashi whose ties with the elder writer were professional as well as personal. Emotional investment alone, however, does not guarantee fine prose. Kobayashi's book provides the reader with much interesting detail about Rohan's work habits, his love of liquor, his dealings with the publishing world and other writers, and even the endless arguments with his second wife Yayoko. Yet despite Kobayashi's obvious regard for Rohan, he manages only to evoke a rather ordinary man who happens to be an extraordinary man of letters. The prose plods along, flat and uninspired, and the narrator's insights do not provide a point of interest. Kōda, by contrast, suggests a man of great emotional complexity and passion. Her success in writing about an unusual father and his unusual daughter in these memoiristic pieces demonstrates an impressive literary talent, not merely depth of emotional involvement in the subject. Alan Tansman has examined the sterling literary qualities of these autobiographical pieces, as well as the constructed nature of the persona.[13]

Other aspects of Kōda's essays continue to hold readers' interest, whether they bear allegiance to Rohan's writings and worldview or not and whether he stands to them as a canonical figure or as a name in history, one vaguely associated with the classics, Buddhism, and pagodas. One admirer, novelist Naka-zawa Kei (b. 1959), who would have encountered the Kōdas not before the 1970s and 1980s, mentions Rohan primarily as a man whose long life spanned several crucial periods in Japan's modern history: from the final years of the Edo period to the Meiji Restoration (even though Rohan was born just at the dawn of the restoration), the age of modernism from Taishō to Shōwa, and prewar and postwar Japan (even though Rohan died in July 1947, a mere two years after the defeat, and spent most of that time bedridden).

The Limits of Conventional Womanhood

One of the qualities that attracts readers lies paradoxically in the fact that the essays form a remarkable portrait of a life that, apart from her connection with Rohan, at first glance seems to lack interest because of its utter conventional-ity. From her adolescent days, Kōda performed much of the domestic work in the Kōda household, even while she was a student. Then she married and had a child, and finally became her father's companion and, during his later years, his nurse. Only near the very end of his life did Kōda begin writing, and even that was not an act of rebellion but one of homage. Again, her biography is sur-prisingly unpunctuated by the customary varieties of social resistance and rebellion:

> My father was a professional writer, but I never for a moment imagined that the day would come when I made money writing. I had no interest whatso-ever in my father's work. In those days, women could get by without thinking about earning money. When I was young, I depended on my father; when I got married, I looked to my husband. After my divorce, I again went back to my father. Such a life was comfortable, I suppose, but I grew tired of its nar-rowness. I occasionally thought of striking out on my own, perhaps starting a small business. It never occurred to me that I might do Father's work.[14]

The memoirs are fascinating because they suggest a life thoughtfully consid-ered and unconventional in nuance, detail, and perspective.

Unlike other women writers of her generation, such as Enchi Fumiko (who also had a famous writer for a father), Uno Chiyo, or Miyamoto Yuriko, Kōda did not of her own accord decide to become a professional writer. Although her memoirs and essays focus principally on the domestic sphere, one must be careful not to equate such a life with restriction and oppression for a number or reasons. The claim that Kōda's "philosophical training made her writing an act of 'symbolic inversion'"—that is, a contradiction of common notions of the nature of domestic space and female work there—stands as highly problematic because it assumes that domesticity, the home, and woman's labor were, during the period Kōda depicts, universally regarded as degraded.[15] While much of women's domestic work may have remained uncompensated, it did not bear the post–World War II stamp of trivia as in the United States, for example, as is witnessed by the prewar Japanese state's effort to render the home an aspect of the public sphere and regard the woman's role as that of public servant.[16] This assertion, furthermore, does not take into account the importance of domestic space in the writings of male writers, for example, or other female writers who focus on activism and social issues. It also conveniently ignores the fact that Rohan performed his labor, writing, at home, as well as the unconventional nature of the family and home where Kōda wrote. For Kōda, domestic space could never be viewed as trivial because it was not conceived in the terms of a binary model that opposes the private versus the public sphere. Spatial form, in fact, plays a less significant role than the vision of a unified moral universe.

As Kōda notes, her father became both "mother and father" to her not so much by virtue of the literal absence of a mother—for two women occupied the role of mother in the Kōda household—but because Rohan had grown up in a family whose poverty and traditional ethos dictated that male children too learned to do housework, which meant that Rohan knew what to teach his daughter about running a home. His own parents, furthermore, had not tolerated idleness, nor had they regarded Rohan's own youthful declaration that he wanted to become a novelist as an excuse from making himself useful around the house. In 1887, after Rohan quit his job as telegrapher in rural Hokkaido and returned to Tokyo to respond to Tsubouchi Shōyō's imperative concerning the future of Japanese literature, his mother Yū set him to work washing rice at the neighborhood well, a task with which he was familiar from the time he was a small boy.[17] For many Japanese in prewar days, productive work ("producing essential goods and income") and reproductive work ("childrearing, cooking, and housekeeping") took place in close physical proximity.[18] The separation, both in spatial and gender terms, of the public sphere and productive work and the domestic sphere and reproductive labor, respectively, did not become the predominant model in many households until after World War II.

In his childhood home, Rohan performed housework both as service to his family and as a form of discipline. Part of his attachment to his first wife Kimi stemmed from his admiration for her capable handling of the household budget and labor—not only because her talents allowed him to devote himself principally to his writing, but also because he could appreciate the demands of managing a home and family.[19] In turn, Rohan deemed it essential that his youngest daughter Kōda learn these skills as well. Kōda describes in an essay:

> It was my father who taught me how to sweep the floor and dust the house. My lessons with him went beyond the realm of cleaning, and he taught me the sort of things one normally learns from a mother. We never made it to the proper placement of hairpins when you're doing a permanent for curly hair, but Father did show me how to powder my face, how to cut up tofu into nice neat cubes, how to re-cover paper sliding doors, the best things to say when I need to borrow money, and even the ins and outs of love.[20]

Rohan's exacting approach to teaching his daughter Kōda the proper ways to handle water or a broom, described in "Incantations" (*Atomiyosowaka*; 1948), demonstrates that, far from disdaining reproductive labor in the home, as is the case in postwar, middle-class America, for example, Rohan regarded such work with utter seriousness and, furthermore, as the perfect opportunity to instill in his daughter his own Confucian-inspired philosophy. His attitudes toward domestic work were characteristically exceptional. Although domestic labor can certainly be carried out as unskilled work, Rohan taught his daughter that the Confucian dictum *kakubutsu chichi* (the investigation of all things) extends to the most quotidian activities. He emphasized that individual behavior and thought should be understood within the framework of a moral worldview—specifically his brand of Confucianism:

> The next morning, the scoldings started early. The glue that I had cooked up the day before seemed too stiff to me and I certainly didn't want him complaining again, so I decided to add some water. But then as I was mixing up the glue, it turned lumpy, and Father's reaction was of course devastating. "Trying to come up with something clever on your own is tantamount to ignoring Confucius' teaching. He wrote that it is best to learn from observation."
>
> When I do something without consulting Father and it turns out poorly, usually the venerable Confucius comes and rests his weight upon me, a four-ton boulder, just to make sure I have understood the error of my ways. Even worse than not having consulted with Father, it seems, was my failure to have shown proper respect to Confucius, and no amount of discussion or apology could absolve me. To a girl raised in the village of Terajima, Minami Katsushika-gun, the revered words of Confucius from many millenniums before seemed distant and murky at best. And how in the world could my making lumpy glue be construed as disrespect for Confucius? And then Father told me

that girls like me, who have no sense of humility, are evil and won't do anyone any good. My life was useless, he said.

Father regarded Confucius as worthy of great respect and used polite language when he referred to him. But in my eyes, it was Father who was absolute, not Confucius. I was in trouble because that Absolute came raining down on me, bringing the Honorable Confucius with him. My heart torn apart, I wished that I could disappear, but I was not allowed even that. One must, he told me, try again, come to life again. Feeling momentarily relieved, I then learned that I still was in error: this time, his approach took the form of an accusation: "Are you going to live your whole life in fear of Confucius? That's a coward's way." It seems that I must discard that desire to disappear and assume a new attitude of fortitude.[21]

The long memoir "Incantations" contains dazzling passages describing in detail Kōda's apprenticeship to Rohan in household work, which she calls her "private lessons in cleaning" *(sōji no keiko),* as one might refer to lessons in a traditional art such as Noh chanting or tea ceremony. Kōda credits this strict upbringing not just to her father but to her grandmother Yū, as well, whom she felt was "always watching her from afar, certainly not willing to allow her granddaughter to be spoiled or raised as an undisciplined country girl." Rohan's study was her classroom.[22]

The Confucian slant of Rohan's teaching reinforced the emphasis on this world: "Confucius' effort to take things at hand—ordinary daily affairs—as the basis for his ethical teaching makes Confucian learning an intrinsically moral activity at whose core is the task of developing a refined knowledge of oneself." Rohan's emphasis on the importance of good physical form also derived from a Confucian approach to self-cultivation: the "ritualizing [of] bodily behavior . . . represents a concerted effort to transform the body into a fitting expression of the mental and spiritual resources within."[23] The initial steps toward the goal of "becoming an exemplar of personal knowledge" involve ritual acts of "elementary learning," such as cleaning the floor and calligraphy. The eights steps of "Great Learning" that facilitate this aim during adulthood include the "investigation of things" *(kakubutsu;* Chinese *ke-wu)*— a "form of knowing in which the knower is not only informed but also transformed by the known." That is, investigation is not simply a "disinterested study of external facts by an outside observer."[24] Much of Kōda's autobiographical writing explores the training that she received from Rohan in ritualized "body behavior" and emphasizes the explicit link between cleaning and self-cultivation. Her claim, moreover, of possessing a well-defined aesthetic and moral sensibility stems from the notion of the transformative power of observation and from her conviction that knowledge is linked to moral improvement.

At the same time Rohan, by providing a good education for his daughter, drew on familial practices in evidence in both the Edo period and earlier in Meiji. The Edo poet-painter Ema Saiko (1787–1861), for example, learned calligraphy, painting, and literature from her father, Confucian and Rangaku (Dutch Learning) scholar Ema Ransai (1747–1838). Other precedents include the venerable sage Ninomiya Sontoku, who gave his daughter Fumiko what a writer in 1909 termed "the best education of the time: she learned to read and write and to sew and cook, as well as the fine arts of tea, poetry, and calligraphy"—best because the Meiji writer sought to extol "hard work, endurance, and education" as feminine virtues in accordance with the state's policies concerning the roles of women.[25] During Edo and Meiji, women were not completely exempt from the encouragement of their fathers because, as Kathleen Uno notes, it "behooved the conscientious head [of the household] to make sure that the heir was carefully groomed to shoulder the household's social obligations and ply its trade. This concern applied especially to eldest sons, but fathers have devoted attention to other children as understudies to the heir." Higuchi Ichiyō's father, for example, recognizing her intelligence and talent, afforded her more attention and better educational opportunities than her less apt brother.[26]

Kōda herself rationalizes her father's focus on teaching her housework by first comparing herself with her siblings. For Utako, the eldest daughter (and, by Kōda's account, the child most beautiful and beloved), Rohan bought special plants and trees for the garden at Kagyūan in order to cultivate Utako's native intelligence and fascination with nature.[27] Rohan, Kōda tells us, meant to make a botanist out of Utako. Kōda, by Rohan's standards, lacked natural curiosity and aptitude for art or learning—or so she tells us—and thus by default he chose to train her strictly in cooking, cleaning, and budgeting. Curiously, he did not include in her home education lessons in tea ceremony or flower arranging required of a young woman being readied for marriage.[28] Kōda remarks on the fact that her father did not demand of his long-awaited, but ultimately dissolute, son Ichirō the same competence in anything that he expected of his daughters. In fact, he spoiled the boy terribly. In the end, both Utako and Ichirō died young. Only Kōda Aya survived, almost too well prepared for the several lives and careers ahead of her. In retrospect, Kōda describes such family dynamics as affecting her in these terms:

The hard outer shell of a chestnut may contain only one chestnut, or some may shelter two, making it a double chestnut, or three—a triple chestnut. If you peel a single chestnut, the nut inside has a nice rounded belly and back. Everyone loves this kind. The meat of double chestnuts have flat bellies, but their backsides are still nice and round. This is the second most well loved type. But a triple chestnut has three nuts inside, and the one in the center is, well, I suppose you'd call it pathetic. It gets pressed in from both sides and smashed flat. That was the way I was—stuck between my sister and brother and crushed flat. . . . And so—and I'm not complaining but—I don't think that I was given much love. . . . My father was the fourth child in his family and got smashed quite a bit too. . . .[29]

The complexity of her relationship with her father and siblings, as well as her maturation as an individual, come through clearly.

Of Kōda's marriage and divorce, Inoue Kazuko asserts that Rohan's extraordinarily rigorous training ruined Kōda's "potential for happiness" in a married relationship. Kōda's many strengths and skills, Inoue writes, "were useless in a marriage that was predicated on the construction of the identity of a wife as one who relied on her husband's strengths. Kōda's sharp perceptions, furthermore, allowed her to see through the fallacy of marriage under patriarchy."[30] Indeed, Kōda has seldom written critically of the system of marriage. But most relationships predicated on the establishment of social and economic bonds would pale against the intensity of emotional and moral unity she describes in the domestic arrangement with her father—an arrangement that elevated the mundane to the moral, spiritual, and intellectual level and was predicated on a complementary model rather than an oppositional one.

From Kōda herself we know surprisingly little about her marriage—save that she was terribly unhappy, especially because her husband was utterly ineffectual in running a business and she had to shoulder nearly the entire burden of both the household and their family shop. In the essay "A Woman's Screams" (Kansei; 1951), Kōda describes the financial ruin, resulting from Ikunosuke's incompetence, which left her vulnerable to humiliation and denigration, suggested forcefully by an attempted rape by a former employee of their liquor business. Her husband's lack of outrage at the indignity she suffered was, according to Kōda, one factor that led to divorce. If indeed, as Inoue claims, Rohan "robbed Kōda of a woman's happiness," it was because, cranky and demanding though he was, he engaged her at a profound intellectual and moral level and took her quite seriously. Despite Kōda's claims of inadequacy in the face of her father's high standards, her memoirs succeed in conveying not only their mutual affection (though expressed only indirectly) but, more important, her own ability to spar with this most demanding of partners—whether it be over the correct way to polish the floor, or poetry, or the best way to recover from a traumatic experience. Repeatedly Kōda describes the pain of "defeat" after a lesson or an argument with her father. But then she reveals that she would acquiesce only after fighting back. Such images stand in stark contrast to other father/daughter relationships depicted in prose narrative, such as Uno Chiyo's evocation of the strict father who would lock up or tie up the daughter.

Indeed, a major source of interest in Kōda's essays lies in the thrill of contact, through narrative, with the rigorous subjectivity of a woman whose world had not been totally ravaged by Japan's defeat in the war or by the death of her father. The familiar metaphor of Japan's phoenix-like rise from the ashes could likewise be applied to Kōda Aya. But in her case, birth seems a more appropriate metaphor than rebirth because the narrative persona emerged for the very first time from the loss that threw much of the literary world into a state of self-doubt. Paradoxically, the act of creating Rohan's daughter in the narrative realm allowed Kōda herself to become something other than Rohan's daughter. Her importance as a writer owes much to her ability to convey optimism in the face of all odds and to evoke women's lives that are predicated on independence and self-reliance.

The Symbolic Order and the Postwar Family

Apart from interest in Rohan and the quality of the prose and voice, Kōda's writings are attractive to readers on a symbolic level, as well, because they focus on the loss of the Father and suggest the possibility of maturity and psychological integrity in the aftermath of such trauma. In prewar canonical fiction, the reader frequently encounters the topos of the death of the Father—in Sōseki's *Kokoro* and Shimazaki Tōson's *The Broken Commandment* (Hakai), for example. Alan Tansman has brilliantly analyzed the critics' appropriation of Kōda's works as signs of cultural conservatism and the nativist discourse concerning the Return to Japan *(Nihon kaiki)*: "Critics agreed with Mishima about the feminine quality of Aya's writing. Most valorized her style as essentially Japanese and thus an antidote to male overintellectualization and overreliance on foreign modes of thought. To these critics 'feminine' language was somehow more authentically native and could restore a true, untainted, and life-sustaining quality to Japanese cultural and literary life."[31]

Kōda's writings must also be read in light of postwar debates that employ what are essentially psychoanalytic categories to consider texts, gender relations, and national identity. A prime example of this fascination with the idea of the Father can be found in the controversy surrounding literary critic and intellectual Etō Jun's seminal work *Maturity and Loss: The Collapse of the "Mother"* (Seijuku to sōshitsu: "haha" no hōkai; 1965–1966).[32] This discourse on the employment of the symbolic order and especially the notions of Mother and Father in postwar culture reaches far beyond issues of individual psychology and addresses concerns about global politics, nationalism, feminism, and family structure. With *Maturity and Loss*—ostensibly a critique of the contemporary Japanese fiction of Kojima Nobuo, Yasuoka Shotarō, and Endō Shūsaku—Etō captured the attention of a broad audience with his far-reaching discussion of the family, gender, psychology, and politics in postwar Japan. Etō adopted the approach of psychologist Erik Erikson to look at Japanese fiction written in the political context of the two decades after the end of the war.

During the first three postwar decades especially, the allure of the psychoanalytic method for Etō, Erikson's work in particular, is clear for several reasons. Certainly a psychoanalytic framework provided a new means for understanding the family and individual psychology by defining a logical progression toward personal maturity and cohesive individual identity.[33] But of even greater significance, perhaps, is Erikson's attempt to explain, with Freudian categories, "the process of American identity formation" and the role of the American mother ("Mom").[34] For Etō, a well-traveled, erudite scholar, Erikson's impressively fair and insightful dissertation on Hitler and Germany, yet another country haunted by its recent past and a postwar identity in flux, must have been compelling. "For nations, as well as individuals," Erikson notes, "are not only defined by their highest point of civilized achievement, but also by the weakest one in their collective identity: they are, in fact, defined by the distance, and the quality of the distance, between these points."[35]

Despite the subtitle of his work ("The Collapse of the 'Mother'"), Etō's thesis hinges on the Father's loss of authority in postwar Japan. Such attenuation of power on a personal level is suggested in the Kojima, Yasuoka, and Endō novels by "the husbands and fathers" who, "exhausted from the war and dazed by the recovery, have without realizing it relinquished their roles as helmsman of the home."[36] This identification of the father as leader also suggests the familiar metaphoric connection between the paternal figure and male figures of authority, such as the emperor, and between the home and nation. Although Etō displaces his anxiety about the emasculating effects of the war by shifting the focus/blame, both in his title and in his essays, onto the Mother/ Female, he ultimately offers a restorative alternative for these broken men:

> To compensate for (or perhaps simply as a reaction against) the capitulation/ unconditional surrender of the father, the mother showers all her affection upon her son and places all her hopes on him. But this boy . . . is every bit as bewildered as his physically debilitated father. He has never sought his mother's adoration, nor has he felt worthy of it. . . . For this son to attain true maturity, Etō claims, he . . . must break away from her influence and thereby assert his independence. . . . This "loss" of Mother is a painful but necessary prelude to "maturity."[37]

Such separation on the part of the son results in disintegration of the family and home as well, rendering them gatherings of lonely, isolated individuals. In the fiction that Etō studies, the Mother becomes deified, forgiving, and accepting of broken, flawed men.[38]

Notably, the novels that Etō discusses do not portray these bewildered men as effeminate. The feminine here is not the weaker sex but indeed is often equated with strength that is imagined as maternal power outside of history. This "retreat from the role of patriarch" did not constitute simply an abrogation of gendered authority within the family: it acknowledged the impossibility of remaining aligned with the prewar and wartime ideology that led Japan into its ultimately disastrous role as an imperialist power and aggressor.[39] Van Gessel takes up Etō's discussion on a personalistic level because, although he acknowledges the symbolic potential of Kojima Nobuo's *Embracing Family* (Hōyō kazoku; 1965)—with the character Miwa Shunsuke as the wounded Japanese Father and his wife Tokiko and her lover George, an American GI, suggestive respectively of changes in women's attitudes and the presence of the U.S. military—he asserts that this novel is "most moving if read as a personal chronicle of one man's home."[40] While not taking issue with Gessel's claim, it is clear that the significance of *Embracing Family* and, in particular, Etō's compelling reading of the novel has had broader implications in postwar Japan.

Etō wrote *Maturity and Loss* in an era when memories of the Occupation still remained fresh and great controversy surrounded Japan's relations with the United States and the global community, as was demonstrated by the outspoken student and citizen protests. A critic deeply enmeshed in politics and debates on Japanese nationalism and identity, Etō did not advance *Embracing Family* solely as a personal chronicle. In *Embracing Family,* the protagonist Shunsuke's life hurtles into chaos and confusion as the house he is building starts to deteriorate underfoot, but especially after he learns that his otherwise dependable wife Tokiko has had sex with a GI named George. The unity of Shunsuke's world is threatened constantly by intruders—not only the soldier but a maid whose presence ironically contributes to making their house feel dirtier, rather than clean, and who acts as the bearer of bad news (such as Tokiko's infidelity). Shunsuke takes his wife to talk with George about their relationship (he must translate for her), and Tokiko has him ask George whether he feels responsible for his actions. When George responds that he has a sense of responsibility only to his parents and his country *(kokka),* it makes Shunsuke furious. In katakana English, Shunsuke tells George to *"Go bakku hōmu Yankii"* ("Go back home, Yankee"). Etō's response to this passage is noteworthy:

> This is the only point in the novel where the word "nation" *(kokka)* appears, and it is significant also as the sole suggestion of the public sphere. Notably it is George, the American, who uses this word. Despite the fact that "nation" is only used once, I can't help feeling that it bears great significance in the work as a whole and possesses a weight comparable to the spread of Shunsuke's strangely "polluted" private world, precisely because of its complete and utter absence from Shunsuke's world. . . . Shunsuke and Tokiko flinch in the face of George's logic precisely because they have been living in a culture that goes to extreme lengths in order to erase the image of the shameful Father *("hazukashii chichi no imeeji").* Although Japan's defeat in the war undeniably contributed to this, the weakening of the Father image cannot be said to have come solely from the defeat. Shunsuke's groan, "Go home, Yankee," is pathetically humorous. This is because the reader feels intuitively that what is motivating Shunsuke is a mentality of exclusion so fundamental that the pullout of U.S. troops from Japan would not solve it.[41]

Although this part of Etō's argument hangs on a minute detail of the text, he uses it to point out precisely what he finds most significant in the novel and in his own political thinking as well—that is, the problematic literal and symbolic relationship between country and individual, the public and private spheres, particularly in the aftermath of the defeat. He follows Erikson's theory of the conflict of shame and autonomy in development of the self (or ego).[42] Shunsuke, in Kojima's novel, has no adequate response to George's claim that one of his main responsibilities is to his country, America, because Shunsuke completely lacks the sense of a strong "Father"—that is, a paternal figure identified with the nation-state. Gessel, and other critics such as Katō

Norihiro, emphasize the progress of Shunsuke's increasing isolation over the course of the novel—initially from his wife Tokiko, on whom he once depended "as the source of his values," the ensuing loss of traditional authority on Shunsuke's part, his alienation from conventional social roles, and finally his feeling of separation from the rest of his family and nature. Shunsuke has lost the authority of traditional familial bonds predicated on a particular role as Father, but he is unable to connect with society in any other way. No longer can Shunsuke assume that his wife will be content with the social and sexual confines of their marriage. Nor may the husband rely anymore on his clenched fist as a means of communicating with his spouse.[43] One sign of *Embracing Family*'s entanglement with the socioeconomic realities of the early and mid-postwar decades—specifically the era of high economic growth—can be seen in Shunsuke's conversion to consumerism. The Father who formerly looked to his wife as manager of domestic needs eventually finds himself in the surprising position of shopping for clothes for his wife. Kojima renders this character's encounter with consumer culture in vivid and minute detail, as Shunsuke discovers new facets of his social and erotic self in the women's clothing section of a Tokyo department store, filled with bare-armed mannequins and attractive sales clerks. In contrast to his wife's purchase and renovation of their house, however, Shunsuke's behavior as a consumer is still inextricably linked to his dependence on the Mother. He is unable to adopt the new values and sense of subjectivity encouraged by economic prosperity and the consumer-oriented promise of a "crystal" life far superior to the "dowdy" (*kakkō warui*) early postwar days.[44] Thus Katō regards Etō's blind spot as residing in the latter's view that redemption and maturity can be found in recovery of the "Father" by Shunsuke.[45]

In Kojima's well-known novel, Shunsuke also finds himself faced with the unprecedented task of raising his children, on his own, after his wife's death. Even more than in his relationship with Tokiko, he fails miserably in his effort to find a basis for authority and a means of communication with his children. The strong reaction to Kojima's *Embracing Family,* especially the character Shunsuke, by generations of postwar critics, including Etō, Katō Norihiro, and Ueno Chizuko, testifies to the power of the idea of the family in postwar discourse. Although Etō's application of Erikson's familial paradigm to Japanese society might be new, the notion of the state as *ie* (household/family/house) has been frequently invoked.

Sociologist Ueno Chizuko has found significance in Etō's commentary on *Embracing Family,* but for different reasons from Katō. In the controversial book *On Men's Literature* (Danryū bungakuron; 1989), Ueno astonishingly professes that Etō's reading of the Kojima novel "moved her to tears." Such praise for a conservative male thinker is striking in the context of this book, which takes the form of a free-wheeling discussion *(zadankai)* among three feminists about novels by male authors. Like Katō, Ueno responds positively to Etō's desire to forge a connection between the individual and politics. She reacts particularly to Etō's view of the character Tokiko. Although Ueno professes that her reaction was emotional, she also seems to have been struck by her own methodological proximity to Etō at the time ("I too was employing Eriksonian methods then") and by their common effort to view Japanese culture and society in a new critical light. This social science methodology, Ueno claims, leads Etō to the insight that, in *Embracing Family,* the wife Tokiko exposes the self-loathing of women under the capitalist system. "And he wrote this in the days before feminist discourse was common in postwar Japan," Ueno states.[46] Ueno also notes the shift in the use of the related *ie* from the time of Sōseki's *Meian* through postwar writers such as critic Honda Shūgo and Kojima himself, as well as the strong affective responses to and symbolic resonance of the family/home and mother.[47]

As for Katō's reading, he especially assumes the masculine/feminine (as well as parent/child) binarism as oppositional. Maturity, in this discourse, accrues the vague definition of separation from maternity and the destruction of the mother. What is striking about his maintenance of this particular paradigm is the denigration of the female element and the persistence in employing an oedipal framework as a tool for understanding the family. Although this viewpoint mourns the denigration of the old father, the drive for maturity implies a search for a new model of manhood, because the categorical rejection of the mother leaves that as the only alternative. Indeed, much prose fiction by male authors in the prewar period intimates such a quest for a second father: a spiritual father.[48] It is against such cultural criticism that Kōda wrote.

For Kōda Aya, the notion of Father became equated with the language of transcendence. Less than his fame or his abilities as a writer, the Rohan evoked in her narrative realm has authority that evokes the teachings of Confucius and, as we have seen, transcends even the authority of that philosophical past:

> I have, since my childhood, had the strong urge to resist the absolute power of this father. For some reason still unclear to me, in my forty-four years of struggle, I have not once succeeded in escaping from this "Absolute." Only that would give me relief. After Father died and was no longer a person in my life,

the "Absolute" became even more absolute. I came to crave the "Absolute" once I could no longer see it with my eyes or hear it with my ears, and for the first time I cried. When Father picked a fight with someone, he never took into account his partner's height, and instead spoke exclusively from his own intellectual level. He would go on and on about matters beyond my comprehension. One minute it would be Socrates, and the next Ninomiya Sontoku. Without warning, he'd switch the topic of conversation from the *Kojiki* to race car engines.[49]

Constant in Kōda's evocations of Rohan the father is the dizzying mixture of the cultural icon (sage, teacher, and literatus), the beleaguered family man, the manic constantly in search of new texts and new cultural phenomena, and the spiritual partner of Kōda, for whom only a man of Rohan's breadth and depth will suffice. For this demanding daughter, a lost man like Kojima Nobuo's Shunsuke would not even register.

Autobiography and Heightened Emotion

Throughout her writing career, Kōda Aya consistently made reference to her relationship with her father, Kōda Rohan, even after she had firmly established herself as an exceptional writer of essays and fiction and no longer needed to invoke his name to attract readers. Her textual uses of Rohan, however, change over time. Precisely because Kōda wrote so much in the way of memoir and autobiographical essays, the reader may be tempted to conclude that one therefore has the equivalent of a more or less complete biography of Kōda Aya. A fundamental problem arises from this neat solution to understanding her life and her essays: this approach ignores the constructed nature of autobiography —that is, the notion that an autobiography, true to biographical fact as it may be, remains nonetheless an interpretation of a life, the authenticity of which is beyond doubt.[50] Thus the reader may be able to confirm from a variety of independent sources the veracity of much that is described in the essays: the identity of visitors to the Kōda home, the exact length of Kōda's residence in her father's house after her divorce, her extreme unhappiness during her marriage to Mitsuhashi Ikunosuke and some of the causes of their marital strife, the length and number of pencils on her writing desk, and even the fact that she wrote with pencils at all.[51] Beyond such historically verifiable facts, however, the nature of Kōda's creation of a narrative of personhood and interiority, the nuances and significance of her relationship with her father, must be understood within the framework of poetics—that is, narrative strategy and modes of self-presentation—because autobiography, unlike biography, takes the form of narration of a life in process and a life interpreted.[52]

The equation of Kōda's memoirs and essays with her life or biography becomes problematic if it ignores the rhetorical approaches she employs to fashion certain types of self-presentation and the aims of different discursive practices. To regard the essays as a transparent medium through which Kōda Aya spells out the facts of her life and her father's is to leave unanswered the question of the power of these essays, which make up the majority of her writings. Of the twenty-three volumes of her posthumous *zenshū* (collected works), only five contain full-length novels.[53] Similarly, only one of the five single-volume editions of her works published in the years immediately after Kōda's death is a work of prose fiction; the rest are essays of varying length. Unlike her father's essays, which include scholarly "objective" works about urban planning, the Bible, Chinese history and literature, as well as more impressionistic sketches of nature and travel, Kōda's essays are almost exclusively autobiographical and trace her activities and feelings throughout her long life. The only exceptions are the later works *Trees* and *Landslides* and several short pieces about pagodas.

Hans Robert Jauss suggests that the power—the "quality and rank"—of a literary work derives from "the criteria of influence, reception, and posthumous fame," in addition to the "biographical and historical conditions of its origins, or from its place in the sequence of the development of a genre."[54] I would like to examine some additional reasons why Kōda's essays remain so powerful today—even as their titles, brevity, and themes suggest ephemera and even though they are marked by repetition. Most contemporary readers of Kōda's early essays would have been attracted to the opportunity to learn more about Rohan's home life and his personality. Within a relatively short period, however, Kōda proved—though all the while professing her status as amateur—that her writerly presence and the perceptions manifest in her narrative provided a great deal of interest, whether or not she wrote about her father, with the result that readers would want to know Kōda's authoritative view on morality, on the family, on old age, and come into contact with her words and style. Some critics have claimed that Kōda's works reveal no literary influence from Rohan.[55] The question of influence between father and daughter, it is generally agreed, lies primarily in Rohan's transmission of the practice of the Neo-Confucian *kakubutsu chichi* ("investigation of all things through observation" with the aim of self-cultivation) and Kōda's gracious mastery of this practice.[56] The question remains: in what ways does *kakubutsu chichi* manifest itself in narrative form? Many critics have labeled Kōda a *seikatsusha* (one who lives), rather than a *sakusha* (one who creates), as if the received capacity for observation and investigation could be known in the world without the medium of narrative or as if narrative itself did not give expression or, more accurately, lend shape to the cognitive processes and the signs of cultivated knowing.[57]

Overemphasis on Kōda's seemingly masochistic tendency for self-denigration and her extreme identification with her father will distract the reader from appreciating her narrative accomplishments. Many of her later essays, such as "Private Tutor" (Kojin kyōju; 1971), start out with a rhetorical positioning of Kōda Aya as someone lacking potential in the arts and scholarship, though a member of a family of talented musicians, writers, and scholars, but end with a celebration of the gifts she received from her father, including the ability to observe nature and the possession of the rhetorical means, both poetic and prosaic, to express the beauty and perceive connections between the natural world and human society. Another prominent feature of the essays is the emphasis on affect. The earlier works convey the complexity of emotion during mourning: anger, grief, joy, depression. In the essays Kōda wrote later in life, she still places great value on expressions of affect; but in these texts emotion, rather than flowing from within, becomes poetic and transcendent. Rather than social intercourse, it is contemplation that gives rise to emotions and aesthetic response. Experiencing heightened emotion, however, does not constitute an end in itself. The ability to observe, to be transformed, and to narrate becomes the foundation of her moral realm. In a 1977 public lecture in Kyoto, Kōda related her initial realization of the transformative power of *kandō* (heightened emotion or aesthetic response). Also remarkable in this speech is its performative aspects: as she approaches in her narration the moment of epiphany, the pitch of her voice becomes significantly higher; the pace of her speech more rapid; and she modulates the volume of her voice precisely to fashion the precision of her description:

> The pencil that started my writing career came rolling over to me. It was not something I sought out. In my family, my father always taught me that I must try whatever is served to us. As children, we were not allowed to refuse something for the reason that we didn't like it or because it was new to us. My parents were especially strict with girls about this. Father instructed me that if I were served a food unfamiliar to me, I must not hold back. He would not tolerate such behavior from me. "Try everything," he said. "If you absolutely can't swallow it, then just spit it out. But that alone would be rude, so, in order

to avoid insulting the other person, you must then say, 'Regretfully, I am unable to partake of this. I beg your kind forgiveness,' and then leave." That's what he told me. For, you see, the inferior child must be told exactly what to do, down to the last detail, down to the last word.

Do you know that if you scribble down a few sentences and get them published, people will address you as "Sensei?" I'd been a homemaker all of my life, and then one morning, all of a sudden, I was "Sensei.". . . Psychologically I couldn't stand all the pressure, and friends told me I needed a rest, so I decided to go to Hakone. It was May, and the mountains there were lovely. . . . The people at the inn where I was staying recommended a walk in the mountains because there were fine bush warblers to be seen there. The whole thing seemed a bit dubious to me, but I went up anyway, and, what do you know, I found one. I couldn't see the warbler because it was high up in the trees, but I knew that it was there when I heard its beautiful song. I listened and guessed that he or she likely had a nicely rounded throat—the song sounded round to me. I heard it singing "hokkekyo," for indeed that is the way the bush warbler sings. It's so pretty, the song, but I wondered how the bird could sing so marvelously with a small little throat like that. They can't possibly have very big bodies. So I was standing there listening to the warbler's song, and then all of a sudden it stopped. Just like that, and the mountain was absolutely quiet. I could hear the quiet. I looked out and the May breeze came blowing from afar, and the green was all waving about like this, and that wind swept lower into the grasses in the fields and about my feet. The May breeze felt wonderful, and I realized what I had just heard. And I felt it. Suddenly, my heart cleared up. I knew that it didn't matter if people called me Sensei or whatever. This is where I exist. . . . I am simply an old woman, a person who knows nothing of art and learning. But I can do things like this and feel. . . . Hadn't I heard something fine and felt it? Had I not been moved? If I go out into the world, I will be moved. I only needed to search for it, and then everything would be all right. With that, the stress vanished from me and I was ready to come home right away. Once home, I enjoyed my life. . . .

I realized something else because of that bush warbler. I was amazed that the warbler, with its tiny throat and lungs, could produce such a voice, from such a small place. I realized that if I too sang from my small, lonely corner, with my meager breath, but with my five senses, I would exist. . . . By that time I was already an old woman, but all the things I had been interested in as a small child came back to me—pebbles of all colors and shapes, dogs, bright yellow rape flowers, the clouds floating by in the blue sky, gourds, moss, tadpoles, the Sumida River, fields of tall grasses. They said to me, here we are. Of all these, I chose to concentrate on trees. At that point, even my feelings of jealousy for my brilliant sister disappeared.[58]

In the last essays about trees and landslides, Kōda most bluntly states her narrative aim: she scrambles up steep slopes and gets strong men to carry her up unblazed mountain paths in her search for heightened emotion, or excitement *(kandō o motomete)*.[59] Thus the heightened emotion previously available within the "narrowness" of her own home life can now be found only by means of a quest. At the same time, Kōda represents herself as someone well qualified to search for, and to narrate, such transcendent values:

> Even if I have no ability as a scholar, I am still able to go out and see things with my own eyes. If I am then able to seize the heightened emotion of land-slides, weave that emotion into words, and convey it to my readers, I will be satisfied. Even a natural disaster of a small scale involves a tremendous amount of energy, and it is inconceivable that one cannot find heightened emotion in a place where the earth has moved with such force. As for the nature of that emotion, sometimes one may feel horrified, and at other times sad and desolate. I hope to convey to my readers the emotion that I have seen and heard, the emotion that speaks of the fate of this country Japan. I would like to be the messenger of that emotion. If one has few prospects as a scholar, then she must use her physical facilities instead, and go out and see with her eyes and listen with her ears.[60]

In this way Kōda situates herself in a new relationship with her narrative Father. In this passage, the implicit comparison of herself with her father ("I have no ability as a scholar") serves as a preface to what she views now as her true and legitimate role: "messenger of emotion."[61]

Another strategy Kōda frequently employs is to describe a criticism session during which Rohan will occasionally praise but most usually complain about her personality or way of doing things or even her resemblance to her dead stepmother. This description is inevitably followed by her own analysis of the veracity—or lack thereof—of Rohan's complaints and finally the conclusion that, negative evaluation or not, her relationship with her father was one characterized by love and deep bonding that has stood her in good stead for the rest of her life.[62] In the memoir "Notes from Sugano" (Sugano no ki; 1948), for example, the reader finds an early example of this method:

> Father has been bedridden for three years, ever since the time of the fire bombings, and though I had grown accustomed to nursing him and knew exactly

what I needed to do, I never did become an accomplished nurse to him. Indeed, nursing Father was one continuous fight. He complained constantly about the way I cared for him. It seems that I did not exhibit sufficient consideration to the invalid and proved inept at managing his affairs—in short, he was not pleased in the least. His feelings of dissatisfaction flew out at me as sarcastic invective. He flung his complaints at me in a rage; his irritation turned to meanness and exploded in my face.[63]

Admittedly, an integral part of her method lies in the compulsion to create harshly lit and often unflattering portraits of a man who was lionized in the public domain—a man whose erudition and ability to wield archaic and difficult styles rendered him an object of awe, even as his novels and essays became increasingly inaccessible even to educated readers. Kōda knocked Rohan down to an utterly human level by presenting him both as a demanding parent who had unreasonable expectations of the child who tried the hardest to please him (and only him) and as a very mortal man of flesh, vulnerable to the ravages of illness and aging. Her characteristic fondness for precision and detail, received as part of Rohan's education in *kakubutsu chichi,* extends to sketches of Rohan himself—whether it be the cold, biting sting of his words or the blood that he coughed onto the sheets of his sickbed during the last days of his life.[64] For example, "Notes from Sugano" contains a passage in which Kōda examines, by the glaring light of a bare light bulb, Rohan's bleeding gums and the bloody strings of mucus that came out of his mouth and nose. After the bleeding stops and Rohan manages to spit out the blood, Kōda asks her daughter Tama to bring the lamp closer so she can examine the contents:

> The bulb illuminated for me not only the red blood in the pail, but every detail of Father's face as well. I detected no trace of fear or despair or laxness there, or, of course, any expression of pleasure. All I saw were his eyes looking, just as he does when he is reading, with the muscles beneath his brows slightly tensed, those eyes looking at the blood. The stink of the blood rose from the pail.[65]

But the practice of repetition—of reducing Rohan to the status of an ordinary man, sometimes cruel, sometimes loving—suggests the profundity of his influence and the extent of their attachment. Only by trying to tame this man, who was larger than life not only in the public eye, but at home as well, could Kōda grapple with her own literary and philosophical inheritance.

At the same time, she did her part in elevating and mythologizing his being. Thus the bond between them cannot be reduced simply to the level of a masochistic daughter and cruel father but remains on the biomythic level of the Chinese lion who pushes its cubs off a cliff in order to make them prove themselves.[66] Through this mythologizing strategy, Kōda achieved a place for herself in the narrative pantheon while at the same time paying tribute to a father whose lessons had given her the enviable ability to view with wonder a world most of us overlook and to write of the strength and love she has come to possess.

Concepts of Humility and Authority

The extent to which Kōda succeeded in sustaining and enhancing this biomyth becomes clear when one reads her daughter Aoki Tama's books *The House in Koishikawa* (Koishikawa no uchi; 1994) and *The Home That I Longed For* (Kaeritakatta uchi; 1997). Although many incidents and the atmosphere of the Kōda home are already familiar to readers acquainted with Aya's writing, Tama allows us a glimpse of an unknown Aya: a woman who was as strict and demanding as her perfectionist father Rohan. Tama also portrays in a more thorough and balanced manner her own father, Ikunosuke. Through both mother's and daughter's narratives runs a similar conceit of self-deprecation. Tama chose only to shoulder the mantle of unworthy daughter (and granddaughter). Aya, however, assumed inadequacy in a much grander manner: not only did she paint herself an unworthy member of the accomplished Kōda family—by virtue of her ordinariness—but she also bemoaned her shortcomings as a writer and an artist, all the while denying any aspirations to art. She only wrote, its seems, for the money, and because she could not find a niche for herself elsewhere, not because she had the god-given talent accorded her father.

I use the term "conceit of humility" here for several reasons. First, self-deprecation has long been considered a virtue in Japanese society, especially among women. In this sense, both Kōda and Tama employed the rhetoric of humility and inadequacy because, in the vernacular, it was among the few acceptable means of self-presentation, especially for women of Kōda's generation. (The unabashed self-assuredness and pride of the writer Hayashi Fumiko, by contrast, was anomalous.) Neither mother nor daughter, furthermore, entered the narrative realm with the ambition of creating an autobiographical self or assuming the role of artist. The persona's sense of inadequacy is attributed to multiple sources: her parents' disappointment that she was not a boy; her feelings that she is neither a good daughter nor a good mother; the constant comparison of self with the extraordinary father; her sense of being different and unloved. At points in the essays, she invokes formulaic expressions of modesty in order to convey her feelings of inadequacy: as a child, when she mistakes the church where Rohan and Yayo's wedding is held for a movie theater (never having been to a church before and uninformed about the event in progress), she concludes, "I am so stupid."[67] At other points she declares herself ugly, lazy, and an unworthy recipient of her father's teachings.[68] One driving force behind this constant self-denigration is the potential for forgiveness and reevaluation: the narrative ultimately leads, not to desire for self-destruction or self-hatred, but rather to resolution and recovery. In the essay "By the Writing Desk," self-forgiveness is expressed in a passage in which Rohan declares to her: "Even people who aren't brilliant have their place in the world."[69]

But there is another reason why I regard textual humility as a discursive strategy for self-presentation. This reason relates to the idiosyncracies of the Kōda household, which in turn resonate with certain social mores in society at large. In that admittedly unusual family, Rohan unceasingly demanded discipline and perfection, linking these qualities with the Confucian dictums that equate laziness with evil (aku) and place even the most mundane of household chores in the realm of spiritual and moral training. Thus Kōda's repeated insistence that her links to Rohan are "through the kitchen," rather than discursive in nature, implies much more than that she only knew Rohan from the perspective of a servant or servile wife who cooked and served his meals. As suggested earlier, ordinary daily activities such as cooking took on an "intrinsically moral" sense as the site of self-cultivation. Thus the seemingly simple assertion suggests, but does not spell out, the degree to which Kōda succeeded in rising to Rohan's challenge—not only in preparing tasty meals but also in making an entire cluster of correct moral and aesthetic choices in the context of the unified realm that she evoked, in narrative, as their home. Rather than buckling under to the unreasonable demands of her father about the proper way to hold a feather duster or handle water in a bucket, she rose to the occasion and succeeded where she could, in the realms of action and observation: "Father taught me to look at nature, since I wasn't suited to art or learning."[70] Similarly, Kōda's constant refrain that her life was "lived narrowly" stands in ironic relation to the body of her essays. The majority of these essays aim precisely at illustrating the depth of a life narrowly lived—if one has the aesthetic and moral wherewithal to perceive and be moved by the sounds of a knife chopping vegetables, by the sight of sparrows in a tiny garden, by the pale face of an aged man as he lay dying. The body of Kōda's essays exists precisely to evoke this vast and profound perceptual realm and this aesthetic sensibility.

Over the course of her career, Kōda produced innumerable essays for inclusion in journals targeted both at specialized audiences (literary journals, women's magazines, periodicals devoted to *shōgi,* poetry, the kimono, and language education) as well as general ones (*Shinchō, Nami, Gakutō,* and others) and also the major newspapers. The essays have subsequently been collected in single-volume editions. In these pieces Kōda stated her views on an astonishing array of topics—and these short pieces inevitably bear topical titles related to nature or culture, literature or politics, objects or people, encounters or incidents: crows, a natural disaster, a famous site, snow, Christmas, gourds, Bashō's poetry, Rohan's complaints, poverty, the month of August, the month of May, weeds, men, rulers, scissors, the kimono, light and dark, ice, furniture, publishers, the emperor, rags, sounds, green soybeans, chopsticks, old age, nicknames, fish, Kyoto women, the *Apollo* mission to the moon, temple architecture (pagodas), her father's career, her childhood, aging, and the changes in Japanese society since the war. Many of the earlier pieces, such as "Dolls for a Special Day," "The Medal," and "The Black Hem," can easily be read as short stories because they are longer and structured around plot and character. Many of them were, in fact, promoted by publishers and received by critics and reviewers as either *shōsetsu* or autobiographical fiction *(jidenteki shōsetsu).*[71] Other of Kōda's numerous *zuihitsu/*essays, published subsequently in bound editions such as *Scattered Clouds, Smoke Over the Moon* (Tsuki no chiri; 1994) or *Reminders of the Season* (Kisetsu no katami; 1993), never tempt the reader to regard them as fiction but are nonetheless highly entertaining and edifying. Formulaic in their repetition of the elements of careful observation, interpretation, and statement of emotional appeal, yet always stunningly beautiful, balanced, and pleasing to read and savor, the essays form the core of Kōda's oeuvre and her public persona.[72] It is through these works that Kōda created and asserted her textual authority.

At this juncture, let us pause to consider the notion of literary authority: the questions of "what allows the text and its creators to maintain the ability to speak within . . . society at a specific time."[73] Kōda, throughout her long career, unabashedly employed the name of her father and his celebrity. Because she earned the high praise of critics and readers for her novels, she could have remained successful without the explicit reminders of Rohan. However, apologetic primarily for the rhetorical and conceptual distance between his idea of art and her own, she cultivated her reputation as Rohan's daughter through her own writings and repeatedly reaffirmed her position vis-à-vis this man.

Rohan, admittedly, did not spawn other literary followers of his own in the orthodox literary establishment *(bundan).* He remained a paradoxically lonely figure who grasped tremendous textual authority but hovered nevertheless on the fringes. He was not one of the writers whose works sold tremendously well, who had a popular following, or about whom critics argued and staked their reputations. Like his contemporaries Natsume Sōseki and Mori Ōgai, Rohan belonged to the last generation trained in Confucian learning and a heavily *kambun* (Japanese written in Chinese) and Chinese-oriented curriculum.[74] While writers such as Sōseki and Ōgai became cosmopolitan by virtue of their travels abroad and the depth of their engagement with Japan's ongoing crisis of modernity and individualism, Rohan did not engage with the "seminal organizational structures" of twentieth-century Japan such as academia or science.[75] Nor did Rohan throw in his lot with those (now canonical) male writers who struggled with issues of the modern self *(kindaiteki jiga)* and the dynamics of Japan's ongoing dialogue with the West. Throughout his long lifetime, Rohan always had something in print. His name inevitably landed on the lists of this century's most influential and accomplished authors, right next to Sōseki and Kawabata. But he dealt with difficult Chinese topics, and his style challenged even intellectual readers; his collected works did not sell well during his lifetime because they overwhelmed and even threatened the reader with signs of erudition, difficult vocabulary, and Chinese historical figures who are far less familiar to many Japanese readers than, say, George Washington. Rohan, moreover, had the reputation of being a demanding man—not an attractive quality to potential students or followers.[76] Thus his erudition and adherence to a literate style, as well as his continental orientation in learning and writing, both enhanced his stature as an alternative path—a possible source of ancestry for Japanese authors and intellectuals—and pushed him to the margins of contemporary culture.[77]

It was such a man with whom Kōda Aya aligned herself—but not without knowing the ambiguous status of his scholarship, viewed by many as dilettantish, his writing, so admired and feared, and his personality, intriguing but thorny. Although she could have used his name merely to find an opening for herself in the literary world and then set him aside to make room for other projects, Kōda emphatically chose to celebrate his life and their life together in her writings and to make a career reveling in what she calls the treasures *(takara-mono)* she inherited from Rohan—that is, the abilities to perceive, to observe, and to concentrate *(isshin)*:

> Conventional wisdom has it that a person never forgets what she learns as a small child, which means that if one is taught music or dance, one can find

pleasure in them forever. All my parents taught me as a child, though, was how to do housework and chores *(kaji zatsuyō)*, and, as times have changed so radically, these lessons of my youth serve me ill.[78]

She invokes the Confucian dictum *kakubutsu chichi* and connects her own ability to observe and analyze with this teaching handed down to her from her father but ultimately evocative of the "seminal power structures" of continental Asian culture, that is, of the elites' role of rectifying heaven and earth.[79]

Paradoxically, what Kōda does not openly claim as her own, especially in her younger years, is the power to record and transmit. In fact, more than once she denies any intention to do so through writing. Her earliest works about Rohan's final days, she states, resulted only from her desire to "observe him carefully" and not from any plan to write about him. Similarly, Kōda flatly insists that when she went to work in the Yanagibashi geisha house as a servant in the early 1950s, she had no intention of collecting materials for a novel or magazine article. The resulting essays about her father, or the novel *Flowing* concerning a maid in a Yanagibashi geisha house, came about coincidentally because she was asked to write about these things. She learned from her father careful observation, not how to wield a brush—or so the conceit goes. The body of her work speaks otherwise. The connection between Kōda and her teacher cannot be found in style or form, but in authoritative voice. If Kojima Nobuo, another postwar writer, leaves his readers with more questions than answers, and creates narrators who exhibit "an extraordinary degree of discursive reticence" and "cannot find answers within" themselves, then the voices in Kōda's narratives write because the gap between tradition and modernity, between the war and its aftermath, did not leave them floundering in the void without any answers.[80] In these works the reader finds a contrasting vision/version of the symbolic order.

If Rohan claimed Sima Qian, the Grand Historian, as one of his principal influences, his daughter took this moral stance too.[81] In premodern Chinese culture, where history stood alongside poetry as the preeminent forms of narrative in the realm, "Sima Qian's embodiment as one in a conceived chain of historical recorders who maintain morality and even, through their records, create the morality of the past" takes the form of a declaration by the "previous holder of this power whose temporal and spatial existence is important in establishing his and his son's moral authority."[82] But because in Kōda's works the persona presents herself as one unworthy of having a privileged relationship with Narrative or Art such as that possessed by her father and his siblings, she receives the mantle of transmitter even as she says she cannot. She writes of the moral order with authority though she says she has none. Among the numerous father-daughter pairs of writers in Japan, Kōda remains among the notable minority of women writers for whom the authority to write does not derive from the figure of romantic, original, creative individual. If anything, Kōda positions herself in a time-honored tradition of learning in Japan, one that is based on a master/disciple relationship (itself echoing the parent/child relationship). Such a structure lays emphasis on transmission of the master's spirit; doing as the master does is the method of learning. In Rohan and Kōda Aya's case, the imbalance of gender is compensated for by Rohan's marginalized position in the world of letters. As Esperanza Ramirez-Christensen has noted: "It is fitting that Kōda became the disciple he never had, the one who permanently inscribes his name and work in cultural history, who rejects 'a woman's happiness,' and appropriates for herself the more authoritative role of transmitter of privileged knowledge."[83]

Although it might seem presumptuous to claim moral authority for an author who writes about kimonos, birds in the garden, and sounds in the kitchen, this is precisely the stance that Kōda Aya assumes: a wise person with the authority to speak about the moral and symbolic order and with the voice that bears certainty. Her stance, as well as her father's, is especially evident when contrasted with those of their literary contemporaries, who, in the face of modernity, lack the wherewithal and certainty to assert their sense of personhood, much less the harmony or disharmony of heaven and earth.

Recalling Kōda's speech about her epiphany at Hakone, Kōda makes no direct reference to artistic or literary precedents for such profound connections between viewer and nature and the subsequent moment of discursive activity that gives rise to the moment in narrative. In the lecture, she claims it as her moment, her way, her emotion. Written all over this revelation and her account of it, however, are traces of multiple cultural and personal moments: Rohan and Kōda's shared acute powers of observation; Rohan's admiration for premodern poet Bashō and for Rohan's contemporary, poet Masaoka Shiki, and especially for their aestheticism.[84] Even in the elder Kōda's prose fiction, the "most basic principle of conduct [of a character] is his artistic impulse" and "because of that devotion, [he] attains a final victory over his rivals."[85] The idea of a way, or *michi*, which Kōda invokes, while ubiquitous in Japanese culture, also resonates with Bashō's career as a poet. Fellow Bashō devotee Masaoka Shiki also linked individual expression and discursive activity with profound beauty and emotion: "My fundamental principle is to express as clearly as I can the poetic quality that I myself feel to be beautiful."[86] Like Shiki, who would characteristically declare that a "brief literary interlude brought me the first . . . solace I had felt in many days," Kōda claims curative powers for observation and composition.[87] The linking of aesthetics and emotion can be traced far back in the Japanese (and Chinese) poetic tradition and is most obviously expressed in the preface of the *Kokinshū,* the tenth-century imperial anthology of poetry. Shiki carried this out in his own modern manner. As critic Itō Sachio has pointed out, Shiki's treatise on tanka and the principle of *shasei* ("copying from life") was "justification for the tanka as an outpouring of the heart—a *sakebi* or lyric cry."[88]

While it is true that the *zuihitsu* essay genre, in its various forms as memoir, reminiscence about people, and meditation on objects, has found great favor with the modern Japanese reading public, generic popularity alone cannot explain the constant demand for Kōda's essays. Her works tend to concentrate on certain topoi: a childhood home (in her case, the semipastoral Mukōjima on the banks of the Sumida River); wandering, loss, her assumption of the homemaker role at a very young age; emotional reactions to natural phenomena or specific sights or sounds; the strictness of her upbringing and her father's teachings at home; expression of inadequacy (personal or professional); interpretation of her father's regard (initially perceived as negative but subsequently as an expression of love). Of all these themes, those concerning the child's inadequacy and desire for acceptance appear with such frequency and consistency during the four decades of Kōda's career that the reader may discount them as her trademarks, as formal aspects of her narrative that function variously as a means of beginning or closure, or as textual self-identification.[89] Even if readers "do not normally read the autobiographies of previously unknown authors, or of authors without a name," Kōda Aya had constructed sufficient public identity and name by the mid-1950s, the first decade of her career—as the publication of her collected works in 1955–1956 suggests—that her constant invocation of Rohan and insistence on her own lack of artistic qualities take on a meaning beyond that of mere self-identification.[90] This is especially true as she earned greater critical praise, and commercial success, and as her works became more widely read than those of the father to whom she compared herself. To some extent her modesty constitutes an acknowledgment of the degree to which the male *bundan* (literary establishment) was entrenched: once her father's name had been chiseled among the pantheon of gods of literature, such as Shiga Naoya, Tanizaki, Sōseki, Tōson, and Kawabata, there seemed no prospect of challenging the centrality of the canon, whether Rohan's works have readers or not, whether his *zenshū* sells or not. This acceptance of literary orthodoxy in the face of reality and change in Japanese letters is a sign of Kōda's conservatism, or perhaps a relic from her many years by

Rohan's side, when she watched streams of editors from the major publishers, journals, and newspapers come to their home in Koishikawa to ask Rohan to write for them, and as Rohan responded by playing the role of erudite celebrity.[91] Famous writers and intellectuals, including Tanizaki, Kuki Shūzō, and Watsuji Tetsurō, also visited their home.

For Kōda, on a personal and professional level, these emblems expressing modest connection with a famous man may have proved useful as a means of deflecting her own sense of guilt about presuming to work as a writer, having come from a household in which writing meant Rohan's style of scholarship, voracious reading of knotty texts, and immersion in continental literary culture. She had not succeeded in contributing to the Kōda family's highly successful endeavors in a variety of fields from classical music to military excursions to economics.[92] Beyond this personal anxiety about textual work, however, Kōda's compulsion to repeat these topoi points to the sources of literary authority in modern Japan—that is, the claims of sincerity, authenticity, and emotional fidelity. These sources might seem natural locally, but in comparison with the fate of literature in twentieth-century China, for example, are noteworthy.[93]

Women with Mythic Origins

The emblematic invocation of Rohan the father suggests an individual and an author so bound to her paternal origins that a sense of individuality outside of identification with the father seems impossible. For some Anglo-European "father-identified daughters" for whom "paternal existence gives shape and meaning to . . . life, to speak directly of [the father's] failings would be to undermine the terms of her own self-image"—in other words, an extreme idealization of the father and resulting suppression of the mother.[94] In contrast, one of the paradoxical and suggestive aspects of Kōda's narratives and careers lies in the ambiguous project of exalting the father while also exposing his human failings—using the father as a reference point, but in an idealized, distanced manner, while exploring in a much more nuanced fashion the two mothers she knew, the other women who played an important role in her life, and the many female characters who are central in her narratives.

Despite the father figure's supposed prominence in Kōda's narrative, she actually writes more in the memoirs about the women in her family than about Rohan. The figure of Rohan takes on exaggerated presence out of sheer repetition and, as well, out of the conceit (and readerly expectation) that the famous man is the central preoccupation of her oeuvre. More than once, Kōda recalls a point in her career when she could write of nothing except memories of her father: "After I had completed *Good for Nothing,* I was stuck; my pencil would not work for me. Of course, I had reached an impasse, because I had neither will nor self-cultivation, and wrote only about my memories of my late father."[95] For many readers and critics whose "horizons of expectations" were aligned with the canon, this apparent focus on the death of the father and its significance in the child's life as entrance into adulthood had great pull, for this topos has occupied a central position in many canonical modern prose works.

Although Rohan did represent an "entire erudite tradition," by no means was this a "tradition inaccessible" to her mothers; if anything, Kōda had available a variety of models, including women in her own family who excelled in Western classical music (her aunts Nobuko and Andō Kōko) and writing (her stepmother Yayoko, a poet and devoted Christian, whose bookshelves were lined with the Bible, Kant, and Socrates).[96] Significantly, these women artists were linked with orthodox and respectable traditions of verse and music whereas Rohan started his career with fiction, a genre held in lower esteem.

The earlier essays, especially, evoke a girl possessing mythopoetic origins. "In the Beginning" (Hajimari), the first section of the autobiographical *Good for Nothing*, starts out with the words: "September 1, 1904. They say I was born in the midst of a storm."[97] She compares herself to the banana *(bashō)* tree, whose huge leaves and trunk may be torn by fierce storms and wind but, because of their resilience, will never fall. By contrast, Rohan describes his own birth within the framework of specific historic events—above all the crucial days at the dawn of the Meiji Restoration:

> I am told that I was born in the seventh month of the third year of Keio in a place called Shinyashiki of Kanda. At the time, my father was twenty-seven years old and my mother was twenty-five. My family still lived quite comfortably in those days, apparently in a spacious house of seventy-some mats. Soon thereafter, I hear, the world began to undergo drastic changes. The year following my birth, the time of the Battle of Ueno, found me strapped to my mother's back as she made her way out of danger to a property in Asakusa. They tell me that I was quite a fragile infant.[98]

An even more powerful link with mythological beginnings can be seen in Kōda's allusion to the Chinese story of the lion who kicks its cubs off a cliff to see if they can prove themselves worthy offspring—described in the story "The Medal" (Kunshō; 1949)—and the analogy she draws between the mythical beasts and her own relationship with Rohan:

> I had lost my way at the bottom of a deep abyss. I cast my eyes upward, toward my father, only to see him dimly, shrouded by mist.

When I was a little girl, Father told me this story as he sat one evening sipping his sake: Once there was a mother lion who pushed her growing cubs off a high cliff in order to test them. The heartiest of the cubs began flapping his legs the moment he realized that he was falling and came floating up again. Another, after landing gently on the ground, shook his head, got back up on all fours, and effortlessly soared up in the air. Yet another cub climbed back to the top by way of a steep, winding path. The father lion judged and ranked them accordingly.

One of the cubs, though, does not try to find his way back to the top and instead just sits there bawling. The lioness sees him and roars, 'Finish him off!' I felt so sorry for this last cub that I started crying, unaware that one day I would become a wretched, unworthy child just like the cub.[99]

This is also an allusion to a poem by Rohan: "The lion cub gazes up at his father / And there is only mist" *(Shishi no ko no oya o aogeba kasumi kana)*. This further alludes to another verse by Rohan about Laotse riding his ox off into the mist.[100]

Another means of evoking a mythological realm in her memoirs can be seen in Kōda's evocation of Rohan as one of the literati (*bunjin;* Chinese w*enren*). This image of Rohan as the last of the literati prevailed in the popular discourse about him, as well, and in fact he cultivated the aura of a writer and thinker, apart from society, fond of poetry, philosophical matters, and liquor. Although Rohan's other biographers mention his fondness for drinking, Kōda's depiction of him constantly sways between, on the one hand, nostalgia for the cups, trays, and other paraphernalia associated with serving him his evening sake, flowers and drinking, poetry composition and wine, and, on the other, gut-wrenching descriptions of the father and husband under the influence, ranting at his wife, making his children cower in the corners, attacking his companions. The more positive and sentimental depictions are striking for their allusiveness, both to the *bunjin* tradition in general and to Rohan's own texts.

As is the case with many of Kōda's works, the general outline of incident and characters in "Fragments" coincides closely with the facts of the writer's life. The Kōda home in Tokyo did burn down during World War II. Kōda Aya did return to build a new house and live on the same site after the war and her father's death. Moreover, Rohan's love of liquor was well known. The reader might also consider Kōda's familiarity with Rohan's literary works and her own predilections as a writer. While the voice in "Fragments" remembers past incidents and emotions in her life, the work itself recalls another narrative, one by Rohan titled "Tarōbō" (1900). Rohan preferred historical fiction and essays, but he also composed vernacular short stories, "Tarōbō" among them. A third-person narrative, the story begins with one man's feelings of peace and contentment when, after a long day's work, he waters and tends his garden. His harmonious relationship with his wife, who serves him sake on the back veranda after his labors in the garden, as well as the lovely garden itself, both afford him great satisfaction. This idyllic, harmonious world is disrupted when the man, slightly drunk, drops his favorite sake cup and breaks it. His wife, puzzled by his great regret and unhappiness over the loss of a mere sake cup, asks him for an explanation. The cup, which he nicknamed "Tarōbō," turns out to be something he received from the father of a young lady he loved in his youth. Even after he and the young lady separated, the man always kept the cup as a reminder of his youthful passion:

> "It's strange to think that I had Tarōbō for so long. It's even funnier that, after I broke it, I started thinking about all those things from the past. Just as they say, 'Hold a piece of sparkling ice in your hands and you will end up with water; the scent of flowers does not stay fixed in the sky.' I've been talking too much, haven't I? Let's have some dinner," he said, and then laughed loudly again. A distant, cold, reserved look now on his face, the man had reverted to his old self.
>
> His wife, smiling as she listened to his ending, sat with her head tipped to one side, as if moved by his story.
>
> "But why did you have to give her up if you loved her so much? I suppose there must have been some compelling reason?" Before she could stop them, the words came out of her mouth, because of the extraordinary sympathy she felt for her husband. The man, however, did not respond to her question.
>
> "There's no point in talking about that now. . . . Who is there to say that the story I have told you is true or false? And is there anyone who will judge for me the merits of having experienced such pain? Only Tarōbō knew all the details of our secret, but now he is gone. How futile to point at the water and talk about how the ice used to look, or to gaze up at the sky and speak of where the fragrance of the flowers has gone."[101]

His wife reacts sympathetically, and in the end the world is a harmonious realm once again.

Kōda Aya's "Fragments" bears similarities to "Tarōbō" at several points. Both stories explore responses to loss and involve characters who find consolation in narrating their memories. Apart from the similarity in image/motif (the liquor and ceramics), the fragment of the tray in "Fragments" and the broken cup in "Tarōbō"—both useless, broken objects—serve the purpose of spurring a memory. In turn, these instances of recollection in each of the works are essential in character development. The reader finds the characters interesting and vivid precisely because they remember. While the world portrayed in "Tarōbō" is small, complete, and harmonious, that in "Fragments" evokes the degree to which everything has changed as a result of the war. The sake cup is the only broken element in Rohan's story. The world depicted in Kōda's piece, however, is vast: no walls left standing, no gardens, only wild onions that grow everywhere. Everything is broken. And ironically the narrator regains her sense of identity only upon finding something significant, a meaningful fragment, in a shattered world. The narrator of "Fragments" concludes the story with these words: "As for the blue and white piece of porcelain, I could not bear the thought of having anyone else see it again, and so I crushed it into a powder and returned it to the earth." The moment of remembrance, the link with the past, and the fullness have been fixed forever in narrative. Ironically, the once highly significant ceramic fragment has lost its value.

In Kōda's narrative realm neither image—neither the wild, drunken Rohan nor the happily imbibing literate—predominates. Thus the reader is left with a portrait of the idealized *bunjin* with a drinking problem or a kindred spirit to the Chinese literate of old who, instead of dwelling in a hut in the mountains, aloof from society, is stuck in a nuclear family with a wife who demands as much time with her books as he does:

> When I woke, I could hear Father's voice aggressively intoning Chinese poetry, and also the unfamiliar sound of his keeping rhythm by tapping on something metal. . . . Deep in the night, all was silent except for Father's angry booming voice, echoing with anger as he recited the verse. Doubtless, he sat on the near side of the long brazier, his legs crossed, a volume of Chinese poems on one knee, drinking late into the darkness. I imagined the black lacquer tray before him covered with dirty bowls and plates, the food set out for him earlier in the evening long gone. Usually when he drinks that much he is all by himself . . . but I peered in and saw Mother leaning up against the pillar. . . . A prayer book lay on the floor before her. . . . No one needed to tell me what was going to happen—I knew. As he chanted the verse, Father's voice grew louder and more piercing in its anger and roughness. Mother sat silent and unapproachable, her body bowed in prayer, and the sight of the two of them made me feel utterly desolate and lonesome, as I was still a child. Father seemed not to care in the least about the devastating effect such behav-

ior had on me, and so I saw him like that repeatedly. For my part, I became so sensitive to any sign of his lapsing into such a state that I was constantly on my guard. I hated that pale yellow volume of Chinese poetry that was Father's, as much as I did Mother's green prayer book and her Bible bound in leather.[102]

Unlike the novelist Enchi Fumiko, who registers surprise when readers inquire about the influence of her famous father, the writer and scholar Ueda Mannen (Bannen), Kōda Aya reveled in creating a body of narrative works describing the relationship of a father and a daughter. Kōda spent many years of her life serving her father, cooking for him, cleaning house, and nursing him. Some readers will view Rohan as a lucky man because he had a daughter willing to serve him like a wife throughout his long life; others will regard his strength and her self-denigration as analogous to, or even as legitimating, the relationship of patriarchy to women. But such a conflation of the individual father with the patriarchal system and equation of Kōda's life with servility renders her works corrupt and pointless. In this chapter I have argued that the narrative realm created by Kōda Aya in her autobiographical essays presents in fact a utopian vision of the family by evoking a unified moral and aesthetic universe and an alternative, in fact, to the despair at failed patriarchy and matriarchy expressed in the texts of many of Kōda's contemporaries.

Notes

1. "Atomiyosowaka," *KAZS* 1:112–113.
2. "Sugano no ki," *KAZS* 1:4–87.
3. Maryellen Toman Mori, "The Quest for *Jouissance* in Takahashi Takako's Texts," in *The Woman's Hand,* ed. Paul G. Schalow and Janet A. Walker (Stanford: Stanford University Press, 1996), pp. 207–208. On the variety of feminist strategies in literature see also Sharalyn Orbaugh, "The Body in Contemporary Japanese Woman's Fiction," in *The Woman's Hand,* pp. 121–124.
4. Alan M. Tansman, *The Writings of Kōda Aya* (New Haven: Yale University Press, 1993), p. 4.
5. As Barbara Herrnstein Smith has written: "To endure as something other than vivid historical artifacts, [literary works] must also be able to serve as metaphors and parables of an unpredictable future. They must, in short, continue to have meanings independent of the particular context that occasioned their composition, which will inevitably include meanings that the author did not and could not have intended to convey." See Smith, *On the Margins of Discourse: The Relation of Literature to Language* (Chicago: University of Chicago Press, 1978), p. 151. Also relevant to

this question of literature and the world is Todorov's assertion that although literary works do "evoke life . . . the absence of a rigorous relation of truth must at the same time make us extremely cautious: the text can 'reflect' social life but can just as well incarnate its exact opposite." See Tsvetan Todorov, *Introduction to Poetics* (Minneapolis: University of Minnesota Press, 1981), p. 18.

6. "Shūen," *KAZS* 1:260–261.

7. Patricia Yaeger, Beth Kowaleski-Wallace, and Ursula Owen note that several frameworks exist for feminists viewing father/daughter relationships: one approach is the Freudian view that "focuses on the sexual bonds between father and daughter, emphasizing the daughter's sexual feelings and her elaborate mechanisms for denying those feelings"; the other approach lies in institutionalized forms of patriarchy that determine "what part women shall or shall not play and in which the female is everywhere subsumed under the male." See Ursula Owen, *Father: Reflections by Daughters* (New York: Pantheon, 1983), p. 3, quoted in Patricia Yaeger and Beth Kowaleski-Wallace, eds., *Refiguring the Father* (Carbondale: Southern Illinois University Press, 1989), p. xiii.

8. See Sharalyn Orbaugh's illuminating "The Body in Contemporary Japanese Fiction," especially pp. 128–129 and 149–153.

9. "Kōen 'Deai to kandō'—Iwanami no bunka kōenkai ni te," *KAZS* 22 (cassette tape).

10. *KAZS* 1:267–268.

11. "Shūkyaku," *KAZS* 2:97.

12. Kobayashi Isamu, *Kagyūan hōmonki* (Iwanami Shoten, 1956); Shiotani San, *Kōda Rohan,* 3 vols. (Chūō Kōronsha, 1965–1968). Other biographical views of Rohan include Saitō Etsurō, *Zōho Kagyūan oboegaki: Rohan ōkina dan sōsho* (Keyaki Shuppan, 1994); Shimomura Ryōichi, *Bannen no Rohan* (Keizai Ōraisha, 1979).

13. Tansman, *Writings,* pp. 22–28.

14. "Eiyaku 'Kuroi suso' ni soete," *KAZS* 6:185.

15. Tansman asserts that "Aya's works can be seen as a symbolic attempt to overcome the contradiction between her social parameters and her personal desires. She overcame it not by rejecting either aspect of her life but by joining them, by rewriting her domestic sphere into an aesthetically and existentially enriching world." See Tansman, *Writings,* p. 6. While I agree that Kōda rendered her world an "enriching" one in narrative, her background was not the bland domesticity of 1960's suburbia but a highly stimulating and unusual family.

16. Sheldon Garon notes that even in the postwar era "reports of the death of women as state agents have . . . been exaggerated. The gendered basis of women's participation in public life has not fundamentally changed since the interwar era. . . . Wives are still held responsible for education, household finances, and the

health and welfare of their communities." See Sheldon Garon, *Molding Japanese Minds: The State in Everyday Life* (Princeton: Princeton University Press, 1997), pp. 191 and 147, n. 19. See also Sharon H. Nolte and Sally Ann Hastings, "The Meiji State's Policy Toward Women, 1890–1910," and Kathleen Uno, "Women and Changes in the Household Division of Labor," in *Recreating Japanese Women,* ed. Gail Bernstein (Berkeley: University of California Press, 1991), pp. 151–174 and 17–41 respectively.

17. "Atomiyosowaka," *KAZS* 1:113; *Misokkasu, KAZS* 2:39. It is worth noting that Rohan's agemates teased him when they saw him washing rice and asked him if he was performing such service because one of the women at home was sick.

18. Uno, "Household Division of Labor," p. 27.

19. *Misokkasu, KAZS* 2:15 ff.

20. "Atomiyosowaka," *KAZS* 1:112.

21. Ibid., pp. 139–140.

22. Ibid., pp. 113–114.

23. Tu Wei-Ming, *Way, Learning, and Politics: Essays on the Confucian Intellectual* (Albany: SUNY Press, 1993), pp. 31 and 33.

24. Ibid., pp. 39–40.

25. Tomeoka Kōsuke, "Joshi ni taisuru Ninomiya Oo no risō," *Shimin* 4 (4) (28 May 1909):61–62, quoted in Nolte and Hastings, "Policy Toward Women," p. 168; Patricia Fister, "Female Bunjin: The Life of Poet-Painter Ema Saikō," in *Recreating Japanese Women,* p. 110.

26. Uno, "Household Division of Labor," pp. 31–32; Robert Lyons Danly, *In the Shade of Spring Leaves: The Life and Writings of Higuchi Ichiyō, a Woman of Letters in Meiji Japan* (New Haven: Yale University Press, 1981), pp. 11–13.

27. *Misokkasu, KAZS* 2:56–59.

28. Again, Rohan may have been following a model such as that of Ema Saikō and her father, for whom painting and calligraphy were not *"hanayome shugyō"* (training for marriage) but part of the education of a literate, or *bunjin.* Fister notes that "the earliest female bunjin . . . were primarily the wives, sisters, or daughters of well known bunjin artists. . . . Many scholars, inspired by the actions of contemporary masters in China, now encouraged women to join their ranks." See Fister, "Female Bunjin," p. 108.

29. "Kōen," *KAZS* 23 (cassette tape).

30. Inoue Kazuko, "Onna no isshō—Kōda Aya to kimono," in *Gengo bunka-bu kiyō,* p. 111.

31. Tansman, *Writings,* pp. 132ff. and 151.

32. Etō Jun, *Seijuku to sōshitsu: "haha" no hōkai* (Kōdansha, 1993). My consideration of Etō's work refers extensively to Katō Norihiro, *Amerika no kage* (Kawada Shobō

Shinsha, 1985); Van Gessel, *The Sting of Life: Four Contemporary Japanese Novelists* (New York: Columbia University Press, 1989); Ueno Chizuko, Mizuta Noriko, Asada Akira, and Karatani Kōjin, "Nihon bunka to jendā: kafuchōsei to sono hihan kara hajimete," *Hihyō kūkan* 2(3) (1994):6–43; Ueno Chizuko, Ogura Chikako, and Tomioka Taeko, eds., *Danryū bungakuron* (Chikuma Shobō, 1992).

33. Julia Kristeva has written of the force of psychoanalysis in similar terms: "I see psychoanalysis as the lay version, the only one, of the speaking being's quest for truth that religion symbolizes for certain of my contemporaries and friends." Kristeva conceives of psychoanalysis as "the locus of extreme abjection, the refuge of private horror that can be lifted only by an infinite-indefinite displacement of speech and its effects." See Julia Kristeva, "My Memory's Hyperbole," in *The Female Autograph: Theory and Practice of Autobiography from the Tenth to the Twentieth Century,* ed. Domna Stanton (Chicago: University of Chicago Press, 1987), p. 225.

34. Erik H. Erikson, *Childhood and Society,* rev. ed. (New York: Norton, 1963), pp. 286 and 326 ff.

35. Ibid., p. 327. In *Origins of Modern Japanese Literature,* Karatani Kōjin cites Erikson's efforts to free psychoanalysis of the rigid oedipal framework.

36. Gessel, *Sting of Life,* pp. 69–70. My discussion of Etō's book draws heavily on Gessel's lucid comments.

37. Ibid., p. 70.

38. Erikson in fact protests the early postwar trend in American psychoanalysis to vilify Mother for all the problems of society and specifically those of its men: "'Mom,' of course, is only a stereotyped caricature of existing contradictions which have emerged from intense, rapid, and as yet unintegrated changes in American history." See Erikson, *Childhood and Society,* p. 291.

39. Gessel, *Sting of Life,* p. 221.

40. Ibid., p. 229.

41. Etō, *Seijuku to sōshitsu,* pp. 69–71.

42. Erikson, *Childhood and Society,* p. 85. Here Erikson is discussing infant development.

43. Critics have been notably silent on the violent aspect of Shunsuke's personality.

44. Katō, *Amerika no kage,* pp. 64–67.

45. Katō discusses this sense of "crystal" on pp. 11–15.

46. See Ueno et al., "Nihon bunka to jendā," p. 36. Etō's claim about the role of industrial capitalism and women can be found in *Seijuku to sōshitsu,* p. 64. Notably, Ueno also wrote the afterword to the 1993 paperback edition of *Seijuku to sōshitsu,* titled "*Seijuku to sōshitsu* kara sanjūnen" (Kōdansha, 1993), pp. 256–283.

47. *Danryū bungakuron,* pp. 210–212.

48. I thank Paul Anderer for pointing out the predominance of the search for a sec-

ond father. The most obvious examples of this are in Sōseki's *Kokoro* and Tōson's *Hakai.*

49. "Atomiyosowaka," *KAZS* 1:140–141.

50. John Sturrock, "Theory vs. Autobiography," in *The Culture of Autobiography: Constructions of Self-Representation,* ed. Robert Folkenflik (Stanford: Stanford University Press, 1993), pp. 25–26.

51. No book-length biography of Kōda Aya has appeared. Most of the works that do describe Kōda's life rely heavily on her autobiographies, although one finds independent descriptions of Kōda in Kobayashi Isamu's and Shiotani San's writings about Rohan. Kōda's daughter, Aoki Tama, gives another view of Kōda in her books *Koishikawa no uchi* (Kōdansha, 1994) and *Kaeritakatta uchi* (Kōdansha, 1997).

52. Folkenflik, *Culture of Autobiography,* p. 15.

53. The distinction between *shōsetsu* (prose fiction) and *zuihitsu* (essay) is blurred. The generic status of a work is often decided by what the dust jacket (that is, the publisher or marketer) labels the contents of a book, by the section of the bookstore where the book is found, or by a critic or reviewer's casual categorization, rather than detailed analysis of the rhetorical aspects of the text with the aim of generic classification. Such generic fuzziness is not unique to Japan. Another obstacle to placing texts neatly into one category or another is the proximity of *watakushi shōsetsu* (personal fiction) and autobiography. For more on these types of prose see Edward Fowler, *The Rhetoric of Confession* (Berkeley: University of California Press, 1988). Karatani Kōjin discusses the constructed nature of interiority and confession in his "Naimen no hakken" and "Kokuhaku to iu seidō" in *Kindai Nihon bungaku no kigen* (Kōdansha, 1980).

54. Hans Robert Jauss, *Toward an Aesthetic of Reception,* trans. Timothy Bahti (Minneapolis: University of Minnesota Press, 1982), p. 5.

55. Interview with Noborio Yutaka, April 1986.

56. Kōda herself, Aoki, Tansman, and all Japanese critics concur on this aspect of "influence."

57. Tansman, in his fine study, discusses Kōda's use of objects in her work. See especially his chapter "A World of Objects," pp. 70–101. Also relevant is Paul deMan's exploration of Yeats' famous line, "How can we know the dancer from the dance?" in "Semiology and Rhetoric," in *Textual Strategies,* ed. Josué V. Harari (Ithaca: Cornell University Press, 1979), pp. 130ff.

58. "Kōen: 'Deai to kandō,'" *KAZS* 23 (cassette tape).

59. *Kuzure, KAZS* 21:24.

60. Ibid., pp. 24–25.

61. "Kojin kyōju," *KAZS* 19:308–310.

62. *Misokkasu, KAZS* 2:38.

63. "Sugano no ki," *KAZS* 1:8–10.

64. "Chichi—sono shi" and "Sugano no ki."

65. "Sugano no ki," *KAZS* 1:23.

66. In contrast, Uno Chiyo describes her relationship with her sadistic father in blunt terms and makes it clear that she became a writer despite his attempts literally to bind her. See Rebecca Copeland, *The Sound of the Wind* (Honolulu: University of Hawaiʻi Press, 1992).

67. *Misokkasu, KAZS* 2:68.

68. *Misokkasu, KAZS* 2:122–123; *Kuzure, KAZS* 21:11; "Gozaimasen," *KAZS* 20:8–9; "Renzu," *KAZS* 1:398; "Zen," *KAZS* 3:135–136; "Sugano no ki," *KAZS* 1:68–69.

69. "Kihen," *KAZS* 15:11.

70. "Kusabue," *KAZS* 21:155.

71. The shifts in generic classification occur in the United States too: what had earlier been promoted as "fiction" because of sensitive material is later packaged as autobiography.

72. Tansman uses the term "persona" in his book.

73. Wendy Larson, *Literary Authority and the Modern Chinese Writer* (Durham: Duke University Press, 1991), p. 161, n. 1.

74. Donald Keene, "The Sino-Japanese War of 1894–95 and Its Cultural Effects in Japan," in *Tradition and Modernization in Japanese Culture* (Princeton: Princeton University Press, 1971), p. 171. Stefan Tanaka, in *Japan's Orient: Rendering Pasts into History* (Berkeley: University of California Press, 1993), examines in detail Chinese studies in Japan.

75. Rohan's tenure at Kyoto Imperial University lasted for less than a year, probably because the university did not sit well with Rohan's self-taught approach—or vice versa.

76. Kobayashi Isamu, *Kagyūan hōmonki* (Iwanami Shoten, 1956).

77. See, for example, "Mō hitotsu no kindai" and Shinoda Hajime's defense of Rohan titled *Rohan no tame ni*. In *Dawn to the West* (New York: Holt, 1984), p. 162, Donald Keene presents Rohan as a "road not taken" by modern Japanese literature.

78. "Zassō to sakana," *KAZS* 21:204.

79. Larson, *Literary Authority,* pp. 15–16.

80. Gessel, *Sting of Life,* pp. 221–222.

81. Tansman, *Writings,* p. 52; Larson, *Literary Authority,* p. 15.

82. Larson, *Literary Authority,* p. 15.

83. Personal correspondence with the author, 14 September 1996.

84. Although Rohan and Shiki admired each other's work, Rohan discouraged Shiki from becoming a novelist.

85. Makoto Ueda, *Matsuo Bashō* (New York: Kodansha International, 1982), pp. 180–181.

86. Robert Brower, quoting from Shiki's "Open Letter" in "Masaoka Shiki and Tanka Reform," in *Tradition and Modernization in Japanese Culture,* ed. Donald H. Shively (Princeton: Princeton University Press, 1971), p. 395.

87. Ibid., p. 406.

88. Ibid., p. 418.

89. Kirk Varnedoe comments that in modern art "impersonation" is "the fundamental modern means of self-expression"; quoted in Jerome Bruner, "The Autobiographical Process," in Folkenflik, *The Culture of Autobiography,* p. 52.

90. "For the lay reader, an autobiography [is] the unique self-presentation of author X or author Y, some public figure this reader already knows, and about whom he or she wants to know more. The lay reader does not normally read the autobiographies of previously unknown authors, or of authors without a name. . . . He becomes an autobiographer because his name is already in the public domain; he has done or written something that ensures him a readership. Although he is in part known already, he may feel he is misleadingly or inadequately known, and write in order to correct that, to impose an image of himself whose authenticity no reader is in a position to question." See Folkenflik, *The Culture of Autobiography,* pp. 22–23.

91. Kobayashi Isamu in his *Kagyūan hōmonki,* for example, writes of the constant stream of editors, writers, and publishers to the Koishikawa home. Kobayashi himself worked as an editor at Iwanami Shoten and maintained a long and intimate relationship with Rohan.

92. See Chapter 1 for more on Rohan and his extraordinary siblings.

93. See Wendy Larson, *Literary Authority.*

94. Kowaleski-Wallace, *Their Father's Daughters,* p. 23.

95. See the newspaper article "Watakushi wa fude o tatsu." See also the afterword to the 1983 paperback edition of *Misokkasu* (Iwanami Shoten), p. 218.

96. Kowaleski-Wallace, *Their Father's Daughters,* p. 11; *Misokkasu,* KAZS 2:72.

97. *Misokkasu, KAZS* 2:4.

98. "Shōnen jidai," in *Rohan zuihitsu,* vol. 1 (Iwanami Shoten, 1983), p. 376.

99. "Kunshō," *KAZS* 1:356–357; translation is my own.

100. Shiotani, "Kaisetsu," in *Chichi—Konna koto,* pp. 191–192.

101. *Rohan zenshū* (Iwanami Shoten, 1951), 3:265–266.

102. "Yu no senrei," *KAZS* 2:97–100.

3

Flowing and the Literature of the Demimonde

In 1955, Kōda surprised readers when she published the novel *Flowing* (Naga-reru), a work about a geisha house in early postwar Tokyo. Readers and critics alike wondered at Kōda's switch from memoirs about her family to prose narrative on a radically different subject—the world of the geisha and prostitute.[1] Kōda had consistently produced sober, mature works focusing on domestic themes and had exhibited even less interest than her scholarly father in portraying passion, sex, and obsession or spinning amatory tales.[2] Yet, in *Flowing*, Kōda chose the floating world *(ukiyo)*, the urban pleasure quarter devoted precisely to these concerns, for the setting of her long prose narrative. Although Kōda had direct contact with this segment of society during her brief tenure as maid in a geisha house, her novel figures not as autobiography but instead places Kōda among the numerous Japanese writers and artists who have found inspiration in the urban pleasure quarter and its inhabitants.[3]

In this chapter I want to examine Kōda's *Flowing* in the context of the Japanese tradition of demimonde literature dating back to the Edo period. The assumption underlying this study is that every literary work observes the rules—the poetics—of a literary type (or genre) while simultaneously altering and redefining that genre. Although Kōda's *Flowing* appeared long after the flourishing of literature about the pleasure districts, the work bears a relationship to its predecessors both in conception and execution. Many authors of earlier demimonde literature had evinced a primary interest in sex and romance. A voyeuristic fascination with the women of the quarter—the objects of desire and consumption—became orthodox in the texts they produced. A number of other writers, especially in post-Edo narrative, banished the voyeur's fantasies and instead portrayed the suffering of women bought and sold in the demimonde. Kōda, in *Flowing*, acknowledges both of these textual constructs, but then gives them a postwar interpretation. The viewer in *Flowing* seeks a consummately aesthetic otherworld, rather than a sexual one, thus creating a niche in the demimonde for the one type of person whose existence seems most at odds with the pleasure quarter: the middle-aged homemaker.

Although the reader encounters in *Flowing* a highly elaborated realm of the senses, the work notably lacks the sex scenes that one might anticipate in a work concerning a world of libidinal commerce, especially given the tradition of demimonde visual arts and literature from the Edo period on. In terms of the contemporary reader's expectations, exploration of sexuality and physicality figured as a central concern in prose fiction in the era when *Flowing* was published. From the end of the Pacific War, the literary scene had been distinguished by an increasing interest in graphic descriptions of sex—whether in reaction to the liberalization of censorship laws after the defeat or in an attempt to locate meaning in the celebration of physical intercourse, when so much of the sense of spiritual communion emphasized in narrative before and during the war had lost its validity. The debate over the place of sex in literature had found a public forum in the early 1950s with the prosecution of the translator of *Lady Chatterly's Lover.* The 1955 publication of Ishihara Shintarō's *Season of the Sun* (Taiyō no kisetsu; translated in 1961 as *Season of Violence*) accrued significance as a literary event not only because of its author's rebellion against the senior literary establishment and its hierarchy, as well as his manipulation of the media, but also because of the novel's affirmation of sexuality in the youth culture.

Unlike authors of Kōda's generation such as Enchi Fumiko (1905–1986) who focused on eroticism and the psyche, Koda had never shown interest in writing overtly about sexuality, with the exception of the story "A Woman's Screams," which deals with rape. In the novel *Kimono* and other works, furthermore, she evokes heterosexual intimacy in a largely negative light. In addition, Kōda's public image of chastity and modesty reinforced the notion of extreme repression of physical sexuality to the extent that even the suggestion of incestuous overtones in her relationship with her father, despite the fact that she lived as his devoted companion for many years, seems utterly absurd. Nonetheless, *Flowing* is indeed a sensual and erotic text, though predominately in the sense of a negative aesthetic.

Eroticism in *Flowing* takes on the particular form of the desiring gaze—specifically the gaze of woman taking pleasure in looking at woman. As Kojima Chikako and others have suggested, the sense of subjectivity in *Flowing,* and later that of *Kimono,* distinguish themselves because, though the protagonists are female, they "adopt a man's perspective"—or, more accurately, the narrative perspective at certain points is "from the point of view of a woman who has borrowed a man's perspective."[4] In *Flowing* this occurs most notably in two famous passages: when the protagonist Rika is looking at the bodies of two experienced geisha, one falling (being knocked down) and one rising (sitting up in bed), but neither in the presence of male partners. This evocation of the pleasure of looking and heavily veiled eroticism constitutes one of the reasons for the work's popularity, especially with male critics. The question remains, though, whether *Flowing* should be regarded as antifeminist because of its subjective adoption of a "man's perspective"—that is, the "female spectator's phantasy of masculinization . . . restless in its transvestite clothing."[5] But Kōda's investment in scopiophilia (erotic pleasure in looking) is much more complex than simple visual transvestism. The mechanisms of readerly response to the "rising" and "falling" geisha passages involve the invocation of the male gaze, but specifically in the context of the urban demimonde and its cultural tradition. The space is one where women perform in the stylized manner with the specific aim of giving pleasure to the male customer. The catch, however, is that the customer himself must also enter fully into the performance as a participant and act the role of nonpaying, emotionally engaged, and sensitive male partner. The demimonde's power as an otherworld, a fantasy realm, relates precisely to the historical change in its economic, legal, and ethical status and concomitant shifts in narrative. In *Flowing* the reader encounters a belated attempt to recapture the elements of fantasy and eroticism implicit in Edo constructs of the courtesan's world, despite the desperation and poverty redolent in the geisha house depicted by Kōda and emphasized in contemporary narrative.

Quest for a Realm of Beauty

Kōda's *Flowing* centers on the experiences of Rika, a middle-aged woman who comes to work as a maid at a geisha house. Formerly an ordinary housewife, Rika has decided to enter this marginal world after losing both her husband and child. It is not so much the poverty and discomfort of her new position as a maid that draw Rika's attention as the novelty of the geisha's social and physical world. Rika falls into the category of *shirōto,* an ordinary, "nonprofessional" person, who observes up-close *kurōto* (professionals, or women of the demimonde) for the first time.[6] The geisha house *(okiya)* where Rika works is located in the geisha quarters along the west bank of Tokyo's Sumida River, an area that has seen better days.[7] The Tsutanoya (the geisha house where Rika works) suffers from financial difficulties and a constantly shrinking number of geisha. Its owner (consistently called *shujin*) herself came to the house after many years of working as a geisha, but even her long experience does not prepare her for all aspects of managing a business. Along with the proprietress, her nineteen-year-old daughter Katsuyo, niece Yoneko, and Yoneko's child Fujiko live in the house. The geisha employed by the Tsutanoya check in at the *okiya* before and after engagements. Among them Tsutaji possesses the perfect balance of professionalism and emotion. Someka exemplifies the aesthetic of *iki* (elegant chic). Nanako, with her frankness and desire for the new, epitomizes the postwar geisha.

The novel includes a large cast of minor characters as well. The most important of these are two "hero-villain" pairs. Kishibojin, the owner's older sister and Yoneko's mother, makes her living by lending money at exorbitant interest rates. This villainous usurer has Someka in her clutches and relentlessly demands repayment.[8] The character Nandori, by contrast, the elegant owner of a *ryōtei* (teahouse), can do no wrong and has a major voice in deciding the Tsutanoya's fate.[9] The other good/bad pair is male. The unsavory Nokogiriyama appears repeatedly to demand restitution on behalf of his "niece," Namie, who was formerly employed at the Tsutanoya. A young man named Saeki (secretary to the owner's former patron), by contrast, comes to the owner's aid several times.

Both in plot and in theme, the notion of a world in decline is central in *Flowing* and is suggested by a number of the novel's subplots. The house must struggle to remain afloat financially because the number of geisha employed there has dwindled considerably.[10] The Tsutanoya's owner, however, avoids the subject of money. Eventually all of the financial problems are resolved, but ironically the proprietress has by then lost control of the house. Nandori and Saeki install Rika as the manager, and the older geisha then moves to the less reputable side of the river to manage a house there. Presumably the infusion of new blood will put new life into the decaying establishment, but the end of the work is ambiguous. Kōda seems to be pointing to the inherent potential for decline and corruption in this closed world ruled by emotions and money.

The Demimonde: An Ideal World?

At this point we must pause to consider why the cultural tradition of the geisha may have attained such significance in Rika's imagination and life. The pleasure quarter traditionally attracted *shirōto* men, but in *Flowing* it is a respectable middle-aged widow who chooses to live there. Although the postwar period, the setting of *Flowing*, witnessed tremendous social and cultural change in the demimonde, the geisha still retained an aestheticism and an otherworldly quality in the popular imagination that would have attracted an outsider such as Rika.

Both now and in the past, the pleasure quarter gained importance for a variety of reasons besides sex. As Howard Hibbett has written, romance, as distinguished from sex, was the principal selling point of the quarter.[11] While some of the women in these urban areas sold only their bodies, others, such as the geisha, possessed artistic and social abilities prized by their patrons.[12] The scholar Takahashi Toshio notes that men in the Edo period regarded the government-licensed pleasure quarter as the only place where one could participate openly in play, an aestheticized life, and liberation *(kaihō)*.[13] The geisha undeniably work as skilled performers of traditional arts, but there is a certain ambiguity in their identity. Their roles parallel those of the prostitute, common dancing girl, and bar hostess in so many ways that any claim that they are primarily artists and performers is met with skepticism.[14] Furthermore, they have traditionally remained within the urban context known as the pleasure quarter, which exists apart from the respectable world, both literally and metaphorically.

While much scandal and heartbreak resulted from respectable, married men spending time in the demimonde, even the wives of such men admired certain aspects of the geisha's life. During Edo, the geisha and courtesan reigned as arbiters of taste and fashion. The kimono they wore and songs they sang set the standard even for "decent" bourgeois women. In the postwar period, a person like *Flowing*'s Rika would have viewed the geisha not as trendsetters but, ironically, as conservators of tradition. The geisha continued to wear kimonos and traditional hairstyles, even though Western styles had replaced them as the standard of fashion. To have done otherwise, however, would have been to lose "that which made them special as geisha."[15] A geisha by definition, then, wears a certain type of costume suitable for such activities as playing the samisen and singing. This is because the profession is firmly grounded in the dynamic yet uniform cultural milieu that was Edo. The dominant aesthetic of *iki* or chic, demanded a certain narrow conception of style and behavior. Western attire cannot be *iki,* because it is not Edo.[16] In postwar culture, the retention of the geisha business signals an effort to sustain practices related to the pre-Meiji past as an aspect of cultural identity, but it also relates to "the anxiety of contamination" expressed in Kuki Shūzō's *The Anatomy of "Iki,"* which stems as much from "anxiety over the *internal* specter of mass culture (and allied possibilities of mass politics) as it is an anxiety over the *external* presence of the West."[17]

While the geisha has, in one sense, become a relic, the profession's iconic significance still has a powerful grip on modern culture. The beauty of the geisha, her music, and dance remain a source of interest, but equally intriguing is her ambivalent role of "maintaining sexual chastity and autonomy while appearing hospitable to every customer."[18] To a person like Rika, the geisha's effort to retain control of her body elevates her occupation and renders it more acceptable than the rest of the demimonde.[19] The geisha never bears the ultimate degradation of the prostitute because she retains her art *(gei)* and her links with the past. Perhaps for this reason, men in high position have traditionally not felt uneasy about consorting with geisha.[20]

Images of the Demimonde in Art

Images of geisha in the visual arts and literature have long been a source of fascination. A respectable middle-aged person like Rika would know the geisha as an important subject of Edo-period art, especially *ukiyo-e* prints and painting. Edo prose narrative similarly glorified the beauty of the geisha and courtesan.[21] Although numerous Edo writers and artists produced texts and pictures with pornographic intent, the majority of canonized works depend for their power on the evocation of the dynamics of romantic and erotic relations outside of marriage and the family and on portraits of women whose identities do not find their basis in the orthodox roles of wife and mother. Premodern writers, such as Ihara Saikaku (1642–1693) and Tamenaga Shunsui (1790–1843), made women of the demimonde intriguing by portraying them as possessing great emotional freedom. During Edo, this quality was attractive to readers because of the rigidity of prevailing Confucian morality.

By Shunsui's day, a growing number of women were literate and of sufficient leisure and means that their presence had an effect on the prose produced by contemporary writers.[22] This female audience also enjoyed reading about the demimonde and made up a considerable part of the market for Shunsui's *Shunshoku umegoyomi* (Colors of Spring: Plum Blossom Calendar; 1832–1833) and other works of the *ninjōbon* genre. In the *ninjōbon,* the female characters, prostitutes and geisha alike, are much more distinctive and individualized than those of the earlier literature of the demimonde.[23] The *ninjōbon* not only developed the women of the licensed quarter more fully as fictional characters, it also attempted to clean up the sordidness of this segment of society by glorifying the women's sincere love.[24]

Although marginal in terms of Edo-period Confucian moral standards, the literature and art of the floating world commanded a central position in the realms of Edo popular culture and commerce. Subsequently, during the Meiji period, novelists and critics rediscovered the writings of Saikaku and Shunsui and celebrated such works as an important part of Japan's literary heritage, in turn making them familiar to modern readers.[25] Japanese scholars in the twentieth century, as part of a "restoration of continuity with a chosen past," have defined texts about the demimonde as part of the literary canon by annotating and including them in collections of classical literature.[26]

One must not underestimate the powerful influence exerted by artistic and literary images of the geisha. The fiction of the pleasure quarter reinforced the notion that the women were artistic beings, not unlike actresses.[27] In his definition of the pleasure quarter, scholar Hirosue Tamotsu reminds us that it existed simultaneously as a liberating force and as a "bad" place *(akubasho)*, a term in fact used to refer to the pleasure quarter. As such, it had a strong affinity with the theatre:

> The pleasure quarter, as well as the romance (love, *koi*) that joined the courtesan and her dapper gentleman, was constructed on the basis of an elaborate fiction. These areas of the city were controlled by money, with the women as the products and the male guests as purchasers. Despite this, a male visitor had to give himself over to the world of love untouched by concerns as vulgar as money. . . . To behave otherwise would be most boorish *(yabo)*. It is precisely this ability to participate in such a tenuous fiction that brings the ideal world of the pleasure quarter into existence.
>
> Such relationships demanded a certain type of discipline precisely because they were not the total fictions of the stage. Separated from the outside world *(shaba),* the courtesans drew their strength from the order of this "bad" place, an order resistant to the outside world. Women of the demimonde stood as a symbol of opposition *(jiitekina shōchō).* To this end, however, a courtesan had to undergo the ordeal of having another woman, a construct, chiseled onto her physical being. The customer, furthermore, was not a mere spectator; as a fellow performer he too had to maintain discipline.[28]

The economic contract implicit in the pleasure quarter would seem to suggest an obvious hierarchy in man/woman relations as manifest in the narrative, fantastic, and aesthetic element as well. Even if Edo-period textual evocations are seldom read by postwar readers, the visual impact of *ukiyo-e* woodblock prints of courtesans and theatrical representations in the form of Kabuki or Bunraku has not faded. And thus the fantasy remains extant, for it is "fantasy rather than history which determines what is reality for the unconscious."[29] Kuki Shūzō's *Anatomy of "Iki,"* one of the central texts that codified the aesthetics of the demimonde and "Japanese" culture, furthermore, makes explicit the perceptual and epistemological hierarchy involved in the particular variety of beauty and fantasy offered by woman. Kuki elevates *iki*—a "phenomenon of consciousness" closely linked with the demimonde culture—to the status of philosophical and aesthetic tenet. Such a tenet may overlap with the aesthetics of other cultures, but in its complexity and historical basis it becomes, in Leslie Pincus' words, "a privileged signifier of the distinctiveness of Japanese culture."[30]

While one can supposedly perceive *iki* in the rhythms and sounds of language, or even in smell, touch, or taste, Kuki regards visual examples as the clearest means of illustrating *iki* in its diversity.[31] To this end, Kuki frequently cites women portrayed in *ukiyo-e* prints of courtesans and narrative passages from Edo texts as visual "natural expressions" or manifestations of *iki*. Indeed, *iki* can be detected in the posture of the body, neck, or feet, in the pattern and colors of kimono fabric, and in the degree of disclosure of the body:

> Wrapping the body in a thin, translucent fabric can be regarded as an expression of *iki* that involves the entire body. The poem "From Akashi faintly I can see through the red silk crepe" *(Akashi kara honobono to suku hichirimen)* describes a man being able to perceive the body of a woman through the fabric of her Akashi silk underrobe. One also encounters the motif of sheer fabric in *ukiyo-e* prints. In these instances, the first words of this poem express *iki* by suggestion of the fabric's sheerness as perceived by the opposite sex. At the same time, the final phrase evokes *iki* by portraying the fabric's function of covering the body. The eroticism of Medici's Venus derives from her effort to conceal parts of her otherwise nude body with her hands, but it is so obvious that the painting cannot be called *iki*. Similarly, the nudes in the Louvre show absolutely no connection to *iki*.[32]

Kuki thus emphasizes that the visual aspects of *iki* lie both in the viewer and in the object of contemplation, which also constitutes a subject. In the matter of cosmetics, while *iki* normally dictates that the face be lightly made up, the thick layer of white foundation on the nape of the neck can be an expression of *iki* because it emphasizes that the back collar of the kimono has been pulled down purposely: "Thus it obliquely suggests a passage to the flesh to a person of the other sex. In contrast to Western décolletage, *iki* does not stoop to exposing a wide expanse of flesh from the shoulders down to the breasts and down the back."[33] Related as it is to the demimonde, *iki* by definition evokes eroticism and beauty, but in his own narrative Kuki reinforces the aspect of pleasure in looking. *Iki* also implicitly involves attraction to the opposite sex and the possibilities of sexual relations.

The question remains, however: is it valid to apply the concept of "pleasure in looking," which dictates a sexual imbalance of active/male and passive/female, to the dominant fiction of the demimonde? Theorists of Western narrative, painting, and cinema have described the "determining male gaze" that "projects its fantasy on the female figure which is styled accordingly. In their traditional exhibitionist role women are simultaneously looked at and displayed, with their appearance coded for strong visual and erotic impact so that they can be said to connote to-be-looked-at-ness."[34] From a feminist viewpoint, the problem with such looking and visual representation lies less in the fact that "woman so frequently functions as the *object* of desire (we all function simultaneously as subject and object)" but rather in the universalization of male desire: "that male desire is so consistently and systematically imbricated with projection and control."[35] In textual and artistic constructions of the Edo demimonde, however, several factors skew this seemingly straightforward imbalance: one is the implication of the male customer in the performance; another is the association of the pleasure quarter with the theater, where male exhibitionism in the form of an all-male Kabuki theatre figured prominently, as did the representation of male Kabuki actors in woodblock prints. Moreover, the glorification of male love *(nanshoku)* in the theater and in narrative functioned as a counterbalance to the heterosexual romance offered to men by the female geisha and prostitutes.[36] In any case, demimonde literature does stress the reworking of "the woman's body as a cultural rather than natural artifact."[37]

Kōda's Rika, in *Flowing,* is in the grip of this elaborate fiction when she first sets foot in the Tsutanoya. At the same time, modern notions about the demimonde temper her vision of the world she enters. From the Meiji period on, the influence of Western and especially Judeo-Christian ideas rendered untenable this view of the quarter as a utopia or fantasy universe. Post-Edo literature showed this in its exposure of the pleasure district as, in the words of Takahashi Toshio, a "shameful part of the urban topography that bore the scars of sinners, akin to those of prisons and slums. . . . The aesthetic notions of *iki* and *tsū* [connoisseurship] crumbled and the desolate barrenness of this gloomy meat market was exposed."[38] Takahashi also points out the refusal of mid-Meiji writers to draw romantic images of the pleasure quarter in their novels and short stories. Examples of this include Hirotsu Ryūro's (1861–1928) *Love Suicide at Imado* (Imado shinjū; 1896) and Higuchi Ichiyō's (1872–1896) "Troubled Waters" (Nigorie; 1895).[39] Although the spatial dimensions of this utopian otherworld have been all but banished from twentieth-century prose, many authors, mostly male, have expressed a continued longing for sexually available, culturally inscribed women, even apart from the spaces that traditionally set the stage for the fantasy. Famous examples include the mistress Ohisa in Tanizaki's *Some Prefer Nettles* (Tade kuu mushi) and Komako, the rural geisha in Kawabata's *Snow Country* (Yukiguni).

In *Flowing*, Rika's quest for a realm of beauty differs from those of the characters and narrators in Nagai Kafū's (1879–1959) "classicist" lyrical elegies about these parts of Tokyo.[40] Repeatedly Kafū mourns the disappearance of Yoshiwara, the decay of Yanagibashi, and, finally, the destruction of Tamanoi.[41] Moreover, he links these last vestiges of the old world to the Edo prose that glorified these romantic otherworlds. Stylistically and structurally, Kafū's works depend a great deal on premodern narrative. Kafū balks at modern culture's exposé of the quarters as a place of economic exploitation and degradation; he instead evokes a "prettified [world] with elegant surfaces and nostalgic mists covering or blurring the worst of reality."[42]

Kafū never denied the misery of the courtesans' lives or their poverty. His ability to tolerate such conditions stems from the fact that the demimonde districts, and the women there, were inextricably linked to their cultural legacy in his mind: "I shall never be able to see the banks of the Sumida apart from the literature of Edo."[43] Kafū could not depict the brutality of the pleasure quarter in the bald, "realistic" style a twentieth-century writer might use to describe a prison or a poorhouse, because the quarter described in such terms would lose its aesthetic value.

A Critical Eye: The Creation of Rika

The very complexity of incident and the large number of characters in *Flowing* have struck some readers as a major flaw of the work. Hanaya Yutaka, for example, commented that *Flowing* reminded him of a modern theater production, but with "too many props . . . the numerous characters seem to be standing offstage, waiting to be pushed on, one after another, by the author."[44] Hanaya's criticism acknowledges the element of intrigue, the exotic setting, and the jumble of characters while it ignores more significant aspects of *Flowing*. *Flowing* is neither on the order of a Kabuki play crowded with colorful, larger-than-life characters nor a titillating glimpse of an exotic world. The events and characters all come to the reader by way of the work's unifying voice and central vision, Rika, and her narrative perspective and presence become a major source of interest.[45] In terms of the book's multiple subplots, however, Rika's involvement is marginal at best. Her actions are limited to dealing with the consequences of events that involve other characters. Like many servant characters in both Japanese and Western narrative, Rika is a "most privileged witness" to "private life."[46]

Kōda employs Rika as a credible and nonironic observer and as a connection between the reader and a secret world. Rika is not, however, a permanent member of the servant class.[47] She has sensitivity, breadth, and intelligence beyond those qualities of her employer. Not only is she the means by which the reader sees the geisha world, but Rika is the most interesting character in the work. The nature of her observations and the quality of her voice constitute the primary text of *Flowing*. In other words, this character does not exist only to guide the reader through a story; if anything, the story, place, and characters provide an opportunity for the astute, sharp-tongued, cultured Rika to perform, to criticize, and to remember. Misapprehension of this guiding force in *Flowing* has led Itagaki Naoko to criticize the work for its failure to recognize the plight of the geisha. Kōda is unable to represent such women as sympathetically and urgently as did Hayashi Fumiko (1903–1951) in her "Treasures from the Sea" (Gyokai; 1940), the critic claims, because she is too "elegant" *(jōhin)*.[48]

If the personality and outlook of this character indeed form the unifying force in *Flowing*, why did the author choose the subject matter (geisha) and construct such a complex web of plot and subplot? As in many of her other works, this artistic decision has to do with Kōda's interest in the past. The geisha, with their kimonos, artistic and social accomplishments, and surroundings, are the past incarnate in postwar Japan—or, as Leslie Pincus puts it, artifacts of a chosen past, so much so that the word "geisha" forms a part of the cliché that represents tired but still extant symbols of the traditional Japanese world: "geisha, cherry blossoms, and Mount Fuji." It is that very cliché against which Itagaki reacts in her criticism of *Flowing*, implying that geisha are not the romanticized dolls that we make them out to be but real human beings who suffer in an economic and social system from which they cannot escape. Kōda does not deny the economic and social realities of such women's lives; indeed, she shows in great detail the hardships they suffer.

Itagaki works within a realist narrative and ethical framework that seeks to expose social and economic inequities—a framework that contrasts starkly with the evocation of fantasy, the unconscious, and desire in Tanizaki's novels, for example. Tanizaki's *Some Prefer Nettles* revolves around the notion of "women as a form of national treasure, or, in Sharon Siever's words, as 'repositories of the past.'"[49] In Tanizaki's text, the elderly but potent father of Misako molds his mistress Ohisa into a work of art, much in the mold of geisha or Bunraku puppets. Such viewing of woman as artifact, inscribed with cultural significance rather than natural, goes part and parcel with the "prewar discursive construction of national (male) identity."[50]

What Kōda is actually interested in here is the survival of cultural and aesthetic elements from the past in the otherwise dark and oppressive world of the geisha. Where is the art, the beauty, and the transcendent eroticism in these supposedly aesthetic beings' lives? And, in spatial and metaphorical terms, how does this corner of the modern urban environment relate to the traditional concept of the geisha quarters as an "otherworld"? Finally, is this aesthetic world accessible only to men? In choosing the demimonde as her subject, furthermore, Kōda draws on a long line of literary and artistic precedents. The use of the literary past can take a conscious form through reference, allusion, parody, and imitation of style and diction. Kōda's *Flowing* holds the reader's interest precisely because she deliberately embeds Rika's link with the cultural past in her *memory*—the recollection of a homemaker who, unlike a man, should not, by the codes of the dominant fiction, project any erotic fantasy on the women of the pleasure quarter. Nevertheless, despite the general squalor of her surroundings, Rika longs for erotic contact with the women—not overtly but as expressed in the delicious and languid instances of simply looking. The geisha life beckons her with its ambiguous blending of high and low, the sensual and the abstract, and its inherent eroticism. The cultural heritage seems all but lost at the Tsutanoya. But Rika, with her breadth of understanding and memory of artistic tradition and aesthetics, is able to find traces of the beauty that traditionally distinguished the world of the geisha. Rika's discovery then enables her to replace her unhappy personal memories with a broad cultural memory.

Rika is smart—so smart that Isogai comments that "a maid like this could not exist in reality." She stands as a central figure in *Flowing,* yet she exhibits no potential for emotional growth or change. Such a static nature, however, is necessary if she is to perceive the place clearly. Her former identity does not matter to those around her: the owner assigns Rika a new name (Haru) without even consulting her. On her first day there, Rika is standing within earshot of Someka and Nanako, who are arguing about something, when suddenly she is addressed by the older geisha:

> Someka said, "Well, you agree with me, don't you, Haru?"
>
> In this world, the women seemed to subscribe to a roundabout manner of expressing things, rather than a straightforward one. Someka had needed an

ally, so she had put this question to Rika, and had used the newly assigned name "Haru": "You agree with me, don't you, Haru?"—simply because Rika was standing conveniently nearby. If it had been a little earlier in the day, before Rika's arrival, Someka likely would be addressing the cat with the same "You agree, don't you, Ponko?" Rika had taken the role the cat used to play in such situations.[51]

Like so many men in the narrative of the demimonde, Rika crosses over into the otherworld that is a geisha house in order to escape the weight of mundane life and with the goal of liberation through the fantasy performed there. For a *shirōto* woman to participate in the production and maintenance of this fantasy, as well as to enjoy the fruits of the geisha's sleight of hand, demands a large measure of self-denial. Rika masters that task. Once inside the filthy entranceway of the Tsutanoya, she becomes, in a sense, a nun, all ties with the illusory world severed. Her stoic capacity for repressing her wants and needs allows Rika to succeed, whereas the owner and the other geisha "fail" because they are driven by pride and their desire for love and money.

Rika tries her best not to feel anything but hunger and cold; crossing over into the geisha world throws her into a state of near amnesia that allows her to fit smoothly into her anonymous role of maid. Memories of her former life as mother and homemaker begin and end in a flash, suggesting her desire to escape them. When she goes out shopping for food one day, she is momentarily overwhelmed with the memory of going out to buy apples for her child when it was "very tiny and weak." Later Rika gives away her only keepsake of her dead child: a coat "that she had treasured, but now the time had come to sever all ties, and she felt no regrets." The sound of a passing car reminds her of "the pleasure of the full life she had enjoyed before—decent furniture, a couple of fashionable kimonos, a nice necklace or two."[52] At Tsutanoya, she hardly ever eats a decent meal because the geisha lick their plates clean, leaving nothing for her. Rika never would have done that to the young woman who had helped her out around the house when she was married. Because of her repression of emotions and memory, Isogai Hideo views Rika as idealized. But perhaps her abstract interest in the erotic and aesthetic potential of the geisha world constitutes the only narrative means for a woman to view a world meant for men.

One notes Rika's fascination with the squalor and filth of the Tsutanoya—its dying dog, the dirt, fleas, mice, menstrual blood, crumbling walls, and dust balls—and her willingness to embrace the poverty that allows this proximity to naturalness. Rika waits for her opportunity to view the geisha in their role as masters of illusion, because she finds them not only willing to let their surroundings return to nature but also crasser and less "civilized" than she would have anticipated. Rika embodies a link between the present and past as represented by the *shiroto* world and the geisha quarters, respectively. The past, however, manifests itself only in memories of family events and members, and these Rika wants to forget. The *kuroto* world, by contrast, finds its inspiration and purpose in a broader past. In *Flowing*, Rika has detached herself from both the present and future orientations of the *shiroto* world. Her alienation from those aspects of her former life appears vividly in a passage that takes place just after she has recovered from her illness and is staying with her sister-in-law:

> On the seventh of January, the Feast of the Seven Herbs of Health, Rika went to visit the cemetery where her family lay buried. What she actually wanted to do was get out of the house and have a talk with someone, but at Rika's age and in her circumstances, with whom could she talk? And what did she have to say, in any case? She did not have a particular desire to speak to her husband or child. All the same, she felt put out at not having any place to go, much less anyone to talk with.
>
> At a time like this, where was there to go? Rika did not feel inclined to tour the hills or stroll along the riverbank, nor was she sufficiently reverent to visit her family's old temple. And she could hardly go to the zoo. The cemetery was her destination. But this time Rika did not go in order to visit their graves. She went to escape from places associated with the grime of living, with the mundane habits of existence. She wanted to go somewhere good, and pure—in short, a place with no kitchen or toilet—that was the kind of place where she wanted to be. The only place like that was the cemetery.[53]

As a point of contrast, Rika's greatest pleasure and deepest involvement in the nonfinancial aspect of the geisha house consist of listening to the owner's daily practice of traditional *kiyomoto* singing and samisen playing for a recital.[54] Rika possesses sufficient knowledge of the arts to be able to judge the owner's singing abilities. In fact, she reacts so perceptively to improvements in the proprietress' performance that her employer becomes suspicious about this woman whom she had assumed to be an ordinary maid. Rika functions as a link between the two worlds because she has lost her past in the *shiroto* world. Her escape from personal memory is an example of Kōda's preoccupation with memory as a subject and as a literary device. Rika has chosen to leave her old life because it contains for her nothing but painful memories. In this case the impersonal memory—the past manifested in the geisha house and its continuity of art and aesthetics—is more stable and satisfying for Rika than the memories her own past supplies.

Art as Life in *Flowing*

In *Flowing*, Kōda vividly evokes this realm of the demimonde in its twentieth-century manifestation, as well as the essential clash between the post-Edo realistic, social perception of the quarters and the traditional, aesthetic version. The surface drama of geisha in debt, in trouble with the law, and the house in decline contributes to this creation. But more than plot, Kōda's use of imagery and narrative voice draws the reader into her conception.

Rika becomes the reader's guide through the geisha house Tsutanoya, and she communicates its atmosphere and quality of life by several means. First, she is constantly aware of the two-sidedness of everything and everyone around her. The behavior of the geisha frequently contradicts Rika's expectations, and the physical reality of the place runs counter to her anticipations as well. Because Rika is an untutored and, at the same time, intelligent and curious outsider, she is the ideal observer. Her moments of discovery and disappointment, furthermore, go beyond the intellectual. Kōda's use of visual, tactile, and auditory imagery, as well as metaphor, gives rise to the rich texture of this evocation of the demimonde's two faces. In fact, the components of voice and imagery play a far more important role in making *Flowing* a coherent narrative than do plot or characterization. These aspects of the novel are not, it must be noted, at odds with the story of the Tsutanoya and its geisha.

The geisha survives as a master of illusion; her world is a product of illusion as well. In *Flowing*, Rika's reactions reveal to the reader the powerful grip of this fiction on culture as a whole. The work opens with the middle-aged *shirōto* approaching the entranceway of the Tsutanoya and experiencing disappointment and surprise at many of the things she sees:

> This had to be the place, but Rika had no idea how to go in. There was no servants' entrance. The street that the house faced was narrow, and people streamed by, one after another. Each one of them turned and looked at Rika, and so, flustered, she decided that she had no choice but to present herself at the front door. As she stepped into the small stone paved entranceway, Rika realized that the door before her must open directly onto a room; the hubbub that emanated from within was such that it made her think of a fight, with some voices shrill and excited, and others low and angry. She stood and waited

a few moments, but the uproar did not cease. So, first stepping back a bit—it would not do to be caught standing right in the middle of the doorway, staring in at them all—she slid the door back about a foot. And, with that, an impressive silence fell over the place. It brought to mind the sudden calm of water fleas in a gutter. Rika felt herself recoil a bit, as if she too had become one of the water fleas. Then she heard a sweet, cooing voice call in from somewhere farther inside than she had anticipated.

"Yes? Who's there?"

Rika called out that she had come to interview for the maid position and mentioned the name of the person who had told her about the job. But when she ventured to peek in through the doorway, she was stunned. Why, it was one of the filthiest places she had ever laid eyes on. Could this be the entrance hall of a geisha house?

"The back door? Oh, don't worry about it. Just come on in through the front." The same voice that had greeted her had suddenly lost its sugar coating and dropped an octave or so. In the entranceway, about twelve-by-twelve feet in size, there was a jumbled mess of footwear and a puppy and its bowl and its droppings. A large, rather grand shoe cupboard lined one wall. The sliding door that divided the entranceway from the front hall stood wide open, and all of its paper covering, from the handle down, hung in large shreds, like some wide, curly-edged seaweed. Tufts of dust floated over the length of the corridor. Dragging its chain and scampering through its own droppings, the dog made its way over to Rika and stood there with its tail wagging. Then, all at once, the two doors along the hallway slid open, and two beautifully made up faces leaned out, as if they had anticipated Rika's arrival.[55]

During the war, incendiary bombs had wiped the city clean, and in one of the ramshackle dwellings that sprang up after the defeat Rika discovers a striking combination of raw nature and cultured bodies, women inscribed with one version of civilization. The fantasy has promised her pristine lotuses. She had not anticipated that they would be growing out of muddy water.

This passage contains a number of impressions and images of the geisha house that recur throughout *Flowing*. Everything at the Tsutanoya seems to have two faces. Even in this initial passage, the house where Rika goes to work as a maid has no back door through which a servant would be expected to enter. This signals the beginning of a chain of betrayed expectations for Rika. For the reader, this initial encounter leads to speculation: is the lack of a "servants' entrance" simply a matter of space (houses too jammed together)? Or does it point to the composition of the geisha world in general, a population of women whose purpose, in one capacity or another, is to serve?

The auditory imagery in this passage also enforces the sense of an illusory, ever-changing world. Rika's first encounter with the Tsutanoya's inhabitants is auditory. When she at last ventures to enter the house, the many raucous voices vanish and are replaced by an "impressive silence." The adjective is telling: the women at the Tsutanoya can put on an attitude of poise and refinement instantly, at the mere signal of a sliding door. They are able to turn off the din, the vulgar voices of everyday life, on cue.

In *Flowing* the narrator does not take for granted the dichotomy of performance and everyday life. Rika, although she never witnesses a geisha party *(zashiki)*, remains acutely aware of the geisha's effortless ability to transform herself: to rise up from the humdrum rhythms of mundane existence and become beautiful. Kōda emphasizes this from the opening passage with the imagery of the "sugar-coated" voice suddenly dropping an octave and the "beautiful faces" shining through the filth of their surroundings. Rika's consternation at the two distinct faces of the geisha is due in part to her realization that the pleasure quarter is not a modern theater, where the audience and actors sit apart and where the play begins and ends at set times. The codes of this world dictate to both the performer and her audience that the geisha is not merely a performer on the stage but an artistic being who dwells in a consummately aesthetic realm.

If *Flowing* had stopped at the evocation of Rika's psychological reactions to the demimonde, it would hardly have been such an interesting work. Kōda balances this cerebral dimension with a rich and constant stream of vivid imagery. For the reader, the most immediate and insistent quality of *Flowing* lies in its representation of a sensual world dominated by sights, sounds, and smells. Here the evocation of a specific place bears less weight than does the texture of a general cultural milieu and its inhabitants. Kōda uses a wealth of onomatopoetic and mimetic expression and colloquialisms to create the mundane rhythms of daily life at the Tsutanoya. This strategy has led Komatsu Shinroku to call Kōda a "writer who, trusting only the five senses *(gokan),* attempts to capture the object of her works in sensory terms" rather than intellectually.[56] Many self-consciously writerly writers such as Tanizaki have elevated perceptions and sensations to a similarly privileged status. But because Kōda is female, writes about women in the home, and has shunned the title of artist, this attention to the sensory world has struck many critics as a product of "one who lives" *(seikatsusha)* rather than one who creates *(sakusha)*. The women in this novel have a frankly physical and sensual presence that betrays the reader's expectations of ethereal, doll-like creatures. Yoneko sits and eats peanuts all afternoon. The proprietress sings *kiyomoto* ballads miserably. Nanako smells of French perfume. Someka eats cold, greasy croquettes. Like the dog and cat who live there, the women are associated with their bodily functions. Rika finds bloodstains on the futon she is given.

Contemporary reality is not all that is being portrayed here. The text includes numerous references and allusions to the past, as well, specifically art and literature. The Tsutanoya's dog, for example, a blaring dramatization of the house's state of decay, also functions as an ironic allusion to the past. In Edo painting and prints, elegant geisha are often portrayed with a dog by their side. The canine companion adds to the geisha's sense of style, usually by virtue of its exotic origins. In *Flowing*, Kōda retains the iconic linking of geisha and dog, but in this case the dog is a wretched mutt. This ironic twist reveals the stark reality of geisha existence. No longer do the geisha perform as the trend-setters of society, foreign pet in tow.

The conclusion of *Flowing* alludes to an earlier literary work—again somewhat ironically. At the end of the novel, the proprietress moves out and Rika takes charge of the Tsutanoya. This turn recalls premodern and early modern fiction: in *Umemibune* (Plum Blossom Boat; 1841), a sequel to Shunsui's *Umegoyomi,* a character named Osono competes with other women for the love of a rake named Hanjirō, but she is not successful in her pursuit. In order to satisfy the happy-ending requirement of the *ninjōbon* genre, however, Osono becomes the owner of a teahouse "which she is instinctively able to manage successfully."[57] Similarly, in Nagai Kafū's *Udekurabe* (translated variously as "Rivalry" and "Geishas in Rivalry," 1916–1917), the heroine Komayo bids for the favor of potential patrons and the love of various men, but fails in all her attempts. Happily for her, though, the proprietress of the *okiya* dies and Komayo takes over the establishment.

One of the most interesting and consistent aspects of *Flowing,* as noted earlier, lies in the evocation of a stark and insistent reality through auditory, tactile, and olfactory imagery and the concurrent suggestions of the persistence of a traditional aesthetic sensibility in the geisha house. At several points in the narrative, however, Kōda merges these two seemingly incompatible realms. The effect is stunning and gratifying—all the more so because the two realms constitute not merely the dichotomy between art and nature but between past and present as well. It does matter that the viewer, the voyeur, is Rika: she finds pleasure in the visual encounter with what momentarily seems a performance apart from history and space. But because of her gender and social background, she then fastidiously rejects her rising erotic interest because of the tainted nature of the interaction being mimicked.

Significantly, the key scenes involve the two older retired geisha in the novel: the proprietress of the Tsutanoya and Nandori, the owner of the *ryōtei* across the river. Unlike the younger female characters in the book, both are geisha to the core, in all likelihood residents of the quarter since childhood. Above all, their lives are vitally linked to the forms, behavior and beliefs of the past. Both have been trained in a range of polite accomplishment such as dance, music, and social interaction. In the two scenes that join the natural and the stylized, the immediate present and the seemingly distant past, these two characters are agents of the synthesis. But Rika's pleasure in looking figures prominently, as does the interplay between the "exhibitionist" women and the desiring viewer. The first incident occurs when the proprietress, Yoneko, Rika, and a doctor have all gathered in an attempt to calm Fujiko (the little girl living at the Tsutanoya), who is very ill and in need of a shot. The child, however, resists the doctor's ministrations with all her might:

> As she stood up to leave the room, the proprietress addressed the doctor: "I'm sorry. I just can't bear needles."
>
> This brought an immediate reaction from Fujiko, who recognized that the only person there who might protect her from the shot was about to leave her. Slipping out of the grasp of her mother and the doctor, the child grabbed onto her great-aunt. Frantically, Yoneko tried to pry her loose, but the child would not let go. . . . Rika did not move a muscle.
>
> Legs buckling, the proprietress began to collapse under the weight of the child hanging from her neck. Fujiko's body was straight and hard, not even vaguely feminine, and she wore a threadbare cotton kimono; her great-aunt, though, showed the soft pink of her legs as they started to bend beneath her. Who else could make a beautiful pose out of tumbling to the floor? The action itself was nothing out of the ordinary: an adult being knocked down by a small bundle of energy. But in the execution of this particular fall, one could detect the unmistakable and remarkable character of the proprietress. The sight dazzled Rika. How fine her form was as she was pushed down sideways, smiling graciously; falling with someone's body pressed up to hers—though it was only a child—and resisting, bending her body gracefully to accommodate the downward pull, yet all the while trying to recover.
>
> Fujiko still clung to the proprietress, so Rika could not see what had hap-

pened to the front of her kimono. The heavy silk of the sleeves, though, had been flung back to expose her upper arms, and her legs lay stretched out, bent slightly at the knees to form a modest, gentle curve. Over the white tips of her *tabi* rested the heavy hem of her kimono.

Rika had never seen a woman's body behave this way: the gradual collapse, the vague sense of resistance to the downward pull as she shifted her center of balance to her hips. What a way to respond to enticement, with this slow fall, the stunning collapse, this most pleasant sense of giving way to disorder.

Could a woman, as she lay herself down—her figure from the moment she began to bend, to yield, until when she reached the floor—could a woman be so bewitching?

I had no idea.

Rika felt embarrassed, but she could not bring herself to look away. She sat and gazed upon the stunning figure stretched out before her.

But it was like a fleeting silhouette. No sooner had Fujiko been pulled off of her than the proprietress propped herself up with her right arm and just as quickly straightened out the errant skirt of her kimono with the other hand. She pulled up the gracefully bent legs and sat with them doubled beneath her. Automatically, she straightened out the collar of her kimono, and then her hands shot up to smooth down her hair. She had quite magnificently regained control. But Rika also sensed a certain reluctance. There had been a splendor in her actions, indeed, but the reluctance that appeared as the proprietress righted herself was unmistakable. She had tidied herself up as a matter of course: this was expected in her line of work. At the same time, she was certainly aware that such behavior brought reminders of what had come before— an impurity. The woman who sat back up, who fixed her tousled hair and mussed clothes, was disappointing and lacked dignity.[58]

Here everything runs counter to Rika's—and the reader's—expectations. The immediacy of the moment, the annoyance at the squirming child, the presence of other faces, noises, and smells—all fade away in the face of the proprietress' gracefully falling figure. In her agile reaction lies all the training of her own past as well as the stylized forms of the cultural tradition: hence the comparison of this scene to "an *ukiyo-e* print by Utamaro."[59] Here is the woman "carved onto the real woman" that Hirosue mentions as part of the performing world of the Edo demimonde. Rika repeatedly disavows previous knowledge of the pleasure of viewing such a choreographed series of moves by the female body and the state of disarray and the allure of the gap of the kimono. Indeed, the sight gives rise to her desire.

Kōda emphasizes the importance of this passage—and the visual impression—not only by extending its length but also by investing it with certain distinctive narrative qualities. First, she creates a pronounced rhythm through repetition of certain key phrases and words: *kuzureru,* give way, collapse; *shinayaka,* bending, curving; *taoreru/taosareru,* fall down, be pushed over; *jojoni,* gradually; *onna,* woman. Aside from making the passage stand out from the narrative, this departure from the straightforward, colloquial style of the rest of the text suggests the quality of the proprietress' fall: different in kind and speed from mundane behavior and action. The narrative also slows drastically and illustrates the observer's temporal sense—that is, an action that occurs in less than a second seems to take an immeasurable amount of time. Furthermore, this passage mimics the fall in its stylization, its bending, curving, and the attention brought to the act of narration itself. It begins with past-tense verbal endings and shifts to the nonpast aspect as the narrator freezes all other action before bringing attention to the fall itself ("Yoneko tries to pry . . . ," "The doctor stands frozen . . . ," "Rika does not move . . ."). What follows is not merely an empirical account of the motions of the proprietress' body as she goes down, but an alternation between Rika's vision and her internal monologue. By the end, Rika realizes not only the stunning beauty of what she has seen and its departure from the ordinary, but also its erotic and traditional aspects. Here she links the urgency of the physical present to the force of the cultural past. Although Rika declares early on in the text that the very state of decay and rawness of the Tsutanoya makes her feel comfortable about working there, these moments of seeing the geisha in action sustain her tenure and thus the narrative as a whole.

Another scene in *Flowing* that evokes the aesthetic forms of the past as they exist within the crass reality of daily life involves the other older female character.[60] She is the restaurant owner nicknamed Nandori. In this famous passage, the narrator provides a careful description of Nandori getting out of bed one morning. She is seen from the viewpoint of Rika, who has come to her room to rekindle the brazier:

> Nandori, still in bed, reached out with her slender fingers and flipped each of the red *yūzen* silk comforters off of her, one by one. Then she sat up, and, leaning back on one arm, drew her legs up to one side. By thus extracting herself from under the covers, she could leave them smooth and unmussed. Her manner of rising was most graceful indeed.
>
> She wore a dark lilac cotton kimono decorated with a pattern of white weeping cherries and pale green willows. Its silver-gray collar had fallen open

a bit during the night. At the waist, she had loosely tied a sturdy sash adorned with a green bamboo and white iron-club pattern. She managed to look gorgeous without even a spot of red in her clothing. Rika could not help but wonder about her nights. Nandori was quite youthful in appearance, but by all accounts she had reached her mature years. Surely she did not share her nights with anyone, nor did she likely desire a companion. But that was only Rika's guess—and Rika was, after all, an outsider *(shirōto)*. A person at the age when the somberness of purple suits her better than red could hardly be inclined to passionate attachments. Nandori's charming manner of rising from bed belied the fact that her only connection with passion was through her memories.

This seductiveness, Rika imagined, came not as an expression of some personal desire but rather from many years of practicing her art. It had been part of her for so long that she would never lose it. And if the grace and elegance that Rika had seen were only a trace of that art, Nandori must have been truly splendid in her younger days.

Nandori slipped her hand back under the covers and pulled out a small folding mirror. She peered into it and smoothed back some stray locks. Sitting up in bed, ever so gracefully and slowly, like a figure in a film in slow motion, and taking the time to check her hair in a little hand-held mirror—somewhere in the deep recesses of her memory, Rika remembered such a morning in her own past. But how long had it been since she had risen with a similar elegance and loveliness? No, for Rika, morning meant leaping out from under the covers and scampering over to crouch by the hearth. It meant dragging herself out of bed, hurriedly brushing her teeth, and bolting down some breakfast.

But not this old woman. The graceful ritual of slipping out of bed, and quietly fixing her hair, had always been part of her mornings. It did not matter where she woke up, or whether anyone was with her or not. She would always be elegant in her every motion, as if a man lay there beside her, and as if she cared for him.

What different lives.

Rika shuddered in her thin robe. The sun had risen high already, but with the shutters still closed and only light from the lamp, the room was cold.[61]

The eroticism of this passage derives again from the "woman inscribed on the woman"—in this case, an older woman who, though alone, gets out of bed as if she had just spent a passionate night with a lover. Nandori represents the quintessential geisha.[62]

Nandori also exemplifies *iki* as the word came to be used in the Edo period and, especially, the demimonde. *"Iki"* has connotations that go beyond the sense of "chic" or "stylish" that it possesses today. From the Edo period, *iki* was one of the central values (or "concepts of behavior" as Alan Woodhull calls it) ascribed to the pleasure quarter.[63] One quality of a geisha or courtesan considered to be *iki,* Kuki Shūzō explains in his classic work *The Anatomy of "Iki,"* is sexual allure *(bitai).*[64] *Iki* demands subtlety in this power of attraction: not a brash, fleshy eroticism, but just enough to create a sexual tension. In addition, *iki* involves the interaction of this feminine sensual element with a spirit of pride and vigor. A geisha who is *iki,* in other words, possesses a certain amount of dash and self-sufficiency. The terms used to describe this second aspect of *iki,* such as *inase* and *ikiji,* are more usually applied to males. Thus the *iki* woman successfully combines desirable feminine and masculine behavioral traits. Finally, *iki* entails a degree of resignation *(akirame),* that is, an awareness of the illusory nature of human emotions. Related to Buddhist notions of resignation, this attitude requires a person to have a "clean heart"—in other words, to recognize the fickleness of human emotions and not cling to any delusions.[65] *Iki* was manifest in all aspects of a woman: her deeds, words, dress, posture, and attitude.

Although *iki* was a concept that thrived in the demimonde, not all of its denizens could boast such stylishness. Kuki points especially to older, more experienced geisha as *iki* because they are most aware of the transitory nature of relations with men.[66] Although *iki*'s principal connection to romantic love lies in its denial of such illusory attachments, Nandori's actions show how little cynicism has to do with this denial. Rather, it is the ultimate integration of life and art. This older geisha's every motion and breath involve art and performance. The performance, however, is not naturalistic or realistic but depends instead on stylization—that is, on the *kata* (forms) that elevate the mundane to the realm of art.[67] In *Flowing,* Rika recognizes this in Nandori's behavior and acknowledges that, far from being an expression of individual style or personality, it comes from "many years of practicing her craft." For an ordinary person—a *shirōto* like Rika—the value of Nandori's performance is twofold. Not only can it be enjoyed for its aesthetic value, but Nandori's art of rising from bed is not stylized to the point of abstraction or impersonality: it has immediacy and sufficient individuality to remind Rika of her own experiences.

At the same time, both Rika and reader realize that they have witnessed an inadvertently intimate moment and that to surrender to it would be to possess less than noble intent. Thus Kōda approaches and then abruptly averts the thrill of erotic fiction that perhaps some readers of *Flowing* have been waiting for: the aim of erotic texts of "quickening of the observer's body." The text alerts the reader to the possibility of responding to "bodies that are not flesh but the construction of phantasies and desires."[68]

The realistic descriptions of the degradation faced by the geisha and the dinginess of the Tsutanoya in *Flowing* show Kōda's awareness of the negative modern vision of the demimonde. At the same time, Rika's insistence on staying in the geisha *okiya* suggests her inability to abandon the search for the elaborate fiction and world of beauty. Rather than be cast back into the vast modern world that promises her no niche, no security, and no promise of pleasure, she is willing to suffer through the cycle of decay again within the tight world of the geisha. This realm offers her a new memory, but of a social order that is a vestige of another age, and the possibility of looking.

One Writer's Vision of the Demimonde

What motivated this highly respected author of memoirs to write about a geisha house and venture into a literary realm dominated by men? Kōda Aya became familiar with Edo demimonde fiction because her father was a great devotee. Rohan esteemed Shunsui's *Shunshoku umegoyomi* not only as a literary work but also as a practical guide to the facts of life for his daughter.[69] Kōda was thus directly exposed to the romantic image of demimonde women by reading this type of *ninjōbon*. When Kōda was a child, moreover, the Kōdas made their home in Mukojima not far from where many geisha and prostitutes worked. Kōda has written of her youthful admiration for these women and their freedom from stifling social rules.[70]

Although scholars often point to biographical factors that influenced *Flowing*'s composition, most Japanese readers approach it as a work of fiction. Some readers perceive in Rika a grown-up version of Kōda as she described her younger self in earlier works, a girl whose personality and outlook have been shaped by her strict, latter-day Confucian father. Isogai Hideo, for example, insists that Rika communicates not merely a "female attention to detail" but an ability to penetrate to the essence of things, which, in turn, shows the influence of Rohan's *kakubutsu chichi* thinking.[71] One also detects in Rika strong traces of the aesthetically sensitive and observant character that appears in other of Kōda's works.

In *Flowing*, Kōda launched a new course in her career as a writer: she gave her first long work of prose fiction a setting that departs from the domestic scene and steps into the world of the demimonde. Rika, the central figure, leaves painful memories behind to enter a world of cultural and aesthetic tradition. Kōda's depiction of Rika's education in the realities of postwar geisha life makes use of contrast—the disparity between Rika's cultural expectations and the actual images of an *okiya* in decline. Seldom does Rika find the glimmer of the past that she had anticipated. Rika finds herself "secretly, unconsciously almost, enjoying the freedom of action and control over the diegetic world that identification with a hero provides."[72] Indeed, the reader cannot help noticing the absence of a male hero and the curious fact that the geisha house continues functioning with barely any evidence of male customers. Kōda employs powerful imagery both in her establishment of the *okiya*'s decline and in her portrayal of the older geisha and their ability to act as icons of a cultural memory in the midst of a changing world.

Notes

1. Although a geisha house is a place inhabited by women, it is not their home. Geisha are professional women who work outside the home, and the geisha house is their office/dormitory.
2. In her apparent lack of interest in sexuality and eroticism, Kōda differed radically from other women writers of her generation such as Enchi Fumiko and Uno Chiyo.
3. Kōda lived and worked at a geisha house in the Yanagibashi area of Tokyo for four months in the winter of 1951–1952, but she left because of poor health brought on by an inadequate diet.
4. Kojima Chikako, "Kōda san no namida," *Shinchō* 88(1) (1991):206.
5. Laura Mulvey, "Afterthoughts on 'Visual Pleasure and Narrative Cinema,'" in *Feminism and Film Theory,* ed. Constance Penley (New York: Routledge, 1988), p. 78.
6. In modern Japanese, the word *"kurōto"* also has the meaning of "expert" or "accomplished practitioner of an art or occupation." It is written with the characters for "dark" *(gen)* and person and historically was used in Buddhism and Taoism to refer to religious people. *"Shirōto"* (white/adorned/person) had the original meaning "layman," but now its use has expanded to signify a "nonprofessional/ordinary/decent person." By extension it also means "a person inexperienced or untrained in the arts or learning" or an amateur. Although some of the *kurōto* in the demimonde are prostitutes, others are not. Geisha, for example, are first and foremost accomplished entertainers.
7. Critics identify the novel's setting as Yanagibashi because Kōda actually worked there and it matches the novel's description of an old but declining pleasure quarter on the "better" side of the river.
8. Many of the characters in *Flowing* are referred to by nicknames. The name Kishibojin, for example, is not the character's real name but a nickname bestowed by

Rika. Kishibojin (Hariti in Sanskrit) is a deity who bore hundreds of children and fed on the flesh of other women's babies. She subsequently received Buddhist teaching and abandoned this practice. She is believed to protect women in childbirth and the health of children. The owner of the *ryōtei* (exclusive restaurant club) across the river is dubbed "Nandori" by Rika after she hears the woman use this quaint expression meaning "gently."

9. *Ryōtei,* translated here as teahouses, are exclusive restaurants or clubs where customers (usually in groups) drink, eat, and often are entertained by geisha. The individual rooms where such a dinner or party would be held are called *zashiki,* the same name used for the events or parties themselves.

10. The main institutions in a Tokyo geisha community include the geisha house *(okiya),* a registry office *(kenban),* and the restaurant or club *(ryōtei).* For the women who work as geisha, the *okiya* is the home base where they receive their work assignments, change into their kimono, and apply their makeup. The *kenban* collects the customer's payment from the *ryōtei* and, after taking off a certain amount as commission, sends it on to the geisha or the *okiya* manager. The *okiya* must pay a fee to the *kenban* for an operating license. See Liza Dalby, *Geisha* (Berkeley: University of California Press, 1983).

11. Howard Hibbett, *The Floating World in Japanese Fiction* (New York: Grove Press, 1960), p. 27.

12. In time the entertainment aspect of the *jorō's* (prostitute's) work disappeared. Geisha, though some may have had sex with customers, were primarily entertainers. Certain types of geisha were, in fact, legally prohibited from having sex with customers, probably in order to reduce competition among the different types of women in the quarters. Entertaining as a geisha became a distinct profession for women during the Edo period (mid-eighteenth century), but the geisha's origins can be traced back to the twelfth-century female entertainers/dancers called *shirabyōshi.* See Laura Jackson, "Bar Hostesses," in *Women in Changing Japan,* ed. Joyce Lebra, Joy Paulson, and Elizabeth Powers (Stanford: Stanford University Press, 1976), p. 133; Saeki Junko, *Yūjo no bunkashi* (Chūō Kōronsha, 1987); and Dalby, *Geisha.* Takigawa Masajirō clearly distinguished between courtesans *(yūjo)* and prostitutes in his *Yūjo no rekishi,* Nihon rekishi shinshō series (Shibundō, 1965), pp. 1–14; this volume also traces the origins of *yūjo* to Korea and China. See also "The Hierarchy of Courtesans," app. 3, in Ihara Saikaku, *The Life of an Amorous Woman and Other Writings,* ed. and trans. Ivan Morris (New York: New Directions, 1963), pp. 285–288.

13. Takahashi Toshio, *Nagai Kafū to Edo bungakuen* (Meiji Shoin, 1983), p. 157.

14. Chieko Ariga contends that geisha are the same as prostitutes because they too are

"entertainment women who sold their bodies to men," and she cites a number of Japanese writers on the pleasure quarter (notably all male) who include geisha in the category of prostitutes. See "Dephallicizing Women in *Ryūkyō shinshi:* A Critique of Gender Ideology in Japanese Literature," *Journal of Japanese Studies* 51(3) (August 1992):571.

15. Dalby, *Geisha,* p. 74.

16. Indeed, Leslie Pincus glosses the title of Kuki's work *("Iki" no kōzō)* as "The Structure of Edo Aesthetic Style." It must be noted, however, that Kuki's examples of *iki* include those from Meiji-period literature, so his consideration of *iki* includes contemporary examples (that is, not exclusively Edo style). When discussing the notion of *iki,* however, Pincus uses the Japanese term rather than attempting to find an English equivalent "in provisional deference to Kuki's central claim that the phenomenon of iki is culturally incommensurable and consequently untranslatable." See Leslie Pincus, "In a Labyrinth of Western Desire," in *Japan in the World,* eds. Masao Miyoshi and H. D. Harootounian (Durham: Duke University Press, 1993), p. 222.

17. Although Pincus is specifically addressing Kuki's anxiety upon returning from a long sojourn in Europe to a Tokyo utterly transformed by its rebuilding in the aftermath of the 1923 Great Kantō Earthquake, this essentially elitist anxiety about preserving class and national identity may continue to play a role. Pincus writes that "Kuki's defense of culture masked a resistance of the few to the rising tide of mass culture, hence his sympathy for the dandy, that purveyor of aristocratic style whom Baudelaire pitted against the undistinguished crowds of mid-nineteenth century Paris." See Pincus, "Labyrinth of Western Desire," p. 231. See also Pincus' excellent book *Authenticating Culture in Imperial Japan: Kuki Shūzō and the Rise of National Aesthetics* (Berkeley: University of California Press, 1996).

18. Takie Sugiyama Lebra, *Japanese Women: Constraint and Fulfillment* (Honolulu: University of Hawai'i Press, 1984), p. 68.

19. Rika may also have felt easier about going to work at the Tsutanoya because of the postwar legal reforms that affected the geisha's working status. These measures aimed at cleaning up urban areas where women entertained men professionally and making the profession more equitable. Until the time of the Allied Occupation, it was not uncommon for poor families to sell daughters to geisha houses. Postwar child welfare legislation banned such practices and set a minimum age limit for geisha apprentices (eighteen). The Diet enacted antiprostitution laws from 1955 to 1958. The sex trade tended to shift to Western-style bars and hotels in the postwar period. See Jackson, "Bar Hostesses," p. 136. For a fascinating consideration of prostitution, extramarital sex, and romance in the postwar period see

Sheldon Garon, *Molding Japanese Minds: The State in Everyday Life* (Princeton: Princeton University Press, 1997), pp. 195–205. Pincus discusses the pleasure quarters in *Authenticating Culture,* p. 186ff.

20. In the early Meiji-period work *Ryūkyō shinshi* (New Chronicle of Yanagibashi; 1874) by Narushima Ryūhoku (1837–1884), for example, the reader finds geisha paired with politicians. The geisha houses provided an ideal spot for political hobnobbing (and still do). The work was eventually banned by government authorities because of its political satire and racy setting. See Jay Rubin, *Injurious to Public Morals: Writers and the Meiji State* (Seattle: University of Washington Press, 1984), pp. 32–37.

21. Examples of such Edo literature abound: early Edo *hyōbanki* (books that evaluate prostitutes and actors) and the *sharebon* of mid-Edo (1745–1850) depict the dandies who visited the quarter and their consorts in excruciating detail.

22. J. Marshall Unger, however, challenges the view that pre-Meiji Japan had extraordinarily high literacy rates and asserts that the "optimistic views of pre-Meiji Japanese literacy need to be scaled back considerably." See his *Literacy and Script Reform in Occupation Japan: Reading Between the Lines* (New York: Oxford University Press, 1996), pp. 7 and 22–35.

23. See Jinbō Kazuya, *Kinsei Nihon bungakushi* (Yūhikaku, 1978), pp. 68–74, on the subject of *ninjōbon*. See also Donald Keene, *World Within Walls* (New York: Grove Press, 1978), pp. 416–435.

24. Immediately following the climactic love scene in *Shunshoku umegoyomi* between Tanjirō and Ochō, the implied author steps in to reassure the reader about the morality of the characters:

> The author prostrates himself to beg the reader's pardon. There are those who would say that to write a story with the above scene is equivalent to advising misconduct among women and girls, and hence, most despicable. Ah! How wrong they are! . . . Though the behavior of the female characters in these works seems lascivious, their actions stem from the depth of their chaste, circumspect Love. I do not write tales of fallen female virtue, of one woman mingling with numerous men, or, most despicable, of lust aroused by money. Although there may be many provocative phrases in these pages, only the unsullied, clear will of these men and women is here set forth. The four women characters—Konoito, Ochō, Oyoshi, and Yonehachi, though each is different in appearance—are all of a pristine, upright nature befitting a heroine.

In *Shunshoku,* Yonehachi is a geisha who competes with Ochō, the daughter of a geisha house owner, for the love of Tanjirō. See Alan S. Woodhull, trans., "Romantic Edo Fiction: A Study of the Ninjōbon and Complete Translation of

Shunshoku Umegoyomi" (Ph.D. diss., Stanford University, 1978), pp. 8 and 278–279.

25. Kōda Rohan, Ozaki Kōyō, and Awashima Kangetsu (1859–1929) were avid students of Saikaku and Edo literature. In the world of aesthetics and philosophy as well, as Leslie Pincus points out, Kuki Shūzō's *"Iki" no kōzō* situated a marginalized historical moment in the center of Japan's self-understanding because the "foe from whom he had to wrest iki was . . . not the West so much as it was Japan's own Enlightenment, under whose reign the culture of the Tokugawa era had become the object of disrepute and neglect." Kuki, a student of Anglo-European philosophy, thus "embraced the European cultural hermeneutic for its methodological capacity to reclaim a selectively cherished past." See Pincus, "Labyrinth of Western Desire," pp. 224–225.

26. The works of Saikaku and Chikamatsu, for example, appear in almost every collection of classical literature. Pincus employs this notion of guaranteeing "continuity with a chosen past" to describe the efforts in late-nineteenth-century European cultural studies and cultural hermeneutics—and later in Japan by philosophers such as Kuki Shūzō—to construct a certain social identity and to resist the leveling of "all cultural differences at the expense of an indigenous past" at a time of crisis. Clearly this philosophical and ethical gesture is related to the canonization of literary texts. See Pincus, "Labyrinth of Western Desire," pp. 229–230.

27. Saeki Junko claims that historically these "pleasure women" were regarded as having shamanistic powers and functioned as "a bridge between the profane world and the sacred one." See Saeki, *Yūjo no bunkashi,* quoted in Tansman, *Writings,* p. 117.

28. Hirosue Tamotsu, *Akubasho no hassō* (Sanseidō, 1970), p. 138. Hirosue also discusses the similar status of the theater as *akubasho* (pp. 102–129).

29. Kaja Silverman, *Male Subjectivity at the Margins* (New York: Routledge, 1992), p. 18.

30. In a chilling reminder of Kuki Shūzō's later enthusiastic complicity with Japan's military aggression in Asia, Pincus quotes a piece of Kuki's from the late 1930s in which he employs the same metaphor of "inscribing" a cultural identity onto the body of the subjugated Other, in this case the Chinese people: "It is our cultural-historical mission to lend spiritual succor to the renewal of our mother country by imprinting our idealistic philosophy in the form of *bushidō* in the innermost recesses of their [Chinese people's] bodies." See "Jikyoku no kansō," in *Kuki Shūzō zenshū,* ed. Amano Teiyū (Iwanami Shoten, 1981), 5:38; quoted in Pincus, "Labyrinth of Western Desire," pp. 224 and 236.

31. Kuki Shūzō, *"Iki" no kōzō; ta nihen* (Iwanami Shoten, 1979), pp. 50–51 and 59.

32. Ibid., pp. 51–52.

33. "Isei ni taishite hada e no tsūrō o honokani anji suru"; ibid., p. 56.

34. Mulvey, "Afterthoughts," p. 62.

35. Silverman, *Male Subjectivity,* pp. 143–145.

36. Kuki does not consider the homosexual aspect of *iki,* if there is one. Paul Schalow has examined the significance of *nanshoku* (male love) in his introduction to Ihara Saikaku's *The Great Mirror of Male Love* (Stanford: Stanford University Press, 1990). See also James Reichert, "Representations of Male-Male Sexuality in Meiji-Period Literature" (Ph.D. diss., University of Michigan, 1998).

37. Peter Brooks, *Body Work: Objects of Desire in Modern Narrative* (Cambridge, Mass.: Harvard University Press, 1993), p. 17.

38. Takahashi Toshio, *Nagai Kafū to Edo bungakuen,* p. 159. An interesting postwar view of the "meat market" is the movie *Gate of Flesh (Nikutai no mon),* directed by Suzuki Seijun and filmed in lurid color, about a group of prostitutes struggling to survive in the chaos of early postwar Tokyo.

39. Takahashi, *Nagai Kafū to Edo bungakuen,* p. 160.

40. Sasabuchi Tomoichi contends that Kafū's love for Edo *gesaku* was "inspired by his reverence for [French] classical literature." See his *Nagai Kafū: Zuiraku no bigaku-sha* (Meiji Shoin, 1976), pp. 395–396. See also Ken Ito's chapter on Kafū and Tanizaki in *Visions of Desire: Tanizaki's Fictional Worlds* (Stanford: Stanford University Press, 1991), pp. 30–63.

41. The Yoshiwara was one of the oldest and largest licensed quarters in Edo/Tokyo until the great fire of 1911, when it was mostly destroyed. When it was rebuilt, the spirit of Edo and romance had disappeared and what remained was a cluster of brothels but no *ryōtei.* Yanagibashi was, along with Shinbashi, one of the great geisha quarters in the late Edo and Meiji periods. The Tamonoi was an area with many brothels near the east bank of the Sumida River that flourished briefly during the interwar period. Kafū spent a great deal of time there during one period of his life. See Edward Seidensticker, *Kafū the Scribbler* (Stanford: Stanford University Press, 1965), p. 86.

42. Seidensticker notes that in Kafū's *Udekurabe* (translated variously as "Rivalry" and "Geishas in Rivalry," 1916–1917) the "highly contrived plot, relying heavily on coincidence, could have been lifted bodily from a nineteenth-century erotic novel, perhaps by Tamenaga Shunsui." See *Kafū the Scribbler,* pp. 86 and 88.

43. Ibid., p. 8, quoting from Kafū's diary.

44. In Takeda Taijun, Hanaya Yutaka, and Shiina Rinji, "Sōsaku gappyō," *Gunzō* 11 (January 1956):216. Noborio Yutaka concurs with Hanaya's opinion, calling the

work "essay-like" and "high-handed, with too much crammed in." See Noborio Yutaka, "Kōda Aya: *Otōto* no keisan," *Kokubungaku kaishaku to kanshō* 50(10) (October 1980):81.

45. Isogai Hideo comments on Rika's centrality to the work in his essay "*Nagareru*— Kōda Aya," *Kokubungaku kaishaku to kyōzai no kenkyū* 13(5) (1968):86.

46. See M. M. Bakhtin, *The Dialogic Imagination* (Austin: University of Texas Press, 1981), p. 125.

47. Tansman suggests that Rika finds satisfaction in her role as a maid because she, like Aya, came from a life of domestic service (for Rika as a wife and mother and for Aya as a daughter). Even in the role of a maid, Tansman intimates, such service seemed familiar and thus comforting.

48. Itagaki Naoko, *Meiji Taishō Shōwa no joryū bungaku* (Ōfūsha, 1967), p. 292.

49. Gregory L. Golley, "Tanizaki Junichirō: The Art of Subversion and the Subversion of Art," *Journal of Japanese Studies* 21 (1995):393.

50. Ibid.

51. *KAZS* 5:22–23.

52. *KAZS* 5:103; 167–168; 28.

53. *KAZS* 5:168.

54. *Kiyomoto* is a style of music originally used in Kabuki, but it was widely performed by geisha at *zashiki* as well. *Kiyomoto* combines a light and cheerful vocal style with samisen accompaniment.

55. *KAZS* 5:4–5.

56. Komatsu Shinroku, "Kaidai," in *Kōda Aya,* vol. 34 of Shinchō gendai bungaku series (Shinchōsha, 1980), p. 384. In her 1977 speech, Kōda emphasizes her reliance on *gokan* (the five senses).

57. Woodhull, "Romantic Edo Fiction," p. 190, n. 14. Woodhull also comments that Osono, the shy-but-bold city girl, is the "type of girl [who] would also have made up a large share of the *ninjōbon* readership."

58. *KAZS* 5:81–82.

59. Yoshii Isamu, "Dokugo no mudasho—Kōda Aya—*Nagareru*," *Chūō Kōron* 113 (June 1956):137.

60. Seidensticker comments that it may "be possible to accept the geisha and her quarters as simultaneously an escape from crass reality and the embodiment of a crass reality." See *Kafū the Scribbler,* p. 88.

61. *KAZS* 5:210–211.

62. Kōda in an interview commented on this "getting-up" scene. See Shiotani, ed., *Nagareru oboegaki* (Keizai Ōraisha, 1957), p. 32.

63. Pincus, *Authenticating Culture;* Woodhull, "Romantic Edo Fiction."

64. Kuki Shūzō, *"Iki" no kōzō* (Iwanami Shoten, 1979).

65. From the cultural standpoint delineated by Kuki, innocent young love was considered *yabo* (boorish, uncouth, raw, rustic) and the opposite of *iki.*

66. Kuki, *"Iki" no kōzō,* p. 26.

67. Isogai Hideo uses the term *"kata"* in his discussion of Kōda's works in *Senzen sengo no sakka to sakuhin* (Meiji Shoin, 1980), p. 271.

68. Brooks, *Body Work,* pp. 52–53.

69. Kōda Aya mentions her exposure during her teenage years to *Shunshoku umego-yomi* in the essay "Plum Blossoms" (Ume; 1950), in *KAZS* 2:404–405. In her essay "Growing Up" (Sottaku; 1949), Kōda writes about giving her own daughter *ninjōbon* to read (*KAZS* 1:219).

70. Shiotani, *Nagareru oboegaki,* p. 3; "Yuki" (Snow; 1952), in *KAZS* 3:211–213.

71. Isogai Hideo, *Bungakuron to buntairon* (Meiji Shoin, 1980), p. 306.

72. Mulvey, "Afterthoughts," p. 69.

4

Narrative Authority and the Postwar Realm: Two Exemplary Short Stories

Many works of fiction by modern Japanese women writers convey a strong undercurrent of female self-repression and anger directed at the sexism of Japanese society.[1] Readers who seek expressions of "'female rage' against patriarchal oppression" in Kōda's writings, however, will not find it.[2] Certainly her earlier works concentrate on the pain resulting from her relationship with Rohan, an unusual, highly critical man, but they also confirm the extent to which Kōda used invaluable tools for living that her father, among others, taught her. Through her works Kōda offers a model of wisdom and the means by which to survive traumatic periods of change. The maturity and generosity of spirit evident in her narratives are qualities valued in times of great self-doubt whether personal or national. It is precisely this doubt that has characterized Japan's prolonged postwar period. In this new world, faced with the challenges of defeat and spiritual crisis, Kōda proved herself an astute and sensitive observer of the varieties of female experience and a proponent of a positive identity for Japan. Although, from "Random Notes" on, Kōda's works tend toward the personal and lyrical, she forges a link between the individual and social change around her. Let us begin this discussion of Kōda's shorter narratives with a look at the social and historical context in which postwar literature evolved. Many postwar writers, Kōda included, had a great interest in themes of cultural identity and self-identity as well as alienation and subversion. My reading of Kōda's stories contrasts with that of some critics who regard her work as apolitical and suggestive of conservatism.

The term "postwar" has a variety of connotations. In some contexts it suggests a war's disruptive force and the profound shadow it inevitably casts on all that follows. The word also presents the possibilities of a new beginning, however, or, conversely, the reaffirmation of a heritage. In Japan's case, defeat in World War II and the ensuing postwar period dictated a large measure of self-negation. Part of the difficulty in Japan's passage through the latter half of the twentieth century has stemmed from the dissonance implicit in forgetting the past while at the same time retaining a sense of identity and direction. The long-term nature of this project is evinced by the persistence of the term "post-war Japan," still used decades after the war actually ended.[3] During the period immediately following the defeat, reactions to the legacy of the war varied greatly. Many turned back to examine the experience with new eyes. On the whole, though, the defeat provided compelling motivation to look to the present and future, rather than to the certainty of history. Many people who had experienced the war as adults, in fact, felt great ambivalence toward their cultural heritage. These feelings of self-doubt, in turn, gave rise to a sense of rupture with the past, to the point that there existed, according to Kenneth Pyle, "widespread self-criticism that Japan lives in a spiritual and moral vacuum with no guiding principle other than economic rationality."[4] Pyle notes a similar sense of discontinuity in the early Meiji period:

> In the new age, then, growing up became a difficult, disturbing, unsettling experience: the thinking and experience of previous generations provided no certain precedents for new tasks; and the disintegrative effects of change on the older generation were in turn reflected in insecurities among the young.[5]

This massive social change had a profound effect on literature after the war as well. Indeed, the vast majority of Japanese novelists and poets had become part of the state's war effort, whether through voluntary participation or through reluctant *tenkō* (ideological conversion). As a result, the announcement of defeat occasioned much soul-searching among them.[6] Women had not stood with weapon in hand at the battlefront, but many had taken up the pen to cooperate with the government's propaganda effort. Millions of mothers had sent their sons off to die for the empire. The fortunate few who could claim no active participation in writing propaganda or government-approved literature still were faced by the chaos and uncertainty of the new age: the values and assumptions of a society seemed to have been lost.[7] Some mourned the passing; others rejoiced at the liberation. The situation was further complicated by the imposing presence of the Allied Occupation forces and Western culture.

Kojima Nobuo's "The American School"

This dilemma of where to start, what to reject, and what to adopt as one's identity is portrayed intriguingly by Kojima Nobuo in his story "The American School" (Amerikan sukūru).[8] In this story the author depicts a group of Japanese teachers of English in a face-to-face encounter with American culture just three years after the end of the war. Of the group, a young woman named

Michiko fares best when the group is placed within the confines of an American military base to observe classes at the base school. Unlike a fellow teacher named Isa, she has no trouble speaking English and seems much more adaptable to the occupiers' ways. Even so, Michiko is able to sympathize with Isa when he is rendered literally speechless with fear:

> Michiko acknowledged to herself that in referring to Isa as "him" and making her remarks in English she had stilled the pangs of guilt which she would normally have felt in this betrayal of trust. And that, she reflected, was no doubt one reason for Isa's hatred of the foreign language: when you spoke it you stopped being yourself. It was too easy to be carried away by the titillation of the words.[9]

Kojima treats the cultural clashes and strangeness that arose during the Occupation with humor. The slapstick comedy and bumbling do not, however, mask the story's major thematic concerns: the problem of retaining a cultural identity in the aftermath of defeat and the difficulties inherent in accommodating alien linguistic and conceptual systems. Isa's identity is no longer complete without a recognition of foreign tongues and cultures. The presence of strange visitors thwarts his desire to live in his usual manner. He can vent his frustrations only by screaming in Japanese at an American soldier who knows no Japanese: "You'll have to speak our language. Speak Japanese or else! What would you do if someone really said that to you?"[10] His language and his values no longer offer the security they once did.

Near the end of the story, Michiko tumbles off her ill-fitting high heels when reaching out for a pair of borrowed chopsticks. For a horrible moment it seems that the embarrassing eating utensils might be spotted by the American hosts. But instead "it remained a secret shared by Isa and Michiko that she had fallen while clutching at this homely artifact of their native land" *(kono yōna Nihontekina wabishii dogu).*[11] The chopsticks are clearly a synecdoche for traditional material culture in its most quotidian aspect. Although the chopsticks, along with language, form the core of culture and identity, the postwar world imposes an order under which the "artifacts" must be kept hidden. The characters, therefore, find themselves stripped of identity and a past. Even those who attempt to resist the new state of affairs must at least pretend to have forgotten all that came before.

This crisis of identity brought on by the shocking defeat figures prominently in the literature of the period and has continued as a matter of central concern. Inseparable from the question of what Japan had lost was the issue of what had survived the ravages of war. The nation as a whole, as it struggled to rebuild and to survive, pondered its status as a defeated people. Novelists and poets considered the value of their literary heritage, their wartime experiences, and the relationship between politics and art. To what extent did the individual bear responsibility for the disastrous project of militarism and cultural imperialism? Had the people, indeed, been duped? The past was tainted.

Several of Kōda's works concentrate on this question of cultural continuity in an age of profound change. As in "Fragments," "The Medal," and earlier works, Kōda maintains her fascination with the personal past of her characters and the insights afforded by a focused remembrance of that past. The two stories examined in this chapter stress the significance of the broad cultural and literary pasts, especially as they relate to women. "Dolls for a Special Day" (Hina) involves the rediscovery of the centuries-old aesthetic of asymmetry and looks at the implications of this cultural value in human relationships, art, and narrative structure. The later work, "A Friend for Life" (Mono iwanu isshō no tomo), approaches continuity both thematically and formally. The narrator discusses the links between generations and the decisions that result in continuity or disruption. To many readers, the voice itself embodies the witty spirit of the *zuihitsu* (discursive essay) in contrast to that of the modern *shōsetsu* (prose fiction).

"Dolls for a Special Day"

Kōda's "Dolls for a Special Day," a story roughly contemporaneous with "The American School," concerns the clash between youthful hopes and the pragmatic demands of adulthood. The story is told in the first person by a narrator in the postwar period who relates how, before the war, she acquired a set of traditional decorative dolls for the celebration of her daughter's first Girls' Day holiday.[12] She buys fancy, expensive dolls though she and her husband can scarcely afford them. Her extravagance in this purchase, the story reveals, ultimately stems from her disappointment at the plain wooden dolls she received during her own childhood. This realization comes only after the narrator has been shown her shortsightedness both by her parents and by the misfortune of another family. Years later, when the dolls are lost in the war, the daughter for whom they were bought shows no concern for their fate.

In "Dolls for a Special Day," in keeping with one of her central concerns, Kōda points to the potential for self-understanding that lies in remembrance. The mature narrator at the beginning states the illumination brought to her by memory: "Most women find themselves in a state of giddy elation after they have their first baby. Youthful exuberance leads them to act without a thought for the consequences. . . . I know. I speak from experience."[13] The story traces this realization that arises gradually through the narrator's habit of examining and reexamining her past.

From the beginning, Kōda emphasizes the narrator and her role as storyteller and bearer of memories. The narrator is thus simultaneously every young mother and the voice of an entire culture. For Kōda this woman—both in her youth and in her mature incarnation—is specifically female and feminine in nature, but the author refuses to equate femaleness and femininity with narrowness and dependence. If, as David Pollack has suggested, young male adult novels of self-discovery in modern Japanese literature characteristically focus on the male character's "relentless absorption with the problems of his miserable self," then Kōda rejects that vision as universal.[14] Instead, subjectivity exhibits the potential for change; the foolishness of youthful enthusiasm and excess is containable, a phase leading to maturity and autonomy.

The voice in "Dolls for a Special Day" immediately proposes an act of contemplation—not of "homely artifacts" threatened by extinction, but contemplation of a continuing cultural tradition: "I have heard that Girls' Day dolls vary in appearance from one generation to the next because they are modeled after the reigning empress. I wonder about that."[15] In one sense, the notion of continuity finds expression in the dolls themselves, which can "be found back in the age of *The Tale of Genji*" and continue to the narrator's day in the postwar era.[16] At the same time, continuity comes in the very act of recollecting the doll display. In contrast to Kojima's "American School," the physical demise of the dolls is not, in the final analysis, a matter of the greatest concern because the persona has the power, through creation of narrative, to resurrect them— not so much as objects of nostalgia but as points of reference linking the past and the present through memory. Such optimism and valorization of remembrance constitute a source of narrative and cultural authority. Even the incendiary bombs that come crashing down to destroy the city (and the small dolls in the story) are incapable of erasing this woman's memory or eradicating the past.

The mature narrator's prologue about the *hina* dolls attests to the enduring qualities of these cultural symbols of beauty and nobility that have enabled them to survive historical cycles of stability and chaos. Her faith in the tenacity of cultural tradition and the validity of female experience can be seen in the decision, at the end of the story, to leave her daughter's set of dolls behind when the family is preparing to evacuate during the war:

At one point he glanced at me and asked, "Aren't you going to pack up Tamako's dolls?"

He seemed perfectly at peace, and showed no sign of irritation. After considering the matter for a moment, I replied, "No, I'll leave them here."

I had decided quickly, but I knew what I was doing—after all, I was no longer young and without experience. And I remembered what my father had said, the talk with my mother-in-law, the dyer's story.[17]

In the original, this final sentence is both more metaphorical and less emphatic about cause and effect. Translated literally, it might read as follows: "In my mind as I responded were the years that had accumulated, what Father had said that time, what my mother-in-law had said, and the dyer's story—all these had become my foundation."[18] In the context of the story, it is obvious that the narrator recalls these old conversations, not idly, but in a concerted effort to connect the present and the past and to learn from this act. The folly of her youth—the dolls—can be dispensed with, for she knows that memory will preserve the important and intangible aspects of culture. The custom of the Girls' Day festival will survive, just as her parents' teaching has survived, in her memory and in narrative.

The structure of "Dolls for a Special Day" and its narrative stance have as much to do with tradition and the notion of narrative authority as do its thematic aspects. In the manner of a discursive essay, the piece begins with a discussion of various aspects of the *hina* dolls and their history. But "Dolls for a Special Day" does not pretend to be an objective account. Indeed, the narrative fairly bursts with the narrator's presence, her opinions, and her highly idiosyncratic voice. The initial paragraph is set in the narrative present and thus creates a sense of immediacy. The impression that the narrator speaks directly to the reader is accomplished, not only through the use of nonpast predicates (*"darō ka," "tsukutte aru," "omoeru," "omowareru," "to iu,"* and so on), but also by the high frequency of verbs of consciousness such as *"omou"* ([I] think). In subsequent sections of the work, the narrative stance alternates between the remembering narrator and experiencing narrator. The flowing, colloquial style brims with confidence and shows no sign of insecurity in the face of foreign cultures or languages. Through her creation of this assured, astute narrative voice, Kōda evokes the sense of authority characteristic in the *zuihitsu* genre. This power to present one's opinion derives not so much from a democratic realm of public discourse or from claims to logic as from the sense that the narrative persona has the proper aesthetic perceptions and sensibilities. The flowing, discursive rhetorical approach, based on familiarity with prior *zuihitsu,* contrasts with the authority of, say, academic or philosophical discourse.

In the *zuihitsu* genre, the presence of a narrator's tone, personality, and perceptions is an indispensable convention. As one modern critic has commented on Sei Shōnagon, the author of *The Pillow Book* (Makura no sōshi; ca. 994) and *zuihitsu* writer par excellence, "she succeeds as a shrewd impressionistic critic and a fine sketch writer, but not as the creator of *shōsetsu* [novels, prose fiction], because she cannot help coming forth as herself in her writings. She is unable to kill her own voice."[19] From a generic point of view, however, Tomi Suzuki comments that the "differences among *shōsetsu, zuihitsu* (essay), and *nikki* (diary) derive not from the form of the subject matter but from the writer's attitude toward what he is writing, by the intensity of the creating spirit, with the *watakushi shōsetsu* as a "medium into which the author pours his spiritual energy."[20]

In "Dolls for a Special Day," the narrator's personality and critical spirit become most evident in her notions about beauty. She describes the *hina* doll set with care and even comments on the differences in doll design at various points in history. At length the sense of cultural insularity gives way when the narrator mentions her impression that Audrey Hepburn in the movie *Roman Holiday* resembles one of the Japanese empresses. In this passage, the Japanese visage, not the Western one, is normative. This stance contrasts greatly with Kojima's portrayal of well-fed, glamorous Americans. Even Tanizaki, with his fascination with the West, portrayed Caucasian whiteness as pure and neutral, while "no matter how white a Japanese person may be, his whiteness has a slight dimness to it. . . . [The Japanese] could not erase the darkness settled deep down in their skin." Tanizaki concludes that "one could see it as easily as some filth at the bottom of clear water . . . so when [a Japanese] stands among Caucasians, it is most unsightly, like a gray smudge on a sheet of white paper."[21]

The lone hints of the West (Hepburn) and modern technology (movies) in the first part of "Dolls for a Special Day," then, are not threatening. In fact, the Hollywood actress is incorporated into the Japanese conceptual mold:

> The other day I went to see a film called *Roman Holiday.* That popular young star named Audrey Hepburn was in it, and when I first saw her I was immediately struck by how old-fashioned her face looked. Very strange, that this visage seemed to me to be from another age, while all her young fans regard her as fresh and new.

Not until the end of the movie did I realize that it was something about the way her eyes were made up. Their sharp, upward curve was Empress Shōken's. The shots of Hepburn in this film about a modern-day queen had reminded me of a photo of the Japanese empress from a half century before.[22]

The narrator as storyteller has more than one tale to relate. She is the old woman who attests to the continuity of culture: her family's set of dolls may have vanished in wartime, but she has survived to witness the tradition's revival and to verify the dolls' significance. More important even than these material traces of tradition, however, is the aesthetic the narrator exemplifies: asymmetry. The age-old preference for such unbalanced beauty manifests itself repeatedly and in a variety of ways throughout the story. At the beginning, the narrator makes explicit mention of its positive value in her description of the composition of the *hina* doll sets. Although the exquisite emperor and empress dolls and their perfect court attendants form the core of the set, she notes that:

On the very bottom row of the stand . . . there are three servant dolls with faces and expressions not unlike those of ordinary people. The doll maker renders their faces slightly less refined and even adds a few minor and somewhat humorous imperfections. The dolls' ugliness draws viewers to them. . . . To my mind, this touch of charm seems necessary as a means of creating an asymmetrical balance, so to speak, in a set otherwise dominated by twelve perfect, ridiculously gorgeous, dolls.[23]

At first glance this lengthy prologue seems merely a pretext for recalling the dolls that represent the misdirected energy of the narrator's youth and the lesson she learned about adult responsibility. In other words, the beginning passage may be thought of as a simple narrative device for introducing the "real" story. And, in one sense, it is. Of equal and perhaps even greater importance, however, is the introduction of the central aesthetic. As expressed by the mature narrator, this preference and method of evaluating the world seems an effortless, inborn aspect of Japanese life. As the story unfolds, however, the opposite proves to be true. The aesthetic of asymmetry reveals itself as part of a conscious tradition, not a mere mindless habit. The eternal transmission of the value and the individual's response to this offering from the past form the core of "Dolls for a Special Day."

In her affirmation of an asymmetrical harmony or balance, the narrator expresses a stance that has informed Japanese arts for many centuries. The aesthetic calls for the slightly lopsided, somberly glazed tea bowl, for the brush-and-ink painting that preserves some unfilled space, for indirection and allusion in verse. Yoshida Kenkō (1283?–1350), by articulating this concept of beauty in his *Tsurezuregusa,* helped to lead the arts away from the well formed and perfect, idealized in Heian times, to the suggestive and asymmetrical:[24]

> I found merit in Abbot Kōyū's words: "It is the petty man who attempts to make complete sets of things. It is preferable to have something missing."
>
> Indeed, in all matters, they say, perfection is bad. Something left unfinished is intriguing and makes one anticipate future growth. Even when they build a palace, they always leave some part unfinished.[25]

In art, incompletion and asymmetry are valued because they allow the viewer to take part in the work's creation. Rather than regarding such asymmetry as a deformity, this aesthetic stance sees it in positive terms as potential for growth.[26]

In "Dolls for a Special Day," this aesthetic of asymmetry possesses such force that it expands beyond the realm of art—the dolls—into the world of social intercourse and ethics. The narrator's parents berate her more for failing to perceive the importance of incompletion than for her irresponsibility with household funds. After the Girls' Day party, the narrator's father expresses his disappointment that she has done things "so well and so completely that afterwards there's nothing left—just a big nothing."[27] Her mother-in-law expresses frustration, too, at not having been able to contribute to the gathering, remarking that "a certain amount of imperfection creates a sense of closeness."[28] But for the elders' decisive action, the tradition of incompletion, in its most human and mundane manifestation, would have been lost. The narrator has learned this lesson, and in her maturity she transmits to her audience the same values: "To my mind, this touch . . . seems necessary as a means of creating an asymmetrical balance" in the doll set.[29] In this way Kōda examines not only the transmission of material culture but also the role of traditional aesthetics as a force in culture.

Even the form of "Dolls for a Special Day" complies with the dictates of asymmetry. The "real" story, which narrates, in a straightforward chronology, the events surrounding the purchase, possession, and loss of a set of *hina* dolls, could stand on its own. But Kōda did not write that story alone: she prefaces it with a lengthy discursive prologue (three pages out of fifteen in the original). This structure conforms to the requirements of asymmetry and finds its origins in premodern and early modern narrative. What Kōda has written here is akin to the "*haikai* short story" of the Edo master of letters Ihara Saikaku (1642–1693).[30] Saikaku incorporated the form and flow of *haikai* (comic linked verse, a genre that flourished during the Edo period) into his writing of prose narrative. The *hokku,* or first verse in a chain of linked verse, had the important function of establishing the tone and setting for the initial sequence of eight poems (out of thirty-six or even more). While all the other links (except the last) in the thirty-six-stanza sequence are modified both by the previous and the succeeding link, the *hokku* has an especially distinctive identity by virtue of the fact that nothing comes before it. Saikaku, recognizing the *hokku*'s potential, used elaborate, allusive prologues to set the theme and tone in *The Japanese Family Storehouse* (Nippon eitaigura; 1688) and other works of prose narrative.[31] This structural feature can be found again in the writings of the revered Meiji writer Higuchi Ichiyō, herself an admirer of Saikaku, in "Child's Play" (Takekurabe; 1895–1896), for example. Both Saikaku and Ichiyō used the *hokku* flourish to great effect in establishing the atmosphere of a particular quarter of the city or people's spirit at certain times of the year. Unlike her eminent predecessors, Kōda, writing in an age aware of the possibilities of psychological realism, does not direct the opening view of "Dolls for a Special Day" to a broad panorama. She examines a microcosm—the searching mind of the narrator and her world—but this does not result in triviality. The prologue establishes the cultural and historical significance of the *hina* dolls; furthermore, it creates the distinctive voice and personality of the narrator.

"A Friend for Life"

During the decade after "Dolls for a Special Day," Kōda produced a number of short stories. Many of these strike the reader as uninspired—as though, indeed, the author regarded writing them as a chore.[32] Absent from these stories are the intensity of observation, the humor, and the graceful style familiar to the reader of "The Medal," "Dolls for a Special Day," and other works. Despite Kōda's skill in evoking a narrative voice and in storytelling, in this short fiction she has difficulty in creating character and constructing plot and, more than anything, balancing these two aspects. Without the characteristic voice and narrative structure, with plot and character wandering aimlessly, these works flounder.

Of all Kōda's writings, the contemplative stories that are furthest from so-called orthodox prose fiction (that is, texts that are plot-oriented or densely populated with well-developed characters) are most successful. "A Friend for Life" (Mono iwanu isshō no tomo) counts among these. From the beginning it reads like an exemplary *zuihitsu:* voice and personality figure prominently; structure does not depend on incident or interaction between characters. The narrator begins by introducing the "friend" of the title—a mirror she has owned for nearly forty years. She recounts its history and deplores its present state, but then she suddenly turns to a discussion of different types of mirrors she remembers from her childhood and her favorites among them. Subsequently the narrative shifts to the topic of the appeal of mirrors, then to anecdotes about mirrors in movies, and then to a funny story. The piece next alternates between sections concerning the narrator's personal experiences relating to mirrors and sections concerning mirrors in general. Thus "A Friend for Life" consists of two types of discourse. On the one hand, the narrator acts as a cultural critic discussing the broad implications and uses of the object we call the mirror. Even in this role, the voice modulates between formality and familiarity with the reader, depending on whether it is relating an opinion (such as "mirrors make people behave in strange ways") or telling a funny story (such as the tale of a land without mirrors). On the other hand, the narrator tells her own story with mirrors as a central motif. The general "commentary" parts connect one woman's story to a broader context and thus elevate the narrator's act from personal confession to public narration. As a teller of tales, she becomes one of the links in the social and psychological process that is culture.

Over the course of this nonlinear narrative, the narrator reveals her motivations for purchasing an imposing, full-length mirror: it represented to her a bright, positive approach to life in contrast to the small, dark mirror her mother had owned. The mirror thus functions, as we shall see, in a symbolic sense. Although the narrator's changing view of herself is one of the story's central themes, "A Friend for Life" is not strictly an egocentric work. Even the syntax of the opening sentence expresses an interest in looking at something larger than the individual. Literally it reads: "A somewhat oversized full-length mirror is what I'm using at home."[33] Syntactic flexibility in Japanese allows for the possibility of a direct object preceding a subject, but even so the order of this sentence points away from the subject and to the mirror. In essence, Kōda does not adhere to a single use of this image. While the metaphorical potential of the mirror image (ego, self, narcissism) is obvious, the author varies her approach to the image—now bringing forward its most immediate symbolic implications, now regarding it in a literal sense as a physical object (a piece of furniture). Perhaps it is here that the reader encounters Rohan's notion of *kakubutsu chichi:* know things of this world well; investigate them thoroughly as a means of self-cultivation. The narrator considers every possible aspect of mirrors, and mirrors are an indicator of her changing self. As we shall see, they allow the narrative to expand to include an examination of generational change and cultural continuity.

In "A Friend for Life," therefore, the reader finds a variety of levels of interest. First there is the story of a woman who survives the breakup of her marriage and becomes a stronger person, more aware of her own emotions. The narrator also presents us with a modern woman who struggles with versions of female identity handed down from her mother's and stepmother's generations. This process of accepting or rejecting the new and the old is approached through retrospection, as in Kōda's other works. The narrator looks back, examines her motivations, and realizes how much the lives of her two mothers have affected her. Thus the opening sentence quoted earlier does not automatically signify the exclusive invocation of the mirror/self metaphor. In fact, it points away from the "I" of the story and toward the image, which eventually evokes a broader range of human activity—specifically issues of generational change and cultural continuity.

This combination of personal confession and general anecdote might seem confusing were it not for the narrator's pervasive humor and incisiveness. Her observant nature and articulate style propel the lopsided narrative. As she recollects her younger days, the narrator clearly expresses the nuances of her youthful motivations, aspirations, and feelings of despair. This side of the story attains depth and beauty because the narrator searches back beyond the first awakenings of adolescence for the forces that have shaped her. As she discovers in pondering the lives of her mother and stepmother and their mirrors, the past holds many answers. The sections concerning mirrors in general, by contrast, allow the narrator to display her curiosity and aesthetic sensibility as she considers the varied significance of mirrors and declares her opinions about each aspect of the matter. Her reactions are impressionistic and brief, not analytical. One is reminded of Sei Shōnagon's terse comments in *The Pillow Book*.[34]

Kōda also lends immediacy and force to the voice by evoking the narrative present as fully as possible. This is accomplished through the frequent use of nonpast predicates and usages that emphasize the presence of a probing mind—such as *"to omou"* ([I] think), *"to kioku shite iru"* ([I] recall that), *"wake ne"* (here, mustn't [I] . . . ?), and so on. The personal tale seems distinctly modern because of its psychological focus. Through the process of tracing the history of a large mirror she has owned for forty years, the narrator reveals her present self and the difficulties that old age has brought her. In the recent past, she relates, "cloudy spots started appearing, one after another, all over the mirror's surface. I suddenly developed a great attachment to the mirror, and though I had never been faithful about keeping it clean, I set out to prevent the blotches from spreading."[35] The mirror, in this way, becomes a metaphor for her own old age but later reverts to its status as a reflective glass, somehow personified: "So I always make sure to ask my rather large mirror to watch out for me."[36]

The mirror motif in this personal story furthermore reveals the narrator's emotional past—in particular, her youthful aspirations and subsequent sobering confrontations with her environment and her self. As a young wife, she asserts herself by purchasing a larger-than-average mirror and situating it prominently: "I was determined to find a place for it in our bedroom."[37] Her mother had owned a small mirror not meant for public display; from the eyes of the narrator as a young woman, it seemed "somber and inferior" to those of geisha she had seen. For the older narrator, too, the tiny looking glass of her late mother pales in comparison to the advances of the modern world. After a determinedly bright start at married life, the narrator's relationship fails and she realizes that even the mirror cannot help her attain the cheerful, optimistic life to which she had once aspired:

> I consoled myself by leaning up against the sturdy legs of my mirror. To think how proud I had felt of it on my wedding day. Now all I could do was crouch up against it and sigh. . . . The mirror served more as a support for my emotions than as a glass in which I could see my reflection. The sunny location I had chosen for it had been part of my effort to avoid sadness and gloom in my life, but ironically it ended up lodging a darkened, tired soul.[38]

In her effort to escape the repressive self-denial of her mother's life, the narrator acquires a mirror that metaphorically and physically refutes her mother's small, dark mirror. Thus when the narrator's home life falls apart, she feels all the more acutely the anguish of her battered pride and lost hopes, embodied as they are in her large mirror: "In the end, I left my husband's house. When I was moving out, I felt keenly embarrassed about having such a grandiose mirror."[39]

The image of the mirror illustrates, too, the narrator's lack of self-understanding and her tendency to avoid confronting her own emotions. Even though she owns a huge mirror, she never looks at her own face or figure in the glass; instead she uses it as a prop against which she can lean her weary body and weep. Only after the narrator returns to her father's home does she realize her own emotional and psychological state:

> One day I shut myself up in my room and was sulking there when Father casually walked in and, without warning, thrust a small mirror up to my face. I saw my surly countenance grimace in embarrassment. How ugly and out of sorts I looked.[40]

Ironically, it is a small mirror, the type she deplores, that brings her to her senses and out of her depression.

The work's seemingly random alternation between personal and general passages brings to the forefront the central issues. Rather than creating a narrator who is motivated solely by a personal, irrational fear of "living darkly" as her mother had, the author stresses the narrator's cultural and social awareness upon which this fear is based. In fact, sometimes even the passages that seem totally personal tend toward the broadly cultural. In turn, this breadth points to the maturity of the narrator and the role of remembrance in self-understanding. The initial passage about the old-age spots on the mirror and the later one concerning her motivation for buying the mirror are linked to each other by memory. The structure of the story, in fact, suggests the nature of recollection: rather than being something carried by the continuous flux of time, memory is shown to be the deliberate act of linking distant points in time. Therefore, the intervening passages do not proceed by means of any discernible narrative logic. Instead they exist for the purpose of defining the voice as belonging to a person who values the past in its many manifestations. At the same time, the structure emphasizes the individual's ties to society. Kobayashi Hideo has pointed out that in the modern Japanese novel, portraying the viewpoint and emotions of an individual character throughout a work does not preclude an examination of society as well—for in a relatively homogeneous society, the individual's life is a microcosm of society.[41] This notion can be applied to Kōda's works as well, with the qualification that society and the individual become apparent, not through the actions and events the character experiences in the course of the novel, but through the character's process of remembering her life and the quality of those remembrances. From this derives her narrative authority.

From the first of the numerous general passages about mirrors, the narrator isolates the primary human motivations for using mirrors: vanity and egotism. The use of similes and the whimsical attribution of various powers to mirrors, rather than to human psychology, conveys the narrator's wit and astuteness:

> On occasion I notice young women behaving in a similar manner when they do their makeup. There might be three or four of them lined up in a row when I walk into the ladies' room of a department store or theater. They will all have their faces only inches from the glass, as if they had decided beforehand on this course of action. The lighting in such places must be a hundred times brighter than in our bath, but still these women feel compelled to thrust their faces for-

ward as if they were long-necked cranes. No matter how well or poorly lit, a mirror seems to possess the power to make women behave oddly.[42]

In the next general passage, this central image is developed further. It concerns the charm or allure of mirrors—in other words, human attitudes toward the seemingly mysterious looking glass:

> Some people believe they can see, not only their own future, but also a departed lover or the holy Bodhisattva in the mirror. And so, for them, the mirror is a boundary between this world and the other. I wonder if such beliefs exist in other countries as well.
>
> Quite a while ago I saw a movie about Orpheus. That filmmaker used the mirror to represent the passageway between the human world and the realm beyond, too, so I guess that people everywhere are interested in such notions. In the movie, a man carrying mirrors on his back appears time after time in the chilled, hushed alleyways. I shuddered at his unearthly, shrill voice as he cried out selling his wares. The use of mirrors in this film impressed me a great deal.[43]

Despite the earlier Kōda's claim that her narrative world was the product of a modest, untalented homemaker, the narrator's concern here with human psychology and belief, foreign films, and symbols in art define her as cosmopolitan and intellectually curious.

Another link between the personal and the broadly cultural in "A Friend for Life" lies in the narrator's examination of mirrors belonging to members of different generations, places, and social strata. Much of her ability to delve into such matters has to do with her process of remembering and, specifically, bringing up memories of her own family:

> My memories about mirrors begin with my mother's dressing stand. Because I lost my mother when I was a very young child, I have only the vaguest recollections of her face. Photographs of Mother merely reinforce the haziness of my memories. I do remember that a hairdresser would come to the house to fix her hair. Mother kept her mirror, stand, and combs on the floor of the closet along with her sewing kit and the iron. She used the folding stand for the long-handled, round mirror. That was late Meiji, so her mirror must have been a glass one, not metal. In any case, it was quite old-fashioned. . . . I do distinctly remember her sitting before the glass, a white cloth draped over her shoulders, having her hair combed. I also have a picture in my mind of her mirror but, oddly, no clear image of her face.[44]

In this section, titled "A Strange Piece of Furniture," Kōda uses the image to evoke the spectrum of female society (and, by extension, society as a whole). The narrator's mother lacks a face and a distinct identity. Only in matters of propriety does she assert herself, and then only as an anonymous voice amid the decent and proper people who defend the mores of society. "A woman in a decent home *(katagina uchi)* does not leave her makeup scattered all over for everyone to see," the mother says, or "A woman ought to be discreet when fixing her hair and applying powder."[45] The narrator draws a further contrast between such "old-fashioned" mirrors and those of the geisha, whose "beautiful mirrors [are] proudly set out for display."[46] Not only are they of different sizes, but they belong to two separate spatial and social realms: the housewife's is covered and hidden in the closet; the geisha's is situated by the latticed windows that face the streets. Between these extremes of modesty and unabashed vanity coexisting in traditional society is the stepmother's mirror. This golden mean, in the narrator's eyes, comes in the form of a mirror set atop a dressing table laden with containers of fragrant perfume and the like. Such a mirror is never put away. In contrast to her mother's conformist values, the narrator's stepmother has her own mind and a place of her own.

In evaluating her stepmother's expression of individual will and demand for privacy, the narrator uses tactile and visual terms rather than moral and social ones: "There was a certain cleanness, a coolness, in her attitude."[47] Thus she characterizes an individual, as well as a generation, in aesthetic terms. She extends her analysis to other mirrors as well:

> When I stopped to think about it, I realized that no one owned old-style mirrors like my first mother's anymore. Instead, everyone used some variation of a mirror attached to a low chest of drawers. The pawnshop lady, somewhat on the shopworn side herself, had a mirror that was always quiet and deserted. In families with many daughters, the dressing tables were constantly in an uproar. A scrap of purple silk was the only spot of color where the fireman's wife sat. At the sundries store, the looking-glass frame shined black with oil. A single flower in a vase decorated the dressing table of the unmarried schoolteacher.[48]

The initial juxtaposition of the old-fashioned housewife and the lovely geisha points to a basic dichotomy in social roles that exists to a degree even in modern society. Women have conventionally been regarded either as proper *(katagi),* self-effacing shadows or as romantic, sensual beings. The stepmother and the women just mentioned, then, represent the broadening of possibilities for women in Japan.

The narrator does not attribute these changes directly to Western influence. While even Kōda would admit to the overwhelming influx of Western culture and material goods from the early Meiji period, she rejects the idea of raw and undigested borrowing. Indeed, the narrator finds the mirrors and bedrooms of Western women—and the very concept of bedrooms, which she encounters for the first time in her youth—intriguing but unacceptable:

> How surprised I was at this very wide mirror (I was used to the tall, skinny ones), the lace doilies on the dresser, a silver hand-held mirror engraved with the lady's initials, hairbrushes, a ceramic powder holder topped with a flower-shaped handle, a jumbled arrangement of dolls and knickknacks, photographs, and a vase filled with fresh flowers. I immediately thought how troublesome it would be to clean such a room, but at the same time I was most impressed by the casual liveliness of her adornments.[49]

After stating her pragmatic, somewhat humorous, viewpoint, the narrator expresses her sense that the Westerners' private bedrooms and the "purity and exclusiveness" associated with them have something in common with the obsessiveness of the "old-fashioned" mothers and their reliance on social definitions of morality and the individual's role in society. The narrator feels distanced from the Western concept of mirrors and bedrooms because they are too self-contained, too isolating. She finds merit in her stepmother's blend of East and West and her ability to circumscribe her own territory and self without shutting others out.

Only after this extended explanation of her culture and her opinions does the narrator return to her own story. In the section "A Place for the Mirror," she recasts the variety of mirrors in less sensual and more abstract terms. Her mother's mirror, in this recapitulation of the mirrors she has seen, is "shabby," "somber and inferior," and "sad." The stepmother's is superior because it shows its owner's ability to "think in much newer ways" and to have a place of her own for the mirror. Even the geisha's mirrors, which earlier were called inelegant, receive praise for being fixed permanently in one spot and pleasing to the eye. This paragraph reiterating the different types of mirrors immediately precedes a paragraph that begins: "I am certain that such feelings have something to do with my attraction to the slightly oversized mirror."[50] In the original, the phrase "these feelings" (*sonna kimochi,* "such feelings") remains ambiguous. Logically the phrase must refer to the narrator's attitudes expressed in the previous paragraph. But the feelings are more than this blunt emotional reaction: they extend back to the complex process of remembering and evaluating described in the previous pages, as well as to the effort to connect her personal reactions to something beyond her own narrow sphere.

In "Dolls for a Special Day," as in her story "The Medal" (Kunshō; 1949), Kōda utilizes the flashback within a straightforward linear narrative as a means of creating character and developing the theme of cultural continuity. The reader's initial sense of formlessness and fragmentation in "A Friend for Life" derives partly from the abandonment of this chronological orientation and the constant shifting between narrative present, recollection, and commentary that does not fit any temporal pattern. Significantly, the commentary passages in this work concern characters and objects rather than place—a typical concern of commentary in modern Japanese prose. Examples of this concern include Tanizaki's *Arrowroot* (Yoshino kuzu; 1931) and Nagai Kafū's "A Strange Tale from East of the River" ("Bokutō kidan"; 1937).[51] In "A Friend for Life," the narrator pays little attention to atmosphere or mood of place, instead concentrating on the placeless, timeless image of the mirror. Temporal and spatial elements are mentioned only in relation to this image. This approach has the effect of emphasizing the mediating observer.

In the case of "A Friend for Life," moreover, Kōda was writing for a special issue of the periodical *Fujin Kōron* (Woman's Forum) on the subject of mirrors.[52] The central image of the story came about, then, largely as a matter of circumstance. Kōda does not put on the robe of the omniscient cultural critic for the occasion. Overall the piece shows a great degree of consistency with her other writings in its approach to the past, treatment of voice, and reliance on elements other than plot or dramatic action to fashion an artistic whole.

Indeed, the juxtaposition of "A Friend for Life" and a piece in the same issue of the journal *Fujin Kōron* called "On Narcissism" (Narushishizumuron) by Mishima Yukio is telling. In his short essay, Mishima steps out of his role as fabricator and creator of fiction and into the role of observer: the objective teller of truths. Against this opposition between fact and art, Kōda's piece can be read in different ways—the musings of the historical author, perhaps, or yet another patch in the artistic whole that Kōda has been weaving during her years of writing. Mishima presents his "argument" in a stiff, cut-and-dried manner with sentences ending in the nonpast predicate, a high percentage of abstract nouns, and few concrete images: "Why are women so happy when they are putting on their makeup? Narcissism certainly cannot be equated with happiness. . . . In any case, 'happiness' is a concept that is difficult for men to understand and of all concepts the most feminine one."[53] Placed against this supposedly neutral narrative, Kōda's work is revealed to emanate from a different impulse. There is no valorization of the objective over the subjective, nor is there an exclusive reliance on the neutrality of an atemporal narrative voice. Humankind, society, and the individual can best be understood in relation to the past.

Kōda's Approach to Identity

Two extremes in postwar narrative are represented by Kōda's "Dolls for a Special Day" and "A Friend for Life," on the one hand, and Kojima's "The American School" on the other. While both writers confront problems of identity in a chaotic age, their formal and thematic interests differ considerably. Kōda leans to the discursive, while Kojima chooses the most orthodox type of short story (in the Anglo-European sense) for describing a new world alienated from its past. The semi-omniscient narrator in "The American School" allows the reader access to the minds of a variety of characters and depicts their varied reactions to the world around them. Kōda, however, employs a limited narrative stance. The assured narrator is well developed as a keeper of memories; her posture alludes, moreover, to classical literature.

The absence of a threatening Other (whether the Allied Occupation forces or a foreign culture) is notable in the two Kōda stories. In "The American School," by contrast, Kojima represents a world where people feel incomplete in their identities when confronted by outsiders. The shadow of war and Japan's status as a defeated nation figure prominently. Language becomes an inadequate tool, and the material aspects of traditional culture are hidden. Memory and narrative authority are beyond the reach of the characters and their world.

Kōda's approach to identity in the postwar period involves an individual female's examination of personal and cultural pasts rather than the portrayal of a multiplicity of reactions to immediate surroundings. Her treatment of memory and the past is multifaceted and subtle. On a broadly cultural level, the narrators' remembrance in the two stories serves as a means of exploring generational change. Kōda uses the image of the dolls in "Dolls for a Special Day" to show how young people learn about the aesthetics of living from the older generation. In "A Friend for Life," the narrator's consideration of mirrors provides insights into changing notions of women's privacy, personhood, and sense of propriety. Significantly, both narrators understand themselves as part of a continuum and acknowledge the weight of their parents' teachings, whether or not they choose to follow those teachings.

Of all the elements that lend coherence to "A Friend for Life" and "Dolls for a Special Day"—the mirror and doll motifs, a woman's lifetime, the force of tradition—the narrator's eye and voice contribute most to the creation of an artistic whole. What is the nature of this voice? Rejecting the casual reader's assumption that one encounters here the "true" voice of the author, one may look to several possible antecedents. The subjectivity and the identification of historical incident with narrative fact suggest the *watakushi shōsetsu* or perhaps the premodern *zuihitsu*. In both genres, critics, writers, and readers have sometimes equated the narrator with the historical author.[54] Not only do these similarities tempt the reader to perceive a direct influence, but it is always gratifying to discover aspects of Japanese tradition vital in modern prose. A question, however, arises concerning the conceptual and artistic impulses of the *watakushi shōsetsu* proponents. Were they actually drawing on the *zuihitsu* tradition?[55] To a large extent, modern notions of narrative voice, fiction and truth, and the *shōsetsu* have influenced our view of premodern genres. Although it is easy to conclude that these two categories merge simply because of their common subjectivity, in the final analysis the connection is more than coincidental. Even if writers of the *watakushi shōsetsu* did not consciously emulate the *zuihitsu*, their exposure to premodern prose doubtless influenced their views of the nature of narrative and fiction.

Whatever the nature of this narrative voice in Kōda's writings, it does share a spirit of reverence for the past with works from classical Japanese literature. For two *zuihitsu* writers—Yoshida Kenkō and Kamo no Chōmei (1155–1215), who lived apart from society as monks and stressed an aesthetic that valued the illusory, the decaying, and the incomplete—there is also an assumption of continuity with the past. Chōmei, even as he lived through a period of natural disaster and political turmoil, placed his trust in the long tradition of Buddhism. As for the *Tsurezuregusa* of Kenkō, the constant reminders of the world's transience belie a firm faith in the past: "To sit alone in the lamplight with a book spread out before you, and hold intimate converse with men of unseen generations—such is a pleasure beyond compare."[56] And again: "In hours of quiet thought, one cannot but be overcome by longing for the past."[57]

The canonical premodern *zuihitsu* writers had a sharp critical eye and were by no means naive idealists. Their works remain central texts in Japanese literature today, not because they represent specific historical occasions or chains of events, but rather because they evoke the "characteristic inner life of the speaker" and his astuteness in observing the world around him and claim on narrative authority.[58] In a similar fashion, the two works by Kōda Aya examined here make the inner life of the narrators and their observations come alive. They also illuminate an important facet of the diversity of women's experience in Japan.

Notes

1. For examples of such works see Higuchi Ichiyō, Hayashi Fumiko, Yosano Akiko, Enchi Fumiko, Tsushima Yūko, Kanai Mieko, and Kōno Taeko.

2. Toril Moi points out that some feminist critics manage "to transform *all* texts written by women into feminist texts, because they may always and without exception be held to embody somehow and somewhere the author's 'female rage' against patriarchal oppression." Such a theoretical stance is problematic, Moi asserts, because such critics view patriarchy as monolithic and fail to recognize the "contradictory, fragmentary nature of patriarchal ideology." Moreover, such theories "cannot cope with a 'male' text that *openly* tackles the problems of women's oppression." See Toril Moi, *Sexual/Textual Politics: Feminist Literary Theory* (New York: Routledge, 1985), pp. 62–65.

3. The attention paid to the fiftieth anniversary marking Japan's defeat and the end of World War II suggests the continued presence of a postwar mentality, as does the controversy over the visits by the Japanese head of state to Yasukuni Shrine, where World War II dead are enshrined. This constant shifting of identity and self-definition in terms of the war continues to play a major part in contemporary literature, despite some critics' insistence that the postwar period is over. See, for example, the famous proclamation of the critic Nakano Yoshio (b. 1903) in 1956 that "it's not the postwar period anymore" *(mohaya sengo dewanai);* quoted in Honda Shūgo, *Monogatari sengo bungakushi* (Shinchōsha, 1965), p. 298.

4. Kenneth Pyle, *The Making of Modern Japan* (Lexington, Mass.: Heath, 1981), pp. 177–178.

5. Kenneth Pyle, *The New Generation in Meiji Japan* (Stanford: Stanford University Press, 1969), p. 16.

6. See Donald Keene's chapters on "War Literature" in *Dawn to the West: Japanese Literature of the Modern Era—Fiction* (New York: Holt, 1984), pp. 906–961. Brett DeBary discusses *tenkō* and its repercussions in her introduction to *Three Works by Nakano Shigeharu* (Ithaca: Cornell University East Asian Papers, 1979), pp. 3–16. See also Alan Tansman's "Bridges to Nowhere: Yasuda Yōjirō's Language of Violence and Desire," *Harvard Journal of Asiatic Studies* 56 (1996): 35–75, in which he discusses the controversial revival of Yasuda in the 1950s.

7. Tanizaki Jun'ichirō, Kōda Rohan, and Nagai Kafū are the most notable examples of writers who did not become involved in the government's effort to mobilize writers for the war.

8. Kojima Nobuo, "The American School," translated by William F. Sibley in *Contemporary Japanese Literature* (New York: Knopf, 1977), pp. 120–144. Although Sibley's translation is good, it is considerably less elliptical than Kojima's original text.

9. Kojima, "The American School," p. 141.

10. Ibid., p. 122.

11. Ibid., p. 143.

12. *Hina matsuri,* the Doll or Girls' Day Festival, is celebrated on 3 March in Japan with decorative dolls, special sweets, and peach blossoms. This modern observance finds its origins in *momo no sekku* (the peach blossom festival on the third day of the third lunar month), one of the five Chinese seasonal festivals *(sekku).* Originally it was also known as *joshi,* or the "upper serpent day," because it was held on the first "serpent" day *(mi)* of the third lunar month (that is, one of the twelve horary characters of the sexagenary cycle used for naming times, dates, and years). By the Heian period, *joshi* had both spiritual significance and entertainment value. The aristocracy on this day participated in *kyokusui no en,* or the "winding water" banquet, to borrow Ivan Morris' translation, which entailed verse composition and drinking cups of sake that bobbed on the garden stream. Participants would float paper or bamboo figurines down rivers or throw them out into the ocean, a ritual that represented the ritual purification of human beings. From the Muromachi period on, it became popular to set up elaborate displays of emperor, empress, and courtier dolls with accessories. See Ivan Morris, trans., *The Pillow Book of Sei Shonagon* (Baltimore: Penguin, 1967).

13. *KAZS* 4:374.

14. David Pollack, *Reading Against Culture: Ideology and Narrative in the Japanese Novel* (Ithaca: Cornell University Press, 1992), p. 66.

15. *KAZS* 4:371.

16. *KAZS* 4:372. Observance of *momo no sekku* dates back to the late Nara period. In *The Tale of Genji,* the *hina matsuri* custom appears at the end of the "Suma" chapter, immediately before Genji decides to leave his place of exile:

> It was the day of the serpent *(mi no hi),* the first such day in the Third Month.
> "The day when a man who has worries goes down and washes them away," said one of his men, admirably informed, it would seem, in all the annual observances. Wishing to have a look at the seashore, Genji set forth. Plain, rough curtains were strung among the trees, and a soothsayer who was doing the circuit of the province was summoned to perform the lustration.
> Genji thought he could see something of himself in the rather large doll *(hitogata)* being cast off to sea, bearing away sins and tribulations.
> "Cast away to drift on an alien vastness,
> I grieve for more than a doll cast out to sea."
> . . . Suddenly a wind came up and even before the services were finished the sky was black.

See Edward Seidensticker, trans., *The Tale of Genji* (New York: Knopf, 1981), pp.

245–246. Significantly, the *hina* dolls are also mentioned in *Makura no sōshi* (The Pillow Book): "Things that make one long for times past: withered heartvine *(aoi)*, the accessories for the *hina* doll stand *(Hina asobi no chōdo)*." See Ikeda Kikan et al., eds., *Makura no sōshi—Murasaki shikibu nikki*, vol. 19 of Nihon koten bungaku taikei series (Iwanami Shoten, 1958), p. 72.

17. *KAZS* 4:386. Kōda's daughter Aoki Tama tells another version of this story in her *Kaeritakatta uchi*, p. 54ff.

18. In the original: *Kotaeru kokoro no naka ni wa hete kita nengetsu ga tamatte iru, ano toki chichi ga itta koto, shūtome no itta koto, somemonoya no hanashi, minna watashi no dodai ni natte iru.*

19. Yoshida Seiichi, *Zuihitsu no sekai* (Ōfūsha, 1980), p. 70.

20. Tomi Suzuki, *Narrating the Self* (Stanford: Stanford University Press, 1996), p. 98. She contends that the *zuihitsu* ("personal essay or *pensee*") became accepted as a "journalistic literary genre comparable in status to the novel, poetry, and drama" in the late Taishō period (1920s). She notes that journals such as *Bungei Shunjū* have contained *zuihitsu* sections since the early 1920s and cites the appearance of the journal *Zuihitsu* in 1923 (pp. 205–206, n. 29).

21. Tanizaki Jun'ichirō, *In'ei raisan,* in *Tanizaki Jun'ichirō zenshū* (Chūō Kōronsha, 1968), 20:547–548. Translations are mine. For a complete English version see Tanizaki Jun'ichirō, *In Praise of Shadows,* trans. Thomas J. Harper and Edward G. Seidensticker (New Haven: Leete's Island Books, 1977).

22. *KAZS* 4:373.

23. Ibid., p. 371.

24. Haga Kōshirō, "'Nihontekina bi' no seiritsu to tenkai," in *Geido shisō shū,* ed. Haga Kōshirō, Nihon no shisō series (Chikuma Shobō, 1971), 7:15.

25. Nishio Minoru, ed., *Hōjōki Tsurezuregusa,* Nihon koten bungaku taikei series (Iwanami Shoten, 1957), 30:156.

26. Earl Miner has aptly called this method in *haikai* and *renga* (linked verse) a "principle of addition." See Earl Miner and Hiroko Odagiri, trans., *The Monkey's Straw Raincoat* (Princeton: Princeton University Press, 1981), p. 44.

27. *KAZS* 4:380.

28. Ibid., p. 383.

29. Ibid., p. 371.

30. My discussion is indebted to G. W. Sargent's introduction to his translation of Ihara Saikaku's *The Japanese Family Storehouse: or The Millionaire's Gospel Modernised* (Cambridge: Cambridge University Press, 1959), p. xxxiii ff., and to Robert Danly's comments on Saikaku and Higuchi Ichiyō in his *In the Shade of Spring Leaves* (New Haven: Yale University Press, 1981), pp. 112–128.

31. Danly, *Shade of Spring Leaves,* p. 116.

32. Kōda repeatedly said and wrote that she takes the same approach to writing as she does to doing the household chores *(kaji zatsuyō to onaji)*. In some of her less successful works, this is obvious.

33. In the original: *Sukoshi ōburina sugatami o watashi wa tsukatte iru.* See Kōda Aya, "Mono iwanu isshō no tomo," *Fujin kōron* 51(7) (1966):119; *KAZS* 15:368 (hereafter "Tomo").

34. Ivan Morris makes note of Sei Shōnagon's commentary in *The Pillow Book.* He regards her repetition of evaluative terms such as *"okashi"* ("charming") and *"medetashi"* ("splendid") as a "deliberate stylistic device"—one likely to irritate Western readers but bound to please Japanese audiences. These ubiquitous adverbs and adjectives affirm and reaffirm the nature of the narrative voice. In other words, they guide readers in their apprehension of the narrator. The significance of the evaluative terms, moreover, shifts from usage to usage, depending on context and matter at hand. The speaker does not pause to explain these highly ambiguous terms. Pervading the work is the assumption that both the writer and reader possess similar outlooks and values. This assumption stems not only from the historical reality of Heian aristocratic life but also from a tremendous sense of authority and assurance. See Morris, *Pillow Book,* p. 264.

35. *KAZS* 15:368.

36. Ibid., p. 385.

37. Ibid., p. 378.

38. Ibid., p. 379.

39. Ibid., p. 380.

40. Ibid., p. 381.

41. "Wagakuni no watakushi shōsetsukatachi ga, watakushi o shinji, shiseikatsu o shinjite nan no fuan mo kanjinakatta no wa, watakushi no sekai ga sono mama shakai no sugata de atte. . . ." See Kobayashi Hideo, *Kobayashi Hideo zenshū* (Shinchōsha, 1978), 3:134. See also William F. Sibley, "Naturalism in Japanese Literature," *Harvard Journal of Asiatic Studies* 28 (1968):165.

42. *KAZS* 15:372.

43. Ibid., pp. 373–374.

44. Ibid., p. 370.

45. Ibid., p. 371.

46. Ibid., pp. 371–372.

47. Ibid., p. 375.

48. Ibid., p. 376.

49. Ibid., pp. 376–377.

50. Ibid., p. 378.

51. Tanizaki's story appears in English translation as "Arrowroot" in Anthony Chambers, trans., *The Secret History of the Lord of Musashi and Arrowroot* (New York: Knopf, 1982). Kafū's "Bokutō kidan" is the title story of Edward Seidensticker, trans., *A Strange Tale from East of the River* (Rutland, Vt.: Tuttle, 1965).

52. *Fujin Kōron,* founded in 1919 and still published today, has been a leading periodical directed at a female readership. The magazine started as a serious forum for the "new woman" and promoted feminist ideals, but with the changing tides of politics it gradually became more popular in its content and appeal. *Fujin Kōron* has featured the works of such writers as Kawabata Yasunari, Akutagawa Ryūnosuke, Ariyoshi Sawako, and Mishima Yukio, as well as translations of the writings of Sartre, Françoise Sagan, and others.

53. *Fujin Kōron* 51(7) (1966):118.

54. For an excellent discussion of the *watakushi shōsetsu* see Edward Fowler, *The Rhetoric of Confession* (Berkeley: University of California Press, 1988). See Nakamura Mitsuo, *Kindai bungaku o dō yomu ka* (Shinchōsha, 1980), pp. 251–256, on the status of the narrator in the *watakushi shōsetsu.* Thomas Rimer, in his *Modern Japanese Fiction and Its Traditions* (Princeton: Princeton University Press, 1978), attempts to link the *zuihitsu* and *watakushi shōsetsu* (p. 78). See also Nishida Masayoshi's discussion of this subject in *Watakushi shōsetsu saihakken* (Ōfūsha, 1973). Janet Walker points to the *watakushi shōsetsu* in its "identification of the author" with "the hero" as an "heir to the traditional genre of the *zuihitsu.*" Furthermore, she writes that the *watakushi shōsetsu* is analogous to certain European literary forms; see Walker's *The Japanese Novel of the Meiji Period and the Ideal of Individualism* (Princeton: Princeton University Press, 1979), pp. 103–104. For a discussion of premodern identification of the expressive or emotional with "truth" *(jitsu)* and the descriptive as fiction or falsehood see David Pollack, *The Fracture of Meaning: Japan's Synthesis of China from the Eighth Through the Eighteenth Centuries* (Princeton: Princeton University Press, 1986), pp. 200–216. William Sibley offers the convincing argument that the narrow scope of *watakushi shōsetsu* arises more from "the writer's unwillingness to give up the accuracy of a single viewpoint for the uncertainties of a wider narrative perspective" than from the simple urge to equate historical author with narrator. These naturalist writers, Sibley contends, were "ill at ease in a complex world of their own making" and preferred accuracy afforded by their own perceptions. See Sibley, "Naturalism in Japanese Literature," pp. 163–165. This notion is confirmed in Kume Masao's (1891–1952) famous 1925 treatise "'Watakushi' shōsetsu to 'shinkyō' shōsetsu": "I simply cannot believe that art *(geijutsu),* in its true sense, means the fabrication *(sōzō)* of another person's life. . . . I can only conceive of art as simply the recreation *(sai-*

gen) of the life that one has lived." See Yoshida Seiichi, ed., *Kindai bungaku hyōron taikei,* 10 vols. (Kadokawa Shoten, 1971–1975), 6:52–53. Consequently, Kume Masao regarded such nineteenth-century European novels as *Madame Bovary* and *Crime and Punishment* as having literary merit but nevertheless being "mere constructs" *(tsukurimono)* or entertainment (and hence without serious purpose). Kobayashi Hideo singles out these aspects of Kume's writing in his discussion of the *watakushi shōsetsu* called "Watakushi shōsetsu ron" in his *Zenshū* (Shinchōsha, 1978), 3:134–135. See also Suzuki, *Narrating the Self.*

55. Nishida Masayoshi discusses the link between classical literature and the *watakushi shōsetsu* in his *Watakushi shōsetsu saihakken,* pp. 27–29 and 242. Irmela Hijiya-Kirschnereit examines this issue in "The Concepts of Tradition in Modern Japanese Literature," in *Tradition and Modern Japan,* ed. P. G. O'Neill (Tenterden, Kent: Norbury, 1981), pp. 206–216.

56. George B. Sansom, trans., "Essays in Idleness," in *Anthology of Japanese Literature,* ed. Donald Keene (New York: Grove Press, 1955), p. 234. In the original: *Hitori tomoshibi no moto ni bun o hirogete, minu yo no hito o tomo to suru zo, koyono nagusamu waza naru.* Sansom uses the word "converse" as a noun in his translation.

57. Ibid., p. 235. In the original: *Shizukani omoeba, yorozuni suginishi kata no koishisa nomi zo senkatanaki.*

58. Barbara Herrnstein Smith, *Poetic Closure* (Chicago: University of Chicago Press, 1968), p. 146.

5

Torn Sleeves and the Anti-Oedipal Family

Never has there been a more dazzling and diverse list of titles available to a reader than in the Japan of the late twentieth century. Heedless of critics' insistence that fiction is dead, hard and soft covers enclose a dizzying array of narratives: some heavy on plot, some not; written by women or men; boldly pornographic or discreetly lyrical; avant garde or conventional in style and conception; realist or fantastic; proposing radical visions or nostalgic dreams. Despite revised economic forecasts, publication of domestic authors flourishes. The thirst for foreign books cannot be quenched, it seems, for translated novels dominate the best-seller list. If the printed word alone cannot satisfy, *manga* (comics) for every imaginable micro-audience flood the newsstands.

Despite the good health of the Japanese publishing industry, the revival of interest in Kōda Aya's works after her death in 1990 was not entirely predictable. During the last years of her life, Kōda had stopped writing. And although the critical establishment had broadened to embrace feminist and poststructuralist points of view, few critics stepped forward to offer new readings of her oeuvre. Despite Kōda's success during her lifetime, in fact, one of her most compelling and accomplished novels languished unnoticed for nearly three decades. Although *Kimono* had appeared serially in a journal during 1965–1966, the novel was not published as a single volume until 1993. After Kōda's death in 1990 at the age of eighty-six, five volumes of her works that had previously appeared in journals were released in book form.

Among the books published in 1993, readers flocked to such novels as Matsuura Rieko's (b. 1958) *The Training of Big Toe P* (Oyayubi P no shugyō jidai), featuring a female protagonist who enjoys unprecedented adventures because of the transformation of her big toe into a penis. The reading public had grown accustomed, even blasé, about the fiction of Yamada Eimi (b. 1959), whose texts "blaze with erotic descriptions of women pursuing sexual fulfillment with a blatant disregard for anything or anyone or any morality that might interfere with that pursuit."[1] Despite such titillating choices, a large audience chose Kōda's novel *Kimono*. But if Matsuura and other writers of her kind focused on women disrobed and genitalia unrobed and out of control,

Kōda, as her title suggests, evokes the clothing people wear close to their skin, not the flesh itself. Although *Kimono,* like Matsuura's novel, sold well, critics at first approached *Kimono* rather unsure about where it fits into contemporary literature—partly because the novel, along with much of Kōda's writing and career, has been viewed as suspect and even ideologically regressive. The outlines of Kōda's biography and the recurring motifs in her works seem to suggest a profound conservatism, and some Japanese critics have viewed Kōda's writings as icons "of cultural conservative rejuvenation."[2] But, in the final analysis, is this the strongest reading?

Literary Daughters and Changes in Literary Criticism

Two factors have contributed to the view that Kōda Aya and her writings are conservative. First, she is among the "literary daughters" of postwar Japanese fiction—a group that includes Enchi Fumiko (whose father was scholar Ueda Mannen) and Tsushima Yūko (whose father was novelist Dazai Osamu). After divorcing her husband in 1938, Kōda returned to her father Rohan's house and cared for him during the last years of his life. To a greater degree than other female writers with famous writer fathers, then, Kōda has been viewed as a "father-identified daughter" because she founded her literary career—wittingly or not—by writing biographical sketches of her father Kōda Rohan and because, though her style and interests do not resemble those of Rohan's much, she compared her own writings to his (inevitably in an unfavorable light). She painted herself the unworthy daughter: the daughter who declared that, lacking the artistry and dedication to art of her father (and the rest of his family, for that matter), she should, by all rights, cease writing altogether. Despite this masochistic expression of humility, Kōda did not in fact abandon the brush but instead went on to have a productive and varied career that spanned four decades.

And second, there are no sexually aggressive women in suits or tight jeans in her works. Kōda's novels, short stories, and essays are firmly grounded in the mundane present. They are conspicuous in their lack of sex, escapist fantasies, mythically potent women, and overt political protest. Many of her stories revolve around capable young women, or wise old women, at home, the only haven for them, even in the midst of troubled families. The farthest afield Kōda goes is the liminal space of the geisha house (in the novel *Flowing*), but even then the subject position rests with a widow working there as a maid.[3]

Other Japanese "literary daughters," whether they mention their own fathers or not, seem to rebel in their narrative against Japan's patriarchal system. Enchi, in her novella *Masks* (Onnamen; 1958), for example, probes the authoritative psychological and seemingly supernatural powers of women and links them with premodern archetypes of female potency. Tsushima Yuko depicts the lives of independent single mothers in an urban setting. One may regard Kōda Aya as a woman "divided against herself" who has embraced the "'phallic' task of her discourse"—a foe of the "'normative' daughter who potentially enjoys 'autonomy.'" In this reading, Kōda's career serves as a literal confirmation of Roland Barthes' assertion that the "absent father is the single source for telling tales" and of Lacan's Father that is outside history—that is, the oedipal dialectic "that insists upon revealing the father as law, as the gaze . . . or as the symbolic."[4] Critic Inoue Kazuko contends that Kōda started her career as a "spokesperson for patriarchy" because she wrote memoirs about her father.[5]

Yet Kōda's work does not reaffirm patterns of male domination and, moreover, defies the "claim of universal patriarchy."[6] In the first place, readers must take into account the configurations of Japanese gender hierarchy, which, although we may regard them as patriarchal, do not demand precisely the same reverence for the father/word/phallus maintained in Anglo-European textual traditions. Kōda furthermore does not espouse the type of female narcissism based on mythical ideals (as does Okamoto Kanoko) or the sexual utopia promised by Yamada Eimi. Kōda expresses a distinctive vision of the home and family life that does not subscribe to "a familial and literary hierarchy" predicated on father-identified daughters.[7] In fact, some of her narratives, especially considered apart from her biography, seek to disrupt male-dominated culture and deny the assumed centrality and universality of masculine values. Otherwise, how would Kōda's writings retain their power among a changing readership and critical establishment? Indeed, even Inoue Kazuko's linking of Kōda with patriarchal power proves to be more a perfunctory acknowledgment of gender theory than a careful examination of the workings of patriarchy or a condemnation. Inoue's insightful reading of Kōda's work does not lead to the conclusion that the author promoted patriarchal values. The fact that Kōda's conceptual basis lies apart from critical approaches such as feminism and gender studies does not make her antifeminist. Indeed, it would be a mistake to obscure Kōda's achievements as a writer simply because her writings do not fit neatly into familiar social and ideological frameworks of Anglo-European feminism. For Kōda the intimate father/daughter bond figured prominently in her career and her narratives. Esperanza Ramirez-Christensen notes that "in the course of writing about her father with a degree of objectivity, Kōda discovered the authoritative voice, one not grounded solely in resentment or resistance of her father."[8]

Another consideration is useful in evaluating Kōda's function in the postwar world of Japanese narrative. That is, a significant change has occurred in the reception of Kōda's works in Japan over the past fifty years—one that tells as much about shifts in the critical establishment as about Kōda's writing. Moreover, non-Japanese and even contemporary Japanese readers bring to Kōda's novels assumptions about her ties with her father and the psychoanalytical implications of this permutation of the "family romance." Yamashita Etsuko, for one, has insisted on the need for a more nuanced understanding of Japanese patriarchy, because many feminist and Marxist critics have employed Western notions of patriarchy as monolithic without attempting to define the differences between Judeo-Christian notions of the family and social organization and those of Japan. Although she has not developed a comprehensive account of Japan's patriarchy, either in a diachronic or synchronic sense, Yamashita's attempts to decenter critical habits that posit an all-powerful, originating Father or a solely phallocentric textual tradition are suggestive. She emphasizes the importance of the *yōshi* (adoption of a male heir) system as a social practice facilitating maternal lineage. In the literary imagination and in symbolic terms, such social practices relate to the centrality of mother figures in canonical modern literary texts.

Yamashita furthermore points out the connection between the sacred and the Japanese-style feminism *(Nihongata feminizumu)* of writer Hiratsuka Raichō, scholar Takamura Itsue, and novelist Okamoto Kanoko. Both Kanoko and Raichō, for example, have associated women's productive and erotic powers with Buddhism and thus with the sacred.[9] Male critics have favored Okamoto Kanoko's writings because of her synthesis of the mother and lover figures, but also because the dual figures tend to synthesize the best of the East (Buddhist compassion) and a passion learned from the West. Hiratsuka Raichō's famous essay that begins "in the beginning, woman was the sun" *(genshi josei wa taiyō de atta)* links the female and the maternal variously to the Shinto deity Amaterasu and to Zen Buddhism, with reference to Nietzsche's thought as well. Yamashita, examining the fascination of the postwar male critical establishment with the "mother," insists that this tendency should be understood not purely in individualistic, psychological terms of a boy and his mother: the *yōshi* system and other social practices, she argues, contribute to the production of "mother complex" *(mazakon)* literature. In other words, Yamashita shifts the blame for regressive tendencies in adult men onto the men themselves rather than finding fault with the mother, who is often described as a *sokubaku* (restrictive force). In any case, any account of gender hierarchy in the symbolic and textual realm must take into account the paradoxical relationship between, on the one hand, feminist writers who seek to resuscitate ancient images of sacred woman and strong mother as a means of enhancing woman's power in an age when female social and economic status are low and, on the other, masculinist authors who view escape from mother/son bonds as the key to radical liberation.

Yet in Kōda's works the symbolic order seems to break down. Contrary to the surface evidence of her status as a father-identified daughter, she writes (especially in *Flowing* and *Kimono*) of worlds of women, where men are marginal, where the imperatives of the Freudian and Lacanian symbolic order are conspicuously weak.[10] Not that fathers are absent from Kōda's texts, for they are not, but her most powerful works decenter heterosexual liaison—not in favor of homosexual union, but in order to define and depict women in other ways. The absence of positive models of heterosexuality in the central consciousness of her texts, it might be argued, serves paradoxically to valorize such relations. But the narrative logic of Kōda's texts does not operate as a means of hovering on the edge of a void or mourning a loss. If anything, autonomy and satisfaction are threatened by the orthodoxy of marriage.

Kimonos in 1960s Japan

As readers we might expect that a writer with such ambiguous ties with feminism and patriarchy would write a book ostensibly about the kimono. The title of the novel *Kimono* indeed suggests Kōda's privileging of iconic and idealized signs of Japan's Official Traditional Culture. But the ambiguity of the term "kimono" exposes the potential for double profit, or irony, in the narrative itself. First serialized in the journal *Shinchō* during the mid-1960s, this novel rode the crest of the kimono boom occasioned by the return of economic prosperity in postwar Japan. While the Pacific War marked the end of the kimono as everyday wear for most Japanese people, the mid-1960s kimono rage reestablished this traditional robe's importance in Japanese culture. But this time the kimono entered the "realm of the decorative," as is suggested by its main functions today in ceremonial and ritual events such as weddings, funerals, and tea ceremony.[11] Indeed, Kōda's novel may be regarded as homage to the end of the age of the kimono, for it is set in late Taishō and early Shōwa (late 1910s and 1920s). The Great Kantō Earthquake of 1923, which destroyed vast parts of the Tokyo–Yokohama metropolitan area and had profound economic and social implications, has also been described as "something of a turning point in Japanese fashion history" because many of the people who lost their homes and property in the fires replaced their kimonos with Western-style clothing. Indeed, the sleeves and length of kimonos were cited by some as a hindrance to people trying to escape the flames after the earthquake.[12]

The history of the kimono, both as garment and as cultural icon, is marked by gender differences. For many urban men, even in the prewar era, Western dress became the standard outfit for work whereas the kimono was something to change into in the comfort of one's own home. More women retained kimonos as their daily wear until the pressures of the Pacific War and government imperatives dictated practicality and efficiency in dress and, later, American and European popular culture held sway during the Allied Occupation and after. The increasing relegation of the kimono to the decorative realm, as well as the postwar marketing of beautiful kimonos targeted at female consumers, bolstered the identification of women and their traditional social roles with the kimono.

Not long after the publication, in 1993, of the novel *Kimono,* Kōda's publisher Shinchōsha capitalized on this postwar image of kimono as art—as signifying Traditional/Exotic Japan and lending an image of "high cultural respectability"—by producing a book called *Inside Kōda Aya's Wardrobe* (Kōda Aya no tansu no hikidashi; 1995) replete with pictures of Kōda's many kimonos (and some of Rohan's as well) and essays by Kōda's daughter, Aoki Tama. During her lifetime Kōda became known as a woman who always wore a kimono in public, a fact that invited the ire of contemporaries who criticized her for being too prim and proper. Only in her later years, when she became interested in traveling throughout the country to see virgin forests and landslides, did Kōda wear long pants and jackets—that is, *yōfuku* (Western clothing).

Kōda's novel *Kimono,* however, refutes this postwar image of the kimono as Official Kimono—an unserviceable silk decorative robe that restricts and binds its female wearer into a similarly decorative and subordinate role. Contrary to the cluster of images that the title suggests and the promotion efforts of the publisher, Kōda succeeds in revealing "how costuming can be an extremely important element in producing pleasures for male and female spectators that are neither ideologically regressive nor immediately recuperable into the sexual agendas of patriarchal dominations."[13] The novel opens with its preadolescent protagonist, Nishigaki Rutsuko, being scolded by her mother and grandmother for having ripped off the sleeves of her kimono:

In the center of the triangular space circumscribed by Rutsuko, her grand-mother, and her mother lay one torn sleeve. Rutsuko's mother was not pleased.

Sky blue with a purple iris design, the scrap had once been the left sleeve of the padded underjacket that Rutsuko wore. But now its upper edge hung torn and frayed, and only the lower hem, lined with red, showed no sign of damage. With its cotton padding spilling out onto the floor, the sleeve looked pathetic.

That morning, after getting dressed, Rutsuko had reached around with her right hand, seized the left sleeve of the underjacket, and ripped it right off. She then stuffed it into the trash can and left for school. It didn't take her mother long to discover the discarded sleeve and to put it out on the floor, ready for Rutsuko's return that afternoon.

"What in the world were you thinking of?" her mother jumped on her immediately, "destroying your own clothes like that?"

Rutsuko tried to explain about how the narrow padded sleeves bunched up around her shoulder, and how uncomfortable it felt, but her mother could not be swayed.

"That's ridiculous," her mother retorted, "I put new cotton wadding in that sleeve—the softest cotton there is. And now you tell me it's too bulky? I've had enough of your lies."

"Okay, Mother, why don't you come to my gym class and try doing exer-cises with all that on your arms?" said Rutsuko angrily. "I can't even hold my arms out straight."

Without missing a beat, her mother asked, "What did you do with the other sleeve?"

"Nothing. I still have it on."

Before Rutsuko had finished her sentence, her mother pounced on her, yanked off her kimono, and then pulled off what was left of the padded gar-ment, one sleeve missing and the other hanging by threads. . . .

[After her mother had left the room], Rutsuko's grandmother asked, "Rut-suko, you never did like that jacket, did you?"

Afraid of another scolding, Rutsuko chose not to reply.

"That underjacket is so pretty, but I can tell that you don't like the way it feels, do you? Tell me, though, it did keep you nice and warm, didn't it?"

"Very warm."

"Don't forget that part. Your mother grew up in the snow country, so of course she stuffs clothes with lots of cotton. . . . So the next time she makes you something with too much padding in it, just pretend that it's cold and snowing outside, and put up with it, instead of ripping off your sleeves."[14]

Feminist critics have seized on this passage as a moment of discursive subversion. For Inoue Kazuko, the kimono becomes a metaphor for the constraints of femininity forced on women by society. She notes that many coming-of-age novels trace the process of women "killing their self" *(jiko o koroshite iku)*, while male protagonists follow the pattern of asserting their sense of selfhood as they become adults.[15] Mizumura Minae concurs with Inoue: this opening section, she declares, indicates that the novel does not concern a woman who wears a kimono but rather a woman who is able to take off a kimono she dislikes.[16]

Rutsuko lives with her extended family in *shitamachi* ("downtown," the working-class area of Tokyo) in the early 1920s, and the novel traces her journey from childhood through adolescence to early adulthood as well as her relationship with her family, friends, and community. Because of the focus on Rutsuko and her two older sisters and arrangements for their marriages, some critics have called the novel a *Makioka Sisters* (Sasameyuki, 1948, by Tanizaki Jun'ichirō) told in Tokyo dialect.[17] To a greater extent than other of Kōda's full-length novels, *Kimono* encompasses a broad range of social relations, historical context, and economy, including the repercussions of the 1923 Great Kantō Earthquake.[18]

In the novel *Kimono* Kōda unearths the motivations for women's desire for marriage and the fissures that lead to consideration of other courses for life. The Nishigaki family has three daughters; the elder two regard marriage as the sole possibility for their adult lives. That in prewar Japan a middle-class woman, who had no pressing financial need to work, would want to marry may seem all too natural a conclusion. Even though she was writing *Kimono* in the 1960s, Kōda's narrative realm does not allow for the daring possibility of escape from the oppressive, capitalist patriarchal system through art—as seen in the prewar stories of Hayashi Fumiko, for example, or in the unfettered eroticism espoused by Uno Chiyo. *Kimono,* in fact, reminds the reader how extraordinary such nomadic and rebellious authors as Hayashi and Uno were.

Kōda's interests lie, instead, in discovering the motives and emotions of ordinary women whose sense of personhood and imagination existed largely within preordained social and cultural definitions. Kōda shows vividly the significance of middle-class wifehood in prewar Japan, the extent to which young women construed marriage as a means of expressing or embodying filial piety, and the degree to which it was possible for women to view marriage practically, in familial, economic, and contractual terms, rather than romantic or personal terms. How these norms came to be internalized can be learned from the recent scholarship on women's history in Japan, which shows the degree to which the state and politics have defined women's roles and sense of personhood.[19]

In *Kimono,* Rutsuko's eldest sister (who remains unnamed) and her middle sister Mitsuko revel in the process of the arranged marriage. Although the beautiful eldest daughter initially attempts to take matters into her own hands by sneaking off on a date with a man of her own choosing, she quickly acquiesces to the demands of her parents to follow the socially sanctioned method of finding a suitable partner: arranged marriage. Selfish and inconsiderate though she is, middle daughter Mitsuko justifies her eagerness to find a husband by claiming that cooperation in arranged marriage and leaving the parental home is her way of being a filial daughter:

> "You just don't get it, do you, Rutsuko? I gave you credit for being a little more grown up than that. Now that sister's gotten married, it's my turn to try. But what am I supposed to do now with Mother sick in bed? I just want to cry. What am I supposed to do when someone invites me out? I just have to get a new kimono . . ." said Mitsuko.
>
> "I can't believe how selfish you are, Mitsuko," Rutsuko retorted. "You already have nice kimonos, like the one you got for sister's wedding. Why don't you wear that one?"
>
> "That one's too fancy for a date. . . ."
>
> "I wish you could hear yourself. Mother's lying in there in rags, and all you can think about is how pretty you want to look."
>
> Mitsuko snapped, "You brat! What does a child like you know anyway? Just wait till you're nineteen years old. If you have something you want to sell, you have to make it look nice—dress it with flowers—or no one will buy it. So I have to look my best so someone will have me. It's my filial duty to get married as quickly as I can. Don't you get it? I don't want to end up like our cousins, the ones who just hang around home and never leave. They're a burden to their parents."[20]

Indeed, Rutsuko later reflects on the financial burden of families with many daughters and the saying that a man with three daughters is condemned to poverty. The parents spend a great deal of money on kimonos for the initial meeting with potential suitors, the dates, the wedding kimonos, and then the trousseau for the bride.

Rutsuko, though, differs greatly from her older sisters. She even bears an unusual name redolent of foreign origins—perhaps even biblical (Ruth).[21] What distinguishes Rutsuko is not her social aspirations. If anything, her siblings know with greater certainty what they want to do with their lives (become wives and mothers) and they achieve those goals. Rutsuko embodies the encounter of women during Meiji and Taishō with the options offered by middle-class life in a parliamentary democracy: some seized the moment for its promise of radical liberation; others floated, however, suspended in the openness of the future.[22] Rutsuko devotes herself socially to the service of her family and privately to her love of kimonos as a source of her own sensual pleasure and also a "form of human relationship" that enables her to understand those around her.

From the start, Rutsuko shows great discrimination in her choice of clothing:

> She had two pieces of clothing that she liked the best. One was a cotton *yukata* that she wore constantly, which was light, soft, and did whatever Rutsuko wanted. It never got in the way, no matter how she moved, and was the coolest of all her summer clothes. The fabric was indeed quite soft, but still Rutsuko thought fondly of its crisp texture when it was freshly washed. Plus, even if it got dirty, Rutsuko's mother didn't get upset, because the *yukata* hadn't cost much to begin with. When someone gave the family cotton fabric during the summer gift-giving season, Mother would sometimes choose a bolt for making a *yukata* especially for Rutsuko, rather than having one handed down from her sisters. Though her sisters might find fault with the pattern of a fabric that wasn't of their own choosing and refuse to wear it, for Rutsuko the way the cotton felt meant infinitely more than the pattern or design.[23]

Moreover, kimonos are the means by which Rutsuko comes to develop her own sense of personhood, which at first presents itself distinctly because it centers on her pleasure in sensual interaction and encounters with cotton, silk, and wool. One afternoon Rutsuko goes to play at the home of her friend Maki, whose father is a Buddhist priest. Maki attempts to fold up the voluminous robe that her father has just taken off:

> Maki sighed, "I can't do it. You try, Rutsuko."
>
> How wonderfully light it was! Light, and felt incredibly good in her hands. As she shook the robe out, Rutsuko caught sight of the diamond design woven into the sheer fabric as they danced up into the air, folding and doubling over each other, then separating, and finally the whole thing settling quietly onto the beige of the tatami mat.

"It's so beautiful!"

Rutsuko felt a violent urge to put on the robe, and so she slipped her hand into an opening. She was pleased at the sight of her own hand through the intricate white net of the cloth, with the diamond-back pattern in relief.

"I really want to try it on. What do you think?"

"Go ahead."

But there was so much cloth there that Rutsuko didn't know how to put her body in.[24]

Gradually, as the text evolves, clothing in Rutsuko's world becomes increasingly multifaceted and complex as she begins to understand that garments constitute a form of self-presentation and the means by which others apprehend her, define her, and desire her. In her early youth, Rutsuko personifies the notion that fashion facilitates liberation: "The empire of fashion indeed signifies a universalization of modern standards, but in the process that promotes an unprecedented emancipation and destandardization of the subjective sphere. . . . To see hedonism merely as an instrument of social control and manipulation is a serious error; in fact it is above all a vector of the affirmation of private individuality."[25]

For Rutsuko, the moments of sensual encounter with woven substance lead to desire for possession: the feel of silk brocade on her foot as she rebels and kicks at a doctor trying to treat her so impresses her that she insists on having a kimono of her own from that fabric. She enjoys the sensation of having the wide trouserlike *hakama* close around her, like a bud tightening. Her innocent celebration of sensuality does not last long, however, for she becomes a woman not so much through physiological change as by becoming the object of man's desire—a process again facilitated by clothing's relationship to the body. After several incidents when men on commuter trains touch and rub up against her, Rutsuko has a long talk with Grandmother, who interprets the incidents as signs that Rutsuko has become a full-fledged adult: a woman *(ichininmae)*:

Well then, I'd rather not be an adult, if that's what it means, thought Rutsuko. It's so vulgar. She makes it sound like once you become a woman, you're at the mercy of all these disgusting men. It's not as if I did anything to provoke them. If that's what it means to be a woman, I don't want any part of it.

"You're overreacting, Rutsuko," said Grandmother. "There are other ways to look at it, you know. You're mad about what happened, but there are some girls who would be excited. They'd think it proved how attractive they are to men."

"Not me."

"People are different—that's all I'm saying. Anyway, enough of your complaints. Think a little more about why those men acted that way toward you. I happen to think it's because of what you were wearing. What do you think of that kimono of yours?"

"I love it! You yourself said that it looks good on me."

"Is that all?"

"What do you mean? What else did you expect me to say?"

"I'll tell you what else. I thought young people were supposed to be so clever! I expected more of you, Rutsuko. I suppose you've never thought about what horizontal stripes do to you? Not that you need to think about it. A mirror will tell you all you need to know."

"So what is it about stripes?"

"They show your body as clearly as if you were naked," explained Grandmother. "Don't you see? Stripes emphasize all of the curves."

. . . That, according to Grandmother, was what had led to all the unwanted attention from various men. And, indeed, this made some sense to Rutsuko. So it was the three—the wearer, the clothing, and the viewer—who all bore equal portions of the blame.[26]

The success of the single-volume version of *Kimono* in 1993 owes much to the nostalgia evoked in the novel for an era when the kimono was not a "national costume," redolent of cultural jingoism or exotic Japan, but simply the clothing that people wore in their everyday life. As Mizumura Minae suggests, even in late twentieth-century Japan, although men may lump together woman and kimono and regard them both as existing in another realm, women in fact view the kimono as exotic—as residing on the other side *(mukō-gawa)* from the quotidian.[27] Still, in the divide between Mitsuko and Rutsuko's attitudes toward the kimono, the reader detects "the inclination to read consumer culture as a dual system of meaning with the economic life of the commodity impinging upon its life as an object of cultural significance."[28] Mitsuko regards a kimono's importance as lying in its utility: it constitutes a tool for improving her appearance and thereby her desirability as a marriage partner. Rutsuko, however, possesses an intimate, highly sensual relationship with kimonos and the fabric from which they are tailored.

Another more significant source of *Kimono*'s power lies in Kōda's brilliant evocation of Rutsuko's sense of interiority in the here and now as an adolescent female. During the 1980s and 1990s, the concept of female adolescence *(shōjo)* has been transformed from a stage of life to a utopian state of mind in opposition to jaded adulthood and the harrowing brevity of youth in the late twentieth century. While earlier, canonical works sanctioned the male literary youth *(bungaku seinen)* as subject, subsequent shifts in readers, the critical establishment, and the literary marketplace have elevated the *shōjo* and her world to a position of legitimacy, at least in the popular imagination.[29] Thus while Rutsuko's sisters express their eagerness to end their adolescence and become women by making themselves into the wives of men, Rutsuko has discovered all the riches of life in her own youth. Her hesitation to marry—even the trouble she has deciding whether marriage, work, or college should be her next step—suggest both the luxury of her middle-class existence and the gratification she gains from the forms and textures of cloth and clothing. Compared to the sensual pleasure that Rutsuko derives from trying on a new type of brocade or the extreme pain occasioned by the donning of a scratchy wool kimono, her first menstrual period is hardly more than a physical and psychological inconvenience:

> The bath felt rather hot to Rutsuko, so she stayed in just for a moment and then stood up to get out. As she stepped out of the tub, Grandmother, who was over by the faucet, let out a cry. Rutsuko glanced down and saw for the first time dots of red blood down on the floor between her feet.
>
> "Oh my gosh," exclaimed Rutsuko. Startled, she crouched down and rested her head on her knees.
>
> Grandmother brought Rutsuko's futon into her own room and kept her company. "Tomorrow, I'll make you some red rice and beans to celebrate. That's what I did for your sisters." Rutsuko, though, would have none of it. Wide awake, she cast her eyes to the light filtering dimly through the small window and said, "I really wish you wouldn't. I don't want something so shameful advertised like that." This was not an occasion for celebration. Rutsuko found it so unpleasant. She felt uneasiness and disgust.
>
> "I was afraid you might react this way, Rutsuko," Grandmother answered. "That you'd find it disgusting and painful. I'll tell you, though, you're the only one who can make yourself feel better. You've got to stop dwelling on the discomfort and try to forget about it. And you mustn't get cranky. That in itself is an advertisement."[30]

Thus the onset of menstruation does not signal to Rutsuko her own reproductive potential. Even the grandmother celebrates this passage into adolescence in the abstract terms of ritual.[31] Indeed, as we shall see, Rutsuko's grandmother, a pivotal figure in the text, encourages her granddaughter's prolonged enjoyment of virginal adolescence. *Kimono* concerns the prolonging of adolescence, on one young woman's part, in contrast to her sisters who regard it instrumentally as a passage to a more significant stage of life: heterosexual union, reproduction, and entrance into an economic contract with someone other than one's parents.

Long known as an author who writes from the "five senses" *(gokan),* Kōda confirms her interest in evoking subjectivity through sensuality—much as Tanizaki valorizes and elaborates "an aesthetic disposition that treats sensations as ideas, and that replaces the force of logic with the irresistibility of the caress."[32] In Kōda's case, this logic of the senses does not, however, align itself with a fascist or jingoistic intent, for Rutsuko's celebration of her own sensuality does not preclude an enlightened awareness of class and gender hierarchy. In her creation of Rutsuko, Kōda evokes a conception of interiority that rests on Rutsuko's tactile experiences with the fabric of kimonos—the various weights and textures of cotton, wool, and silk—and the garment's myriad styles and her visual perceptions of the colors and patterns of her own clothing and that of others. While some writers employ the body as a means of evoking the individuality of experience, clothing too attains great significance textually. For as Barthes has written, clothing constitutes

> an excellent poetic object; first, because it mobilizes with great variety all the qualities of matter: substance, form, color, tactility, movement, rigidity, luminosity; next, because touching the body and functioning simultaneously as its substitute and its mask, it is certainly the object of a very important investment; this "poetic" disposition is attested to by the frequency and the quality of vestimentary descriptions in literature.[33]

While part of the reader's journey with Rutsuko takes the form of exploring the social realities of a woman's life and the dynamics of her family, much of the pleasure of *Kimono* derives from the celebration of the feel and meaning of the clothing we wear close to our skin. Although the novel is told in the third person, the idiom of the voice remains in close proximity to that of Rutsuko—as evidenced in the constant fascination with (or rather the compulsion to judge and to raise to the level of extreme pleasure) the fabric and form of fashion. This is not the world of the voyeur or the woman as exhibitionist (as in Kōda's *Flowing*), although Rutsuko learns about that world, too, again from her grandmother. Rutsuko is constantly taught to endure *(gaman)* what she finds unpleasant, to bend her will, yet she remains strong, vibrant, and most of all certain of her own powers of discrimination and judgment. It is cloth that is the object of her pleasure: through garments she is able to gauge the quality of people around her and understand the workings of social and economic class.

Contrasting Figures: Five Generations of Women

If modern Japanese narrative contains an overabundance of indecisive, drifting men who are crippled by the spectacle and contradictions of modernity or the conflicting demands made of their sex—simultaneous authority and dependence—the normally clear thinking and discriminating Rutsuko finds herself burdened by the uninviting possibilities made available to the modern woman in the 1920s. Although Rutsuko considers work and college in her future, she settles, in the end, on an arranged marriage to an eye doctor, a man from the provinces of whom her father and grandmother do not approve. When Rutsuko seeks advice and support, her grandmother, who has cared for her so long, rebuffs her, claiming that Rutsuko's resolve to marry means that she, as Rutsuko's older female relative, has finished with her duties. In the end it is Osono, her father's mistress, who attends to the details of the wedding and Rutsuko's bridal wardrobe and offers her love and understanding.

In many of Kōda's writings, the sense of history and the workings of ideology emanate from her delving into the processes of generational change, especially among women. Rutsuko's confusion about her future stems precisely from her sensitivity to the lives of women around her. Her practical sisters and grandmother regard Rutsuko as stubborn and selfish because of her discriminating taste in kimonos. And while she understands all too clearly their relationship to clothing, she cannot adopt their instrumental approach or their ambitions as women. In any case, the sisters marry and leave: both from the center of the narrative and from Rutsuko's consciousness. What remains a fundamental dilemma to Rutsuko, however, is the tension embodied in the contrasting figures of her own mother and her father's mistress Osono.

Rutsuko's father, a native Tokyoite, married a woman from the countryside who is dependable and conscientious but retains much of the provincialism of her rural upbringing. Although his daughters do not know it, the father has for years also consorted with the elegant Osono, a fellow Tokyoite, who seems to work as a geisha. Rutsuko's first encounter with Osono is accidental, but she feels immediately drawn to the older woman, partly because she shares with Rutsuko a love for the kimono:

> "Your kimono is gorgeous. I just adore that plaid, but then plaid has always been one of my favorites. It looks wonderful on you. Are you fond of plaids, too?" asked Osono.

"Yes, I prefer them to florals," explained Rutsuko. "And this one's my special favorite."

"Oh, I can see why. People usually look good in fabrics they like."

"How true. But you know something about this kimono? I've had to mend it a million times! I've had it since I was little, and now I can only wear it under *hakama*. And see, it's faded a lot up here around the shoulders."

"We're so alike. Once I pick a favorite, I just can't throw it away. The older it gets, the more personality it has. Don't you think so?"

"I couldn't agree more."

"You want to hear something funny? I have a couple of old kimonos that I just keep in a drawer. I never even wear them. My friends laugh at me for wasting space like that, but I can't help it."

"I guess this one will end up in a drawer some day too."

"I wish I could keep all the kimonos I've ever worn."[34]

According to the grandmother, Rutsuko's mother was aware of her husband's relationship with Osono but, being from the snow country, she did not put up a fuss and instead "was tough" *(gaman shita)*. Although Rutsuko frequently feels exasperated at her mother's lack of discrimination about clothes (as illustrated by the overstuffed padded jacket or the scratchy wool kimono that made Rutsuko break out in hives), she loves her mother. When her mother falls ill, Rutsuko nurses her faithfully and empathizes with her mother's anxiety over the father's betrayal. The logic of the narrative—and, so it seems, of the mother's life—ultimately renders her dispensable, however. Soon after her eldest daughter has come to visit her parents for the first time as a new bride, the mother begins to show signs of heart trouble, as if, with her firstborn safely married, she has no further function. Similarly, the chronology of Osono's appearance in the narrative and the mother's subsequent death (though the mother is unaware of Rutsuko's encounter with Osono) suggests that her mother has been supplanted by a kindred spirit in Rutsuko's consciousness. Indeed, even as Rutsuko sits faithfully by her mother's sickbed—willing to comb her oily, unwashed hair and bathe her body and feet (although her sister, revolted by the smell, refuses to)—she notices the shabbiness of the futon and bedding her mother has chosen for herself. Against her mother's wishes, Rutsuko moves her to the silk futon normally reserved for guests and finds a clean, fresh robe to replace the worn one from which the mother is loath to part. Rutsuko, unlike her mother, understands how clothing functions as a means of self-presentation and separation of private and public. Although she puts on her mother's old apron when she takes her place in the kitchen at mealtimes, Rutsuko refuses to wear it all the time, as her mother had done, because she does not wish to be seen by others in something so shabby and poor.

Not only do Rutsuko and Osono have in common a fine taste for fabrics and a sense of style and sensuality, but Rutsuko admires Osono's role as loving partner to her father. After the family has fled their home in the aftermath of the Great Kantō Earthquake and fires, they stay for several days in Ueno Park where they are safe from the flames. In the midst of the masses of homeless people crowded into the park, Rutsuko spots Osono:

> Among the line of people straggling slowly past, Rutsuko caught sight of a spot of white that had stopped moving altogether. It was, she quickly realized, the white of a bandanna tied in a knot on top of someone's head. And then Rutsuko saw that it was the woman, her father's woman—Shimura Sono, the source of Mother's pain and sadness; the person she encountered the day she went with Yūko to pick out a kitten; the woman she felt so comfortable talking with. Without a thought as to the consequences of her actions, Rutsuko rushed over to Osono and stood before her, speechless in her excitement. In an instant, their eyes and arms met. Rutsuko did not know what to say, so she silently led Osono over to where her family sat.
>
> "Father, Grandma, it's Miss Shimura."
>
> "So you're safe? Good," said Father, a note of hope in his voice.
>
> Sono just stood there, her head bowed slightly, staring at the ground, and then, raising her hands to cover her cheeks, barely managed to say, "I'm so glad all of you are safe." She seemed overwhelmed by the chaos of the park, and Rutsuko thought she might be crying.
>
> Rutsuko stood by awkwardly, in an indescribable state of agitation, until at last Grandmother broke the stilted silence by offering Osono some sweets. . . . Osono had already found out that the office where Father worked had burned down, and that Rutsuko and the others had evacuated early on. Although Osono did not say so, Rutsuko guessed that she had gone about asking after the family's whereabouts. And so, there in the midst of that chaos, Rutsuko saw with her own eyes the love that her father and Osono had to hide from the world. It made her think of her own mother. And though she tried her best not to, she compared Osono and her mother. She could hardly label Mother's feelings for her father as shallow. But then she knew that Mother had never felt for him with the depth that Osono did, nor had passion motivated any of her behavior. The quality of emotion belonged to different realms.

Mother lacked subtlety and was not a person of deep feelings. Her evenness and lack of discrimination were desirable traits in a mother and homemaker, but perhaps those qualities in a wife, in a woman, left Father unsatisfied.[35]

The older unmarried woman also represents a rare model of independence and strength. Eventually Osono announces her intention to return home despite the devastation wreaked by the fires. In Osono's bravery, Rutsuko discovers an inspiration she never found with her own mother:

> Osono seemed already to be planning ways to carry on with her life. Rutsuko guessed that Osono had garnered this strength over the many years she had lived on her own. No matter what it took, she would gather all her resources and find some way to make a living. It was the same attitude a man would have: a sense of gallantry that a homemaker did not possess.[36]

Kōda does not resort to tradition versus modernity as a point of contrast between the two women. But this is not because she is unaware of other means of autonomy and self-reliance for women, as is demonstrated in the characters of Rutsuko's two best friends and classmates, Kazuko and Yūko. Whereas Kazuko's family is so poor that she starts working while still in school, Yūko comes from the ranks of the nobility. Rutsuko admires Kazuko for her entrepreneurial resourcefulness in starting a delivery business and subsequently working as a nanny for an American family and then as an office worker. Yūko travels to Europe on her own and attends college.

In some ways *Kimono* seems like an apology for *Flowing,* a novel that presents in uncritical terms the geisha institution—or, at least, in that novel Kōda does not consider the implications of the demimonde romance for the wife waiting faithfully at home. To the last, Rutsuko feels ambivalent about her relationship with Osono because of the affair's effect on her mother, but in the end it is Osono who triumphs as Rutsuko's spiritual mother. The bonds they share are passion and independent-mindedness. That readers today could conceive of the novel *Kimono,* written in the 1960s by a woman in her sixties, as fresh, new, and even feminist in intent, relates to Kōda's attentiveness to female adolescence—or, more accurately, the preheterosexual innocence and purity of the *shōjo,* a central preoccupation in twentieth-century narratives. At the same time, the narrative alludes to premodern literature. Although Kōda portrays Rutsuko as admiring the passion in Osono's relationship with her father, the beauty of their love harks back to Edo dramas. Osono may have something of the independent working woman about her; the father may work for a stockbroker; but the depth of their forbidden relationship alludes to the repressed, smoldering emotions of the Edo courtesan and her merchant-class lover in Kabuki or Edo prose.

In the context of Kōda's oeuvre, it comes as no surprise that the grandmother also claims a central position as wise woman and adviser to Rutsuko. Frequently in the narrative, Rutsuko's interaction with her grandmother takes the form of a lesson with Rutsuko asking questions and the grandmother holding forth wisely. And Grandmother seems to have all the answers about everything from the emotional to the practical: Rutsuko's personality, her relationship with her sisters, Osono and her mother, endurance, narcissism, the family budget, ways to raise money in the aftermath of a horrible earthquake, and, naturally, kimonos. Such is Grandmother's authority and wisdom that one critic insists, in an autobiographical reading, that Rohan's personality is expressed in the grandmother figure. In contrast to other Kōda novels, such as *Little Brother* and *The Fight,* which feature novelist fathers, in *Kimono* Rutsuko's father works in a brokerage firm. Because this father is so dissimilar to the literate Rohan, the Rohan figure must exist elsewhere in the text, Inoue Kazuko suggests. Inadvertently this feminist critic gives credence to the notion that any authoritative figure must be an expression of male authority without considering the possibility of female assumption of such a role.[37] The identification of the grandmother with Rohan (the Father) also ignores the increasing tendency in Kōda's prose to assume the voice of wise woman and authority herself, especially in her essays, as well as to recognize the influence of older female relatives in her life. While to some extent Kōda's idea of narrative authority draws on Rohan's model of transmitter and historian, she carves out a distinctly separate role for herself: one with different philosophical and ideological assumptions that rejects the notion of self-conscious artist and intellectual.

Inoue furthermore insists on identifying the spirit of endurance *(gaman)* that Grandmother teaches to Rutsuko with the "masochism of the good wife/wise mother *(ryōsai kenbo),*" which she terms the "dark side" of women. She notes that Grandmother tells Rutsuko to grin and bear it on several occasions, most significantly when she is forced to wear clothing chosen by her mother. But Inoue fails to mention that, in the narrative as a whole, in stark contrast to these minor instances of youthful surrender, Rutsuko's strength and aesthetic judgment triumph. As is evident in the backlash against the popular 1980's NHK television series *Oshin,* which featured the ultimate in patient heroines, it is tempting to condemn all instances of women enduring adverse conditions simply as remnants of feudal gender roles that teach women to grin and bare it rather than protest. But in reading *Kimono,* it is misleading to high-light the isolated cases in which the grandmother urges Rutsuko to accept her mother's dictates. To do so is to reduce the grandmother and Rutsuko's rela-tionship to a flat, unnuanced one not borne out by the text as a whole. Her rural-born mother, resentful of Rutsuko's aesthetic sense and desire for plea-sure, persists in her misguided attempts to clothe her family properly. And her sisters, who hoard the new and the best kimonos, all too easily capitulate to the clothing tastes of their husbands' families. Over the course of the narrative, poetic justice prevails: these women who lack sufficient aesthetic and practical judgment and inner strength when it comes to wardrobes are punished; the mother suffers from a weak heart and dies; and the vain sister who capitulates to her husband in matters of clothing and life suffers horrible burns over her face and body when trying to flee from the fire in the Great Earthquake. As if confirming the importance of possessing a vital sense of interiority, both moral and sensual, Rutsuko emerges from the earthquake unscathed, along with her precious grandmother, not greatly disturbed that her family's house, along with her own wedding trousseau, has burned to the ground. She regrets only that if she had known she would be left with only the clothes on her back, she would have changed into something better before fleeing her home.

In the text it is Grandmother's words that give rise to the story of Rutsuko's prolonged adolescence, a period of wonder and innocence, and sustain it: "It's the truth—you're only a girl for a short time. It won't be long before you're an adult too. The same thing happens to all of us. But you're the baby of the fam-ily, Rutsuko, and it pains me to see you grow up so fast. I wanted you to be my little girl for just a while longer." [38] Ultimately Rutsuko does grow up. With the family home lost in the earthquake, Rutsuko and her grandmother con-tribute to the family earnings by selling household goods on the street. It is at this time that Rutsuko begins to feel attracted to men. Tentative about her interest in work outside the home, reluctant to ask her father to send her to college in the aftermath of the earthquake and the hardship it has brought the family, Rutsuko meets a number of possible suitors. But in the end she is deter-mined to marry a man whom she initially rejected: a doctor from the country-side who seeks to promote his new business in Tokyo. The man also seeks a native Tokyoite for a wife, and Rutsuko, who is well liked in her neighbor-hood, seems the perfect candidate. Opposed to the match, Rutsuko's whole family cooperates only reluctantly in the wedding plans, and Rutsuko finds the resulting discord so upsetting that she increasingly regards her fiancé as a means of escape.

Though highly discriminating in matters of clothing and a model daughter, Rutsuko, as Mizumura notes, makes the wrong choice in men.[39] On her wedding night, Rutsuko finds herself repulsed by her husband's kisses but acquiesces to his advances anyway. Wearing the soft, floral-pattern robe given to her by Osono, Rutsuko follows her new husband to bed. In the extraordinary closing passage of the novel, Rutsuko finds herself being disrobed by a man for the first time:

> Rutsuko yielded to the pressure of his body, and lay exactly where he had pushed her down. She felt so many new sensations, all at once, and his bare chest rubbing on hers, and her underrobe being stripped away from her waist and hips, not by her own hands but by his. The ceremonial wedding night was proceeding as planned.[40]

The disturbing symmetry of the beginning and end of the text suggests a means by which Kōda challenges the primacy of heterosexual contractual relationships and emphasizes the centrality of female bonds, primarily in a social and ideological sense, as a core aspect of subjectivity.

Although the installment that ends with the foregoing passage was not scheduled to be the last during serialization of the novel *Kimono,* Kōda wrote nothing more. Kojima Chikako claims that Kōda abandoned the novel because she was deeply involved with the reconstruction of a pagoda in Nara and did not have time.[41] In any case, critics have reacted differently to what became, in the single-volume publication, an extremely striking conclusion. The male critic/writers Mizukami Tsutomu and Muramatsu Tomomi, for example, assert that the final passage of *Kimono* is "clean and sensual." The moral of the story, they say, is that Rutsuko learns that the kimono is not just something that a woman takes off herself: men will take it off for her.[42] Inoue Kazuko opposes their view and points to another male critic (Akiyama Shun) who has similarly misread the attempted rape in Kōda's short story "A Woman's Screams" (Kansei; 1949) as a "fight between a man and a woman."[43]

Since the publication of her novel *Flowing,* which depicts life in a postwar geisha house, critics have frequently associated Kōda with the concept of *iki* (elegant chic). Critic Yoshimoto Ryūmei (Takaaki), Muramatsu Tomomi, and others employ such notions in order to identify Kōda and her writings with the idea of an essentialized Japan having a traditional cultural order comprehensible in ahistorical terms: a unique Japanese subjectivity. Stemming from Kuki Shūzō's influential *The Anatomy of "Iki,"* a key text in the essentialist discourse on Japanese culture in this century, *iki* is articulated as a concept of behavior

that posits sensuality and beauty, as well as pride and self-sufficiency and resignation, as imperative aspects of a chic and valued woman of the pleasure
quarter, or object of desire.[44] Yoshimoto's insistence on relating Kōda's fiction
to such aesthetic categories resembles the critical stance that links the works of
modern women writers to those of Heian aristocratic women. This vague and
ultimately ahistorical appeal to nativist sensibilities, while seeming to elevate
women's writing to the status of great tradition, can also function as a means
of denigration and marginalization.[45] In contrast to critical strategies that
understand men's writing in the context of their age and intellectual history,
through reference to such notions as the "modern self" *(kindaiteki jiga),* the
easy labels of "feminine sensibility" and "feminine writing style" allow the
critic to ignore the troublesome and potentially subversive aspects of Kōda's
narrative.

The very publication of this open and ambiguous work *Kimono,* and its
positive critical reception both by old-guard critics and feminist readers, signal
changes in the critical establishment in Japan.[46] Critics such as Yale-educated
Mizumura, feminist scholar Inoue Kazuko, and novelist Nakazawa Kei find in
Kōda's writing not only a challenge to the idea of male orthodoxy but also a
model of strength and resilience firmly grounded in history. But they also write
in an age when feminist critics have attained a measure of authority that
enables them to challenge canonical readings of literary texts.

Notes

1. Nina Cornyetz, "Power and Gender in the Narratives of Yamada Eimi," in *The
   Woman's Hand,* ed. Paul Gordon Schalow and Janet A. Walker (Stanford: Stanford
   University Press, 1996), p. 426. Cornyetz concludes, however, that Yamada's "writing of Japanese woman and African-American male remains locked inside the conventional dominance/submission dialectic that underlies" dominant configurations
   of race and patriarchy in Japan (p. 453).
2. See Janet Walker's review of Alan Tansman's *The Writings of Kōda Aya* (New Haven:
   Yale University Press, 1993) in *Journal of Japanese Studies* 21 (1995):448–451.
3. Kōda's *The Struggle* is a notable exception. Set in a tuberculosis sanatorium, the
   novel explores the lives of staff and patients, both male and female.
4. Patricia Yaeger and Beth Kowaleski-Wallace, *Refiguring the Father: New Feminist
   Readings of Patriarchy* (Carbondale: Southern Illinois University Press, 1989), pp.
   304–305 and xi–xii.
5. Inoue Kazuko, "Onna no isshō—Kōda Aya to kimono," in *Gengo bunkabu kiyō*
   (Hokkaidō Daigaku, 1994), p. 109.

6. Brett DeBary, "Not Another Double Suicide: Gender, National Identity, and Repetition in Shinoda Masahirō's *Shinjūten no Amijima*," *Iris* 16 (Spring 1993):81–83.

7. Elizabeth Kowaleski-Wallace, *Their Fathers' Daughters: Hannah More, Maria Edgeworth, and Patriarchal Complicity* (New York: Oxford University Press, 1991), p. 11.

8. Esperanza Ramirez-Christensen, correspondence with the author, 14 September 1996.

9. Yamashita Etsuko, *Mazakon bungakuron: sokubaku toshite no "haha"* (Shinyōsha, 1991), pp. 12–13 and 220–222.

10. My reading of Kōda's works is informed by the debate surrounding Gilles Deleuze's revisionary theory of mother-centered, pre-oedipal theory aimed at challenging Freudian and Lacanian positing of the centrality of the phallus.

11. See Hirozawa Sakae, *Kurokami to keshō no Shōwashi* (Iwanami Shoten, 1993), pp. 34–45; Liza Crihfield Dalby, *Kimono: Fashioning Culture* (New Haven: Yale University Press, 1993), pp. 130–137; and Keiichiro Nakagawa and Henry Rosovsky, "The Case of the Dying Kimono," in *Dress, Adornment, and the Social Order,* ed. Mary Ellen Roach and Joanne Bubolz Eicher (New York: Wiley, 1965), pp. 311–321.

12. Nakagawa and Rosovsky, "The Case of the Dying Kimono," pp. 318–319.

13. Gaylyn Studlar, "Masochism, Masquerade, and the Erotic Metamorphoses of Marlene Dietrich," in *Fabrications: Costume and the Female Body,* ed. Jane Gaines and Charlotte Herzog (New York: Routledge, 1990), p. 230.

14. Kōda Aya, *Kimono* (Shinchōsha, 1993), pp. 3–5.

15. Inoue, "Onna no isshō," p. 112.

16. Quoted in Koyama Tetsurō, "Bungaku tsuiseki: Kōda Aya futatabi," *Bungakukai* 6 (1993):216.

17. Mizukami Tsutomu and Muramatsu Tomomi, "Taidan Kōda Aya no sekai," *Nami* (January 1993):44.

18. There are, as well, other points of similarity between Kōda's novel and Tanizaki's: the contrast of regional cultural differences (Tokyo and the provinces in *Kimono;* Kansai and Kantō in *The Makioka Sisters*); changing family fortunes in the context of rapid historical and social change; a focus on women's lives; and a focus on the details of domestic life.

19. See, for example, Gail Bernstein, ed., *Recreating Japanese Women, 1600–1945* (Berkeley: University of California Press, 1991).

20. Kōda, *Kimono,* pp. 147–148.

21. Inoue Kazuko comments that Rutsuko, like Ruth who serves the widow Naomi and whose name means "sorrow and regret," is burdened with the fate of leading a sorrowful life; see "Onna no isshō," p. 111. Takahashi Hideo suggests that this

biblical name is related to Kōda's experience in the mission school that she attended as a girl. He further notes that Uchimura Kanzō's eldest daughter was named Rutsuko after Ruth in the Bible. See Takahashi Hideo, "Kōda Aya no muaku naru jikan," *Shinchō* 94 (1994):209.

22. Although set in early Shōwa, Uno Chiyo's novel *Confessions of Love* (Irozange; 1935) is a good example of a character who has lost her sense of direction.
23. Kōda, *Kimono,* p. 11.
24. Ibid., pp. 15–16.
25. Gilles Lipovetsky, *The Empire of Fashion: Dressing Modern Democracy,* trans. Catherine Porter (Princeton: Princeton University Press, 1994), p. 148.
26. Kōda, *Kimono,* pp. 173–174.
27. Quoted in Koyama, "Bungaku tsuiseki," p. 216.
28. Jane Gaines and Charlotte Herzog, eds., *Fabrications: Costume and the Female Body* (New York: Routledge, 1990), p. 13, commenting on Walter Benjamin's work.
29. Yuri Sachiko, "Josei sakka no genzai," in *Kokubungaku kaishaku to kanshō bekkan: Josei sakka no shinryū,* ed. Hasegawa Izumi pp. 72–73. See also Honda Masuko et al., *Shōjoron* (Seikyūsha, 1988), and Honda Masuko, *Jogakusei no keifu* (Seidōsha, 1990), p. 178ff.
30. Kōda, *Kimono,* pp. 102–103.
31. Inoue discusses the portrayal of menstruation in modern fiction in "Onna no isshō," p. 114.
32. Gregory L. Golley, "Tanizaki Junichirō: The Art of Subversion and the Subversion of Art," *Journal of Japanese Studies* 21 (1995):371–374.
33. Roland Barthes, *The Fashion System,* trans. Matthew Ward and Richard Howard (New York: Hill & Wang, 1983), p. 236.
34. Kōda, *Kimono,* pp. 205–206.
35. Ibid., pp. 267–268.
36. Ibid., p. 270.
37. Inoue, "Onna no isshō," p. 111.
38. Kōda, *Kimono,* p. 171.
39. Quoted in Koyama, "Bungaku tsuiseki," p. 216.
40. Kōda, *Kimono,* p. 357.
41. Kojima Chikako, "Kōda san no namida." *Shinchō* 88(1) (1991):206. Kojima suggests that Kōda intended to continue the novel and have Rutsuko engage in an affair to escape her unhappy marriage. In an interview with the author on 7 July 1998, Aoki Tama argued that Kōda planned to write more of *Kimono* because she wished to explain what the kimono meant to older women.

42. Mizukami Tsutomu and Muramatsu Tomomi, "Taidan Kōda Aya no sekai," *Nami* (January 1993):42–47.

43. Inoue, "Onna no isshō," p. 112.

44. Kuki Shūzō, *"Iki" no kōzō* (Iwanami Shoten, 1979).

45. Yoshimoto Takaaki, "Kōda Aya ni tsuite: shirōto no iki," in *Shinchō Nihon bungaku arubamu: Kōda Aya* (Shinchōsha, 1995), pp. 97–103.

46. Yuri, "Josei sakka no genzai," pp. 71–81.

6
Epilogue

An encounter with the body of texts written by Kōda Aya raises many tantalizing questions about the status of reading, literary production, and criticism, few of which have clear-cut answers. In the preceding chapters I have attempted to address some of these questions. As Edward Said has written:

> Criticism adopts the mode of commentary on and evaluation of art; yet in reality criticism matters more as a necessarily incomplete and preparatory process toward judgement and evaluation. What the critical essay does is to begin to create the values by which art is judged. . . . Critics create not only the values by which art is judged and understood, but they embody in writing those processes and actual conditions in the present by means of which art and writing bear significance.[1]

For a writer who focuses on seemingly conventional or even regressive topics—kimono and geisha and life at home—Kōda's works resist neat classification in generic terms, as well as on the scale of tradition versus modernity. Partly this stems from Kōda's own consistently humble posture in her career as a writer and her professed distance from such categories as Art and Literature. Although she fashions stories out of incidents that would seem for all the world to relate to the life she lived, no one wants to read the stories simply to find out about her life. Not only does the style of the text present itself in an utterly arresting manner, not only are the conceptions of social relations, gender, and personhood surprisingly fresh and unconventional, but readers have also been attracted to the intelligence, ferocious curiosity, and wit of the teller of stories as well as the rhythm and beauty of Kōda's words.

Critics are not in the least perturbed when they discover discrepancies between the stories she tells and independent reports of the same historical incidents or individuals. Katsumata Hiroshi, for example, enthusiastically endorses Kōda's insistence that she was born "in the midst of a storm" even though his research has turned up a newspaper weather report indicating that the skies over Tokyo were clear on the day she was born. The actual climatological conditions do not matter, Katsumata writes, because everyone in Kōda's family, even her daughter, and most of all Kōda herself lent silent approval to this legend. It was only fitting that Kōda should have come into the world during a storm and that a powerful star dominated the sky that night.[2]

Every reader and critic cooperates with the effort to allow Kōda's discursive performances to float in the ambiguous border zone between essay and fiction, between autobiography and novel. So much the better that she refuses the mantle of art—unlike those pretenders who have scant control of language and little understanding that people should aspire to optimism and maturity rather than succumb to, or even revel in, the pessimism of an exposed and lonely ego, or the allure of the strip show. In the end, it works nicely, this figure of the storm, because it leads smoothly to the metaphor of the bashō leaves, tattered and torn by the storm, yet still intact, ever flexible. The resilience, strength, and maturity of the persona differ sharply from the masochistic, self-sacrificial spirit of *gaman,* or endurance: *gaman* is an attitude prescribed for women—an attitude of persevering and not complaining about the oppression of patriarchy, the exploitation of the brutal capitalist, the barrenness of Japan's rural landscape, the bankruptcy of unexamined habits of heterosexual marriage. As a writer Kōda participates in the construction of discursive worlds, what Ken Ito calls in his discussion of Tanizaki "world building," not for the sake of "the contemplation of ideal worlds" but rather to problematize "the desire behind such worlds."[3] If Tanizaki in his creative endeavors "explores the tense relationship between human subjectivity and the material world where it seeks satisfaction . . . the awesome energies invested by the imagination in remaking the exterior world, as well as the exterior world's resistance to being fantasy," Kōda discovers worlds where the Confucian strategies of observation and self-cultivation lessen the distance between unfettered desire and an unruly universe by altering the conception of both.[4]

If anything undergoes symbolic inversion in the discursive realm created by Kōda Aya, it is most certainly the family romance and the symbolic order, but always in the spirit of generosity and humor that characterizes her work. Far from being shameful, even in his dotage, the father proves to be infinitely wise and solid and willing to share his method of knowing the world and thus the means for becoming a moral and mature individual. He holds his daughter to the highest standards of cultivating herself and her world. Never portrayed as a saint, Kōda's Rohan also has ordinary tendencies and thus will lose his temper, drink too much, and interrupt his children's lessons in the Confucian classics in order to take them to the riotous streets of Asakusa and into its bawdy dance halls. The early postwar reading audience, for whom food was scarce and electricity unreliable, relished Kōda's portraits of such a father—portraits of authority, that is, dissimilar to the father figure who communicated with his fist. Rohan taught discipline, but not that of the military, and impressed firmly on his daughter the importance of narrative and the written and spoken word —and made it all intriguing and seductive:

> Father is a good storyteller. When we were little, he did a marathon storytell- ing series for us. My brother and I would sit, all ears, on either side of the lac- quer tray put before him for his evening sake. And he would use his hands as he told the story, picking up a chopstick for the brave samurai's sword. Then it would become the monk's staff, and the lid of the soup bowl turned into the lady's broad hat, or a warrior's helmet. Sleep the farthest thing from our minds, we begged him for more—"And then what happened?" Finally it would be time for bed, so Father would say "And then the unfortunate creature plum- meted into a deep canyon. The end"— only to leave us with the promise of another installment the following evening.[5]

For postwar readers, such a father was more than an object of nostalgia. He "represented culture and traditions that one could still believe in," even with the defeat.[6] Even the archetypal evil stepmother undergoes a transformation, for Kōda's evocation of Yayo contains a mixture of the stepdaughter's resent- ment with a large dose of compassion for this woman's dilemma. Nothing is as it appears: the powerful father cannot be folded into the monolithic and oppressive patriarchy signifying the state and orthodox concepts of masculin- ity; the Christian mother figure offers not a lick of comfort and nurture to needy children. The husband constitutes the most pitiable figure, for he has no mind of his own, no strength to resist the temptations of the world, no stan- dard for deciding how to act. The independent-minded daughter, who initially rails against all of these models, ultimately forgives them, learns from them, and subsequently finds her own way, rather than seeking revenge and burning up in anger.

Despite claims that the status of women's writing in Japan is unique because of the centrality of texts written by women in the premodern Japanese canon, a major task of feminist critics in the latter half of the twentieth century still remains: to reveal the gender-based assumptions behind the formation of the modern canon and the category of "women's literature" *(joryū bungaku)* in Japan. Not that women's writing is suppressed in the marketplace, for book- store shelves, women's literature sections, and best-seller lists abound with titles written by women. In terms of critical assessment and canon formation, however, it does not suffice to claim that the literary establishment has always taken women's writing seriously simply because *The Tale of Genji, The Pillow Book,* and many of the greatest works of the premodern tradition were all written by women. Rather, one must pose other questions. Do critics, reviewers, and school curricula regard writing by women as worthy of careful reading and explication, and as evocative of transcendent meanings, as have texts included in the canon dominated by male writers? Do we still trivialize writing by women? Can separate ever be equal? Does criticism challenge the "ideology of the subject [as male] by developing alternative and different notions of subjectivity?"[7]

Kōda Aya's writings do not fit neatly into any school or category of literature; nor does her career as a writer. She does not easily slide into the category of Feminist; nor can her works be labeled Antifeminist. Although she maintained a public persona of modesty and adherence to traditional styles by wearing a kimono throughout her life, Kōda's narratives invert conventional gender and familial roles, decenter the heterosexual romance, alter notions of sensuality, and create a realm of narrative authority rare in postwar letters. In resistance to essentialism, which posits a monolithic femininity, feminism, or even women's writing, this study contributes to understanding the differences between writers, especially women writers, with the aim of de-essentializing "the category of Woman."[8]

Notes

1. Edward Said, *The World, the Text, and the Critic* (Cambridge, Mass.: Harvard University Press, 1983), p. 53.
2. *Shinchō Nihon bungaku arubamu* (Shinchōsha, 1995), pp. 3–6.
3. Ken Ito, *Visions of Desire: Tanizaki's Fictional Worlds* (Stanford: Stanford University Press, 1991), pp. 2–3.
4. Ibid., pp. 3–4.
5. *KAZS* 1:246–247.
6. *Shinchō Nihon bungaku arubamu,* pp. 50–51.
7. Diana Fuss, *Essentially Speaking: Feminism, Nature, and Difference* (New York: Routledge, 1989), pp. 95–96.
8. Ibid., p. 28. I refer the reader to two important books that were published as this book was still in press: Joan E. Ericson, *Be a Women: Hayashi Fumiko and Modern Japanese Women's Literature* (Honolulu: University of Hawai'i Press, 1997); Kanai Keiko et al., eds., *Kōda Aya no sekai* (Kanrin Shobō, 1998).

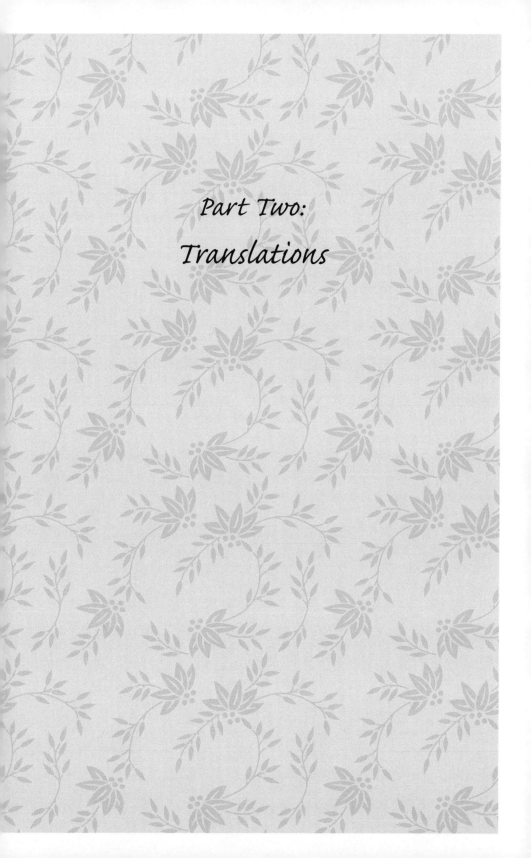

Part Two:

Translations

Fragments

I live among the charred ruins of Omotechō in Koishikawa. This is where Father spent about twenty years of his life, from the late Taishō period until a month before our neighborhood was destroyed in the fire bombings. When I first moved back here, I felt stunned at the sight of those horrible wild onions that grew everywhere and would not go away, and at the vast expanse of burnt, broken roof tile that covered the ground completely, like asphalt. But I have gotten over that and now find it all quite splendid.

The burnt ruins are a treasure chest, and the earth yields so much. Buried in it are things that, above the ground, had purpose but now, broken, are useless, like fragments of china and dishes, and warped pans and spoons. While the soil seems willing to settle back into its old routine, now dancing up in the wind, now sinking down under the falling rain, the things in the earth are content only if they can push their way up out of the soil so as to see the sun once again. Every object that appears has some memory attached to it, especially the things directly linked to Father. When I come across one of those, I feel like raising my face to the sky in celebration of the opportunity to remember, and at the same time like lying down on the earth to cry over my loneliness.

Just this morning, I could scarcely believe my eyes when I saw a glint of dark blue in the ice that covered the ground. It was a fragment of a tray Father had adored—a nice Kyoto piece of Shōnzui ware with a low rim. It had been in our house for nearly forty years, from the days when Mother was still alive. I imagine that Mother used it to carry a bottle of sake, a cup, and some tasty morsel out to Father each evening.

My stepmother was Christian and abhorred Father's evening cup of wine as something sinful. Even so, she could not prevail over the stubborn man she had married, so she too had poured him sake. She had no appreciation whatsoever of the various implements used for serving spirits. I remember when I was little seeing the wine cups and tray and everything crammed into a big, sturdy cake box from the bakery. When I was a bit older, I was given charge of all the household chores because my stepmother suffered from rheumatism. By that time, the sake cups and all had decreased drastically in number and were stored in a flimsy, shallow wooden box.

Because I had to do all the cleaning and chores at home, plus my school-work, my main consideration when it came to washing up after dinner was speed. I was terribly rough with the dishes, and one Imari plate and Oribe dish after another fell victim to my rough ways. And the lovely little sake cups with the lacy designs, sadly, were with us only briefly before they went the way of all things. Father, amazed at my violence, would say, "You should marry a demolition man." Then he would rest his chin on the palm of his hand and sigh. I felt bad.

It was different with that blue and white tray. I handled it with special care because I knew how much Father loved it. It never got broken, but one day I did smash his favorite cup. He decided, right then and there, to change his habits rather than wait for me to become less clumsy. He switched to sherry glasses for his evening sake. One could buy sherry glasses anywhere, and, because they were all the same, Father would not grow unduly fond of any particular one only to lose it.

I married the son of a liquor wholesaler in Shingawa. Father had not purposely chosen a man who could supply him with a free lifetime supply of liquor. It was just a happy coincidence. The brewery we did business with was located in Nishinomiya. Someone told me that the president of the company, a Mr. Itō, often reminisced about our wedding reception. He had been deeply impressed when Father spoke of his feelings about parting with his only daughter. One cold and windy day in February, we received from the gentleman two bottles of sake wrapped up nicely and decorated with a branch of rose-colored plum blossoms.

A young apprentice delivered the sake. He wore the usual striped cotton kimono fastened tightly with a stiff sash. He sat before me, posture erect, and briskly said, "We sincerely hope that your father will enjoy this." He explained that the bottles contained the first pressing of sake. He had come from Nishinomiya especially to deliver it to Father. Without a moment's delay, I picked up the bottles and went out into the cold, windy evening.

Father was very pleased. I poured the white, thick liquid into one of those sherry glasses and floated a plum blossom on top. Lifting the glass to the light, Father gazed at it and smiled, "Very pretty."

After watching him put the glass to his lips and taste the spirits—"Nice. Quite nice."—I went home.

But then, the next morning, all hell broke loose. I got a sound scolding from my stepmother on the phone. She announced that she did not want so much as a drop of that drink of the devil in her house ever again. Apparently Father had poured one glass after another for himself, sometimes downing it without ceremony, sometimes putting a plum blossom on top for decoration, until he was thoroughly soused. I felt both happy and sad about what had happened. Of course, Mother was not being totally unreasonable. But since Father ordinarily did not drink excessively, I decided that every year I would send him a gift of freshly pressed sake. I knew that would make him happy.

One winter some years later, Father sent me a letter from Izu where he was vacationing: "Steam rising from the hot springs, the blossoms of the plum, the color of the bitter orange—please join me." Unable to resist such an invitation, I took the train down to Izu with my young daughter. Fortunately I had just received Father's annual bottle of new-pressed sake from the brewery. The town looked lovely during our ride from the station to the inn, with lights coming on in houses and shops and a gentle snow falling.

"So you came after all!" Father said when we arrived. I noticed that he was bundled up in one of the quilted jackets provided by the inn. When I gave him the yearly gift, he was all smiles, "Excellent timing! And it's snowing too. What more could a man ask for? The only treat I have to offer you is the bath."

So saying, Father got up and led us to the hall along which the inn's several bathing rooms were located. He showed us to the smallest one at the very end of the corridor. The maid said apologetically, "That's the one we use ourselves. It's awfully small." But I had already begun untying the jacket over my kimono.

The sound of water pouring into the bath came from inside. Not wanting to waste a moment, I slid the door open. Adorned with a beautiful plum branch heavy with white blossoms, it was a splendid bath. My daughter and I splashed about and had a thoroughly good time.

When we returned to the room, we found Father already sipping sake. A small plum branch with many pink buds lay on the table across from him. Quite clever of the lady who ran the inn, he said, to use her bonsai trees for our enjoyment. A visitor to a new place, I was overwhelmed.

Some years later, I got divorced and my link with sake was severed. Later my child's father—my ex-husband—fell ill and died. More years passed, and I heard that the sake warehouse in Shingawa and its many long years of tradition were gone, victims of the new age. Just this past summer, Father traveled to the world beyond, never to return. As for the blue and white piece of porcelain, in all its beauty, I could not bear the thought of having anyone else see it again, so I crushed it into a powder and returned it to the earth.

[February 1948]

The Medal

In those days, I wore a black striped apprentice's kimono with a chintz sash so threadbare that you could barely see the floral print. A long, straight apron hung firmly from the waist of that sash, like a shield, like a plaster cast, like a fire door.

With the resounding failure of my husband's business, I had fallen from the status of proud young mistress of a prosperous Shingawa liquor wholesaler to manager of a for-members-only sake shop. This way of describing our store makes it sound reputable, but in fact it was a miserable little place without so much as a vendor's permit, much less a regulation-size storefront.

It was late April 1937. The papers in those days always had some amazing news in them—from the attempted military coup of February the year before to the start of fighting in China just three months later. A ferocious gale had come sweeping through, causing small whirlwinds some days and, at other times, a tremendous commotion that stirred up everything, even the dust in the forgotten corners of the world. I was just a speck of dust in one of the narrowest, most remote niches.

With only one telephone and a single errand boy at my disposal—and an ashen-faced husband with whom I wished to spend as little time as possible—I worked myself to the bone. That day I had gone out to make a delivery at a customer's home in Horinouchi. It was my first trip there, and I wasted much time searching for the house. My shop boy had mixed up east and west on his hastily drawn map.

The lady of the house made no attempt to hide her anger at my tardiness, and, just as I was about to leave, she spitefully saddled me with five empty bottles. Taking empties was part of the job, of course, so I could hardly refuse, but it seemed unfair. None of my other customers would have burdened me with such a load because they all knew that I made my rounds on foot, rather than by bicycle. That day, though, I had no choice but to bundle the bottles up in my net bags, two on one side and three on the other, and lug them home.

True, I did have strong arms in those days. In fact, I did not balk at any test of strength, because I hated my reputation as Mr. Kōda's dainty, fragile daughter, a flimsy specimen raised in a hothouse, easily knocked over by the slightest gust of wind. I surprised many a customer by maneuvering those forty-five-gallon barrels that weigh two hundred pounds. There was a trick to it, you see, but none of my customers knew that. And even those big two-quart sake bottles that weigh more than six pounds—I had once carried half a dozen of them up five flights of stairs because one of the customers had no elevator. So, for me, a load of five empty bottles on the way down was really nothing. It was the woman's attitude that bothered me that day.

Even then, the arrogance that came from being born in the distinguished Kōda family and the haughtiness remaining from my days as mistress of a fine house would not disappear, no matter how I might try to rid myself of them. I had become physically stronger and more able by the day, but my mind would not accept the changes in my life so easily.

And the way I dressed! Born and bred in an old merchant family, my mother-in-law saw to it that I was fitted in a striped kimono, the garb of apprentices. The chintz sash became part of the outfit because it was woven of the same material as the kimono and would not hike up or slide down when I was working, the way silk does on cotton. The "sail apron" I wore got its name from the sturdy canvas sailcloth from which it was made. Wide like a sumo wrestler's ceremonial apron, my aprons had gigantic liquor emblems printed across the front. With slogans such as "The Rose of Wines," "Very Finest Quality," "Famous the World Round," or the names of breweries or shops plastered all over, the aprons worked as billboards too—some of the most colorful, eye-catching affairs you have ever seen. Another part of the attraction was the woman wearing them. I had a Western-style hairdo, rather than a Japanese bun, and was on the tall side and not plump, as most liquor merchants' wives tended to be. In the end, such aprons are put to best use when the daughter of an eminent gentleman like Mr. Kōda wears them—or, at least, so my husband liked to think.

A kimono worn by a woman immature in her emotions can be a powerful thing. Or, to put it another way, clothes have the strength to control one's psyche. To me, the striped outfit was a uniform; it gave me a sense of direction and a feeling of pride in my work. The apron shielded me from all arrows; it acted as a cast to brace me against all blows. It was a metal fire door behind which I could hide the anguish of my heart.

A year earlier, the *Asahi News* had carried an article about me on the local news page. The headline ran "Modern Bacchus Rohan's Daughter Opens

Liquor Store—From Housewife to Entrepreneur—All Smiles at Year's End."
Of course, I knew that the reporter had no reason to portray me in a favorable
light, but everyone else insisted that the article was complimentary. My husband decided that we should express our appreciation, and so he immediately
dispatched our apprentice on a mission to deliver a "shot" of sake, brushing
aside my objection that it would be a waste of good spirits.

Just as I had predicted, the boy came home sulking.

"And then, the guy had the nerve to say, 'What kind of fool do you take
me for? I'm a reporter for the *Asahi,* you know. You've got me all wrong,'" he
reported angrily.

Though I have long forgotten that reporter's name and everything else
about him, I still remember him fondly. He was like a breath of fresh air to me.
Next to him, my crestfallen husband seemed so pathetic. In the face of both,
my striped outfit and apron kept me safe and my emotions hidden.

The delivery had taken far more time than I had expected, and I felt rushed
and out of sorts as I headed home. With the heavy load of empties, I had no
choice but to take the bus, though I hated to spend the few sen I had earned
that day on the fare. The stink of stale alcohol from the bottles assailed me, and
the back of the bus where I sat swayed horribly.

It was late afternoon, a time when liquor stores tend to be quite busy. I
thought of my leisurely husband, who would take what seemed like hours just
to write out a receipt or paste on a label. I imagined the boy, who lapsed into
sloth the moment I took my eyes off him. I felt like running back there to right
the situation.

After the bus had passed Hibiya and had just a little farther to go before it
reached Tsukiji, I glanced out toward Shinbashi to the right. The peak of each
and every tiled roof glistened brightly. In the opposite direction, darkness had
fallen over Kyōbashi. I could not see the sun; perhaps it had already begun to
set.

We reached Sukiyabashi bridge. That passageway of water, the water at
sunset, the water of my childhood home, so long ago, the Sumida River. The
sight let loose a current of longing in my breast. In my mind I could picture
each of those thousand waves on the darkened shallows, as the water flowed
slowly in the last peaceful rays of evening sunlight. Then I saw something that
made me jump. Way behind the bus, in the direction I was facing at the time,
the name Rohan flashed on in lights and then disappeared.

A moment of panic. He must have had a stroke. That was the only explanation for his name being up there, I thought as I stared back at the news being

spelled out in lights on the Asahi News Building. At Owarichō, the next stop, I made my way off the bus and ran back toward the flashing news sign.

Once at the intersection, I stood beside the police box and watched the band of lights shining across the sign. None of it registered in my mind. Then the five letters came up again. I watched and waited, convinced that what followed would say that he had suffered a stroke. Nausea overcame me, and I tried pressing back with the base of my tongue to keep anything from coming up, but it welled up again and again. An acrid liquid coated my teeth.

I set the bottles down and went around to the back of the police box. The place stunk of urine, and my eyes and nose watered from pain. The handkerchief I wiped my face with came away a dull brown.

I raised my eyes to the sign once again.

JAPAN'S FIRST MEDAL FOR CULTURAL MERIT

Ever so calmly, the name Rohan moved across for the third time.

The evening sky changed from pink to lavender as I watched. It was time for me to go home. I pulled up the lower edges of my apron, stuffed them into my sash, and then picked up the two loads of bottles. Before me, slender, pale green willow branches swayed in the dusk. Melancholy lingered around me. My head throbbed with pain. I hurried off for home, this time on foot.

Just as I had feared, the sake barrels were empty. This small crisis had my husband at his wits' end, so I felt certain that he was unaware of the news. Without so much as a word having passed between us about Father's award, I left for the warehouse.

Customarily, liquor wholesalers lock up the front gates of their warehouses before sunset, unless they are expecting a special shipment, and the main entrance to the shop will be shut tight as well. After the clerks have all gone home, the only ones left are the fellows who sleep upstairs—those hotheaded young men called the "barrel rollers."

The place had the feel of a bachelor's flat, with the boys all sitting around playing *shōgi*, shooting the breeze, and munching on snacks. Some of them leapt to their feet when I came in, others sat up attentively, but none of them failed to extend their congratulations. They had been trained to speak politely and always cheerfully.

"We were very happy to hear the news about your father. Our heartiest congratulations. He must be terribly pleased."

Their eyes conveyed their simple feelings of happiness for Father. These were men who spent their days laboring, without a moment for reading, and doubtless they had little notion of why Master Rohan suddenly enjoyed such fame or how prestigious the medal was. At that time, though, I myself had no understanding of such things. If asked, I would not have been able to tell who this man Rohan was or to explain the glory of his award. Still, I felt very happy at their kind words. Seized by an urge to celebrate, I thought of treating everyone to some buckwheat noodles or sweets. Why not be extravagant and have a party with them in Father's honor? They may not fully comprehend the implications of what happened, but at least they were sincere when offering their congratulations.

In my nearly empty pockets, though, I could find only the three yen and twenty sen from the delivery that day, a few other coins, and a couple of bus tickets. So much for that idea. My days as the generous, hospitable lady of the house were a thing of the past. I had nearly forgotten that I did not make enough money to serve three decent meals to my own family.

One of the boys stood up and went out, the storehouse keys rattling in his hand. I heard him starting up the three-wheel motorcycle. This wholesaler was very good about deliveries after hours.

"Shall I give you a lift?" he offered, as he flipped over the grimy cushion on the back seat. The side of the pillow that I sat on could not have been any cleaner than the other, but his courtesy pleased me all the same. We roared through the wind; I felt warm inside but the air was cool on my skin. I could see stars in the night sky.

That evening, though I felt too exhausted to pay Father a visit, I could think of nothing but his home in Koishikawa. It was never kept up as well as it should be, for Father lived apart from his wife.

All those newspaper reporters who would come by and the scads of other visitors—where would he ever find enough dishes or places for them to sit? And the young maids usually took care of things quite nicely, but without a lady of the house there at a time like this, how would they manage? I imagined the poor girls running around in a panic.

I did not even know if he had received the medal yet. What if the ceremony required formal dress? Where would he get a top hat and proper footwear?

And so I fretted on and on as never before about this detail and that, although I knew the empty workings of my mind to be fruitless. At length I rescued myself from these feelings of distress and pledged that I would go straight over the next day and extend my congratulations. My resolve, though, lacked both determination and goodwill, as if I had used up my supply of enthusiasm when chatting with the fellows down at the warehouse. I felt desolate and dismayed at my wretched heart. Had I forgotten the old saying, "Another man's joy is my own"? What other child would fail to rise to the occasion when her father was being so honored? He was my only father, and I his only child. Is this any way to behave? I had lost my way at the bottom of a deep abyss. I cast my eyes upward, toward my father, only to see him dimly, shrouded by mist.

When I was a little girl, Father told me this story as he sat one evening sipping his sake: Once there was a mother lion who pushed her growing cubs off a high cliff in order to test them. The heartiest of the cubs began flapping his legs the moment he realized that he was falling and came floating up again. Another, after landing gently on the ground, shook his head, got back up on all fours, and effortlessly soared up in the air. Yet another cub climbed back to the top by way of a steep, winding path. The mother judged and ranked them accordingly.

One of the cubs, though, does not try to find his way back to the top and instead just sits there bawling. The lioness sees him and roars, "Finish him off!" I felt so sorry for this last cub that I started crying, unaware that one day I would become a wretched, unworthy child just like the cub. At the time, I pitied the defenseless little thing and pleaded for more compassionate treatment.

"Aya, I feel sorry for it too. But real lions just wouldn't stand for that kind of spineless behavior, so that's the way the story has to end," Father explained.

Every time he told me the story after that, I would get upset at the part where the mother lion castigates the little one. I just hated her for that. One time, a moment before Father got to that point in the story, I jumped in and yelled at him: "Finish her off!" I wanted to show him the full measure of my indignation at those who have the upper hand and my total sympathy for the underdog. Father chuckled, for I had unwittingly spit out almost the very same words spoken by the lion, though my intention had been to attack that unjust creature. My eyes brimmed with tears as I sat there across from him. Father seldom told me the lion story after that.

For a long time I was not even aware of the words that had come out of my mouth that day. All I knew was that I had felt a certain exhilaration saying what I did. Several decades later, I found myself listening to Father tell the same story to my young daughter. I sat there, interested to hear how tame the story had become. Instead of using the words "Finish him off," Father said: "And then some other beasts heard the baby cub whining, and they came and ate him up."

His granddaughter reacted quite differently.

"What happens if you get eaten up?" she asked.

"You die."

"What happens when you die?"

"You're not alive anymore."

"Yeah, and what does that mean 'you're not alive anymore'?"

"That's the end of you."

After a moment she said, in her own version of adult horror, "Oh no, not that!"

Only then did I remember what I had yelled out as a child. I felt ashamed and amazed at myself. The human mind works in odd ways indeed.

I know nothing about the breadth of my father's learning, nor do I pretend to understand the scope of his art. I could not tell you what came to him as a matter of luck, what he accomplished through his own talents, nor about his stature among men. Though I may be vastly ignorant, I do have enough sense not to entertain the foolish notion that he is some kind of lion of literature, a king among writers. He was just my father. From my own biased viewpoint, I would say that Father possessed some lionlike qualities, but they were those of a lion who would finish you off or give you the push-off-the-cliff test.

This line of thinking, as always, agitated me terribly. Next to me in their beds, my husband and daughter slept peacefully, but my emotions ran wild as I lay there in the dark.

How has he come to be chosen over other men? What trick of fate has linked him with a child so ordinary?

The patch of dampness on my pillowslip grew larger and larger, and the tears had the effect of soothing my agitated mind. At last I fell into a slumber.

The next morning I found myself in yet another frame of mind. When I was in second grade, my father's second wife came to live with us. My family handled the whole affair quite poorly and so, before I even laid eyes on my new mother, the entire population of the school had branded the image of the wicked stepmother into my mind. This remained a sore spot with me. I wanted to prevent my own daughter, who happened to be in second grade at the time, from misperceiving the situation at hand. The excitement over Rohan and his medal of honor could easily transform her childish innocence into conceit.

I decided it would be best to have a good talk with her. But first I wanted to hear how she felt.

"I don't know. It all depends if Grandpa is happy about it. Is he?" she asked me in reply. What was I to say? Fortunately, my daughter had no clear idea about what the medal actually was and seemed not to notice my difficulty in answering her.

"If Grandpa's happy about it, then so am I. If he doesn't like it, then neither do I," she announced blithely.

I watched her spindly legs as she pattered down the stone step and into the entranceway, her leather satchel rustling on her back as she went. I trusted the child's instincts.

That afternoon I went to the house in Koishikawa. I had not been there for a long time. Father and I did not intentionally avoid each other, but somehow we always seemed to be working at cross-purposes. Most unfortunately, I had neglected to keep in touch. Precisely because the bonds between us were so tight, many things already complicated our relationship—from money matters to issues of duty and emotion. Father seemed to feel sorry for me, but at the same time there was no mistaking his coldness and irritation. My apprehension was such that the mere thought of seeing him made my entire body tense up.

Father was an unusual man. He would point out the beauty of blossoms or clouds in the sky with the very whip he had cracked a moment before. With the same knife he had just used to rive your innards, he would slice up a wedge of some delicacy for you. No one else I knew could perform such feats. There was something very solid about him. I felt all at once like a contrite sinner and a puppy dog who is eager to please. I wanted to cut all ties with him, but at the same time I needed him to recognize me as worthy of his love.

A shiny black automobile was parked in front of the house. I slipped in through the kitchen door, hoping to avoid notice, and took off my sailcloth apron. Brightly decorated barrels and bottles of sake lined the room. Lobsters and seafood overflowed from a basket made of young bamboo, with early spring greens added for a touch of color. Although I had come expecting such a mountain of splendid gifts, the sight made me flinch. I stole forward and set down the small bottle of sake I had brought as a gift from the store.

The house was in an absolute uproar, with nothing in its place and not a maid in sight. The sitting room I found in the greatest disorder. Calling cards, letters, and fancy envelopes inscribed with "Our Congratulations" and the amount of money enclosed were strewn all over. A huge mountain of papers and the like covered the top of the tea cabinet, its drawers stuffed so full that they would not close. Half-empty teacups without saucers littered the straw-matted floor. Father's favorite cushion lay crumpled and askew, with an unfamiliar handkerchief draped sloppily over it. I sat down and waited.

Before long someone came pattering down the stairs, only to go straight by the room where I sat, through the hall, and into the kitchen. I decided to announce my presence. It turned out to be the maid. She came to the door, glanced in at me, and said abruptly, "Oh, I didn't know you were here." She did not even bother to say hello or bow. Her stylish kimono and thick makeup caught my eye.

"Isn't it wonderful about Father?" I ventured, trying to break the ice, but she was halfway back to the kitchen before she muttered her terse reply, "Yes, we've been so busy."

I could hear a door rattling open and shut.

I got up and went into the kitchen to see who it was. All of the seafood had vanished, save one small box.

"Who was here just now?"

"Oh, nobody. I don't recall the name."

I could not believe it. As troubled as I felt about this puzzling incident, all I could do was return to the sitting room. There I sat, dismayed about what had come to pass.

New visitors arrived and others were on their way out. Dressed as always in a rather loosely tied kimono, the woman scurried back and forth across the room, allowing numerous glimpses of her immodesty. I was glad at least that I had not brought my daughter along.

Father came down from upstairs and said hello as he trotted by on his way to the bathroom. I went up and put away his bedding.

When I had finished congratulating him, Father seized the opportunity to turn the conversation to me: "I hope you're doing all right?" Like a warm, soothing mineral spring, his words had the effect of relaxing me completely. I could see signs of strain in his face.

"You must be worn out from so much company."

"All I know is that everybody around here has gone crazy. The place is an awful mess, and they seem to think I'm duty bound to see every single person who comes to the door."

He got up to greet some more guests, "Wait here. I'll just be a minute." Ignoring his invitation, I excused myself. Father told the maid to give me some of the fish.

Back at home, I opened the bundle she had made up for me, only to find the same lone package I had seen left in the kitchen. It was flounder, and the skin looked dry.

My daughter seemed to be enjoying all the excitement. As she was eating a piece of the fish from her grandfather, she told me about the events at school that day.

"When my teacher was explaining about the Cultural Medal, all the kids started asking if Grandpa was an important person, and she said yes. And then everybody said they wanted to see the medal."

What an innocent bunch.

The next day, I took her with me. Father had applied some pomade to his normally unruly beard. The medal, in the shape of an orange blossom, looked much lovelier than I had expected. He hung it around his granddaughter's neck, and she, glancing down to see it on her white schoolgirl's blouse, broke into a big grin. I thanked him for the fish.

"How did you like the sea bream?" he asked her.

"A whole lot," she replied, ignorant of the difference between expensive sea bream and an ordinary fish like flounder. Not that the flounder hadn't been the best money can buy. In my mind, though, I felt sure that, for many years to come, this particular fish would serve as a reminder of how deceitful women can be.

Neither my husband nor I had the means to host a party for Father, so we had no choice but to suppress our desire to do so. The following month, though, my Aunt Nobuko took it upon herself to have a celebration for all the relatives at her house.

The pawnshop would not lend me any money, so I was obliged to wear my faded striped kimono. When I arrived at the party, one of my cousins stared at me wide-eyed and exclaimed, "Where on earth did you get that outfit?"

I was grateful for her frankness, which I preferred infinitely to silent contempt. And somehow, amid all the piano music, the flowers, the blossom-shaped cushions, the fancy food, and the refined conversation, I managed to make it through the evening, in a seat far away from Father's.

In June a more formal celebration took place in Tokyo Hall, sponsored by Koizumi Shinzō, Shibusawa Keizō, Saitō Mokichi, Iwanami Shoten, Chūō Kōronsha, and other publishers. Mr. Kobayashi of Iwanami Shoten visited our house three times to urge us to attend. On the morning of the party, he came again and implored, "Mr. Kōda will be so lonesome if no one from his family comes."

I would not be swayed by his emotional plea, but the fleeting sound of his footsteps as he was leaving and the silence that followed made me feel most desolate. I bit my lip, trying to convince myself that I should remain detached about Father's award.

That evening, in response to the congratulatory speeches, Father made the comment that a comfortable life is not a prerequisite for artistic creation. Such composure on his part in the face of all the publicity and emotions surrounding the medal made me see him as a fine, upstanding man, and a solitary man as well.

Higuchi Ichiyō's nephew Higuchi Etsu once said about us: "The parent dons a medal, and the child an apron." I made a show of laughing at his comment, but only because I wanted to hide my weakness. In fact, that apron chafed against my hands and my heart with its unyielding roughness.

The medal somehow survived the war, and Mr. Higuchi's words remain with me too. They capture those years quite accurately. Sometimes the feel of the apron comes back to me so vividly that I have it wrapped firmly around my lap once again.

[*February 1949*]

Dolls for a Special Day

I have heard that Girls' Day dolls vary in appearance from one generation to the next because they are modeled after the reigning empress. I wonder about that.

The sets of Girls' Day dolls familiar to us today generally contain fifteen figures. Twelve of the fifteen—the emperor and empress, ladies-in-waiting, five-member musical ensemble, the Minister of the Left, and the Minister of the Right—are, as one might expect, exquisite examples of male and female beauty. On the very bottom row of the stand, however, there are three servant dolls with faces and expressions not unlike those of ordinary people. The doll maker renders their faces slightly less refined and even adds a few minor and somewhat humorous imperfections. The dolls' ugliness draws viewers to them; the familiarity of the faces puts people at ease.

To my mind, this touch of charm seems necessary as a means of creating an asymmetrical balance, so to speak, in a set otherwise dominated by twelve perfect, ridiculously gorgeous dolls. Even so, the doll maker must practice some restraint here, for no one would be pleased if the dolls' noses were too pug, if they had Neanderthal foreheads, or if their expressions were too foolish. I am certain that no one would object if the set included only the pretty dolls, so it is intriguing that it contains these three common figures which, in their own small way, bring the whole ensemble down to earth.

Doll makers would have no trouble finding models for the ordinary servant dolls or in making these images of working people appealing. How, on the other hand, did they manage to create dolls with the countenances of the empresses, who have always been so remote and shrouded in mystery? The practice of displaying dolls on Girls' Day can be found back in the age of *The Tale of Genji*, and I gather that the custom of celebrating the holiday on the third day of the third month, as we do today, has been traced back to the Muromachi period. As to whether or not craftsmen in past eras ever actually had opportunities to see the empress, some people say that they used the wife of the reigning Tokugawa shogun as their model, not the empress, because the Tokugawa clan actually wielded more power and influence. But certainly even the shogun's lady sat cloistered behind myriad walls hidden from the world. How would it have been possible in the days before photography to know the face of such an august personage?

I must admit that the faces of the dolls I have seen actually do resemble those of the empresses. When I was a girl, the dolls all looked like Empress Shōken, wife of the Meiji emperor. They had slender faces with eyes that curved upward—a rather severe countenance, to be truthful. My daughter's dolls, which were made around 1930, had the same eyes, the same swell of the cheek, and the same soft curve of the chin as the present empress—or at least I thought so. They were much gentler in appearance than the ones I had.

No one, on the other hand, pays much attention to the emperor and minister dolls. While the female dolls may have certain features borrowed from an empress past or present, the male dolls do not seem to have any specific models. The only requirement is that they are devastatingly handsome.

The other day I went to see a film called *Roman Holiday.* That popular young star named Audrey Hepburn was in it, and when I first saw her I was immediately struck by how old-fashioned her face looked. Very strange, that this visage seemed to me to be from another age, while all her young fans regard her as fresh and new.

Not until the end of the movie did I realize that it was something about the way her eyes were made up. Their sharp, upward curve was Empress Shōken's. The shots of Hepburn in this film about a modern-day queen had reminded me of a photo of the Japanese empress from a half century before. The shape of the eyes brought the two images together for me. Of course, Audrey Hepburn's makeup man could not have been thinking of a specific Japanese empress when he applied that eyeliner, but it is altogether conceivable that he struck upon a Japanese look as a means of making the actress appear refined and dignified. Any resemblance was merely in my mind and doubtless unintentional. It just goes to show how great beauty transcends time and national boundaries.

The empress was, when all is said and done, a lovely woman. No wonder the doll makers wanted to borrow her countenance for their creations. They might have seen Her Majesty in real life—if they were fortunate enough to catch a glimpse of her as they stood among the well-wishers lining the streets when an imperial procession passed by. Come to think of it, by the Meiji period photographs were not out of the ordinary, so they may well have used one as a model.

Usually women become parents at a younger age than men do. Except for those possessed of an unusual share of maturity, most women find themselves in a state of giddy elation after they have their first baby. Youthful exuberance leads them to act without a thought for the consequences, and their elders can but sit and frown.

I know. I speak from experience. My child made me the happiest person in the world, and I wouldn't stop at anything to show how much I loved her. I knew as well as the next person that it is unseemly to proclaim to the world one's affection for a boyfriend, husband, sister, or brother. But I made the mistake, as many young mothers do, of thinking it acceptable to show my maternal love with complete openness. Every little thing one does for the child has to be just right, and it only gets worse on holidays and other special occasions. Young mothers tend to become blind to reality. Then they start concocting this kind of self-indulgent demonstration of sentiment.

Embarrassed as I am to admit it, I too was overtaken by this kind of willfulness. Girls' Day was drawing near, and even this rather insignificant holiday took on the proportions of a grand event in my mind—it was, after all, to be my daughter's first. I would plan the most wonderful party, the best I could manage. In my case, by the way, such determination to act meant that I had to carry out my plan to the letter. When I decided to do something, I would usually have my way.

So with every intention of buying the best dolls that could be had, I went and prowled through Jikkendana, which was still in business at the time. Next I scoured all the department stores in town. The celebration had to be perfect—even if I had to spend beyond our means. And that is precisely what I did. I forgot all about doing "the best I could manage" and stepped blithely into the realm of the extravagant. While in no position to be throwing money around, I became even more reckless when I discovered the perfect doll set. Once I had that, I just had to buy all the accessories for her too: those fancy little cushions, the adorable miniature dishes, the lacquered trays, the tiered lunch boxes. I bought them all.

Then there was the matter of decoration for the doll platform and curtain stand. If I were to leave them plain, the delicate faces and gorgeous costumes would lose their subtlety. I needed something that would create a backdrop— a curtain, perhaps. Not just a ready-made one, though, for that would be too prosaic. Better to have a curtain custom made, with a full snowflake cherry blossom pattern in several shades of pink and white on a pale green background. That would do the trick. Time was short, but I had the dyer come over anyway. I ordered a curtain in the finest crepe.

I became completely wrapped up in this idea of making everything perfect. I decorated the ceiling with silk peach blossoms and put up sprays of tiny yellow flowers all around the edges of the doors. Over the platform I spread a fresh, brilliant crimson length of felt. Once I had the food planned down to the smallest detail, I sat down with fancy, red-edged cards and wrote out little menus. The guest list included my mother-in-law and my parents—the proud grandparents.

But when we had finished all the preparations and there was nothing left to do but wait for the big day, the curtain still had not come. It was evening when I called to check on it, but the person who answered the phone told me that both the dyer and his wife had gone out a little after noon and still were not back. When I insisted on talking with someone who would know about my order, she curtly replied: "They're all out and there's no one here who can help you." In the dolls' room, which I had fixed up so nicely, the space where the curtain should have hung gaped, like a mouth, jeering me. The glass beads on the empress' crown flickered red and glistened with an emerald glow. The sight only irritated my frazzled nerves.

Nine o'clock came and went. There was no point in waiting any longer. From the beginning I had known that my order might be too late. If the curtain had still not arrived by morning, I would just have to find a substitute. I could always send someone out to buy a cheap, ready-made one, or I could conjure up something out of whatever scraps of fabric I had on hand. At this point, I would just have to make do. Clearly things were not going to turn out as I had hoped.

An air of gloom filled the house. Even the young nursemaid, who had been so excited all day, lost her cheer when she at last got up to lock the door. I had buried the red embers in the hearth and was dressing for bed when I heard a pounding at the front gate. The girl and I glanced at each other wide-eyed. Although we had not given up hope completely, this loud announcement gave us a start.

"I have arrived with your order."

The dyer's old-fashioned manner of speaking reassured me that it was the person we had been waiting for. But the moment I saw his face as he stood there beneath the light at the front door, I realized that something must have happened. He was haggard, his chin and upper lip were covered with black stubble, his cheeks were hollow. His eyes flashed with a fierceness that warded off expressions of kindness and concern. He also looked totally exhausted. Once in the sitting room, only with the greatest effort was he able to grumble an apology for his tardiness.

"We had to rush a bit with your order, but I believe it turned out well. I do hope this is satisfactory."

And with that, cherry blossoms scattered over the floor. It looked lovely, but I had no patience for his impersonal little speech. I had been waiting for that curtain all day.

"What happened? What held you up?"

The dyer, throwing a sharp glance in my direction, replied with a simple "Sorry, ma'am."

The dyer's wife made kimonos for a living. Skillful at her trade and with a mind of her own, she would only take on apprentices who planned to become professional seamstresses themselves. She had hired quite a number of young women, it seems. Although the old saying has a Tokyo man and a Kyoto woman as the perfect couple, the dyer and his wife, who were the reverse of this ideal order, got along very well in their personal life. When it came to their work, however, neither would compromise.

Just the day before, the dyer told me, they had had an argument. "The baby had been whining all morning, but my wife couldn't look after her because she was busy with the apprentices and also had a rush order to do. So I had to look after the baby. I was mad, all right, but I went ahead and took the kid to the bathroom. But she kept whining, even when I tried playing with her. I told my wife it was all her fault. I said to her, you spoil her rotten, and that's why she gets out of control like this."

The anger he had been directing at his wife then found a new object—the baby. He gave the child a whack on its bare bottom and stalked out of the house. All through the night, the child squirmed and cried, and by morning she had come down with a fever. Both parents tried holding her and rocking her on their backs, but the tears would not cease. Still barely able to stand on her own, the child could not, of course, tell anyone what was wrong.

Around noon, they called the doctor over and were shocked to find that the father's spanking had left a distinct, red imprint of his palm and each of his fingers on the baby's little bottom. And then the doctor made a grim diagnosis: she had a needle in her bottom. The father had unluckily spanked the baby right over a spot where the needle had lodged.

In the uproar that followed, the sewing girls rushed around getting everything ready for the trip to the hospital while the usually high-spirited wife sat in a state of shock immobile. This was because the husband, who was constantly hounded by his ever-so-careful wife, always ended their arguments with the words, "If you'll just be careful with those needles of yours till the girl grows up, I'll put up with any complaints you have."

The baby was admitted to the hospital and operated on immediately. A big needle used for sewing cotton had jammed into the hipbone and the head had broken off. The bone was chipped.

"I kept listening at the operating room door, but I couldn't hear a thing. But she pulled through it fine in the end. That's why I'm so late with your curtain."

Flames flared up from one of the coals I had put in the hearth, and the sharp smell filled the room. I sat, my shoulders tense, and listened.

It was March already, but still only the second of the month. The light of his bicycle a dim glow as he rounded the corner, the dyer quickly disappeared into the darkness. The air was frigid—a bitter kind of cold, I suppose you'd say. Even in the few moments I had been standing there, the harshness of the early spring chill had wrapped itself firmly around my already stiff shoulders. It felt heavy to me. A big chunk of the joy of the next day's celebration with the grandparents had crumbled before me.

The following day, the three elderly people seemed to enjoy our afternoon party. Dutifully they sought out my little projects and each had their own words of praise. I felt as if I had gotten an A-plus on a calligraphy lesson. In particular, they all commented on the fine-looking curtain. That was the last thing I needed. I could not even look at my own daughter without thinking of the dyer's poor baby who had suffered that terrible operation, and each compliment about the curtain made me wince. Still, I kept quiet about what had happened.

The next morning, a phone call came from my father's house. After thanking me for my hospitality, Mother passed on a message: "Your father would like to speak with you when you have a free moment." I had no idea what he wanted, but I could tell that he was going to scold me. But when I arrived at his house, Father genially thanked me for the party and commended me for my efforts.

"Did you plan all that yourself or did the two of you do it together?"

"Well, he was the one who suggested that we have you over. But I did the rest myself."

"And those dolls you bought—those were your idea?"

"Yes."

"What did he think of them?"

I could not answer him. My husband had indeed complained about all the money I was throwing around. Obviously, Father had sensed that.

"You really went all out. Outdid yourself. It's nice to do your best because you're having company. But I'm having a hard time swallowing your way of putting on a show. That's why I called you here today. I can't stand a woman who doesn't even know how to try hard. But I'm not terribly fond either of women who do everything so well and so completely that afterwards there's nothing left—just a big nothing. Of course, I'm glad you can do things so ably, but then what do you have to show for it? And you claim that it's all for your child, but what did she get out of all your hard work? Everyone is entitled to her share of happiness, but there has to be a limit. When a parent goes and does everything for a child, I can't help worrying about what will happen to her in the future. Luxury isn't how much a person's got, you know, it's how he uses what he does have. What you did was quite inappropriate for a child that small. In my opinion, you may even have taken away some of her potential for happiness. Your mother-in-law is an understanding woman and was kind enough to praise your extravagance as talent. But I personally felt that I had to say something to you about this whole business."

Although my father's words were indirect enough—he had kindly called my squandering of money "taking away her happiness" and my reprehensible overdoing of everything "the ability to accomplish a great deal"—still I felt their pressure as if they were touching some sore spot. Indeed, he had his point. My feelings at that moment were not unlike the sense of weight and collapse I had experienced at the gate when I was seeing the dyer off, but emotionally things were not as simple as they had been before.

In any case, the money I had used was not money for which I had to go begging. We had put out our own money and energy to have a nice party and what did we get? Complaints. It did not seem fair. How could he say that I had "used up my child's happiness"? Such thoughts swirled through my mind. To add insult to injury, I realized that hidden in my father's words was the message that I should go to my mother-in-law with an apology for my extravagance. And so, though somewhat against my will, I started off for her house.

I felt better once I was on the train. The blank faces of the passengers sitting across from me swayed back and forth as the train rumbled through the busy town. For some reason this collection of passive, unexcited faces had a calming effect on my nerves. The sense of tranquility that pervaded them reminded me of a field of big, round onion flowers swaying gently in the breeze.

And so, imagining that a clear blue sky stretched above my head, I contemplated the whole situation. What bothered me most was the accusation that I had used my daughter as an excuse to be as extravagant as I pleased. The words "you did too much" bothered me as well. My determination to act, even when it meant overstepping my limits, was reprehensible. My original plan to do things to the best of my ability out of love for our daughter had turned into an unchecked exercise in stubbornness. But he didn't need to tell me that.

If I were to put my husband in among the onion flowers there before me, he would be one of the more slender, immature blooms. He was not much of a presence: a thin little onion plant without much knowledge of the world. But my daughter and I depended on his slim existence. That was an accurate picture of our situation, but still nothing to be distressed about. Instead that overblown, gorgeous dolls' room, which I had created, loomed clearly and painfully before me. I loved my husband and my daughter—why had I let myself get so carried away? I felt disgust at the fact that I had allowed myself to be overwhelmed by pride and greed in my effort to do things right. Even so, when the wave of self-contempt had receded, there remained in me a glowing sense of pride that I had overcome so many obstacles and actually accomplished something. Even deeper within me, there lurked a mass of resentment directed at my father.

"Admit it, Father, you made a big fuss when you were young and you had your first child. Look at all those nice Girls' Day dolls sister had. But then when my turn came along, I was just the second child, so I ended up with some dumb old wooden emperor and empress dolls. You didn't even bother to get me any of the other dolls. That's unfair. I didn't want Tamako to have to settle for such pitiful dolls, and that's why I went ahead and got all that."

My feelings flowed along unfettered, but occasionally they would get stuck in slow waters.

My mother-in-law was ten years older than my father.

"Well, to be honest with you, after I got home that day I really had mixed feelings. I just didn't know what I should say and what I should keep to myself. Your father gave you a scolding for overdoing it, did he? To me, it's not so much that you overdid things, but that you didn't leave anything for us to do."

I had fixed everything up so completely that even the child's grandmother could find no place to express her affection. At least if there had been something missing, the following year she could have had the pleasure of buying something for her granddaughter. Now what did she have to look forward to?

"I think that a certain amount of imperfection creates a sense of closeness. But I can hardly scold you for being too perfect. I'm not about to complain about a daughter-in-law who makes sure that everything is just right. Why, I'm very proud of you! But it would have been so nice if you could have left a couple of spaces empty. I know that your talent is responsible for how beautifully everything turned out that day, but it was lonely for me because you had things so perfect."

I listened to her frank words as those of an older and wiser woman, not merely as the advice of a mother-in-law or grandmother. Indeed, my own father had shown his concern, but he tended to be overly blunt and say exactly what he had on his mind. I could appreciate his message, too, but the way he expressed it just made me want to fight back. I was more comfortable with my mother-in-law's approach to the whole matter because she told me honestly of her own feelings and her sense of loneliness. During my three years of marriage to her son, she had always praised me for doing things just right. I had thought that everything was fine between the two of us. Only now was I made to realize the ever-present yet inexpressible loneliness she had to suffer in the face of such a know-it-all daughter-in-law. Because she too was a woman, I could understand how she felt. It was almost as if I were getting a glimpse into my own future. That stiff, tense feeling I had when talking with my father simply melted away when I was with her. And, having lost that tension, I really let down my guard.

"But, Mother, you should have seen the dolls I had."

She somehow managed not to crack a smile.

"Certainly, I know you have good reason to complain. But I think you'd better stop doing things for Tamako because of your own feelings of deprivation. Given the way you are, I'm sure you'll do as much for your next couple of babies, but how are you going to manage if you have five or six girls?"

That caught me completely off guard. Although it seems too lacking in foresight to be true, the matter of a second or third daughter had never even occurred to me. That scared me.

"You're absolutely right. I couldn't do all that again if I had another child. I'd just have to give her some of those plain wooden emperor and empress dolls. And then she'd be miserable, just like I was!"

My shortsightedness was so stupid that it was actually funny. After a bit I was laughing so hard that tears streamed down my cheeks.

"So you have to learn not to take things quite so seriously, don't you?" she said with a smile.

*

Seven or eight years after that, my husband and I were divorced and my daughter and I moved back to my father's house. Her whole set of Girls' Day dolls was sent back there too, along with old, empty dressers and some other things.

Every March I could not escape the emotional sting of the dolls and the curtain.

The years passed. The fire bombings came incessantly and left Tokyo in total chaos. It was no time to be putting out the dolls. Everyone thought that the end was near, and this precipitated much unexpected foolishness. My daughter had grown up and was always occupied with her duties in the student service corps. The dolls must have been the last thing on her mind.

But consistent with the irrationality of the times, I put out the dolls for display just as I had every other year. The twelve dolls were as elegant, beautiful, and dazzling as ever, and the three servant dolls kept smiling in their slightly vulgar way. How they had aged since the day when I bought them! No one would expect dolls to grow old, but the faces of these had indeed become thin and tightly drawn. The white of their foreheads and cheeks had taken on a translucent quality, rather like the color of a silkworm's cocoon. The brilliant black eyes had already lost their sparkle and were tainted with a feeling of middle age.

The dolls had a small but very special feature that led me to choose them in the first place. Usually only the most expensive and elaborate dolls have five individual fingers on each hand. The most common type simply has a separate thumb and then grooves between the other four fingers; dolls of slightly better quality would have both the thumb and the little finger separated from the rest. Even though our dolls were not of the highest quality, the fingers were all divided.

Gone was the softness of those long, slender, graceful fingers that would look so perfect holding an elegant cedar fan. The silver trimming on the three shelves had become tarnished and black, and the edge of the writing desk was nicked. The brushes in the ink-stone box had been eaten by insects and the tips bent out of shape. The corners of the *go* and *shōgi* boards were chipped, and several of the playing pieces were missing. The strings of the koto had slipped off the bridge, and the lacquer of the flowered cart was peeling. Even the green of the curtain had faded and the shiny flecks that had adorned the cherry blossoms had fallen off. The dolls had grown old, I had grown old; only my daughter remained at the height of youth and splendor. More than ten years had passed and I could harbor no hopes about the coming year. It was a most casual parting.

By about the middle of that month, Tokyo had been transformed into a frazzled, burnt-out wasteland. More and more people were leaving the city to seek refuge. Railroads, trucks, and freight shipments had been almost totally cut off by the time we began to prepare for evacuation to the countryside. But with the help of a friend, we somehow managed to get hold of two trucks. As we arranged to leave the city, our primary concern was the safe transport of whatever books and papers we could fit in. My father, being very old and weak, was himself unable to choose the volumes he wanted us to take and could only watch as the heavy boxes, hastily chosen and hastily packed, were carted away.

At one point he glanced at me and asked, "Aren't you going to pack up Tamako's dolls?"

He seemed perfectly at peace, and showed no sign of irritation. After considering the matter for a moment, I replied, "No, I'll leave them here."

I had decided quickly, but I knew what I was doing—after all, I was no longer young and without experience. And I remembered what my father had said, the talk with my mother-in-law, the dyer's story. And in any case, I had taken a good look at them just a month or so before in the midst of a world in total chaos.

"Well, if you insist, Father, I'll ask Tamako about it."

To my question, Tamako replied without a moment's hesitation, "I'd rather have the space used for books than for those dolls!"

Her grandfather, hearing her response, simply said, "Is that so?"

That was the last of the dolls.

[*March 1955*]

A Friend for Life

I have a rather large full-length mirror at home. It is an old mirror, one that I bought nearly forty years ago. Not surprisingly it has begun to wear out. Last year, cloudy spots started appearing, one after another, all over the mirror's surface. I suddenly developed a great attachment to the mirror, and though I had never been faithful about keeping it clean, I set out to prevent the blotches from spreading. "A little care and attention," I thought, "will surely restore its youthfulness."

One day when the man from the glass shop was over working on something for me, I asked him to have a look at the mirror. He examined it and said there was nothing he could do.

"But I don't think you should rush into buying a new one. Use this one as long as it's got life in it. I personally would prefer not to replace it," he explained.

Now if this were an older man handing out such advice, I would not have given it a second thought. This young man with his personal opinion about everything, though, amused me a great deal. I decided to follow his advice and keep the mirror.

"I'm sorry to have wasted your time."

"Nonsense! To tell you the truth, last year when I came over here to install that wall mirror for you, I caught a glimpse of this one. So the other day when you phoned about a mirror that needed looking at, I knew right away that you meant this big one. No need to apologize, ma'am. I feel like we're old friends, this mirror and I," the fellow replied with a big grin. Then he went on his way.

Only then did I understand that from the glass man's point of view, every mirror he encounters becomes an acquaintance of sorts. One's outlook does depend on what one does for a living. Even so, he struck me as a quite unusual young man for this day and age.

The full-length mirror had been part of my trousseau. All the other things I had as a bride are gone now, reduced to ashes when Tokyo was fire-bombed during the war. Because the mirror was taken to the countryside, it survived.

It may seem odd that this was the only item out of my trousseau to leave Tokyo with me. Simply put, it caught somebody's eye. I myself felt no particular attachment to the mirror at the time. In fact, I had never even considered taking along such a bulky, fragile piece of baggage. The fellows who came to help us move, though, decided they wanted to save it from destruction. For some reason, people tend to take a fancy to big mirrors like that old one.

This was a custom-made mirror, but the shop had actually made it for someone else, not for me. By some miscalculation, the mirror turned out larger than originally planned and the customer who had placed the order refused to take it. When I spotted it looming there in the shop, I immediately took a liking to it. I had no idea that it was a reject. I learned of the mirror's history only when I asked why it had been marked down so low. Conspicuous because of its size, this mirror has been abandoned by one person, bought by another, transported to the countryside by men who were perfect strangers, and now doted on by the glass-shop owner.

In places not devastated by the war, many women still have mirrors that belonged to their grandmothers. By comparison, my forty-year-old mirror is a youngster. It will be my only possession to have lasted an entire generation, or perhaps I should say one lifetime, since I will likely use the mirror until it comes time for me to leave this world. When I first saw it in that shop, I certainly had no notion that something so fragile would be with me after so many years or that it would serve me longer than anything else.

A Strange Piece of Furniture

My memories about mirrors begin with my mother's dressing stand. Because I lost my mother when I was a very young child, I have only the vaguest recollections of her face. Photographs of Mother merely reinforce the haziness of my memories. I do remember that a hairdresser would come to the house to fix her hair. Mother kept her mirror, stand, and combs on the floor of the closet along with her sewing kit and the iron. She used the folding stand for the long-handled, round mirror. The surface of the mirror itself would most likely have been glass, not metal, by that time in the late Meiji. In any case, it was quite old-fashioned, as it had no doubt come to her when she was a young bride. I do distinctly remember her sitting before the glass, a white cloth draped over her shoulders, having her hair combed. I also have a picture in my mind of her mirror but, oddly, no clear image of her face.

She used neither powder nor rouge, but only a razor. Her toilette seems to have consisted of shaving off unwanted hair and shaping her eyebrows. Mother treated her razor with great respect. She would wrap it in a scrap of crimson silk before putting it back into its holder, a long, narrow lacquered box. So Mother's dressing table was indeed a simple affair. She took the mirror and stand out of the closet only when she needed them. The moment she was done, she put them away. Mother seemed to have a rule about not leaving these things out.

It was the same at my friends' houses. Their mothers would set up a mirror in a well-lit spot on the veranda or beside a window—but, again, only when necessary. Once finished with their mirrors, they would return them promptly to the closet, just as my mother did. Some had the type of mirror attached to a low dressing table with drawers, but even these were shoved away into some dark, inconspicuous corner when not in use. I imagine it was this way because we lived far from the enlightened metropolis in a village where people stubbornly kept to the old ways. "A woman in a decent home does not leave her makeup scattered all over for everyone to see," they would insist, or "A woman ought to be discreet when fixing her hair and applying powder." Mirrors, clearly, were not of the same order as sewing boxes and other ordinary household items.

One had only to go over the next hill to find houses with beautiful mirrors proudly set out for display. That was the area where women in the entertainment business—geisha and the like—lived. One could see the mirrors by peeking in through the openings between the wooden slats that covered the front windows of the houses. All the children in the neighborhood knew that late afternoon was the time when the ladies made up their faces, and we loved to go and watch them. Our mothers did not approve of such expeditions, though, and were constantly scolding us and telling stories about those evil women. But I much preferred their lovely, cheerful mirrors to our dark, solemn ones, which were always in the closet anyway, and I would occasionally steal over to take a peek. I'm sure that my behavior made my mother all the more insistent about decent, proper ways.

We did have one other mirror at home. A long glass about two feet tall hung on the wall in the bath. A lamp sat to its left, making the mirror easier to use at night than during the day, when the light would shine in from behind and make the mirror's surface strangely shallow and glaring. Things reflected in it looked dark. Despite these drawbacks, it was the only mirror in the house left out all the time, so the maids and I would always be running in there and putting our faces up close to it.

On occasion I notice young women behaving in a similar manner when they do their makeup. There might be three or four of them lined up in a row when I walk into the ladies' room of a department store or theater. They will all have their faces only inches from the glass, as if they had decided beforehand on this course of action. The lighting in such places must be a hundred times brighter than in our bath, but still these women feel compelled to thrust their faces forward as if they were long-necked cranes. No matter how well or poorly lit, a mirror seems to possess the power to make women behave oddly.

The Magic of Reflections

One often hears about the magical powers of mirrors. Certainly the mirror's ability to reflect creates this feeling of mystery. The objects around the viewer look so different in the mirror—what was one may multiply into two or even three. Objects that had appeared to be piled up come apart. Something might look real in the mirror, but then when you try to touch it, you can't. It seems to be there but it makes no sound. Is it real or just an illusion? Sometimes you can see through things in a mirror. Some things seem actually to be alive inside the mirror, but once the reflection stops moving, the illusion of life is gone. The mirror's power resides in this ability to confound.

When I was little, every child knew that if you opened all the doors on the night of the full moon, let your hair down, clamped a razor in your teeth, and looked into the mirror, your fate would appear in the mirror when the bright moonlight struck it. The very idea both terrified us and thrilled us, but in the end no one actually dared to try it. Mirrors are thus linked with fortunetelling and the spiritual world.

I am not certain whether people attribute that power to the mirror itself or regard the mirror as a mediator—a medium between the heavens, the gods, and human beings. Some people believe they can see, not only their own future, but also a departed lover or the holy Bodhisattva in the mirror. And so, for them, the mirror is a boundary between this world and the other. I wonder if such beliefs exist in other countries as well.

Quite a while ago I saw a movie about Orpheus. That filmmaker used the mirror to represent the passageway between the human world and the realm beyond, too, so I guess that people everywhere are interested in such notions. In the movie, a man carrying mirrors on his back appears time after time in the chilled, hushed alleyways. I shuddered at his unearthly, shrill voice as he cried out selling his wares. The use of mirrors in this film impressed me a great deal.

I once heard a funny story about a land where there are no mirrors. One day a man manages to get hold of a mirror, but what he sees when he peers into it is the face of his father as a youth. His wife becomes suspicious of his behavior and she too takes a peek in the mirror, only to find the face of a young woman! They get into an argument and a priest comes to act as a mediator. Everyone calms down and, in the end, the bald-headed monk pays obeisance to the mirror. The part at the beginning about the man seeing his own father's face shows the power mirrors have over people. We tend to see mirrors as being shallow and reflecting the world accurately, but one must realize that they have a certain depth, a mysterious darkness as well.

Things I Learned from My Stepmother

My real mother's mirror was far too conservative and old-fashioned for my taste. I liked my second mother's looking glass much better. It had a little chest of drawers with a mirror attached to the back. On top Mother kept her powder containers and perfume bottles; inside there were hair clips and combs. A wonderful scent emanated from the dressing table and, best of all, it sat imposingly—and permanently—in the sunniest spot in the whole house. My stepmother did not cover the mirror with a cloth either. The sight of it made me glad, because I had discovered a mirror far superior to any I had known before. It was so different.

My stepmother believed that a person should learn from a young age to distinguish between what is her own and what is not. She strictly prohibited me from so much as touching her mirror. I learned my lesson well and was satisfied with simply looking at her dressing table.

I remember that some people, both close relatives and casual acquaintances, regarded Mother's behavior and manner as cold and distant. They assumed it was because she was a stepmother. Personally I found refreshing her insistence that each of us clearly mark off her own territory. There was a certain cleanness, a coolness, in her attitude. It got rid of the hot air that frequently leads to all kinds of confusion and resentment. My stepmother taught me this and likely had to bear the criticism of others because of it.

I sometimes try to imagine what it would have been like had my real mother not died. In any case, my two mothers had very different personalities, backgrounds, and ideas. I resisted both of them at different times in my life, but in the end I accepted my stepmother's ideas on the subject of mirrors. I have passed these along to my own daughter as well. For practical reasons I was unable to give her a mirror of her own, but I did make a point of explaining to her that although we may share the same dressing table, we should not use each other's combs or hair clips without asking permission. When we did have to borrow something, even if just for a moment, we would always ask the other person first.

My daughter now has a three-year-old daughter of her own and is free to bring her up as she pleases. I shall try to refrain from stating my opinions in such matters. My stepmother's teachings have been passed on for three generations, but who knows what will happen when my great-grandchild comes along. There is nothing earthshaking about her notion of personal possessions. I realize that. At the same time, I truly appreciated my stepmother's spirit in this matter, for she desired only to keep her dressing table all to herself and remained exceedingly generous when it came to food or money. This is one memory of Mother that I am able to recall with complete and unconditional pleasure.

As the years passed and I grew up, I stopped going to see the pretty mirrors on the other side of the hill. I remained intrigued by the way the size of a mirror influences our perception of it. Large mirrors seemed so luxurious and wonderful. Small ones, on the other hand, struck me as confining and loathsome. To my way of thinking, the bigger the better—but with one exception. I could hardly call those huge makeup tables of the geisha elegant or high class, so I relegated them to the bottom of my list. I soon realized the problems with my method of evaluation. When I stopped to think about it, I realized that no one owned old-style mirrors like my first mother's anymore. Instead, everyone used some variation of a mirror attached to a low chest of drawers. The pawnshop lady, somewhat on the shopworn side herself, had a mirror that was always quiet and deserted. In families with many daughters, the dressing tables were constantly in an uproar. A scrap of purple silk was the only spot of color where the fireman's wife sat. At the sundries store, the looking-glass frame shined black with oil. A single flower in a vase decorated the dressing table of the unmarried schoolteacher.

After I entered the girls' middle school, I encountered mirrors superior to any I had seen before. Girls I knew from well-to-do families had their own dressing rooms. Their mirrors had expensive mulberry frames, and some were rimmed in lacquer and bore the family crest in gold. There was always a plump, oversized cushion to sit on, too, which made it all very elegant.

Uniquely Western Bedrooms

I found most refreshing the makeup table that I saw in a foreign lady's bedroom: a standing chest of drawers with a mirror attached to the top. How surprised I was at this very wide mirror (I was used to the tall, skinny ones), the lace doilies on the dresser, a silver hand-held mirror engraved with the lady's initials, hairbrushes, a ceramic powder holder topped with a flower-shaped handle, a jumbled arrangement of dolls and knickknacks, photographs, and a vase filled with fresh flowers. I immediately thought how troublesome it would be to clean such a room, but at the same time I was most impressed by the casual liveliness of her adornments. It struck me as quite revolutionary. I came away thinking of how well mirrors go with lace and also about the unusual location of the mirror. I had never seen a bedroom before, so the rarity of it all set my mind to work.

Women in other countries have bedrooms, places of their own where no one else is allowed. That is where they keep their mirrors. Only the owner of the room uses that mirror; no one else may gaze into the glass. I find this stubborn sense of purity and exclusion a bit surprising, but at the same time I feel attracted to it. This strictness reminds me of my first mother and the other neighbor ladies who would be quick to put their mirrors out of sight and constantly assert the importance of correct and decent behavior. It also has something in common with the dressing rooms found in good homes in Japan, which belong to the lady of the house and her daughters. While other family members are not forbidden to enter, something about the room makes them reluctant to venture inside. No matter how much it costs or how plain or fancy it may be, a mirror encourages people to take possession of it and the space around it. That seems only right.

A Place for the Mirror

Women in other countries and well-to-do Japanese wives have a place to put their mirrors. My real mother did not. I doubt that she even thought of having a place for it. All she possessed was a spot to hide away the glass. I suppose this has something to do with the reason I remember her mirror as a shabby and cheap one. Indeed, of the three types of mirrors, I regard my real mother's as the least desirable. My stepmother, who was able to think in much newer ways, went ahead and set up her mirror without regard for the opinions of others. She seized a place for herself. Her mirror had something vital and cheerful about it.

Perhaps she was correct. While it would not do to have just anyone look in and see you sitting in front of your mirror, it seems awfully sad not even to have a place to put the thing. One must have somewhere out in the open to keep it. There was great beauty in the boldness of those geisha who placed their mirrors in the most important room in the house. I felt a sense of pity and regret both for my mother and for her mirror, so somber and inferior by comparison.

I am certain that such feelings have something to do with my attraction to the slightly oversized mirror. I wanted to buy that mirror even after I found out that it had been rejected by another customer. I felt determined to find a place for it in the corner of our bedroom. In keeping with the scale of the full-length mirror, I ordered a three-way makeup mirror, and a rather fancy one at that. The maroon velvet chair and matching footstool satisfied my desire to be surrounded by luxury. How wonderful I felt when I was able to stake out a prime spot for the set in our new home. Mr. Kafū once wrote that even nice girls take on a disagreeable, unmanageable bent when they get married. I was hopeless from the start. In time, I lost whatever diligence I had possessed.

My life was not going smoothly. I could not handle the problems that confronted me and became unbelievably nervous and stubborn. At times, any little thing would set me off in a rage; often I would get upset and break down in tears. I had so many things on my mind. In those days I consoled myself by leaning up against the sturdy legs of my mirror. To think how proud I had felt of it on my wedding day. Now all I could do was crouch up against it and sigh. In that house, it was the only place where I felt calm. The mirror served more as a support for my emotions than as a glass in which I could see my reflection. The sunny location I had chosen for it had been part of my effort to avoid sadness and gloom in my life, but ironically it ended up lodging a darkened, tired soul. I did, in any case, feel most peaceful when I sat by my mirror. My parents were probably unaware of my state of collapse. But I knew they were concerned about all the conflict and despair that surrounded me. My father offered words of encouragement.

"People's lives are fraught with troubles, certainly, but those problems are just like weeds. Insignificant garbage, weeds, that's all they are. If you look at it that way, it doesn't seem so awful, now does it? So you see, all you have to do is eradicate them, clean them up."

I liked the way he phrased his suggestion—a forceful "eradicate" rather than some weak-kneed expression like "solve." His words stuck in my mind, but in my enervated state I found it difficult to rise to the occasion. I could only cringe at his kind words.

I might add that although Father had used the phrase "clean up," he had not, of course, meant for me to take it literally. He wanted to remind me that I knew where the problems lay and that I should begin attacking the ones closest to me. In those days, though, I spent much of my time sitting glumly beside my mirror, its stand cluttered with all sorts of odds and ends. When Father told me to clean up, I promptly set about straightening up and polishing the mirror. In fact, I've been strict with myself about keeping it clean ever since. Even now I have a mess of things all over the top, but at least I am in the habit of regularly polishing the mirror surface to a brilliant shine. The first time I wiped the glass, I was shocked to discover how dirty a mirror can become. One usually does not notice the dust; a mirror will reflect even when covered with a heavy layer of grime. And once you get used to this, you may end up looking at yourself and trying to make yourself presentable with powder and lipstick, unaware that you are seeing yourself through a haze. But who bothers to dust mirrors? If even smoothly polished glass attracts dust, how much more would accumulate on a troubled heart?

In the end, I left my husband. When it came time to move out, I felt keenly embarrassed about being the owner of such a grandiose mirror.

Father Shows Me the Mirror

After I returned to my parents' house, some time passed before I regained my peace of mind. It was around that period that I began looking carefully into the mirror. Various events prompted me to do so.

One day I got into a terrible argument with Father. I had fallen into the bad habit of picking a fight with anyone and everyone. It did not take much to set me off on a brazen attack. Usually my opponent would not respond. Father was no exception that day. He simply stood up and walked out of the room. In my mind, however, nothing had been settled. I followed him and proposed that we talk some more.

"Young lady, I will have nothing whatsoever to do with you if you continue to behave in such a vulgar manner. I don't like you speaking to me so rudely and sitting in that disrespectful posture. You wouldn't act that way toward a stranger, so why do you have the nerve to treat me like this? A little respect, if you please. Let's talk this out in a civilized way."

I had pushed him too far, and he was not going to let me get away with it.

He had more subtle means of showing me the folly of my ways. One day I shut myself up in my room and was sulking there when Father casually walked in and, without warning, thrust a small mirror up to my face. I saw my surly countenance grimace in embarrassment. How ugly and out of sorts I looked.

"The mouth gives vent to the human heart through words; the face through its expressions. This mirror tells you what is in your heart now."

His demonstration had the desired effect, and finally I was able to talk reasonably. I would never have expected a mirror to play such a role in one of my encounters with Father. A mirror catches much more than the stationary figure that poses before it, the pretty face one wants to see.

There is a personality type called the repeater. Such a person may read a novel and find it moving, and some trace of the emotional effect will remain part of her. But with each day that passes, more and more facts and events pile up on top of that memory and the original emotions are obscured. Even though it may not be forgotten entirely, the experience of reading has as well as vanished. Then, one day, something happens to trigger her memory and it all comes back, though only so vaguely that she feels compelled to read the book again. This time she understands everything with great perspicacity, even the details she overlooked before. She feels satisfied that she has a clear grasp of the work and now can remember it well. As far as personality types go, she falls roughly into the careless category. But repetition—reading something twice or perhaps three times—may elevate her to the ranks of the meticulous. A sloppy yet careful type, we might call her.

I am such a person. As a girl I was taught this lesson about mirrors and understood the point of it. It made only a slight impression in my memory, though, and in time sank to the bottom, utterly useless. I am the kind who has to do something twice before I really master it.

Only a Pretty Face for the Mirror

"Women are strange indeed. Are they truly as fond of mirrors as they would have us believe? Even though they ought to try and see their bad sides—anger, jealousy, disappointment in love, irritability, curtness—I think that they only want to see a pretty face when they look at a mirror. A woman may be in the middle of a big fight, but when she goes up to a mirror to fix her makeup, what do you know? She's as sweet as an angel all of a sudden."

"Not that women actually stay in front of the mirror long enough to find a face that truly satisfies them. The kind of satisfaction they are seeking comes from a face that is momentarily frozen. In reality, though, your face is always moving. Don't they realize that? Living creatures are constantly in motion, changing, active, so how can you be happy with a face that is not? There's more to life than posing. People shouldn't be content with such false images of themselves."

"A person who gazes at herself in the mirror all the time seems to be entrusting the expression of her emotions to her countenance. She also thinks that her face is secure there in the mirror, but what is there to assure her of that?"

"I was under the impression that a three-way mirror would help a clumsy person see herself from behind, but that doesn't seem to be the case. You haven't improved one bit."

"Look at your feet in the mirror! You ought to do something about that unsightly way of walking of yours."

"I wonder what the world would be like if there were no mirrors. Certainly it would make life easier. Because there would be fewer tasks to attend to—a lot less useless things to take up your time."

"A mirror isn't going to shave off your various bumps, but it might help you find ways to make your cheekbones or bottom look a little better. A mirror has no mouth, though, so it will neither tell you what to do nor complain. That's what is wonderful about a looking glass. It will help you to avoid embarrassment—and for free."

"If you want to know whether mirrors tell the truth or not, try tilting a full-length mirror forward a bit. You'll look thin. Tilt it back and your legs get short. If a woman looks slender in the mirror, she thinks it's because she has a nice figure. But if she appears short and pudgy, then she'll blame it on the mirror. Most people get upset when they look at themselves in a mirror positioned correctly."

*

It takes me two times to catch onto anything, even if I pay careful attention on first exposure. I was over thirty when I had to relearn this particular lesson. Certainly this incident made me feel even more attached to that mirror.

My life alone began when I was nearly sixty and my only child got married and moved away. Because I had been preparing for this new life, I was able to adjust quite nicely, aware that it would bring me both pleasure and loneliness. My daughter married a doctor who had been living on his own instead of with his parents, as many single young men do. Their marriage, then, meant that our situations reversed—he now had companionship, while I was alone. One day my son-in-law said something to me that seemed a typical line for a doctor, but I appreciated it nonetheless.

"You know how they say that when one partner in an elderly couple dies the other spouse is likely to pass away not long after? Well, it actually happens that way quite often. I hear that it's because when people have lived together so long, each member of the couple is good at keeping an eye out for the other. They know each other so well that one would notice immediately if the other's voice were a bit shaky or eyes looked a little tired. But then with that mutual support gone, the surviving spouse is likely to get sick without noticing the warning signs. So I want you to be extra careful from now on, okay, Mother?"

"You know, you're right. I'll have to watch myself once I start living alone."

And indeed, when I was by myself, my old familiar mirror proved useful in yet another way. The three-way mirror had burned during the war and was no longer with me. I had to ask my big, ponderous mirror to watch for signs of poor health.

It has no mouth and neither complains nor tells me what to do. And as a result, I have to do all the talking. When I fail to get enough sleep, the mirror shows me my taut, sallow skin. That is its way of answering me. I listen to these warnings and go to bed early. The next morning I ask the mirror again for its opinion.

People need mirrors much more when they get old—not only for their health, but also so they can pay proper attention to their hair and clothing. Some say that old folks do not have any use for mirrors, but I disagree. I depend more and more on my mirror as the years go by. Regardless of what kind of shape your hair is in when you are young, you never have so little hair that your scalp shows through. When one grows older, though, the hair thins out and a mere combing will make the hair clump together in unsightly stripes, exposing the scalp beneath. Bald men may have their charm, but women with thin hair are not attractive in the least. So I always make sure to ask my rather large mirror to watch out for me and check on my appearance.

"If my hair gets any sparser, I won't make you suffer. I have a wig ready for that day. Just bear with me for a little while longer."

I need my mirror to help me out.

Look Carefully

There is a very beautiful woman here in Tokyo who is known as a master of traditional Japanese dance and music. Once I had the good fortune to meet her. Somehow we got on the subject of her hands. I had not made a point of asking about them, nor did she bring up the topic. But to my great delight, we spent some time talking about it.

In Japanese dance, the ability to arch one's fingers back gracefully is essential. But, she told me, she had always had trouble with that movement, even as a child. There is no word for this but bad luck—because in dance, of course, the hands are a vital tool. Many times her inability brought her to the verge of tears, but she knew that crying would not help the situation. Instead she would practice bending her fingers back while soaking in the bath each evening and pray for the impossible to become possible. I was amazed that a lady so well respected for her skill as a dancer had met with such difficulties. Though I have not seen her since, I think of her often and enjoy looking at photographs of her occasionally.

At one point I came across a picture of her standing in front of a mirror—I think it might have been a three-way mirror. I do remember that it was an extremely large one. While the juxtaposition of a dancer and a mirror is a natural subject for a photograph, I realized then for the first time how artistic, how beautiful, this dancer's use of mirrors was. She must have been strict with herself before the mirror, always striving to look lovely. I imagined her gazing into it sternly, judging her own poses as ugly, her posture slovenly. At other times, surely she let down her guard and perhaps even collapsed in tears from exhaustion. And I, too, had memories of such painful, oppressive times. Her mirror was fortunate to have been put to such good use.

All those mirrors I saw as a child: my mother's little mirror (the one she was always putting away), my stepmother's mirror (grand, though not large, and one that was all her own), and then the large, bright ones belonging to the ladies of the lilting voices and powder puffs on the other side of the hill. Of the three, I liked the big ones the best. When I was still very young, I felt certain that, after all I had seen, I knew what was best for me. I wanted something specially made for me, and yet I happily accepted a castoff. Later I sat miserably against the frame of that big mirror.

Now I cannot live without it. We have grown old together and, in its reflection, dotted now with age spots, I have at last found a little peace. I readily acknowledge the mirror as my lifelong friend. I must, however, confess that once in a while I neglect to polish it during my daily chores, being the occasionally careful, but more usually careless, type that I am.

[*1966*]

Chronology

1904   Kōda Aya is born in Terajima Village, Minami Katsushika-gun, Tokyo (present-day Higashi Mukōjima, Sumida Ward, Tokyo), the second child of Kōda Rohan and Kimiko, on 1 September.

1907   Brother Shigetoyo (Ichirō) is born.

1910   Mother Kimiko dies.

1911   Enters Terajima Elementary School. Rohan is awarded honorary Doctor of Literature degree.

1912   Elder sister Utako (b. 1901) dies of scarlet fever. Rohan marries Kodama Yayoko.

1917   Graduates from elementary school and enters Joshi Gakuin, a missionary school for girls in Kōjimachi. During the summer she begins home lessons with her father as well as rote memorization of the Confucian classics with a tutor.

1922   Graduates from Joshi Gakuin. Attends a tailor school for several months.

1923   Flees her Mukōjima home in aftermath of Great Kantō Earthquake.

1924   Moves to a new residence in Koishikawa, Tokyo.

1926   Bedridden because of typhoid fever. Brother Ichirō dies of tuberculosis.

1927   Moves to a new home in Koishikawa, which Rohan calls Kagyūan (Snail's Hut).

1928   Enters arranged marriage to Mitsuhashi Ikunosuke, third son of a liquor wholesaler in Shingawa.

1929   Daughter Tama is born.

1934   Consults with Kobayashi Isamu about her wish to divorce.

1936   Moves back to father's home temporarily but then returns to husband. Opens a small liquor shop in Tsukiji. Moves to several different apartments.

1937   Moves shop to Hatchōbori. Rohan is awarded First Medal for Cultural Merit.

1938   Husband Ikunosuke has surgery for lung disease. Formal divorce is finalized. Returns to father's home with daughter Tama.

1939   Studies Bashō's poetic sequences with Rohan.

1943   Attends birthday party for Rohan along with Saitō Mokichi, Koizumi Shinzō, Mushanokōji Saneatsu, and others.

1944   Nurses her bedridden father.

1945   Stepmother Yayoko dies. Because of Allied Forces' incendiary bombing, evacuates with Rohan and Tama to Yayoko's hometown in Nagano prefecture. In May their Koishikawa home Kagyūan is destroyed in the bombing. In September the Pacific War ends. In November, Shiotani San helps Kōdas find a house in Sugano, Ichikawa City, Chiba prefecture.

1946   Her aunt, musician Kōda Nobuko, dies. Rohan moves into the Sugano house. Rohan celebrates eightieth birthday.

1947   Asked by Noda Utarō to write about Rohan's physical condition. On 30 July, Rohan dies. In August her first essay, "Random Notes," appears in the journal *Geirin Kanpo*. Writes "His Last Hours" (Shūen) and "Father's Funeral" (Sōsō no ki). Moves back to Koishikawa.

1948   Writes "Incantations" (Atomiyosowaka) and other memoiristic essays.

1949   Publishes the essays "Good for Nothing" (Misokkasu) and "The Medal" (Kunshō). Writes essays on the occasion of reissuing Rohan's *Collected Works*. Publishes first book: *My Father—His Death* (Chichi—sono shi).

1950   Edits Rohan's *Letters* (Rohan shokan) for publication. A newspaper article announces that she may cease writing. Publishes the book of essays *This Kind of Thing* (Konna koto).

1951   Publishes the book *Good for Nothing* (Misokkasu); edits a volume of Rohan's letters; completes the short story "A Woman's Screams" (Kansei) and two other short pieces and a book.

1952   Edits a volume of Rohan's short essays. Her Koishikawa home is designated an Important Cultural Site by the city of Tokyo.

1953   Edits another volume of Rohan's short essays and publishes two essays.

1954   Publishes "Black Hem" (Kuroi suso) and five other short pieces. The seventeen-volume *Rohan zenshū* is published.

1955   Serialization of *Flowing* (Nagareru) begins in the journal *Shinchō* (January–December). Publishes "Dolls for a Special Day" (Hina) and a volume of short stories with the title *The Black Hem* (Kuroi suso). Edits a volume of Rohan's writings on poetry.

1956   Serialization of *Little Brother* (Otōto) begins in *Fujin Kōron* (January–September 1957). Awarded Yomiuri Literary Prize for *The Black Hem*. Film version of *Flowing* receives a prize from the Ministry of Education. *Flowing* receives the Shinchō Literary Prize. Edits another volume of Rohan's writings. Publishes fifteen essays.

1957   Receives Geijutsuin Prize for *Flowing*. Publishes numerous essays and short stories, including *Notes on Flowing* (Nagareru oboegaki).

1958   Publishes seven-volume *Collected Works of Kōda Aya* (Kōda Aya zenshū). Publishes numerous essays and books. *Little Brother* is produced as a play.

1959   Publishes the novel *Sorrow of the North* (Hokushū) and numerous essays and several volumes of essays.

1960   Film version of *Little Brother,* directed by Ichikawa Kon, receives Ministry of Education Prize.

1961   Grandson Takashi is born.

1962   Publishes "Living Alone" and other essays.

1963   Aunt Ando Kōko, violinist, dies. Granddaughter Naoko is born.

1965   *The Struggle* is serialized (January–December); *Kimono* is serialized (June–August 1966).

1966   Publishes "A Friend for Life" and many other essays.

1968   Publishes "Ashes over the Moon" and other essays.

1971   Publishes "The Pagoda at Hōrinji Temple." Speaks in various cities in an effort to raise funds for reconstruction of Hōrinji Pagoda in Nara. Starts series of essays on the subject of trees (last installment published in 1984) in journal *Gakutō*.

1972   Continues efforts on behalf of Hōrinji.

1973   Receives Women's Literature Prize for *The Struggle*.

1975   Publishes more essays about the pagoda.

1976   Travels to study landslides and publishes a series of essays on landslides *(Kuzure)*. Chosen as a member of the prestigious Nihon Geijutsuin.

1977–
1988   Publishes many essays, principally about trees.

1988   Suffers a stroke.

1990   Dies of heart failure on 31 October.

Bibliography

The seven-volume *Kōda Aya zenshū* was published by Chūō Kōronsha in 1958–1959. The twenty-three-volume *Kōda Aya zenshū (KAZS)* from Iwanami Shoten, an annotated edition, was published from 1995 to 1997. The following bibliography includes Kōda Aya's writings that have not appeared in either of the *Zenshū* at the time of this writing, as well as editions to which I have referred frequently. All Japanese publications are published in Tokyo unless otherwise noted.

Works by Kōda Aya

Chichi—Konna koto. Shinchōsha, 1956.

Chigiregumo. Kōdansha, 1993.

Hokushū. Shinchōsha, 1972.

Kimono. Shinchōsha, 1993.

Kisetsu no katami. Kōdansha, 1993.

Kōda Aya zenshū. 7 vols. Chūō Kōronsha, 1958–1959.

Kōda Aya zenshū. 23 vols. Iwanami Shoten, 1995–1997.

Misokkasu. Iwanami Shoten, 1983.

"Mono iwanu isshō no tomo." *Fujin Kōron* 51(7) (1966):119–129.

Tō. Shinchōsha, 1973.

Tsuki no chiri. Kōdansha, 1994.

"Watakushi wa fude o tatsu." *Yūkan Mainichi Shinbun,* Tokyo edition, 7 April 1950, p. 2.

Translations

"The Black Kimono." Translated by E. G. Seidensticker. In *Modern Japanese Stories,* edited by E. G. Seidensticker et al. Tokyo: Japanese Publications, Inc., 1958.

"The Black Skirt." Translated by E. G. Seidensticker. *Japan Quarterly* 3(2) (1956):196–212.

"The Medal," "Hair," "The Black Hems," and "Dolls." Translated by Alan M. Tansman. In Alan M. Tansman, *The Writings of Kōda Aya: A Japanese Literary Daughter*. New Haven: Yale University Press, 1993.

Secondary Sources

Akiyama Shun. "Kaisetsu." In *Kuroi suso* by Kōda Aya. Shinchōsha, 1968.

Anderer, Paul. *Other Worlds: Arishima Takeo and the Bounds of Modern Japanese Fiction*. New York: Columbia University Press, 1984.

Aoki Tama. *Kaeritakatta uchi*. Kōdansha, 1997.

———. *Kōda Aya no tansu no hikidashi*. Shinchōsha, 1995.

———. *Koishikawa no uchi*. Kōdansha, 1994.

———. "Oboete iru koto" (pt. 1). In *Kōda Aya zenshū* 8:3–8.

Ariga, Chieko. "Dephallicizing Women in *Ryūkyō shinshi:* A Critique of Gender Ideology in Japanese Literature." *Journal of Japanese Studies* 51(3) (August 1992):571.

Armstrong, Nancy. *Desire and Domestic Fiction: A Political History of the Novel*. New York: Oxford University Press, 1987.

Bakhtin, M. M. *The Dialogic Imagination*. Austin: University of Texas Press, 1981.

Barthes, Roland. *The Fashion System*. Translated by Matthew Ward and Richard Howard. New York: Hill & Wang, 1983.

Beichman, Janine. *Masaoka Shiki*. Boston: Twayne, 1982.

Bernstein, Gail, ed. *Recreating Japanese Women: 1600–1945*. Berkeley: University of California Press, 1991.

Brooks, Peter. *Body Work: Objects of Desire in Modern Narrative*. Cambridge, Mass.: Harvard University Press, 1993.

Brower, Robert H., and Earl Miner. *Japanese Court Poetry*. Stanford: Stanford University Press, 1961.

Bruss, Elizabeth. *Autobiographical Acts: The Changing Situation of a Literary Genre*. Baltimore: Johns Hopkins University Press, 1976.

Cheever, Susan. *Home Before Dark: A Biographical Memoir of John Cheever.* Boston: Houghton Mifflin, 1984.

Cohn, Dorrit. *Transparent Minds: Narrative Modes for Presenting Consciousness in Fiction.* Princeton: Princeton University Press, 1978.

Copeland, Rebecca. *The Sound of the Wind: The Life and Works of Uno Chiyo.* Honolulu: University of Hawai'i Press, 1992.

Dalby, Liza. *Geisha.* Berkeley: University of California Press, 1983.

————. *Kimono: Fashioning Culture.* New Haven: Yale University Press, 1993.

Danly, Robert Lyons. *In the Shade of Spring Leaves: The Life and Writings of Higuchi Ichiyō, A Woman of Letters in Meiji Japan.* New Haven: Yale University Press, 1981.

DeBary, Brett. "Not Another Double Suicide: Gender, National Identity, and Repetition in Shinoda Masahiro's *Shinjūten no Amijima.*" *Iris* 16 (Spring 1993):57–86.

Drummond, Richard H. *A History of Christianity in Japan.* Grand Rapids: Eerdsman, 1971.

Eakin, Paul John. *Fictions in Autobiography: Studies in the Art of Self-Invention.* Princeton: Princeton University Press, 1985.

Elam, Diane. *Feminism and Deconstruction.* New York: Routledge, 1994.

Ericson, Joan E. *Be a Woman: Hayashi Fumiko and Modern Japanese Women's Literature.* Honolulu: University of Hawai'i Press, 1997.

Erikson, Erik H. *Childhood and Society.* Rev. ed. New York: Norton, 1963.

Etō Jun. *Seijuku to sōshitsu: "haha" no hōkai.* Kōdansha, 1993.

Folkenflik, Robert, ed. *The Culture of Autobiography: Constructions of Self-Representation.* Stanford: Stanford University Press, 1993.

Fowler, Edward. *The Rhetoric of Confession: Shishōsetsu in Early Twentieth-Century Japanese Fiction.* Berkeley: University of California Press, 1988.

Fuss, Diane. *Essentially Speaking: Feminism, Nature, and Difference.* New York: Routledge, 1989.

Gaines, Jane, and Charlotte Herzog, eds. *Fabrications: Costume and the Female Body.* New York: Routledge, 1990.

Garon, Sheldon. *Molding Japanese Minds: The State in Everyday Life.* Princeton: Princeton University Press, 1997.

Gessel, Van. *The Sting of Life: Four Contemporary Japanese Novelists.* New York: Columbia University Press, 1989.

Golley, Gregory L. "Tanizaki Junichirō: The Art of Subversion and the Subversion of Art." *Journal of Japanese Studies* 21 (1995):365–404.

Haga Kōshirō. "'Nihontekina bi' no seiritsu no tenkai." In *Geidō shisō shu.* Vol. 7 of *Nihon no shisō.* Chikuma Shobō, 1971.

Harari, Josué V., ed. *Textual Strategies.* Ithaca: Cornell University Press, 1979.

Hibbett, Howard. *The Floating World in Japanese Fiction.* New York: Grove Press, 1960.

Hijiya-Kirschnereit, Irmela. "The Concepts of Tradition in in Modern Japanese Literature." In *Tradition and Modern Japan,* edited by P. G. O'Neill. Tenterden, Kent: Norbury, 1981; distributed by University of British Columbia Press.

———. *Rituals of Self-Revelation: Shishōsetsu as Literary Genre and Socio-Cultural Phenomenon.* Cambridge, Mass.: Harvard University Press, 1996.

Hiraoka Toshio. "Kōda Rohan." *Kokubungaku kaishaku to kanshō* 34(1) (1969): 67–72.

Hirosue Tamotsu. *Akubasho no hassō: denshō no sōzōteki kaifuku.* Sanseidō, 1970.

Hirozawa Sakae. *Kurokami to keshō no Shōwashi.* Iwanami Shoten, 1993.

Honda Masuko. *Jogakusei no keifu: saishiki sareru Meiji.* Seidōsha, 1990.

Honda Masuko et al. *Shōjoron.* Seikyūsha, 1988.

Honda Shūgo. *Monogatari sengo bungakushi.* Shinchōsha, 1965.

Ienaga Saburō. *Japan's Last War: World War II and the Japanese.* Translated by Frank Baldwin. Oxford: Basil Blackwell, 1979.

Ihara, Saikaku. *The Great Mirror of Male Love.* Translated and introduced by Paul Gordon Schalow. Stanford: Stanford University Press, 1990.

———. *The Japanese Family Storehouse: or The Millionaire's Gospel Modernised.* Translated by G. W. Sargent. Cambridge: Cambridge University Press, 1959.

———. *The Life of an Amorous Woman and Other Writings.* Edited and translated by Ivan Morris. New York: New Directions, 1963.

Ikari Akira. "Kōda Rohan to Edo bungaku." *Kokubungaku kaishaku to kanshō* 57(7) (1992):37–47.

Ikeda Kikan et al., eds. *Makura no sōshi—Murasaki Shikibu nikki.* Vol. 19 of Nihon koten bungaku taikei. Iwanami Shoten, 1958.

———. *Zuihitsu bungaku.* Vol. 5 of Ikeda Kikan kansen shū. Shibundō, 1969.

Inoue Kazuko. "Onna no isshō—Kōda Aya to kimono." In *Gengo bunkabu kiyō.* Hokkaidō Daigaku, 1994.

Ishikawa Jun, Ōno Susumu, Kōda Aya, and Maruyama Saiichi. "Tōkyō kotoba." *Tosho* 365 (1980):2–20.

Isogai Hideo. *Bungakuron to buntairon.* Meiji Shoin, 1980.

———. "*Nagareru*—Kōda Aya." *Kokubungaku kaishaku to kyōzai no kenkyū* 13(5) (1968):83–87.

———. *Senzen sengo no sakka to sakuhin.* Meiji Shoin, 1980.

Itagaki Hiroko, ed. *Kindai joryū no bungaku.* Shintensha, 1972.

Itagaki Naoko. *Meiji Taishō Shōwa no joryū bungaku.* Ōfūsha, 1967.

Ito, Ken. *Visions of Desire: Tanizaki's Fictional Worlds.* Stanford: Stanford University Press, 1991.

Iwabuchi Hiroko, Kitada Sachie, and Kōra Rumiko, eds. *Fueminizumu hihyō e no shōtai: Kindai josei bungaku o yomu.* Gakugei Shorin, 1995.

Iwaya Daishi. *Monogatari joryū bundanshi.* 2 vols. Chūō Kōronsha, 1977.

Jauss, Hans Robert. *Toward an Aesthetic of Reception.* Translated by Timothy Bahti. Minneapolis: University of Minnesota Press, 1982.

Jinbō Kazuya. *Kinsei Nihon bungakushi.* Yūhikaku, 1978.

Kamei Takeshi. "Bunshō to iu mono." *Gakutō* 53(4) (1956):36–38.

Kanai Keiko, et al., eds. *Kōda Aya no sekai.* Kaknrin Shobō, 1998.

Karatani Kōjin. *Kindai Nihon bungaku no kigen.* Kōdansha, 1980.

———. *Origins of Modern Japanese Literature.* Translated and edited by Brett DeBary. Durham: Duke University Press, 1993.

Katō Norihiro. *Amerika no kage.* Kawada Shobō Shinsha, 1985.

Kawai Hayao. *Bosei shakai Nihon no byōri*. Chūō Kōronsha, 1976.

Keene, Donald. *Dawn to the West: Japanese Literature in the Modern Era—Fiction.* New York: Holt, 1984.

———. *World Within Walls: Japanese Literature of the Pre-Modern Era, 1600–1867.* New York: Grove Press, 1978.

Kenner, Hugh. *Joyce's Voices.* Berkeley: University of California Press, 1978.

Kobayashi Hideo. *Kobayashi Hideo zenshū*. Shinchōsha, 1978.

Kobayashi Isamu. *Kagyūan hōmonki*. Iwanami Shoten, 1956.

Kōda Rohan. *Kōda Rohan zenshū*. Chūō Kōronsha, 1957.

———. *Pagoda, Skull, and Samurai: Three Stories by Rohan Kōda.* Translated by Chieko Irie Mulhern. Rutland, Vt.: Tuttle, 1985.

———. *Rohan zuihitsu.* 5 vols. Iwanami Shoten, 1983.

Kōda Shigetomo. *Bonjin no hansei*. Kyōritsu Shobō, 1948.

Kojima Chikako. "Kōda san no namida." *Shinchō* 88(1) (1991):204–207.

Kojima Nobuo. "The American School." Translated by William F. Sibley. In *Contemporary Japanese Literature: An Anthology of Fiction, Film, and Other Writing Since 1945,* edited by Howard Hibbett. New York: Knopf, 1977.

Komatsu Shinroku. "Hito to bungaku." In *Amino Kiku, Tsuboi Sakae, Kōda Aya shū.* Vol. 40 of Chikuma gendai bungaku taikei. Shinchōsha, 1980.

———. "Kaidai." In *Kōda Aya.* Vol. 34 of Shinchō gendai bungaku. Shinchōsha, 1980.

Kornicki, Peter F. *The Reform of Fiction in Meiji Japan.* London: Ithaca Press, 1982.

———. "The Survival of Tokugawa Fiction in the Meiji Period." *Harvard Journal of Asiatic Studies* 41(2) (1981):461–482.

Kowaleski-Wallace, Elizabeth. *Their Fathers' Daughters: Hannah More, Maria Edgeworth, and Patriarchal Complicity.* New York: Oxford University Press, 1991.

Koyama Tetsurō. "Bungaku tsuiseki: Kōda Aya futatabi." *Bungakukai* 6 (1993): 216–219.

Kuki Shūzō. *"Iki" no kōzō; ta nihen.* Iwanami Shoten, 1979.

Kuriyama Riichi. "Bunjinron." In *Fūryūron*. Kobun Shobō, 1929.

LaFleur, William R. *The Karma of Words*. Berkeley: University of California Press, 1983.

Lane, Richard. "Saikaku and the Modern Japanese Novel." In *Japan's Modern Century*, edited by Edmund Skrzypczak. Rutland, Vt.: Tuttle, 1968.

Larson, Wendy. *Literary Authority and the Modern Chinese Writer: Ambivalence and Autobiography*. Durham: Duke University Press, 1991.

Lebra, Joyce, Joy Paulson, and Elizabeth Powers, eds. *Women in Changing Japan*. Stanford: Stanford University Press, 1976.

Lebra, Takie Sugiyama. *Japanese Women: Constraint and Fulfillment*. Honolulu: University of Hawai'i Press, 1984.

Legge, James, trans. *Confucian Analects, The Great Learning, and The Doctrine of the Mean*. New York: Dover, 1971.

Levy, Helen Fiddyment. *Fiction of the Home Place: Jewett, Cather, Glasgow, Porter, Welty, and Naylor*. Jackson: University Press of Mississippi, 1992.

Lipovetsky, Gilles. *The Empire of Fashion: Dressing Modern Democracy*. Translated by Catherine Porter. Princeton: Princeton University Press, 1994.

Maeda Ai. *Kindai Nihon no bungaku kūkan*. Shinyōsha, 1983.

Masumune Hakuchō. *Sakkaron*. Shinchōsha, 1954.

Matsui, Midori. "Little Girls Were Little Boys: Displaced Femininity in the Representation of Homosexuality in Japanese Girls' Comics." In *Feminism and the Politics of Difference*, edited by Sneja Gunew and Anna Yeatman. Boulder: Westview, 1993.

Matsuzaka Ken. "Kōda Aya o yomu koto no 'gorieki'." *Bungei Shunjū* 71(5–6) (July 1993): 392–395.

Mawatari Kenzaburō. *Joryū bungei kenkyū*. Nansōsha, 1973.

Miner, Earl, and Hiroko Odagiri, trans. *The Monkey's Straw Raincoat and Other Poetry of the Basho School*. Princeton: Princeton University Press, 1981.

Minowa Takeo. *Kōda Rohan*. Special issue of *Kokubungaku kaishaku to kyōzai no kenkyū* 28(6) (1983).

Miyao Shigeo. *Tōkyō meisho zukai—Sumida zutsumi*. Boku Shobō, 1969.

Miyoshi, Masao. *Accomplices of Silence: The Modern Japanese Novel.* Berkeley: University of California Press, 1974.

Mizukami Tsutomu and Muramatsu Tomomi. "Taidan Kōda Aya no sekai." *Nami* (January 1993):42–47.

Mizuta Jun. *Saikakuron josetsu.* Ōfūsha, 1973.

Mizuta Noriko et al., eds. *New Feminist Review 2: Onna to hyōgen.* Gakuyō Shobō, 1991.

Moi, Toril. *Sexual/Textual Politics: Feminist Literary Theory.* New York: Routledge, 1985.

Morris, Ivan, trans. *The Pillow Book of Sei Shonagon.* Baltimore: Penguin, 1967.

Mulhern, Chieko. *Kōda Rohan.* Boston: G. K. Hall, 1977.

Mulvey, Laura. "Afterthoughts on 'Visual Pleasure and Narrative Cinema.'" In *Feminism and Film Theory,* edited by Constance Penley. New York: Routledge, 1988.

———. "Visual Pleasure and Narrative Cinema." In *Feminism and Film Theory,* edited by Constance Penley. New York: Routledge, 1988.

Murō Saisei. "Kōda Aya no hyōjō." In *Kōda Aya.* Vol. 69 of Gendai Nihon bungaku taikei. Chikuma Shobō, 1969.

Nagai Kafū. *Geisha in Rivalry.* Translated by Kurt Meissner and Ralph Friedrich. Rutland, Vt.: Tuttle, 1963.

———. *Kafū zenshū.* Iwanami Shoten, 1964.

———. *A Strange Tale from East of the River.* Translated by Edward Seidensticker. Rutland, Vt.: Tuttle, 1965.

Nagase Mayumi. "Kōda Aya—Sakuhin ni miru sono seikatsusha no kage." *Nihon bungaku ronsō* 6 (1981):68–70.

Nakagawa, Keiichiro, and Henry Rosovsky. "The Case of the Dying Kimono." In *Dress, Adornment, and the Social Order,* edited by Mary Ellen Roach and Joanne Bubolz Eicher. New York: Wiley, 1965.

Nakamura Masaya. *Iki.* Shūeisha, 1981.

Nakamura Mitsuo. *Kindai bungaku o dō yomu ka.* Shinchōsha, 1980.

Nakamura Yukihiko. "Bunjin ishiki no seiritsu." In Vol. 9 of *Iwanami kōza Nihon bungakushi.* Iwanami Shoten, 1959.

Nakano Shigeharu. *Three Works by Nakano Shigeharu.* Translated by Brett DeBary. Ithaca: Cornell University East Asian Papers, 1979.

Naruse Masakatsu. "Rohan no buntai." *Bungaku* 8(8) (1940):44–48.

Nihei Aizō. "Rohan ni okeru fūryū no tenkai: *Fūryūma* no hassō to zasetsu o megutte." *Nihon kindai bungaku* 27 (1980):15–28.

Nishida Masayoshi. *Watakushi shōsetsu saihakken.* Ōfūsha, 1973.

Nishio Minoru, ed. *Hōjōki Tsurezuregusa.* Vol. 30 of Nihon koten bungaku taikei. Iwanami Shoten, 1957.

Noborio Yutaka. "Kōda Aya: *Otōto* no keisan." *Kokubungaku kaishaku to kanshō* 50(10) (1980):168–169.

———. "Kōda Aya *Nagareru* no Rika." *Kokubungaku kaishaku to kyōzai to kenkyū* 25(4) (1980):168–169.

Oketani Hideaki. *Bungaku to rekishi no kage.* Hokuyōsha, 1972.

Okuno Takeo. *Joryū sakka ron.* Daisanmonmeisha, 1974.

Penley, Constance, ed. *Feminism and Film Theory.* New York: Routledge, 1988.

Pincus, Leslie. *Authenticating Culture in Imperial Japan: Kuki Shūzō and the Rise of National Aesthetics.* Berkeley: University of California Press, 1996.

———. "In a Labyrinth of Western Desire." In *Japan in the World,* edited by Masao Miyoshi and H. D. Harootounian. Durham: Duke University Press, 1993.

Pollack, David. *The Fracture of Meaning: Japan's Synthesis of China from the Eighth Through the Eighteenth Centuries.* Princeton: Princeton University Press, 1986.

———. *Reading Against Culture: Ideology and Narrative in the Japanese Novel.* Ithaca: Cornell University Press, 1992.

Pyle, Kenneth. *The Making of Modern Japan.* Lexington, Mass.: Heath, 1981.

———. *The New Generation in Meiji Japan.* Stanford: Stanford University Press, 1969.

Reichert, James. "Representations of Male-Male Sexuality in Meiji-Period Literature." Ph.D. dissertation, University of Michigan, 1998.

Rimer, Thomas. *Modern Japanese Fiction and Its Traditions.* Princeton: Princeton University Press, 1978.

Roden, Donald. "Taisho Culture and the Problem of Gender Ambivalence." In *Culture and Identity: Japanese Intellectuals and the Interwar Years,* edited by J. Thomas Rimer. Princeton: Princeton University Press, 1990.

Romines, Ann. *The Home Plot: Women, Writing and Domestic Ritual.* Amherst: University of Massachusetts Press, 1992.

Rose, Jacqueline. *Sexuality in the Field of Vision.* New York: Verso, 1986.

Rubin, Jay. *Injurious to Public Morals: Writers and the Meiji State.* Seattle: University of Washington Press, 1984.

Saeki Junko. *Yūjo no bunkashi.* Chūō Kōronsha, 1987.

Said, Edward. *The World, the Text, and the Critic.* Cambridge, Mass.: Harvard University Press, 1983.

Saitō Etsurō. *Zōho Kagyūan oboegaki: Rohan ōkina dan sōshō.* Keyaki Shuppan, 1994.

Saitō Mokichi. *Kōda Rohan.* Senshin Shorin, 1949.

Sasabuchi Tomoichi. *Nagai Kafū: Zuiraku no bigakusha.* Meiji Shoin, 1976.

Schalow, Paul Gordon, and Janet A. Walker, eds. *The Woman's Hand: Gender and Theory in Japanese Women's Writing.* Stanford: Stanford University Press, 1996.

Seidensticker, Edward. *Kafū the Scribbler: The Life and Writings of Nagai Kafū.* Stanford: Stanford University Press, 1965.

———. *Low City, High City: Tokyo from Edo to the Earthquake.* Rutland, Vt.: Tuttle, 1984.

Sherif, Ann. "A Dealer in Memories: The Fiction and Essays of Kōda Aya." Ph.D. dissertation, University of Michigan, 1991.

Shimomura Ryōichi. *Bannen no Rohan.* Keizai Ōraisha, 1979.

Shinchōsha. *Nihon bungaku arubamu: Kōda Aya.* Shinchōsha, 1995.

Shinoda Hajime. *Kōda Rohan no tame ni.* Iwanami Shoten, 1984.

Shiotani San. "Kaisetsu." In *Chichi—Konna koto* by Kōda Aya. Shinchōsha, 1956.

———. *Kōda Rohan.* 3 vols. Chūō Kōronsha, 1965–1968.

———, ed. *Nagareru oboegaki.* Keizai Ōraisha, 1957.

Shively, Donald H., ed. *Tradition and Modernization in Japanese Culture.* Princeton: Princeton University Press, 1971.

Sibley, William F. "Naturalism in Japanese Literature." *Harvard Journal of Asiatic Studies* 28 (1968):165.

Silverman, Kaja. *Male Subjectivity at the Margins.* New York: Routledge, 1992.

Smith, Barbara Herrnstein. *On the Margins of Discourse: The Relation of Literature to Language.* Chicago: University of Chicago Press, 1978.

———. *Poetic Closure.* Chicago: University of Chicago Press, 1968.

Spengemann, William C. *The Forms of Autobiography: Episodes in the History of a Literary Genre.* New Haven: Yale University Press, 1980.

Stanton, Domna, ed. *The Female Autograph: Theory and Practice of Autobiography from the Tenth to the Twentieth Century.* Chicago: University of Chicago Press, 1987.

Suzuki, Tomi. *Narrating the Self: Fictions of Japanese Modernity.* Stanford: Stanford University Press, 1996.

Takahashi Hideo. "Kōda Aya no muaku naru jikan." *Shinchō* 94 (1994):208–211.

Takahashi Toshio. *Nagai Kafū to Edo bungakuen.* Meiji Shoin, 1983.

Takeda Taijun, Hanaya Yutaka, and Shiina Rinji. "Sosaku gappyō." *Gunzō* 11 (January 1956):216.

Takigawa Masajirō. *Yūjo no rekishi.* Vol. 3 of Nihon rekishi shinshō series. Shibundō, 1965.

Tamura Mitsuru, ed. *Joshigaku hachijūnen shi.* Joshigakuin, 1951.

Tanaka, Stefan. *Japan's Orient: Rendering Pasts into History.* Berkeley: University of California Press, 1993.

Tanizaki Jun'ichirō. *In Praise of Shadows.* Translated by Thomas J. Harper and Edward G. Seidensticker. New Haven: Leete's Island Books, 1977.

———. *The Secret History of the Lord of Musashi and Arrowroot.* Translated by Anthony Chambers. New York: Knopf, 1982.

———. *Tanizaki Jun'ichirō zenshū.* Chūō Kōronsha, 1968.

Tansman, Alan M. "Bridges to Nowhere: Yasuda Yōjirō's Language of Violence and Desire." *Harvard Journal of Asiatic Studies* 56 (June 1996):35–75.

———. *The Writings of Kōda Aya: A Japanese Literary Daughter.* New Haven: Yale University Press, 1993.

Todorov, Tsvetan. *Introduction to Poetics.* Minneapolis: University of Minnesota Press, 1981.

Torrance, Richard. *The Fiction of Tokuda Shūsei and the Emergence of Japan's New Middle Class.* Seattle: University of Washington Press, 1994.

Tsumura Setsuko. "Ikizukai no kikoeru kotoba." *Shinchō* 88(1) (1991):202–203.

Tu Wei-Ming. *Way, Learning, and Politics: Essays on the Confucian Intellectual.* Albany: SUNY Press, 1993.

Ueda Makoto. *Matsuo Bashō.* New York: Kodansha International, 1982.

Ueno Chizuko, Mizuta Noriko, Asada Akira, and Karatani Kōjin. "Nihon bunka to jendā: kafuchōsei to sono hihan kara hajimete." *Hihyō kūkan* 2(3) (1994):6–43.

Ueno Chizuko, Ogura Chikako, and Tomioka Taeko, eds. *Danryū bungakuron.* Chikuma Shobō, 1992.

Unger, J. Marshall. *Literacy and Script Reform in Occupation Japan: Reading Between the Lines.* New York: Oxford University Press, 1996.

Uno Chiyo. *Confessions of Love.* Honolulu: University of Hawai'i Press, 1989.

Uranishi Kazuhiko. "Kōda Aya chosaku mokuroku." *Kokubungaku* (June 1994): 92–154.

Walker, Janet. *The Japanese Novel of the Meiji Period and the Ideal of Individualism.* Princeton: Princeton University Press, 1979.

———. Review of *The Writings of Kōda Aya,* by Alan Tansman. *Journal of Japanese Studies* 21 (1995):448–451.

Washburn, Dennis C. *The Dilemma of the Modern in Japanese Fiction.* New Haven: Yale University Press, 1995.

Woodhull, Alan S. "Romantic Edo Fiction: A Study of the Ninjōbon and Complete Translation of *Shunshoku Umegoyomi.*" Ph.D. dissertation, Stanford University, 1978.

Yaeger, Patricia, and Beth Kowaleski-Wallace, eds. *Refiguring the Father: New Feminist Readings of Patriarchy.* Carbondale: Southern Illinois University Press, 1989.

Yaguchi Jun. "Sofu Rohan to no aimegusumigoshi no kiseki: Aoki Tama cho *Koishikawa no ie.*" *Bungakkai* 48(11) (November 1994):271–274.

Yamashita Etsuko. *"Josei no jidai" to iu shinwa.* Aoyumisha, 1991.

———. *Mazakonbungakuron: sokubaku toshite no "haha."* Shinyōsha, 1991.

Yanagida Izumi. *Kōda Rohan.* Chūō Kōronsha, 1942.

Yoshida Seiichi. *Zuihitsu no sekai.* Ōfūsha, 1980.

———, ed. *Kindai bungaku hyōron taikei.* 10 vols. Kadokawa Shoten, 1971–1975.

Yoshii Isamu. "Dokugo no mudasho—Kōda Aya—*Nagareru.*" *Chūō Kōron* 113 (June 1956):137.

Yoshimoto Takaaki. "Kōda Aya ni tsuite: shirōto no iki." In *Shinchō Nihon bungaku arubamu: Kōda Aya.* Shinchōsha, 1995.

Yuri Sachiko. "Josei sakka no genzai." In *Kokubungaku kaishaku to kanshō bekkan: Josei sakka no shinryū,* edited by Hasegawa Izumi. 1991.

Zwinger, Lynda. *Daughters, Fathers, and the Novel: The Sentimental Romance of Heterosexuality.* Madison: University of Wisconsin Press, 1991.

Index

affect in narrative, 23, 30, 33, 52;
    linking of aesthetics and emotion, 60;
    as transformative, 50
Allied Occupation, 106–107
"American School" (Kojima Nobuo),
    106–109, 111
"Amerikan sukūru." *See* "American
    School"
Anatomy of "Iki," 77, 79–80, 95, 151
Anderer, Paul, 69n. 48
Aoki Tama, 10, 27 n. 47, 53; books by,
    54, 136; portrait of parents, 54
Ariga, Chieko, 98–99 n. 14
Ariyoshi Sawako, 14
artifacts of a chosen past, 83
asymmetry as aesthetic value, 112–113
"Atomiyosowaka." *See* "Incantations"
authority in narrative, 30, 56, 58, 118,
    124; Kōda's compared to Rohan's, 149
autobiographical sources for Kōda's writ-
    ing, 31, 39
autobiography, 54; constructed nature of,
    48–49, 72 n. 90

Bashō. *See* Matsuo Bashō
Black Hem, 56
Black Kimono, 18
body of woman as cultural artifact, 81
Brower, Robert, 25 n. 32
bungaku seinen (male literary youth), 143
bunjin. See literati

"Chichi: sono shi," *See* "Death of my
    Father"

Chigiregumo. See *Scattered Clouds*
Chinese concepts of literature, 58
Christianity, 7–9, 34, 153–154 n. 21
clothing. *See* kimono
conceit of humility, 54–55
Confucianism, 9, 32, 33, 38–39, 47, 55;
    Meiji writers' education in, 57
consumerism, 46
Copeland, Rebecca, 71 n. 66
Cornyetz, Nina, 152 n. 1

Daigaku. See *Great Learning*
daisan no shinjin (third generation of new)
    writers, 14
Danly, Robert, 127 n. 30
Danryū bungakuron. See *On Men's Litera-
    ture*
"Death of my Father," 30
demimonde, 73, 102 n. 41; affinity to
    theater, 79, 81, 89; Edo literature
    and art, 77–79, 100 n. 21; as fantasy
    realm, 85, 87; impact of modernity
    on, 81, 87; Kōda Aya's knowledge of,
    17–18, 96; literature, 73, 79, 81–82,
    84–85
"Dolls for a Special Day," 56, 108;
    aesthetic values, 112; narrative stance
    in, 110–112, 114; structure compared
    to *haikai* short story, 113–114
domestic space, 37, 121
domestic work, 37–38; as moral training,
    55

Embracing Family, 44–48

Enchi Fumiko, 14, 36, 66, 133; focus on
  eroticism, 74
Endō Shūsaku, 43
Erikson, Erik, 43, 45, 69 n. 38
eroticism, 14
essentialism, 159
Etō Jun, 43–47

families in literature, 44; as utopian, 66
fashion felons, 150
father figures in literature, 33, 43, 45, 47,
  133, 149; death of father as theme,
  62; in early postwar literature, 158;
  in Natsume Sōseki and Shimazaki
  Tōson's fiction, 42
father/daughter artist pairs, 59, 132;
  examples in Edo and Meiji periods,
  40, 68 n. 28; power imbalance in, 66
father-identified daughters, 61, 67 n. 7,
  132–133
female readers, 78, 100 n. 22
feminism in Japan, 134–135
feminist criticism, 125 n. 2, 134, 138,
  151, 158
feminist fiction, 31
Five-Story Pagoda (*Gojū no tō,* Kōda
  Rohan), 3, 22
Flowing (*Nagareru*), 18, 30; as antifeminist, 75; character development in, 83;
  as erotic text, 74, 94–96; famous passages, 74–75, 90–94; imagery in, 85,
  87–88, 90; memory in, 85–86; merg-
  ing realism and fantasy in, 90, 96;
  narrative voice in, 82–83, 87; plot of,
  75–76; reference and allusion in, 90,
  92. *See also* demimonde; pleasure in
  looking
Fowler, Edward, 26 n. 36
"Fragments," 34, 63–64, 108
"A Friend for Life," 19, 108; imagery,
  117–119; and Mishima Yukio's essay,
  122; narrative stance in, 114–115;
  and *The Pillow Book,* 116; style in,

116, 121; summary of, 114–115;
  themes and structure of, 115–116,
  122
Fujin Kōron (journal), 122, 129 n. 52

gaman (endurance), 149, 157
Garon, Sheldon, 67–68 n. 16
gaze: as gendered, 75, 81. *See also* pleasure
  in looking
geisha, 77; compared to prostitutes, 78,
  98 n. 12, 98–99 n. 14; as conservator
  of tradition, 83; and law, 99 n. 19; in
  literature and art, 78–79, 100 n. 20
geisha house, 17–18
Geishas in Rivalry (Nagai Kafū), 90, 102
  n. 42
gender in literature, 37, 138, 149; female
  identity, 116, 120; male identity, 23
  n. 4, 84, 109; masculinity as universal,
  133; woman as repository of past, 83,
  152
generic classification, 56, 70 n. 53, 71 n.
  71, 124, 156
Gessel, Van, 23 n. 4, 44–46
Gojū no tō. See *Five-Story Pagoda*
gokan. See sensations
"A Good Day," 19
Good for Nothing, 9, 30, 34; Kōda's birth
  described in, 62
Great Learning, 9, 39
Great Kantō Earthquake of 1923, 135,
  138, 147
"Growing Up," 104 n. 69

haikai linked verse, 113–114
Hayashi Fumiko, 14, 54, 83, 138
heightened emotion. *See* affect in narrative
heterosexuality in literature, 135
Higuchi Ichiyō, 40, 81; affinities with
  Saikaku, 114
hina matsuri (Girls' Festival), 126 n. 12
"Hina." *See* "Dolls for a Special Day"

Hirosue Tamotsu, 79, 92
"His Last Hours," 12
"Hitorigurashi." *See* "Living Alone"
Hokushū. See *Sadness of the North*
Hōrinji Temple, 22, 151
Hōyō kazoku. See Embracing Family

I-novel. See *watakushi shōsetsu*
identity crisis: as theme in postwar litera-
    ture, 107–108
Ihara Saikaku, 78, 101 nn. 25, 26; short
    fiction and poetry of, 113–114
iki (chic), 77, 81, 94; characteristics of,
    95; Koda associated with, 151–152
"Iki" no kōzō. See The Anatomy of "Iki"
inadequacy. *See* humility
"Incantations," 38
individual and society in literature, 105,
    118
Inoue Kazuko, 41, 138, 153 n. 21
Isogai Hideo, 85, 96
Itagaki Naoko, 83
Itō, Ken, 157

Jauss, Hans Robert, 49
"Jigane." *See* "Ore"
"Just My Age," 19

Kagyūan, 6, 24 n. 7, 40
"Kakera." *See* "Fragments"
kakubutsu chichi (investigation of all
    things), 9, 13, 38–39, 49, 53, 58, 96,
    115
Kanai Mieko, 32
kandō. See affect in narrative
"Kansei." *See* "A Woman's Screams"
Karatani Kōjin, 69 n. 35, 70 n.53
kata (forms), 95
Katō Norihiro, 45–47
Ki. See Trees
kimono (clothing), 135–136, 140; func-
    tion in literature, 144; as self-presenta-
    tion and liberation, 141

Kimono, 19, 22; allusion in, 148–149;
    compared to *Flowing,* 144, 148; com-
    pared to *The Makioka Sisters,* 138,
    153 n. 18; critical reception of, 132,
    142, 148, 151; grandmother in, 143,
    149; as homage to kimono, 135; mar-
    keting campaign, 136; narrative per-
    spective, 144; opening passage,
    136–138; summary, 145–148, 150;
    themes, 138–140, 144–145, 150; as
    unfinished novel, 151, 154 n. 41
*Kisetsu no katami. See Reminders of the
    Season*
kiyomoto singing, 86, 103 n. 54
Kobayashi Isamu, 35, 72 n. 91
Kōda Aya: birth, 5; mythopoetic version,
    62, 156–157
Kōda Aya: childhood, 5–10; divorce, 11,
    29, 41; education, 9–10, 17, 32,
    38–40; female role models, 17,
    61–62; and feminism, 133; maid in
    geisha house, 17–18, 58; marriage,
    10, 41; opinions on politics, 19–20;
    professions, 10, 17
Kōda Aya: conservatism, 31, 60, 132;
    refutation of conservative image, 41,
    105, 133
Kōda Aya: critical reception, 15, 23, 30,
    102–103 n. 44, 131, 152
Kōda Aya: domestic work, 36; linked with
    moral and spiritual training, 38–39,
    55
Kōda Aya: eroticism, 74, 132
Kōda Aya: essays, 13, 52; characteristics,
    50; as genre, 110; about old age, 19;
    about Rohan, 30; significance, 55;
    topics, 49, 56, 60. See also *zuihitsu*
Kōda Aya: family, 5: Andō Kōko (aunt),
    16, 62; daughter (*see* Aoki Tama);
    father (*see* Kōda Rohan); Kōda
    Kimiko (mother), 5, 7, 37; Kōda
    Nobuko (aunt), 7, 16, 25 n. 29, 62;
    Kōda Shigenobu (grandfather), 5;

Kōda Shigetoyo (Ichirō [brother]), 5, 10, 40; Kōda Utako (sister), 5, 7, 40; stepmother (*see* Kōda Yayoko); Koda Yū (grandmother), 5, 37, 39; husband (*see* Mitsuhashi Ikunosuke). *See also* Kōda Family

Kōda Aya: humility, 16, 33, 35, 41–42, 50, 54–55; as theme in essays, 60

Kōda Aya: influences: Edo-period fiction, 4, 96, 104 n. 69; Rohan, 49, 53, 56, 58; Western novels, 4

Kōda Aya: public image, 74, 136

Kōda Aya: short stories, 114; narrative voice in, 123–124

Kōda Aya: style, 12, 30, 89, 110; compared to Rohan's, 49, 58, 64–65; as "feminine," 42

Kōda Aya: themes, 4, 30, 49, 108–109; compared with Rohan, 63–65; cultural identity, 105, 123; father figures in, 149; gender hierarchy, 133; generational change, 119, 145; marriage, 138–139; parent-child relations, 32; sexuality, 151; struggle with focus on Rohan, 61–62

Kōda Aya: writing career: 11–12, 14, 96; abandons writing, 15; attitudes toward art, 54, 56, 58, 89, 157; lasting contributions to literature, 31, 42, 156; motives for writing, 30, 58

Kōda Family: residences, 6–7, 10–11

Kōda Rohan, 3, 37; career, 3–4; death, 11; drinking, 34–35, 63; and Edo literature, 101 n. 25; education, 57; relationship with *bundan,* 29, 57; remarriage, 7; stature as a writer, 56–57

Kōda Rohan, writings, *Gojū no tō* (see *The Five-Story Pagoda*); poem by, 63; "Tarōbō," 63–65

Kōda Yayoko (stepmother), 7–8, 10–11, 24 n. 18, 34–35, 62

Kodama Yayoko. *See* Kōda Yayoko

Kojima Nobuo, 43, 44, 48, 58, 106, 123. *See also* "American School;" *Embracing Family*

"Kojin kyōju." *See* "Private Tutor"

Konna koto. See This Sort of Thing

Kōno Taeko, 14, 31

Kuki Shūzō, 61, 80, 95, 101 nn. 26, 30. See also *The Anatomy of "Iki"*

"Kunshō." *See* "The Medal"

"Kuroi suso." *See* "The Black Hem"

kurōto (professional), 75, 97 n. 6

"Kusabue." *See* "Whistle of Grass"

Kuzure. See Landslides

Landslides, 20–22

literary authority. *See* authority in narrative

literary prizes, 19

literary daughters. See father/daughter artist pairs

literati, 3, 10, 63

Little Brother, 10, 18

"Living Alone," 19

Mainichi Shinbun, 15

makoto. See sincerity

male love, 81, 102 n. 36

Masaoka Shiki, 11, 59

Matsuo Bashō, 11, 59

Maturity and Loss: The Collapse of the 'Mother' (Etō Jun), 43–47

"The Medal," 56, 108, 122; Chinese lion story in, 62–63

memory in narrative, 109–110, 118

mirrors, 116–117, 120

Mishima Yukio, 122

Misokkasu. See Good for Nothing

Mitsuhashi Ikunosuke (husband), 10, 41, 54

Miyamoto Yuriko, 36

Mizumura Minae, 138, 142, 151

"Mono iwanu isshō no tomo." *See* "Friend for Life"

moral authority, 59
Mori, Maryellen Toman, 31
Mori Ōgai, 57
mother figure in literature, 134, 158;
   in *Kimono,* 148

Nagai Kafū, 82, 90
Nagareru. See *Flowing*
nanshoku. See male love
narrative voice: in Kōda's works, 30
Natsume Sōseki, 57
ninjōbon (books of sentiment), 78, 90, 96
Noborio Yutaka, 102–103 n. 44
Noda Utarō, 11, 25 n. 33
"Notes from Sugano," 12, 16, 30, 52–53
novelist: low status of profession, 5, 62

objective fallacy, 122–123
Okamoto Kanoko, 32
okiya. See geisha house
"Onai doshi." *See* "Just My Age"
On Men's Literature, 47
Orbaugh, Sharalyn, 14, 66 n. 3
"Ore," 20
Otōto. See Little Brother

Pacific War, 11, 19, 63, 106; anniversary
   of defeat in, 125 n. 3; and cultural
   identity, 105–106; and Tokyo, 88
patriarchy, 66, 132, 134; and Japanese
   gender hierarchy, 133
The Pillow Book (Makura no sōshi), 111
Pincus, Leslie, 80, 83, 99 nn. 16, 17, 101
   nn. 25, 30
pleasure in looking, 75, 81; in *Flowing,*
   84, 90–92; heterosexual and homosexual gaze, 81
pleasure quarters. *See* demimonde
poetics, 48–49
poetry, 113–114
postwar fiction: characteristics in, 14, 123
postwar period, 105–106
prewar fiction: self as central tenet, 14

privacy, 37, 121
"Private Tutor," 50
psychoanalytical criticism, 43, 47,
   133–134. *See also* Erik Erikson
publication format, 56, 131, 135–136;
   journals, 56, 122; serialization, 151;
   single-volume editions, 56; *zenshū*
   (collected works), 18, 49
Pyle, Kenneth, 106

racial difference: perceived, 111
Ramirez-Christensen, Esperanza, 59,
   133–134
"Random Notes," 12, 30, 105
realism, 82–83
"Record of the Funeral," 12
Reminders of the Season, 56

Sadness of the North, 18
Said, Edward, 156
Scattered Clouds, 30, 56
Sei Shōnagon, 111. See also *The Pillow
   Book*
Seijuku to sōshitsu. See *Maturity and Loss*
sengoha (postwar school) writers, 14
sensations *(gokan),* 89, 140–141; sensual-
   ity as subjectivity, 144
sex in postwar literature, 74
Shinchō (journal), 135
Shiotani San, 13, 35
shirōto (non-professional), 75, 85–86, 95,
   97
shitamachi (Low City), 6, 138
shōjo (female adolescence), as cultural phe-
   nomenon, 142–143
"Shūen." *See* "His Last Hours"
*Shunshoku umegoyomi (Colors of Spring:
   Plum Blossom Calendar),* 6, 96, 100 n.
   24
sincerity, 12, 15
Smith, Barbara Herrnstein, 66 n. 5
Smoke Over the Moon, 56
"Sōsō no ki." *See* "Record of the Funeral"

"Sottaku." *See* "Growing Up"
The Struggle, 18–19
"Sugano no ki." *See* "Notes from Sugano"
Suzuki, Tomi, 12, 127 n. 20
symbolic inversion, 36–37, 157

Takahashi Takako, 14, 31
"Tama no ii hi." *See* "A Good Day"
Tamenaga Shunsui, 6, 78
Tanizaki, Jun'ichirō, 32, 82, 122, 157;
fantasy in works by, 83; sensations in,
89; and race, 111
Tansman, Alan, 31, 35, 42, 67 n. 15, 70
n. 70, 103 n. 47
This Sort of Thing, 30
Tō. See *The Struggle*
Todorov, Tsvetan, 67 n. 5
Tokyo place-names: Koishikawa, 10–11,
61; Kōjimachi, 7, 9; Mukōjima, 5–7,
9–10, 24 nn. 7, 16; 60, 96; Sumida
River, 6–7, 75, 82; Tamanoi, 24 n.
16, 82; Ueno Park, 147; Yanagibashi,
17, 82, 97 n. 7; Yoshiwara, 102 n. 41
Trees, 20, 22
Tsuki no chiri. See *Smoke Over the Moon*
Tsurezuregusa (*Essays in Idleness,* Yoshida
Kenkō), 113
Tsushima Yūko, 133

Udekurabe. See *Geishas in Rivalry*
Uemura Masahisa, 8, 24 n. 19
Ueno Chizuko, 46–47
Uno, Kathleen, 40
Uno Chiyo, 14, 36, 42, 138
urban pleasure quarter. *See* demimonde

voyeurism, 73

Washburn, Dennis, 12
watakushi shōsetsu, 12–13, 15, 18, 26 n.
36, 129–130 nn. 54, 55
Watsuji Tetsurō, 61
"Whistle of Grass," 19
wish-fulfillment in literature, 138
women and the state, 139
"A Woman's Screams," 41
women's writing, 158–159
world building in Tanizaki's fiction, 157
World War II. *See* Pacific War

Yamada Eimi, 131, 133
Yamashita Etsuko, 134
Yasuoka Shōtarō, 43
Yoshimoto Takaaki, 151

"Zakki." *See* "Random Notes"
Zhu Xi, 9
zuihitsu (essay) genre, 110–111, 124, 127
n. 20